DEPUTY RICOS: TALE 3

DARKER THAN
BLACK

ELIZABETH A. GARCIA

Cover Art: Margarita Garcia, Pixalpod.com
Editing: Lee Porche
Print Format: Lynn Hubbard

ISBN-10: 149522337X
ISBN-13: 978-1495223372

A Few Words About *Darker Than Black*

Before the sun has a chance to rise on the majesty of Big Bend country, sheriff's deputies Ricos and George are called to the Rio Grande near the Texas resort town of Lajitas, where there is an informal crossing point. A dead body has been found at the edge of the river on the U.S. side.

Later that day, a severed foot is reported by fishermen farther upstream. Then there's a burning wreck, a series of break-ins, and a new truck is stolen.

A large stash of cocaine is discovered. Then another. "Stereotypical Mexican drug dealers" are seen hanging out in the Ghost Town. A handsome special agent from the D.E.A. comes to town.

The deputies are soon overwhelmed with the amount of crime taking place in their normally serene community. As Deputy Barney says to Deputy Margarita, "What in Lawman Hell?"

Can these crimes possibly be related?

Who is behind the millions of dollars worth of drugs?

Where is the rest of the body belonging to the feet?

Will Deputy Ricos ever date again?

What's up with the break-ins?

Who would steal a truck in such a small place?

Why is Margarita accused of protecting a Vietnam veteran everyone else thinks is crazy and dangerous?

How does she end up running for her life in a Mexican town?

Come along for the ride and find out.

DEDICATION

For my extraordinary sisters,
Martha Waltman and Mary Lou Egger,

There are no words to describe what
you mean to me.

Acknowledgments

Thank you to my daughter, Margarita Garcia, for exactly the right cover, and to Amber Garcia for taking the photograph. Thanks also to Tamara Sands for her invaluable help.

I'm fortunate to have astute first readers, intrepid souls who are willing to take a chance on a new Deputy Ricos novel. They read my first effort, second effort, etc. You know who you are, and I'm eternally grateful to you.

My editor, Lee Porche, caught every manner of error an author can make. She approaches her work (and mine) with good humor and with enthusiasm. Thank you, Lee.

Thank you also, to Lynn Hubbard, who did the print formatting for this novel.

Like all my novels, this one came out of my imagination. Therefore, any resemblance to anyone living or dead is purely coincidental. I love to make stuff up, so if something isn't exactly where it's supposed to be, you know why, right?

More than to anyone else, I owe a huge thank you to my readers.

Peace and love,
Elizabeth A. (Beth) Garcia

CHAPTER 1

The whole mess started with a dead body in the Rio Grande.

My partner and I beat the sun to the scene that morning. The sky, the multi-colored clay hills, the mountains, the muddy water, the green growing things, the rocky cliff faces—all of it—was bathed in a soft pink glow.

Barney cut the engine. "Damn it, Ricos."

"Don't start. I don't like it, either. I was getting ready to go for a run."

He glared at me, heaved a longsuffering sigh, flung open the door, got out, and headed for the river in great strides. Within seconds he bellowed, "Ricos!"

"I'm getting the camera," I claimed. Dead bodies make me throw up.

"Well get it already and get over here!" He was standing about thirty yards away with his hands on his hips, staring down at what I presumed was the corpse.

With stage lighting-like magic, the pinkish glow faded and was gradually replaced by a muted golden color.

"*Now*, Ricos!"

"Keep your shirt on!" What was his hurry? The poor guy was dead.

As I walked up beside my partner, the sun burst over the mountains in the east, effectively turning up the house lights.

A male was sprawled in the shallow water at the bank. He was young, I thought, but his face was in the mud so it was just a guess.

"He's not bloated or nibbled-on," Barney observed.

"Nope," I agreed without looking. The idea of either thing made my stomach hurt.

"We haven't seen the other side of him yet, though."

I thought Barney was trying to make me throw up.

"His skin isn't discolored either, so he hasn't been here long."

The victim was wearing blue running shorts, blue shoes, and red, white, and blue-striped socks. His t-shirt had been white before he landed in the Rio wearing it. His hair was brown but wet, so hard to say what shade.

Barney grabbed one of several onlookers and the two

men carefully lifted the lifeless man to higher ground and turned him over.

"Usted lo conoce?" asked the helper.

My partner wiped mud from the dead man's face. "No, I don't know him."

Both men turned to me. I shook my head. I had never seen him before.

The shorts bore a once-white Reebok logo on the left side. The front of the t-shirt proclaimed, WILL RUN FASTER FOR BEER in a red and blue design. So he was a stylish, athletic, white man—a runner who looked about my age, twenty-six. I found that both sad and unnerving.

Barney spoke with the lookie-loos, all Mexicans curious about the dead gringo. The group was primarily men, but there were a few timid women standing in a cluster and speaking in hushed tones. Nobody had seen anything helpful. They had crossed the river in a metal rowboat and said they couldn't have missed the body in the shallows near the usual landing place.

The Lajitas Crossing takes its name from the small resort town that sits above it on a bluff, and from the Mexican settlement of Paso Lajitas directly across the river. It is an easy, flat-bottomed ford where the current is usually not fast. A truck can be driven across at lower water levels, or a person who doesn't mind getting wet can wade or swim. The boat is kept on the Mexican side, operated by the community. Since there is no U. S. Customs station, it's illegal to cross back and forth there, but border-dwellers have been doing it for as long as there have been people here. We don't see the river as a dividing line as much as something that connects us.

"Ricos, you want to step over here?"

No. I did not.

"There's no identification on him," advised my partner, who was actually working the scene.

I stepped up to take photographs. "Maybe if we show photos around somebody will know him," I said, but it lacked enthusiasm.

About that time, the ambulance from Terlingua Fire and Emergency Medical Services pulled up, and my friend Mitch hopped down from the driver's seat. He's head medic and executive director of the organization. Their office and clinic are seventeen miles from where we were standing.

"Hey, Mitch."

"Hey yourself." He crushed me in a bear hug and shook Barney's hand. "What we got here?"

"Floater," Barney said, "except he wasn't in the water long enough to float."

Mitch leaned over the body but didn't touch it. I could tell he wanted to. Dead bodies and gruesome wounds fascinate him.

After a few seconds, he said, "I don't see any injuries," and he sounded disappointed.

"I don't see any either," agreed Barney.

"The little finger on his right hand looks broken," I said. "Don't you think it's probably a defensive wound?"

Barney frowned and wordlessly handed Mitch a pair of gloves. He put them on and knelt to examine the finger. "You're right, Margarita. It's broken."

"He must have struggled with somebody," suggested Barney.

"I don't think he just happened to drop dead while admiring the historic Rio Grande." I stated the obvious then added, "He was probably overdosed and dumped here."

Both men frowned. "Maybe," they said doubtfully in unison.

"Should we take him back to the clinic?" asked Mitch. "We can put the bright lights on him."

Perfect. They were going to make me throw up yet. I agreed to Mitch's suggestion only because Barney did.

My partner called the sheriff to tell him where we would be. He was on his way from his office in Alpine, eighty miles away. Our office in Terlingua is an extension of his. Barney and I work in the southern end of Brewster County, the largest county in Texas. It's also the least populated and most scenic, with more mountains than people. When it comes to mountains, we've got them: high, low, wide, skinny, round, jagged, smooth, naked, wild, astounding mountains.

Barney rode with Mitch and the body while I took our Sheriff's Office Explorer to do a quick canvass of Lajitas to show people the photographs.

As I pulled away from the river, I noticed that the layer-cake cliffs of the distant Mesa de Anguila looked spotlighted. The temperature was ideal. Birds swooped at the water as if to capture the sparkles bouncing across its surface. The sky was clear and such a deep blue it looked painted. It was a perfect day for a river trip. Murder should never have been part of it.

The hotel office was my first stop, but the manager had never seen the man in the photograph. A woman working the front desk exclaimed, "I would've remembered a looker like him." The others murmured and nodded in agreement.

I got the same comments in the restaurant and the convenience store. No one had seen him, but all were fascinated by the grim pictures and wanted to know what had happened to him.

An older woman sat alone on a bench on the boardwalk of the hotel that looked like a scene out of the Old West, admiring the scenery. I showed her the photo and asked if she'd seen him.

She studied it before she spoke. "I've never seen him until now. He sure was a handsome young man. I bet you think so, too."

I smiled, but it seemed unprofessional to comment.

"Maybe he broke one too many hearts," she suggested with a wink, "and the last one got him back."

Sure;that explained it.

* * *

When I walked into the medics' office, which is on the other side of the building from ours, Running Man was there under the lights. He lay on an examination table and was covered by a sheet. Somehow that made it worse.

"Look at this," Barney said in place of hello.

I went to his side and he handed me a pair of exam gloves. "What does this look like to you, Ricos?"

I peered at one lifeless arm. Mitch held his gloved finger near a tiny red spot that appeared to be a needle mark. Barney gave me a knowing look. I didn't bother to mention that this had been my suggestion at the river.

"Look at his eyes," Mitch said, and I didn't want to. He held the right eye open for me, then the left. They were bloodshot with dilated pupils, and they were blue.

"I think we're looking at death by drug overdose," Mitch continued, "and I bet the crime lab will confirm it."

"Runners don't do drugs," I said.

"He doesn't have any other marks like this," Mitch told us, "so he hadn't done it before, or not often anyway."

Our sheriff, Ben Duncan, came in at that point. He is a tall, trim, professional-looking man in his mid-sixties. His thick hair is all white. That's what looking at dead bodies and chasing criminals will do for you. I thought for the hundredth time that I should get out while my hair was still dark.

"Good morning, Margarita." My boss and I shook hands, and then he greeted Barney and Mitch. They brought him up to speed on probable cause of death.

The sheriff looked over the body, taking his time.

"Is the hearse coming?" Mitch asked. "Or do you want me to transport him?"

The sheriff raked one hand through his luxurious hair. "The hearse will take him to the crime lab. They should be here soon."

Our closest crime lab is in Midland, 230 miles away. A funeral home in Alpine does the transporting, but Mitch does it when they can't.

When the sheriff finished observing, Barney and Mitch re-covered the dead man.

"You don't have any idea who this is?" asked the sheriff.

"No sir." Barney glanced at me. "There was no identification on him and so far, nobody has recognized him."

"Margarita, you took photos?"

"Yes sir. I already showed them around in Lajitas."

"I want you to keep trying. Somebody in Terlingua is bound to know who he is. Barney will call you after the J.P. comes, and then we'll join you."

Our Justice of the Peace serves as coroner but only as far as pronouncing death. Past that, he does nothing with the dead and isn't trained in forensics. He handles small claims court, marries people, certifies deaths, and serves as a judge for local traffic court.

It was a relief to get out of there. Carrying photographs of a corpse is a few degrees less creepy than being in the room with one.

CHAPTER 2

The Terlingua Ghost Town was a good place to start because there are always people hanging out on The Porch. Maybe someone there had seen him.

At one time, the Ghost Town was an abandoned cinnabar mining village. Now it's occupied by various businesses and private homes. It sits high enough to provide breathtaking vistas of mesas, mountains, and miles of desert landscape. Under a sky that goes on and on.

A wooden bench stretches across the front of the main building, a store built in the 1930s. Because of the view and proximity to cold beer, it's a popular gathering place. It's so well known to locals that when you say The Porch, everyone knows which one. From it we watch the play of sunlight and shadows on the landscape, the changing colors of sunset, and the weather. Discussing rain is a favored pastime in Terlingua. The question heard most often is *you think it'll rain?* We live in a desert, so no; most likely it isn't going to.

When I walked up, a few people I know were drinking beer and talking about Willie Nelson and the making of the movie *Barbarosa* in the Big Bend area in 1980.

"About that time," old Jeff Smith, a long-time, long-haired, long-winded local was saying, "the Terlingua Medics were trying to raise money to buy a defibrillator."

"What the heck is that?" someone asked.

"It's used to electronically stimulate the heart after a heart attack," explained Jeff. "They needed it for the ambulance so it could be used en route to Alpine. It was an important piece of equipment the medics didn't have because it cost around seventy-five hundred dollars—and this was in 1980."

I sighed and took a seat. I hadn't even been born in 1980.

Jeff smiled at me in greeting but didn't stop talking. "One day some of us were sitting here and Willie Nelson joined us. People were talking about the defibrillator and how badly it was needed. Willie pulled out his checkbook and wrote a check to the Medics for the exact cost of the machine. We couldn't believe it.

"After the defibrillator was installed in the ambulance, Mary Harrison had a heart attack, and it was used on her during the ambulance trip to Alpine. Later she bragged to everybody that Willie Nelson had jump-started her heart."

Everyone laughed at that.

"Hey, Margarita, have you heard the one about the blond deputy?"

I groaned and claimed to have heard that one, which got a laugh. There usually had to be a law enforcement joke when I showed up, and the subject was often a blond even though my hair and eyes are dark. I jumped in with my questions and passed the photos around the assembly of seven local residents and two people I had never seen before.

"I saw him last night," claimed Jeff. That figured. He sees and knows all and likes to talk about it whether it's accurate or not, typical news pundit. "He was eating at the Starlight with some Mexicans. They looked like a stereotypical bunch of drug dealers with one wholesome, out-of-place white dude."

The group chuckled at that description.

"Did you know any of the men?"

"No, none of them, and I'm not saying they were drug dealers, only that they looked like you'd expect them to look, you know?"

Jeff asked if I thought they had killed the runner.

"No. I don't know that. The problem is I don't know anything. There was no identification on him, so I don't even know who he is or where he's from."

"You need to find those men and question them."

Aye Dios. No wonder I feel the need to drink. "Yes Jeff, that's the plan, but it appears they left the area."

"Well, there's your proof of guilt."

"That doesn't prove anything," countered someone more reasonable than Jeff.

"They went that-away!" Jeff cried. He swept his tobacco-stained hand towards the rest of the world—so not helpful.

"Adolpho Estevez was with them," said a young river guide called Rio, "and Luis Garza, too." Then he added, "Hi, Margarita," with a big grin.

"Hi, Rio." I returned the grin. "Are you sure about the kids? Those boys are still in high school."

"Yes, I'm sure it was them. Kids or not, they were hanging with those men."

After I found out all I could from the Porch People, I walked over to the Starlight Theatre, a restaurant at the other end of the Porch. I knew they wouldn't open until five o'clock, but I tried the door anyway. It was locked, so I stepped to the side of the building for privacy and called the school office.

"Adolpho and Luis haven't attended classes in three days," advised the secretary. "Their parents don't know where they are. Nobody does."

"If you hear anything, please call me."

"I will, Margarita."

I sprinted to a nearby gallery and showed the sad photos to Darla, the clerk. Her fashion statement was tie-dyed everything except faded bellbottom jeans. She looked like she had stepped out of the 1960s, even though she hadn't been born then.

"Yes, I remember him. He asked me to hold a copper lampshade. Let's see; I have it right here."

Darla pulled an exquisite hand-hammered piece from behind the counter. There was a tag on it that read "hold for Bill Hayfield." I had a name.

"I don't guess he'll be coming back for this," she said sadly.

"No, but please continue to hold it for now."

"He was staying at the El Dorado," Darla volunteered, and then she blushed. "I only know because I asked. He said he was engaged."

"Did he say where he was from?"

Her face scrunched up in thought. "I don't think he said. If he did, I don't remember. He wanted the lampshade for his fiancée but didn't have his wallet because he'd been running."

"When was he in?"

"Yesterday morning. He said he'd be back today. You should ask at the Trading Company. I know he went in there, because I was watching." She reddened again.

It's the Terlingua Trading Company that occupies most of the old company store building. The Porch sitters had been so entertaining I hadn't checked there. I walked back over, ducked the blond lawwoman jokes, and went into the store.

The manager, Nell, was dressed in sharp but casual attire: blue Bermuda shorts and a crisp blue-checkered blouse. I called a greeting to her.

She returned the greeting, but stared at me over

bifocals. "You're here in uniform." It sounded like she was accusing me of something.

"Yes. I'm working, inquiring about this man." I handed her the photos. "Do you have any idea who he is?"

Her expression told me she recognized him. "He's dead?"

"Yes, I'm sorry to say he is. He didn't have any identification on him. Do you know his name?"

"He's dead in the river?"

"That's where we found him. Do you know anything about him?"

"Was he murdered?"

"The cause of his death has not been officially determined."

"Unofficially?"

"Nell, what do you know?"

"Of course I don't know anything. He was here yesterday and bought a few things. Why do you think he was murdered?"

"Did he tell you his name or where he was from?"

"It was Bill something, from Austin. I think he said he was a banker. He sure was nice—and nice-looking. Every woman in here was admiring his ass."

I cleared my throat.

Nell volunteered more information. "He bought some souvenirs to take to his fiancée. Well, he didn't buy them since he'd left his wallet in his room, but he asked me to hold them. He said he was staying down the road at the El Dorado."

"Do you still have them?"

"No, because he came last night and paid for them."

"Did he say anything else?"

"It was all small talk. He liked it here and said he was going to bring his fiancée back for a visit."

"Did he pay with a credit card?"

"I don't know. I can look at yesterday's receipts if you want."

"That would be helpful, Nell."

She went to her office while I perused the store. It has a fine collection of locally-made and imported gifts, but I like the book section best.

Nell returned. "He must have paid cash because I don't have any credit card slips with his name, and I found this." She handed me a receipt with the name "Bill Hayfield" at the top and a list of merchandise he had purchased. "Hold" was scrawled next to his name, but that had been scratched out and replaced with "paid."

"May I take this?"

"Sure. I don't need it. I made a copy."

"Thanks for your help, Nell."

"Come by when you're not working. We have some new cowboy stuff that Kevin would really—" The color drained from her face, and she seemed unable to speak another word.

"It's okay Nell, I do it, too."

"I'm so sorry. Sometimes I forget he's gone."

"I know. It's all right." I smiled at her and ducked out, a familiar ball of emotion blocking my throat.

Sometimes I forgot, too. Other times I refused to believe it. My husband Kevin had been killed in a rodeo accident two and a half years before.

On The Porch I took a deep breath. In the distance were the hazy peaks of the Chisos Mountains, the heart of Big Bend National Park. To understand the park's vastness, you need to know it's larger than the state of Connecticut, with three distinct habitats: river, desert, and mountains.

From nearly everywhere in Terlingua, the Chisos Mountains are a commanding presence of rough, reddish-brown stone. Viewed from afar they appear barren, but in fact they support a variety of plant and animal life, including conifer forests; yet not one tree is visible from a distance or from the desert floor.

"I have a good one for you, Margarita," someone called behind me as I took out my cell phone. There was loud laughter.

"You'll love this!" claimed someone else.

I smiled at them, indicated the phone, and then walked off the Porch and back to my vehicle. The El Dorado confirmed that a William Hayfield had been registered there, but "this morning he checked out." That was truer than they realized.

"Please don't clean that room. I'm on my way there now."

Then I called Barney with the news.

"We were about to call you, Pard. We'll meet you there in ten."

"I'll be at room six."

I didn't say I would be *in* the room. Who knew what we would find in there? My imagination is as big as the national park at my doorstep.

CHAPTER 3

There were no dead bodies in room six, but next to a window was a round table with a small mound of cocaine on it. A syringe, a glass of water, what appeared to be a mixing vial, a razor, and a straw lay next to it. There were a couple of dusty lines where the drug had been laid out. There was also a whiskey bottle on the table and a half-full glass of what looked and smelled like whiskey.

My first thought was *who parties like this so early in the morning?* No way would it be a runner. Besides, the scene looked too contrived.

"This doesn't fit," I said as I turned my back on the whiskey. Man, the smell made me want some. "Hayfield looked as healthy as a horse in spite of being dead and was dressed like he'd just been for a run or was planning to go on one. Either way, he wasn't a druggie. Somebody wanted it to look that way, though."

"That's what I'm thinking, too," agreed Barney.

"Also," interjected Sheriff Ben, "you don't overdose and then throw yourself into a river eleven miles away."

We agreed, and he left to speak with the desk clerk about the man who had rented room six. Barney and I wandered around examining the scene.

"Our vic sure bought a lot of souvenirs," observed my partner.

He referred to a blue Terlingua Ghost Town ball cap with the skiing skeleton logo. "It's a dry heat." The tag still hung from it. There was a similar visor, one shot glass with a desert theme, a Big Bend National Park photo calendar for the coming year that was still wrapped in plastic, and a hand-painted tile with a hanging chili ristra.

"He was planning to go home today," I said, and then told Barney the details of my conversations in the Ghost Town.

"There was no abandoned vehicle at the river," he pointed out. "If nobody else was involved, and he was doing coke like that, he would've had a vehicle. And look at this bed." Barney's 6' 6" frame was bent over it. "See these brownish drops? I bet someone tried to force whiskey down him."

I walked up next to my partner. "Yep, I agree. Some kind of serious struggle happened on this bed."

His left eyebrow rose and he turned his head to me. "Maybe it was wild sex."

"Could be that, except we have a dead man, and I don't believe he died from an accidental overdose of sex."

Barney laughed. "Yeah, he was too young for that to be the cause of death." He studied the bed a few more seconds. "What the hell, Ricos?"

"Don't look at me. I can't explain anything."

Barney put on gloves and handed me a pair. "We have to bag things."

We began doing that.

"I've got a wallet here," he announced. "No money or credit cards, but there's a Texas drivers license that names William Hayfield from Austin. Looks like our dead guy. He was twenty-seven."

He handed it to me, and I agreed it was our man. I took photos of the room and then helped Barney place all the souvenirs in evidence bags. After that he began fingerprinting the surfaces, starting in the bathroom.

Sheriff Ben returned. "The maid says she's seen five men hanging around this room, including the victim. They've been here two days and had the room next door, too. Do you know a couple of local boys named Adolfo Estevez and Luis Garza?"

"Yes I do. One of the guys on The Porch told me they were with them. They're high school students."

"Both the maid and the desk clerk recognized them."

"They haven't been at school for three days, and their parents claim not to know where they are."

"We could get a search warrant," Barney said to the sheriff. "Maybe we can find something relevant."

"We probably won't need a warrant," was Sheriff Ben's opinion. "I imagine all I have to do is ask permission to have a look."

That was more than likely true. His manner usually caused people to help rather than hinder him.

"The manager says these same men have been here before," our boss continued. "It was a few months ago, and the kids were with them then, too. They suspected they were dealing drugs, but nobody thought to call the law."

"Typical." Barney raised one eyebrow at me.

"According to the motel staff, that big Dodge Ram pick-up parked out there is Hayfield's." The sheriff pointed to it as he spoke. "I had the office run the plates, and it checks out. The other men were in an old brown Chevy Blazer. The plate was stolen." That news was not a shock to anybody.

While Barney and I finished up in the room, Sheriff Ben called the Austin Police Department to check the address on the driver's license and the next of kin address and phone number we got from the wallet. He waited, and after a while they confirmed that William Hayfield lived at that address, in what they described as an upscale neighborhood. They promised they would get back to us with the next of kin information.

The sheriff wandered around observing but seemed lost since my partner and I had things under control. After a few minutes, our radios crackled in unison, and the dispatcher asked Sheriff Ben to call Sergeant Landon in Austin.

Barney and I went next door to see if that room had a story we could read. It didn't appear to, but I nosed around while he tried to lift a few prints.

After a while, Sheriff Ben stepped in. "According to the Austin guys, Hayfield was a major player but was not known as a user. The Drug Enforcement Agency had been watching him for nine months, hoping to find his connection in Mexico."

Obviously, they weren't watching him closely enough.

"The next of kin listed were his parents," the sheriff continued. "They thought he was on a business trip to Germany. They believed he worked for an international investment company and said he spoke fluent Spanish and German. He called them yesterday and they assumed he was still there. He said he was doing great and asked if they'd seen his fiancée. He promised he'd be home within the week and would call later, and that was it."

"Did they say anything about cocaine use?"

"That wasn't mentioned, but they did say Bill was planning to marry a woman named Debbie Whitson in December. They asked to be allowed to break the news before the police descended on her, which seemed reasonable. Austin P.D. will call me after they speak with her. They're running a background check on Hayfield, too."

"Did anybody mention running?" I asked.

"His parents claimed he was training for an upcoming marathon."

Barney turned to me. "That'd rule out cocaine use, don't you think, Ricos?"

"Yes, I'm sure it would."

Sheriff Ben received a call and stepped out. When he returned, he brought us up to speed. "The DEA's take on Mr. Hayfield is that he was a serious businessman. He made the deals and organized delivery arrangements, but he never carried drugs or used them. He was never sloppy and didn't take chances. Special Agent David Small told me he'd eat his badge if Bill Hayfield died of a drug overdose by his own hand."

"Alrighty then," exclaimed Barney, making us laugh. "What's next, Sheriff?"

"I want you and Barney to inspect Hayfield's truck. I suspect you'll find nothing incriminating, but you may turn up some detail that will help us. While you do that, I'm going to the Garza home to speak with Luis' parents. If they grant permission to search his room, I'll call and we'll proceed. I'm going to want your help, Barney. After that, we'll go to the Estevez home. Margarita, if I call Barney away, please finish and then secure the crime scene until we return."

The sheriff drove off, and Barney and I put on gloves and opened the truck using the remote button on the key without taking it out of the evidence bag. The first thing I noticed about the interior was how clean it was. There was an empty coffee mug in the cup holder, driver's side. There were sunglasses in a case on the seat. That was it for clutter.

There was a cell phone charger and cord but no cell phone. We assumed the perpetrators left with the phone, pager, laptop, and any other devices that might have given us a clue.

The glove compartment held an owner's manual, a small framed photo of an attractive woman, an unmarked map of Mexico, and a couple of tissues.

While I bagged those items, Barney fingerprinted the doors on both sides, inside and out. Curious people began stopping to see what was going on, but we sent them away as politely as we could. The "Dead Runner in the River" story was running amok; it had already morphed into something it wasn't. There was no bullet hole in his head or anywhere else on his body, but that rumor had started. And there were no victims in room six. A gang of drug dealers had not been "taken out by local deputies." Nor had a man gone crazy and killed his whole family. Thankfully.

"Who starts this shit?" Barney wondered out loud, but I didn't think it was a question he expected me to answer.

We were nearly finished with the truck when our radios crackled with Sheriff Ben's voice. "It's a go, Deputy."

"Ten-four, Sheriff," Barney responded.

We say little over the air because of bored people with scanners who listen for information they can mis-repeat until it doesn't even faintly resemble the truth of our original communication.

Barney finished up what he was doing and headed to the Garza home. When the truck had been checked to my satisfaction, I put the evidence bags next to the other ones on the bed and secured the vehicle. Then I waited, seated in a small sliver of shade, by the door of room six.

In not quite an hour, Barney and the Sheriff came back and brought me iced tea. The two squatted nearby, aligning themselves in separate patches of shade.

"We didn't come up with much," said Sheriff Ben, sounding disappointed.

"We found over one thousand dollars in Luis Garza's room," Barney said. "That's a lot of cash for a high school student, but alone it doesn't prove anything."

"Señora Garza told us her son does odd jobs." Sheriff Ben paused to drink tea. "She thinks he saved the money from his work. We took some of the bills for fingerprinting, along with a hairbrush for DNA. There was a t-shirt wadded up in a corner of Luis' room which appeared to have a small blood smear on it, as well as a stain that smelled like whiskey."

"Nothing incriminating was found in the Estevez home," explained Barney. "We took a toothbrush of Adolfo's for a DNA profile. When I described the men to his mom she was upset, but said she had no idea who they were. She thinks her son has been in trouble for some time. He'd become distant and was gone for long periods and never admitted where he'd been when he returned. He talked about leaving school, but last week he told them he wanted to join the Marine Corps when he graduates."

"I hope he has a chance to graduate," I said. "These boys are in way over their heads."

Sheriff Duncan decided to close the room and remove

the crime scene tape from the parking lot. We were sure we had what we needed, or what we could get, from room six. He would order it kept undisturbed until he heard back from the crime lab. We put tape across the door after we locked it.

Barney and I walked over to the motel office to inform the manager that she was to let no one enter that room until the sheriff released it. She was agreeable, though she was understandably anxious for things to get back to normal.

We agreed to meet back at our office. When we got there, the sheriff sat in his truck a long time, talking on his cell phone.

"Maybe he's calling the Rangers." I thought that because it's customary for the Texas Rangers, the best investigators in the state, to be called in by rural law enforcement for help on serious crimes.

Barney looked up from his mail. "He called them already. They're covered up right now, so Sheriff Ben told them we would handle it."

I went into my office and called Terlingua's answer to the CIA, Sylvia's Café. Sylvia, the English-born owner, always seems to know everything going on in the community. She is known to say, "If I don't know about it, it can't be happening."

I always had to get past her well-meaning worries first: I was too young to be alone all the time; I needed a husband; I ran too much and didn't eat enough meat; my job was too dangerous. She was like a second mother, only worse.

Why do people think if your husband dies you should grab another? It isn't that easy and first you have to get over the one that is gone. No one could tell me how to do that, only that I should. Not helpful at all.

"Sylvia, I won't be alone the rest of my life."

"Yes you will if you don't ever give anybody a chance."

"Okay, look; I need to talk to you about a murder."

"I heard you found a dead man with a great ass at the river."

I couldn't imagine who had related it to her in that way.

"Shame," she added.

"Sylvia, did you see four Mexican men and one white man riding around in an old brown Chevrolet Blazer? Two were boys, Adolfo Estevez and Luis Garza."

"Sure. I saw them. Two of the Mexicans ate breakfast here yesterday morning and the man with the killer butt joined them after they were already eating. Adolfo and Luis weren't with them then, but I saw them later riding around."

"What did the two Mexican men look like?"

She dragged on her cigarette then blew it out, taking her time. "One had a big mustache, one of those droopy ones, and was wearing sunglasses every time I saw him. He was short and stocky. They called him Soto or Sotol; I'm not sure. He spoke broken English and did most of the talking. He and I passed how-are-yous, and he did the ordering with the waitresses."

"And the other one?"

"He was taller and wore his hair pulled back in a ponytail. He was a nice looking man, except for a nasty scar high on his left cheek. I don't think he spoke English."

"Could you guess their ages?"

"Scarface was forty, more or less, and the other man was in his mid-thirties. The runner was around your age, but you saw him. Is it true about his ass?"

I refused to get sucked in to that line of conversation. "Anything else?"

"Well, the one with the moustache wore a lot of gold jewelry and had an attitude. He thinks highly of himself, but he isn't much. Now the runner—"

"Yes, I know about the runner."

"You need to find yourself a live one like that."

"So you don't mind if I date drug dealers?"

"For heaven's sakes, I don't mean that at all, and you know it."

"Thank you for your help, Sylvia."

"Let me know what you find out."

Whatever I found out, she would probably know it before I did.

Sheriff Duncan had come in to the office and was telling Barney about his conversation with the Austin P.D. "They spoke with Mr. Hayfield's fiancée who was certain he never used drugs. The two were planning to marry soon, and she was devastated he'd been killed. She told the police Bill called her last night, excited about coming home."

I related some of the conversation I'd had with Sylvia. The sheriff said her description of the men matched the one he got from the desk clerk. He added that Hayfield was registered in his name, but the other two were registered in the name of Francisco de la Villa and no one knew if that was really the name of either man. The clerk said the other guests referred to a "Sotol." He thinks Sotol is the nickname of the gold laden leader.

I told him what Sylvia had said about the jewelry.

The sheriff let out a long sigh. "So, what we have are five guys who appeared to be friends. One went for a run, and when he came back, he was murdered by the others and his body was dumped in the river. The perps disappeared before the body was discovered. Is that about it?"

Barney and I agreed that it was, which meant we hadn't come very far from where we had started that morning.

    * * *

Barney slammed the phone down and cursed.

"We're heading to the river again, Ricos," he yelled as I came out of my office to see what the heck was going on.

"For?"

"Some fishermen got tangled up with something and when they pulled it—"

"I don't think I want to hear the rest of this."

"Damn right you don't. Come on. I'll catch you up on the way."

He didn't say anything else until we got in his Explorer. "You know where those black rocks go down to the river like steps, upriver from Lajitas?"

"Sure, I know the place."

"It appears there's a body caught up under there on a ledge or something. They got their line caught around a foot, but they got freaked when they pulled it out so they called 911."

"They pulled out a foot? Are you talking about a foot *only?*"

"Well, I don't know. They reported a foot."

"Jeez, I hope they've got that wrong."

"Ricos, whatever this is, I have a feeling it'll be a lot worse than the dead runner."

CHAPTER 4

Two men sat together at the top of the black rocks, looking grim. Fishing gear was strung all over, but nobody was using it. The Terlingua EMS had been called as a matter of protocol, so Mitch and another medic called Galveston were already there, staring at the floating jumble of fishing line, water weeds, trash, and one entangled foot. This was the scene we saw before we got out of the vehicle.

"It's only a foot," I said, and more to myself than to Barney.

He sucked in a breath then let it out slowly. "What in lawman Hell?"

When we lifted the jumble out of the river, Mitch stated his opinion. "It belongs to a male."

Yeah, we could see that.

"The rest of him is probably still in there," Galveston added.

We thought that, too.

Barney and I looked at each other. We shared a non-verbal communication, the gist of which was that *somebody* had to get into the river to look for the rest of the body. He didn't want to; I didn't want to; who else was there? The medics? Inappropriate. The fishermen tourists? Even less appropriate. Our whiny, wordless exchange was over when Barney started removing his boots.

I brought the ragged sneakers he keeps in the back of the Explorer and set them down next to him. Good thing my ratty old river sandals were still there.

It was too cool to get wet, but that wasn't the thing. It was eerie as hell. I had been in the Rio Grande so many times I couldn't guess how many, and it was never scary before—so dark and brooding. And the river smell I love? Forget it.

I tried to concentrate on the surrounding sights and sounds: the bilingual gurgle of water tumbling over stones, the friendly breeze that lifted my hair, sunlight dazzling the surface of muddy water, birdsong, and somewhere a burro braying. We were dwarfed by towering cliffs too, but gazing up didn't help. Every time my hand touched anything my stomach rolled. Immersed in water, all things are wet and cold.

Barney, being taller, ventured farther into the river. I felt along under a ledge beneath the rock formation where the fishermen and medics sat silently watching us. When my hand closed around cold flesh, I couldn't make my head believe it was anything else.

"I have something, Barney."

He turned to me, soaked to his waist. He started to speak but didn't. Then he began slogging towards me, pushing against the water. By the time he reached me, I had pulled out a severed foot.

Mitch, the least horrified, took it from me as I began to climb out and went to compare it to the other one. Galveston offered a hand up and then helped Barney.

"They match," Mitch said over his shoulder.

"We need a rescue crew to see if we can find the rest of him," suggested Galveston.

"Radio it in," Mitch said to him, "and ask the national park for help, but make sure they understand we're searching for a body, not rescuing a live person."

Our volunteer fire department is prepared for search and rescue to a point, but the park's crew is more highly trained and has better equipment.

* * *

The feet were lying on an examination table when Barney and I walked in to talk to Mitch. We had been delayed by interviewing the fishermen and getting their contact information.

"I think these feet belong to a fairly young man," he said in greeting. "I don't mean a child, but they aren't an old man's feet. Also, they were taken from an already-dead body."

Thank God.

"They were cut off with a saw, probably a chainsaw," he continued. "I believe the crime lab will confirm it. The sheriff wants me to keep the feet refrigerated until the rest of the body is found. I don't have a way to do that unless I put them in our staff fridge and I can't do that. Will you put them in yours? I'll wrap them well."

We stared at him mutely.

"Less people are using yours, right?"

Barney sighed. "Yes, we'll take them. But for the record, we don't want to."

Mitch thanked us and added, "Probably in a few hours,

we'll have the rest of him."

That wasn't going to be so easy.

* * *

Barney came into my office and plopped himself down in the overstuffed chair. *"Que paso?* You look very pale."

"I was thinking about the feet."

"Stop thinking, Ricos; you're gonna make yourself throw up."

"Have you noticed that I haven't?"

"I noticed." He put his left foot up on his right knee. "You know they haven't found a body yet—or any sign of one."

"Yeah, I heard the radio."

"Where do you suppose the rest of it is?"

"I don't have a clue, but it might not be in the river. Maybe somebody only cut off the hands and feet so we couldn't identify the victim."

"But there are no hands," he reminded me.

"Well, if I was going to dismember a body, I'd put the parts in different places."

"Sometimes you scare me."

"I'm just sayin'."

"Do you think the feet belong to a drug dealer?" Barney asked.

"Since we've just had a drug-related murder it's not hard to imagine another, but the perps must be different—or the victims were handled differently for some reason. We have to find the rest of the body, or at least the hands. It's not like I can show photos of feet around and get a positive identification."

"Maybe you would if you showed them to the right person. Anyway, if you can get your head off dismembering bodies, Julia and I want to buy you dinner tonight."

"Really? That's nice."

"My brother's visiting."

"I knew there would be a catch."

"That's a terrible thing to say to a friend. Anyway, my brother is better looking and younger than me, but he's smaller."

"I suppose he's also rich and famous."

"No, but he will be. Look, I know you'll like him if you give him a chance. You find me irresistible, right?"

"Barney, I've asked you not to set me up."

"This is my brother, Ricos. Do me a favor."

"Oh, I don't think so. I know what you think about it, but I'm not ready."

"It's just for tonight, Ricos. Let your hair down. See what happens. You might have some fun."

CHAPTER 5

I slammed into my house and threw first my things and then myself onto the sofa. It seemed like I often went home mad and frustrated. It had everything to do with my empty home and nothing to do with drug dealers and murderers. Sometimes running set me right, sometimes not.

Barney's invitation to meet his brother didn't help. I had already forgotten most of what he told me about him except his name, Ted. It wasn't eating with friends that made me chew my nails. It was being set up with other peoples' single men. Everyone I knew had a brother, nephew, cousin, or friend who was an eligible bachelor. When I was ready I would find my own man. I was capable and had done it before. Nobody had set me up with Kevin.

It was hard to say no to Barney but also hard to imagine dating his brother. What if I didn't like him? What if I did? Barney and I had to work together, and I didn't need him to know anything about my personal life. He was too curious as it was.

I hadn't had a date with a stranger in a long time and dreaded making small talk. Stress overwhelmed me as I dressed, so I told myself it wasn't a date, only dinner with friends. But my palms were sweating. I tried to concentrate on looking nice, not too dressed up but dressed up enough. After changing my clothes several times, I decided on a yellow sundress with spaghetti straps that had a white bolero jacket so it wasn't too revealing. Then I almost changed back into jeans.

I sat on the edge of the bed to get my breath. Barney would have laughed if he could've seen me. He thought I was cool and self-confident.

Bottom line—this was Kevin's fault. He was gone, and I was left to fend for myself. He thought I was stunning in anything I wore, and once you've been treated that way it's hard to be demoted to normal. Kevin thought I was smart, sexy, witty, the whole nine yards. That's how it is when you look at a person through love-filled eyes.

My hair is shoulder-length now, and I usually wear it in a French braid when I'm working, to keep it out of the way.

Following Barney's advice, I let it down and brushed it out. It was wavy from being bound all day, but looked all right. At least it was different. Barney had probably been speaking metaphorically, but now it was done. Next: the wedding ring.

I took a deep breath, took it off, and stared at my naked finger. Then I put it back on, took it off again. I set it beside a photo of Kevin and me on our wedding day. Then I put the ring into a drawer. I wasn't going to wear it again.

I cried a while and had to wash my face and re-apply mascara. That was my one concession to make-up besides lipstick. I stared at myself in the mirror and thought I looked pretty good; are you watching Kevin? I almost started crying again.

By the time I went to meet the group at the Starlight Theatre, I was worked up. I needed to drink—or thought I did—same thing. With me it was drink or run since I couldn't do both, and I chose running almost always. Sometimes running was inconvenient and drinking seemed easier. But running made me feel sane and like I had a grip. Maybe it was tenuous, but it was something.

Before my eyes had a chance to adjust to the dim lighting, I told the hostess I was meeting the Georges. Anybody could have found a table with the two biggest men in the county, but she led me there anyway. Somebody at the bar whistled as we passed the row of every-night drinkers. Not long ago I had been one of them, and I couldn't go back to that.

When Barney and his brother stood to greet me, it brought to mind Twin Peaks, a pair of matching mountains near Alpine. Barney had said his brother was smaller and better-looking. He might've been an inch or two shorter and twenty pounds lighter, but he was still huge. As for better-looking, yes he was, not that there is anything wrong with Barney. Ted has the same startling blue eyes and sand-colored hair. They could almost pass as twins.

The admiring look on their faces made me feel slightly more at ease.

"Can I get you something to drink?" Ted asked after we had been introduced.

"I'd like a club soda with lime, please."

Everyone else was drinking beer. Man. I wanted one.

Ted bowed out to get my drink.

"Your hair looks great like that," Julia said.

"Thanks."

Barney studied me. "What are you trying to do?"

"What is that supposed to mean?"

"What do you think of my brother?" he demanded to know.

"For Heaven's sake, she's only just met him," Julia said. "He seems nice."

"You're nervous, Ricos," Barney observed accusingly.

"Yes. I am."

"You need to get out more. Anyway, there's nothing to worry about with Ted. He won't do anything inappropriate, or I'll hurt him. This is only dinner with friends."

"I wish you would've set him up with someone more fun."

"Ricos, I don't know anyone more fun than you."

"Where do you get that?"

"Stop worrying."

We didn't have much time to argue before Ted was back with my pseudo drink.

After we ordered dinner, he asked, "Do you like being a deputy? Except for having to work with my brother, I mean."

That got a laugh out of everybody and was something I could talk about. He said he had been a professional football player until an injury put him out of the game. Now he was in medical school at Baylor in Houston. He relaxed, I relaxed, and before long we were having fun.

After dinner, we took our party to Barney and Julia's, but soon they wanted to go to bed, and that left us without options. I thought it would be nice to take somebody to bed, but he was Barney's brother, and it seemed too weird. I hadn't been with anyone but Kevin in five years, so that part was daunting. I nearly started to hyperventilate before I made my getaway.

I got home a little after midnight and packed a cooler with ice, water, and sodas, and strapped it to the rear of my ATV. The moon was so bright I didn't need any extra light, and it wasn't even full yet. The lacy, oblong leaves of the towering mesquite tree in my backyard looked silvery and stirred lazily in a slight breeze.

Soon I was bumping along, enjoying the moon-drenched scenery, missing Kevin. Everywhere I went seemed like a field of landmines. If I made a misstep, all those memories exploded in my face.

I moved fast, trying to force myself to be happy. The more quickly I moved the further behind I left murder, drugs, dismembered bodies, and other depravities. The potholed dirt road wound around near Cimarron, a mountain I think of as mine. It dominates the view from my neighborhood and from the front of my house. When there is enough rain, water cascades down the sides in torrents, although most of the time it's dry. The truth is I watch it rain or shine and even at night. Cimarron is majestic and stands like a lone sentry, set apart from other mountains. From a distance, its sharp spires and pointy red rock outcroppings make it look like a giant prehistoric creature lying down in a great expanse of desert.

I passed through a neighborhood, but my destination was some sandstone bluffs west of Cimarron Mountain.

The road going up the bluffs is steep and narrow, winding precariously in places. It ends up high, overlooking Tres Outlaws Canyon, Terlingua Creek, and much of the surrounding area. It is a great spot for stargazing and moonbathing and is a place I had never been with Kevin, making it less dangerous than other places.

The moonlit scenery was breathtaking. In the distance were the dark shapes of mountains silhouetted against the silvery sky. Everything glowed.

At the top, I parked the ATV to one side, spread out an old quilt, opened a soda, and sat down to marvel. To the southeast sat the bright, nearly-round circle of moon that had turned the world to magic. I felt like a queen in a storybook land surveying her kingdom from on high.

Terlingua Creek was below to my right, and the leaves of the cottonwood trees lining the bank shimmered. La Kiva, a popular bar, sits off the road, past the bridge that spans the creek. Lights winked through the gently swaying pine, cottonwood, and palm trees surrounding it. Cars came and went but I couldn't hear them, only saw their lights. The dominant sound was the wind, although I sometimes heard a few notes of the music that escaped the bar.

Below was a small canyon called Tres Outlaws. Through it winds a creek called, not surprisingly, Tres Outlaws Creek. Like all desert arroyos, it only runs when there is rainfall to be carried away. Tres Outlaws empties into Terlingua Creek.

There were a few houses in the sculpted canyon, hidden from the rest of the world by towering walls. Lights twinkled from a couple of them; the others were dark. Two people sat on the porch of one home, and occasionally I heard the murmur of their voices before the breeze whisked the sound away.

I moved the quilt near the edge of the bluff and peered over the side until I had vertigo from looking straight down the canyon wall. Then I saw something that almost stopped my heart. Three shadowy figures peered around and went into one of the silent houses. They were dressed in dark clothing, but the bright light of the moon gave them away. One of them was a man suspected in the morning's murder, along with Adolfo and Luis, the local boys I knew. The man with them was the one with the ponytail. Only Sotol was missing. I wondered if they had already killed him. Did the feet belong to him?

No light came on inside the house, but after a few seconds, there was the glow from a cigarette in one of the windows. What to do? I was unarmed and didn't even have my cell phone. The thought of starting the ATV and having those men waiting for me when I reached the bottom of the cliff was terrifying. So I waited.

After ten minutes the wind picked up, and that was the only noise besides the pounding of my heart until I heard something that sounded out of place—a motor. A vehicle was approaching the house. It looked like an old Chevy Blazer, brown maybe. Anyway, it was dark, like the house and the men, and another dark man got out of it, stood by the vehicle, and lit a cigarette. Gold jewelry flashed in the light of the match.

After a few seconds, the other men joined him and began to unload boxes from the back of the Blazer. I counted four. They appeared heavy, judging by the struggle. I didn't think these guys were moving in, not with four boxes, and not in the wee hours of the morning with no light. Besides, they couldn't move here if they had murdered William Hayfield.

What I thought was that those boxes held drugs or some other contraband, and they were only stashing them in an empty house until they could move them north. They had killed the man in charge and were on their own. It was ironic that the "wholesome-looking white man" had been the heaviest player, not the "stereotypical Mexican drug dealers."

I pulled the quilt around me. The wind had begun howling through the canyon, but it wasn't that giving me chills. It was watching ruthless men, and a couple of boys who had no business with them. They were cold-blooded murderers, and I was feeling way out of my league.

Tres Outlaws was so named because of three outlaws who had used the canyon as their hideout in the heyday of the cinnabar mines. They robbed trains up north, and though the law often pursued them, they always gave up when the bandits made it to the vast desert country of what is now south Brewster County. The name would have to be changed to "Quatro Outlaws" if these guys stuck around, I thought, entertaining myself.

For a short time the men sat on the porch. I assumed they were talking but couldn't hear a murmur because of the wind. All I saw was the glow from cigarettes. After more time passed, they checked the door, got in the Blazer, and drove away. I watched until they rounded a bend and then started my ATV. Afraid to use the headlights, I made my way back down the rutted path by the light of the moon.

I drove to the unpaved canyon road, left my ATV in some brush two houses over from where I had seen the men, and approached on foot. I tried the doors and found them locked, but the back door faced the sheer wall of the canyon where I would be unobserved by neighbors. It was locked with a simple key lock that I worked open within a minute.

The house was stuffy and smelled of cigarettes. Moonlight cast eerie shadows, but there was no furniture so it was easy to move around.

The boxes were stacked in the closet of the smaller bedroom. They contained whitish bricks of what I suspected was cocaine. I wet my finger, ran it along one of them, and tasted it. Yep.

I looked around enough to see that nothing had been left except four identical boxes, so the scenario was what I suspected; they were stashing the drugs. Where they had gone to spend the night was anybody's guess. The thing I knew for sure was that they would be back.

I exited by way of the rear door and picked my way back to the ATV. When I got to my house, I called the Sheriff's Office dispatcher in Alpine and asked him to notify the appropriate parties. Border Patrol would be the closest and illegal drugs come under their jurisdiction. I explained that I had seen suspicious activity by men we suspected of murder so had probable cause to search the house.

I changed into my uniform and then stood around while

three Border Patrolmen and one officer from I.C.E. (Immigration and Customs Enforcement) searched the house and confiscated the cocaine. Supposedly, I was standing guard in case the suspects returned. It felt more like I was being kept from under foot, me being a girl and all—and a lowly deputy sheriff at that. Confiscating contraband is big boy work.

I wondered about calling the biggest boy I knew and couldn't decide which would make Barney madder, being awakened or missing the excitement. I decided to let him sleep and was relieved to see there was nothing exciting about any of it. He wasn't missing anything he couldn't live without.

The men were making a final sweep of the house when I looked up. There were headlights on the bluff. I stepped into the shadow of the Explorer to watch. Two figures came to the edge, black silhouettes against the light. A third joined them with what looked like a rifle. He knelt at the edge of the bluff and took aim. I bent over, scurried behind my vehicle, and took out my Beretta.

"Rifle!" I yelled to two men stepping onto the porch. "Don't come out yet."

Being men, they ignored me. Maybe they didn't hear me. As they moved towards their truck, two shots were fired in rapid succession. One of the men fell to the ground in a heap. The other grabbed his injured leg and made a leap towards the rear of the Border Patrol truck.

"Ronnie!" he called to his downed partner.

The injured man groaned in response. "I'm okay. My shoulder—"

"Don't move," I yelled to the officers, took aim, and fired. A man cried out, the rifle spun into the air and flew off the bluff into blackness. The silhouettes disappeared and within seconds a motor revved.

The other two lawmen burst out of the house, weapons drawn.

"Call for an ambulance," I screamed, "and stay back!"

That was when I called my partner.

One of the Border Patrolmen, the uninjured Officer Farris, jumped up into his truck. Without invitation, I threw myself into the passenger seat and we peeled out in a spray of gravel and dirt. We sped to the bottom of the bluff but had missed the perps. A cloud of dust hung in the distance. They were fleeing on a seldom-used road that crosses Terlingua

Creek and disappears into the back country.

I wanted to give chase. "I know that country better than anybody," I said when he hesitated. "I've run back there countless times."

He didn't take his foot off the brake. "We already know who we're looking for so there's no need to chase them down."

I didn't know if he was afraid of the criminals, afraid of getting lost in the desert at night, or afraid of going into danger with me as his only back-up. I have yet to meet a lawman who wants to work with a woman. But in fairness, maybe he only wanted to go back to bed.

"Get out," I ordered. "I'm going to follow them."

"You can't take my truck and besides, you shouldn't go alone."

"Well then, let's go."

"No, I'm saying we aren't going. We'll be sitting ducks out there."

"But I know that country."

"It's too late. We've already lost them."

Yes, we had, because of his head being so far up his butt.

Back at the scene, I was relieved to see Barney talking to the others. He was wearing blue jeans with a uniform shirt that wasn't buttoned or tucked in. That was unlike him, but it was after three-thirty in the morning, and he'd been sound asleep.

The ambulance arrived and left with the two injured men. One had taken a bullet in the thigh; the other had one in his shoulder. Neither injury was life-threatening, but that didn't stop the pain from being terrible.

When the medics took off, Barney pulled me aside. He still had sleep creases on his right cheek. "How did you get in on this, Ricos?"

"I was on the bluff with my ATV, and I saw those guys taking boxes into the house. I checked it out, went home, and called it in."

"Damn. Don't you ever sleep?"

"Sure, but it was such a beautiful night I thought I should admire it. Aren't you the one who advised me to get out more and enjoy life?"

"How come you didn't call me?"

"I didn't think you'd be needed. It was routine until they started shooting."

"They must've come back and seen those trucks parked around their stash and went up there to scope it out. Those are some pissed-off guys about now."

"I could've gone after them, but Officer B.P. Pussy was afraid to go. Or he was afraid to go with a woman."

"Give the poor guy a break. You don't want to go into the back country with anybody from Border Patrol, do you?"

"Well, no. I didn't want to, but I was in his truck."

He laughed at that. "If I'd been here, we would've gone after them."

"Yeah, and we would've brought them in, dead or alive."

"You know it, Ricos."

In our minds, we are the roughest, toughest crime fighters in the West. It doesn't matter what others think.

CHAPTER 6

On Monday morning I went into my tiny office, but I checked the hill outside my window before starting to work. The scene was flawless with all boulders in their assigned places, and the sheer rock face still gleamed on top. A regular visitor, a red-tailed hawk, was cruising above it. I delighted in watching her soar and dip, except she terrorized the songbirds. They hid among the branches and brush whenever her shadow darkened the landscape.

I was standing at the window when Barney arrived noisily.

"Ricos!" he yelled.

"Yo!"

"You aren't gonna believe this."

I walked out to the front. "I hope there hasn't been another murder."

"I was called early this morning to a breaking and entering."

"Are you serious?"

"As a tax audit. Somebody broke into the Terlingua Store last night and stole cash, food, beer, and cigarettes."

"That's a first since I've been on the job."

"Of course we never found severed feet before, either."

"Why wasn't I called?" I wondered.

"At first, I thought it was a prank. When I got there it turned out to be true, but it wasn't like I needed help. I picked up some good prints from where the glass in the back door was broken out." He sighed. "This is ridiculous."

"It feels like we woke up in the wrong place."

"Yeah, and we didn't even sleep together. How could we be having the same nightmare?"

I laughed at that.

"The sheriff says our drug dealer murder case is being turned over to the Texas Rangers," Barney said. "It turns out they've been tracking the activities of Francisco de la Villa, aka Sotol, for some time. They've got evidence linking him to at least three other drug-related murders in Texas."

"I still wonder if he isn't linked to the feet."

"Too bad they're not his."

"Yep," I agreed.

"From now on, everything goes to the Rangers' field office in Midland. Sheriff Ben says the DEA is involved, too. They've done long-time surveillance on Hayfield."

"And they couldn't have followed him here?"

"Apparently not. According to them, he was connected to the Martez Cartel out of Monterrey, major drug traffickers. Sotol is one of their henchmen." He sighed as if it was the end of life on Earth. "So the bottom line is they took us off the case."

"Does that upset you?"

"Not really. It means a change of gears. I hate it when they do this to us."

"Yeah," I said, "it makes it seem like we're only a couple of incompetent yokels, and we know we're not."

"No dead body has turned up, and the river search won't be continued much longer. A corpse will wash up somewhere sometime or not. Meanwhile, we still have the feet. The sheriff says if the body isn't found today he's going to send somebody for the feet and get them to the crime lab. What should we do now?"

"Let's go check out the sandstone bluff," I suggested.

"For?"

"There might be blood or something else they left behind, like the rifle. Maybe we can get prints from it. We should've looked for it before now."

"Well it was three or four in the morning. I don't know about you, but I wasn't functioning. I'm usually sleeping at that hour."

"Granted," I agreed.

"Why go up there? It's not our case now."

"True, but the Rangers don't know firsthand what happened and I do. And going there will get us out of here. Besides, you need to see the bluff. It's incredible."

"Count me in," he said, and a few beats later, "Did you like my brother?"

"Sure. I liked him."

"But not that much."

"Look. I had a nice time, but that's as far as it went. And that's as far as it'll ever go because he's your brother. I wish I could make you understand. It's nothing against him."

"It's something against me?"

"No, not that either. We work together, and it seems too

weird to date your brother. Anyway, I'm not ready for anything serious with anybody."

"Nobody said it had to get serious. You could just have some fun."

"He lives in Houston. Anyhow, let's drop it. You know what I mean."

* * *

First we searched the weeds below the cliff and found the rifle after a few minutes. I took photographs then Barney pulled on gloves and lifted prints before we moved it. After that, we headed up the rutted road in his Explorer. About halfway up we decided to walk because there was no place at the top to turn around such a large vehicle.

"How did you find this place?" Barney asked.

"I took a run up here one day. Now I think of it as mine."

"To hear you tell it, all the scenery is yours."

"Yeah, well."

"There's blood on your bluff."

"Yep, I see that."

"So you hit one of them."

"I assumed that when he yelped and his rifle flew into the air."

"How do you do that in the dark and at that distance?"

"Uh—I take aim. And there was moonlight. Besides, he wasn't that far away."

"Showoff. I'm going to gather some of this blood as evidence."

"Knock yourself out." My boots were already hanging over the edge. Big Bend scenery is one big show-off, and I was powerless to look away.

"Ricos!" Barney yelled so forcefully it startled me.

"What?"

"I've got a finger here."

"Bag it. May it'll tell us something."

"Damn, you're cold."

"No I'm not. Cold would be if I'd shot him in the chest, and I could have. He only lost a finger."

"Oh, he lost two. Maybe I should make a collection."

"That would be gruesome. Talk about cold."

"I could keep them in a jar on my desk. This would make five if I had the others."

I shot off a few fingers in another case, too.

"That would make people stop and think when we're interrogating them."

I laughed at that.

After a while Barney sat next to me. He was silent, watching the same stunning view I was watching: the Mountain-Desert-Canyon Show under the Big Sky.

He took a deep breath. "We do live in a beautiful place, don't we?"

"Yes. I never stop being in awe of it." The sun glittered off something shiny in the distance, probably a pool of water in an arroyo.

"Would you go to dinner with Julia and me again?"

"Sure."

"Would you be angry if we invited a friend to go along?"

"If you're setting me up with one of your single friends, brothers, brothers-in-law, uncles, or cousins, then yes, I'd be angry."

"Jeez Ricos, you have to give men a chance."

"I want to find my own man. What is it you can't understand about that?"

"I want to help you. I know some good men."

"I'm sure you do. You have an intelligent and nice-looking brother. If I was in the mood, maybe I'd go out with him. I'm not ready."

"You promised you were going to look, but I don't think you are."

"I have to do it my way. But I appreciate your concern and hope you understand."

He was quiet a while and seemed thoughtful. Then, "I guess if Julia died, I wouldn't want you to bring me all your single friends."

"Exactly. You'd want to find your own woman. It has to be natural."

"Okay, Ricos. I get it."

"Where do you think the Border Patrol took all that cocaine?" I was staring down at the house, which made me think of the drugs.

"They're all high as crack ho's about now. I bet they turned in three boxes and kept one to play with."

"That's a hell of a way to talk about our fellow law enforcement professionals."

"Don't you ever wonder about them?"

"Would you do something like that?" I wondered.

"Only if it was beer or cash, and the cash only if it belonged to criminals."

"And the beer?"

"I'd drink the beer."

I laughed and elbowed him. "Let's go take a look at the route the criminals took when they left here, Beer Boy."

"What for?"

"Maybe we'll learn something."

"This isn't our case."

"It's criminal activity going on in our community. It can't hurt to look around. Besides, it'll be more fun than the office."

"You have a point. But how will we know where they went?"

"Tracks."

"Oh yeah. Well, lead on Daniel Boone."

We took my ATV because it's smaller, easier to maneuver, and can go more places than the Explorer. I strapped on a cooler with water and sodas. We would've ditched our uniforms for shorts, but I didn't have anything that would fit Barney.

"Besides," he reminded me, "if people see us running around in shorts they'll report to the sheriff that we're playing. Some busybody will tell Julia."

"There are a lot of bored people in our community."

"Yeah, Ricos, and there's the faction that doesn't want anyone to be happy."

"No kidding."

Contentedly married couples like Barney and Julia make them sweat and bare their teeth.

Once we passed the base of the bluff, picking up the tracks was easy since there was only one set. It got more complicated at the creek, where multiple tracks crossed and re-crossed, ATVs playing in the mud.

Terlingua Creek only flows during rain, but it's wet in places from natural springs that exist throughout its length. Some are large and make great swimming holes; others are small, but all are critical to wildlife. Native cottonwood, desert willow, and mesquite trees grow in clumps along the bank in places. In the wettest areas, there's a variety of wildflowers and native grasses.

Past the creek, the Blazer's tracks went up an overgrown road towards a canyon. The growth was recently mashed, making the trail easy to follow.

I drove because I know that area, and Barney was behind me on the passenger seat. Fortunately, my ATV was built to carry a load. Kevin always insisted we buy top-of-the-line.

The canyon goes off into the desert behind Cimarron Mountain. I'm less familiar with that view, but it's awe-inspiring from any angle. Back there, the fallen-down boulders seem even more gigantic, the landscape wilder and less friendly. The canyon, formed by two steep cliffs, was dark with shadows. I stopped to check the ground for tracks.

"I think this is spooky." The small voice came from the hulk sitting behind me.

"It's a little dark right now."

"You run back here—alone?"

"Yes, but I usually stay along the creek so I can wet my face."

"But you've been into that canyon?"

"Yes, several times. It's beautiful. I think there's a mountain lion living in one of those caves up there. See the tracks?" They had been made in wet ground, which made them pronounced and left clear impressions that could still be read many weeks after the last rain.

"Do you think those guys are still back here?" Barney asked.

"I doubt it. This is the 21st century. I don't think outlaws want to hide out in caves nowadays. They want running water, refrigerators, air-conditioning, internet access, you know."

"Women just aren't impressed by caves anymore," he pouted.

"If we ever were."

"Why would those perps come back here?"

"I would guess to hide out or to stash something."

Inside the canyon, the tire tracks stopped and footprints began. Three sets led into the canyon and back several times. My guess was the fourth man had been left in the Blazer. He would've been bleeding from the loss of his fingers and must have been in terrible pain.

"What do you think, Ricos?"

"I think they left something. Should we take a hike?"

"I'd rather drink beer in the shade, but I don't guess you brought any."

"That's right, Beer Boy. Come on."

The dirt in the arroyo was hard-packed and rocky. Where brush grew in clumps it caught debris during flooding. It still hung there, as if suspended in a web.

We didn't have to go far before the footprints wound over a mound of dirt to what appeared to be a shallow cave.

"Do you think a mountain lion will be in there?" Barney wondered.

"No. This cave is too small. But look at this."

Stuck into the opening and covered by brush were three more boxes full of bricks of cocaine.

"They returned to offload these boxes and saw activity at the house," I supposed. "That's why they went up to the bluff to take a look."

"I wonder why they didn't just bring them all at once."

"The boxes were probably coming across the river in small loads. Sotol brought the first ones, so maybe he got tired of waiting at the river and brought what he had, then took the other men back to help."

"Makes sense."

"This won't fit on my ATV. I could strap them on and take them back to the office if you waited here."

He glanced around like he was seven years old instead of thirty-two, big enough to be two deputies, and armed. "I don't like that idea."

"Can you think of a better one?"

"Not right offhand."

"I know. I'll run and you drive the ATV. When we get to my house we'll put the boxes into the Explorer."

"Now you're thinking with your whole brain, Ricos."

"Yeah, you should give yours a test run sometime."

We strapped the boxes on but had to leave the cooler. No big deal, because we could go back for it. The important thing was that lowly south county Deputies Ricos and George had made a major drug bust. The danger in that didn't occur to us then.

* * *

We arrived at the office only to be called to the scene of a vehicle fire at Big Hill. That's in Presidio County, but since we're close and it takes their sheriff's office an hour or more to get there, responding to their calls for help isn't unusual. The Presidio County line is approximately eighteen miles from our office, and is just past the Lajitas Resort.

State Highway 170 between Terlingua and Presidio is curving and mountainous with spectacular scenery. Big Hill is the steepest grade in Texas and is so named because of a sign at the top of the mountain that reads, BIG HILL, as if any conscious person wouldn't figure that out before they reached the sign.

We arrived ahead of the ambulance and fire crew. The burning vehicle was so engulfed in flames there was no hope of stopping it with or without a fire truck, nor did I think it could be reached by one. There was also little hope that anyone had survived the crash. Still, Barney and I picked our way down the steep slope to see if someone had been thrown from the vehicle.

The wreck was burning near the river, far from the top of the hill. It was terrifying to slip and slide our way towards the blaze. To lose footing could mean tumbling into a raging inferno. Twice we had to go back and find a different route because of the overpowering heat.

The fire crew arrived soon after we did, but by then the flames were beginning to recede, and there was more smoke than fire. Barney and I determined that no bodies had been thrown from the vehicle, either alive or dead.

Mitch, who had driven the ambulance, and Rudy, the chief of the volunteer fire department, made their way to us. Another medic stood by the road with the other firemen to slow traffic and discourage stopping.

We stood together, quietly watching.

"This vehicle didn't come off the mountain," I said. "It was already here."

All three men gaped at me but Barney was the first with a question. "What makes you think so?"

"There's no path." I pointed back up the steep side. "In order not to leave any kind of track it would have to have fallen from the sky. It isn't a plane. It looks like a truck and there was a truck body here before. It had been here since before I was born."

"What are you saying?" asked Rudy.

"Someone set fire to that old wreck that was already here."

"Why would anyone do that?"

"I have no idea. I'm just saying this isn't a new accident but the site of an old one. The only way it could burn is if someone set fire to it."

Three men looked at me as if I'd claimed the Rio Grande was running upstream. I ignored them and made my way closer to the river.

"Come on down here," I yelled to Barney.

Along the cliff that drops down to the river, there were footprints and disturbed plants. Below, there were more footprints drying in the mud along the bank and a clear indication that a canoe or some other type of boat had been beached there, maybe only a short time ago.

"Damn," sighed Barney, "it'd be hard to get up here from the river."

"It would be hard, yes, but not impossible."

The men started arguing about what kind of craft had been beached there, but none of them seemed anxious to scale down to the shore. I scrambled back up.

"We should look for them," I said. "They have to take out someplace."

Barney seemed torn between coming with me and staying to bullshit with the guys. They wondered if they should get the fire marshal to come or wait and sift through the ashes themselves when the wreck cooled off. Given the slightest chance, men will want to argue and dick around. I thought we should try to find the arsonists because I wanted to know the purpose of the fire.

"What's the big deal about burning some old wreck?" Barney wanted to know.

I don't think he was convinced that a truck hadn't sailed through the air from the road and crashed there. I was convinced it hadn't. There is a thick rock retaining wall down the side of the mountain. I made Barney drive all the way to the top to prove that no part of it was disturbed. There was no way to crash-land in that location without leaving the road by way of the wall. And if the truck had somehow jumped the wall, that sort of accident would leave a mark. By the time I convinced him of that, we had given the culprits ample time to get off the river and disappear.

"Give me one good reason to burn an ancient wreck, Ricos," Barney said accusingly on the way back to the office.

"Other than to watch it burn, I can't think of one."

He sighed. "So now we have murderers, thieves, *and* arsonists in a place where we almost never had anything more than petty stuff."

"I guess the so-called 'real world' not only found us but

is going to pound us to death."

Later that evening, I thought of a reason to burn something besides the perverted thrill of watching it. I was running towards Cimarron Mountain and trying not to think about the fire or criminals. Sunset was working its magic on the landscape, but a thought came to me anyway. A fire in a vehicle could be about several things. One was to get emergency response crews away from Terlingua, but why? I had no answer to that. As far as we knew, nothing had happened in our absence. Another reason for setting a fire would be to destroy evidence of something, like a corpse.

CHAPTER 7

Before going to work the next morning, I called Rudy, the fire chief, to see if he had stuck around to sift through the ashes or if he had called the fire marshal. He said he had done both things. He was convinced the fire had been set but seemed shocked when I asked about human remains.

I didn't want to set my as-yet-unproven theory in front of the whole community, so I held back my suspicion of murder. Maybe I was only being paranoid.

Rudy said he had found no sign of a human being. He said the fire marshal would not come since he would have to come from Midland. The marshal opined that there had been no loss of life or property, and he saw no reason to make the trip. Even if it had been arson, no criminal charges would be filed, and he thought it should be considered vandalism at the most. Rudy seemed to concur with that opinion and declined to go back to the scene with me because he had to go to work at his regular job. So did I, but I could go as part of my work and planned to.

When I laid out my thoughts to Barney, he felt it would be a waste of time to sift through ashes. I care about my partner and enjoy working with him, but sometimes I wonder what it would be like to work with a woman. Barney is never shy about telling me I'm an idiot, although he never uses those words. He gets his point across with body language, which in his case is like reading a billboard.

I went to the scene alone, which was easier than trying to talk Barney into doing something he didn't want to do. The blackened wreckage was intimidating, and okay, it was scary being there alone. It was a wild place once I got away from the road. I love wild places usually, but this one now had a freakish element.

One side of Big Hill forms the American side of a steep, shadowed canyon called Dark Canyon. It's beautiful but is most impressive when looking up at it from the river. Looking down at a charred spot on a ledge-like piece of land in deep shadows was disturbing. The creosote bushes and prickly pear cacti were half-black, or in some cases, completely charred and collapsed in heaps. All plant life within the immediate circle of the fire had been consumed.

The site was also difficult to reach, and once I arrived it made me feel vulnerable since getting away from it was just as difficult. I forced myself to be calm and began poking around. I was afraid I wouldn't find anything and more afraid I would. Either outcome felt unacceptable for different reasons.

Whoever had set the fire used an accelerant that made it burn hot and fast. Most of what was left was ashes, and many of those had been blown away by the winds of night. At one time, the truck had been discolored by rust and full of weathered holes, but still recognizable as a truck. Now it was a twisted, buckled wreck of metal.

I put some of the ashes into an evidence bag. Then I discovered what looked like a melted, deformed belt buckle. I put it into a different bag. From amid the rubble, I picked up several pieces of what could've been bone fragments. They looked like charred bone, so I took them. I thought maybe Mitch could tell me.

He couldn't. He put on gloves, took them out and studied them.

"I can't say for sure," he said. "Whatever this was has been burned too long."

Mitch even looked at them through a microscope and let me look too. Both of us thought it was bone.

"The crime lab will be able to make a definite determination," he assured me.

I called Sheriff Ben from my vehicle and told him the whole story, from the fire to my finds among the ashes. He listened with interest and said my theory sounded plausible. Since we'd already had one drug-related murder, and maybe another, it wasn't a stretch to think we could've had a third. He said he would send someone later to pick up everything going to the lab.

* * *

That afternoon I was sunk into the overstuffed chair in my office with my boots on the desk, watching the scenery. It helps me think. And my hill makes sense when nothing else does.

Colorful songbirds flitted from thickets of mesquite brush to small desert willows and back again, as if unable to decide which branches would be the best for singing and showing off. Everything is perfect out there in every season and in all weather. I know because I check constantly to be sure.

At the top is a formation of red-brown rock that perches there like a pillbox hat on a scruffy head. Giant boulders litter the sides, some in jumbled groups and others, solo. Their sizes vary from tractor-trailer to basketball.

October had come to the Big Bend country. The heat of a long summer had backed off, and colors were changing. The mesquite were on their way to golden, native climbing vines blazed red-purple practically overnight, and the Torrey yuccas had formed fat green seed pods that had mostly fallen to the ground already. The ones that hadn't were wrinkly dry and brown.

A man came from the Drug Enforcement Agency to pick up the cocaine. I heard him enter and listened while he and Barney talked law enforcement. Men love that stuff. The conversation came back to me and my sneaking-around-in-the-dark capabilities, but I wasn't about to go out there and beat my chest. I leave the chest-beating to Barney. DEA Special Agent Whoever would be unimpressed by my skill and bravery anyway.

A couple of cactus wrens were so worked up I could hear their squawking from inside with the window shut. I got out of the chair and stood at the glass to see what the fuss was about. Nothing, far as I could see—typical Terlingua residents.

Barney was giving me all the credit. He told Mr. DEA that I shot one of the culprits while protecting four Border Patrolmen, which did sound a little hero-ish. He went on to say that I was the one who discovered the drugs in the first place and had insisted on checking the bluff and then the canyon, where it turned out they had stashed still more boxes.

"How did Deputy Ricos know where the men would be?" the agent asked in a deep, pleasant voice.

"She didn't. She happened to be out riding her ATV in the moonlight."

"She?" He interrupted Barney's story. "Deputy Ricos is a *woman?*" He sounded just incredulous enough to make me want to go in there and kick him in the nuts.

"Does she do that a lot? Run around all night in the backcountry?"

"I guess you'd have to ask her that."

"Is she here? I would like to meet her."

I wanted to escape through the window, but the damn

things don't open. Instead I went behind my desk so I would seem professional. The two men entered, filling my office. The DEA guy seemed regular-tall, not Barney-tall. Anyhow, it didn't matter. He looked into my eyes and smiled, and it made me feel all warm inside, like a shot of tequila going down, and blood started pounding in my ears.

"Deputy Ricos, meet Special Agent Diego Romero from the DEA," Barney said.

"So you're Deputy Ricos." He took my hand. "I'm Diego Romero."

"I'm Margarita Ricos." It was amazing I remembered my name.

"I was expecting someone bigger," he said and turned crimson, "a man. I mean older, no, I mean an older man—a bigger—deputy." He was blabbering.

I felt like I had a mouth shot full of Novocain. My tongue was numb. My hand was so warm in his it was probably melting, but I just grinned and grinned and couldn't even feel my face—pitiful.

We held hands across my desk. I expected Barney to make a wisecrack, but he seemed speechless too. Maybe he had succumbed to the flying pheromones.

Diego Romero had turquoise eyes and they sparkled. I'm sure I noticed other things about him—no, I didn't—but none of it mattered. Even the color of his eyes didn't matter except that I happened to be looking into them. He had eyes a person could fall into and drown, and I was sinking fast.

"Well," he said, "I guess I should get that cocaine back to my office." He sighed and let go of my hand. I tried to find something casual to do with it, but it seemed like not a part of me anymore.

I wanted to ask him where his office was. Did he need help getting the drugs back? Had he seen the national park? Would he like to take a bubble bath with me?

When he and Barney left, I followed them outside like a puppy. I watched them load the cocaine into an unmarked government van. I didn't even glance at my hill; that's how serious it was. Then I had the sobering and depressing thought that I would never see him again.

"Well," Diego said when the drugs were loaded, "congratulations to both of you. This is about a million dollars worth of pure cocaine."

Barney shrugged. "I guess we should've kept it and

retired."

Nobody laughed. In fact Agent Romero and I were gazing at each other. He was going to drive away, and neither of us saw the humor in it. He shook our hands, got in his vehicle, started it, and pulled out with one more longing look in my direction.

Barney and I went back inside and incredibly, he didn't say one word to me about that strange encounter. Or maybe he did, and I didn't hear him.

* * *

I ran along the edge of Highway 170 for two miles and then back to where I had parked my car. That section of road follows the Rio Grande. My timing was perfect. I watched the sun drop behind the wild mountains in Mexico to the west, and when I headed back, saw the moon rise above the Chisos Mountains. In the day's afterglow, the bright, nearly-round orb was tinged pink and hung over purple-red peaks to the southeast.

I sat to rest on a rock wall above the river and watched darkness fall across land and water. The Rio seemed to grab the moonlight and throw it back. Along the banks wet sand gleamed. Tiny Mexican split tail bats swooped over the river, rising and dipping in an undulating dance, hunting flying insects, looking luminescent.

I stayed there a long time, lulled by the sights and sounds of night descending on the desert. For a while I lay on my back, my arms under my head, and watched the sky. The usually in-your-face stars were subdued by the big, bright moon.

I thought about the feet we had found in the river, and that led to William Hayfield, murdered over drugs. Special Agent Romero had said the drugs we confiscated were worth a million dollars. Together with the first load, that was three million dollars worth, more or less. I couldn't get my mind around it, or around him—or more to the point, the way he made me feel.

Thinking of Diego Romero made me feel guilty, as if I was cheating on Kevin, but he was dead and besides, I hadn't even touched the man except for a handshake. In one moment I reminded myself harshly that Kevin was never coming back, and in the next I believed he was. No wonder I had started drinking.

* * *

A surprise was waiting when I got home. Someone had been in my house. The hall light was on, and things in my living room had been moved, drawers opened that I left closed. I was unarmed, and my first thought was to return to the Mustang for a personal pistol I kept there. Before I did, an arm went roughly around my neck from behind, and something hard was shoved against my ribs.

"Shut up and listen," said a young voice trying to sound tough.

"Adolfo? Luis?"

"Shut up. They're going to kill you," he growled into my ear. "I can't stop them."

"Put the gun down."

"No."

Luis was still a lanky teenager and not heavy. I reached around behind me and brought him up and over my shoulder in a fast move, slamming him hard to the floor. The gun flew across the room and landed near the door to the kitchen. I had learned the move in a self-defense class and was always amazed when it worked.

I dropped down, straddled Luis, and glared at him. "What do you think you're doing?"

He gaped at me, sucking in air. "I'm trying to warn you."

"I mean what are you doing with those murderers, Luis? Have you lost your mind?"

"I—I didn't think they would murder him. If I don't do what they say, they'll kill me too."

"I have the solution for that—jail." I got off him and picked up his pistol. "Do you know how to use this thing?"

"Sure. I know how."

"Get up. I'm taking you in."

"You can't do that. They'll think I talked and they'll kill me."

"I saw you and Adolfo helping unload cocaine. You helped murder Bill Hayfield, too. I can't just turn my head and let you go."

"I came here to help you," he said and began to cry. "My death will be on your hands."

"No, it'll be on yours. You should've thought this out before you got involved with gangsters."

"They're not gangsters."

"What would you call them?"

"Fuck you."

It always came to that with the bad boys. If they couldn't get their way, they started with the cursing and insults. I had been called everything and was practically immune to it. Sticks and stones, you know. Words may never hurt me. That is untrue, but the words of criminals seldom have an effect.

"You're under arrest Luis, for cocaine trafficking and being an accessory to the murder of William Hayfield. I'll call your parents from my office."

"But I didn't do the murder."

"You have the right to remain silent. Anything you say can and will be used against you in a court of law. You have the right to have an attorney present during questioning. If you cannot afford an attorney, one will be appointed for you. Do you understand these rights?"

"Yes."

I took Luis to the holding cell in our office and called his parents. They sounded drunk or stoned and said they would come in the morning. I didn't want to keep their son overnight, but they left me no choice.

Luis got quiet.

"They're for sure going to kill you now," he said after a long silence.

"Try not to worry about me, and get some sleep. Tomorrow I'll take you to the county jail in Alpine."

"They might break me out tonight," he said hopefully, but I thought even he knew how lame that sounded.

I went into my dark office and sat in the overstuffed chair. Moonlight shimmered on Cactus Hill. I set my feet up on the desk and studied it. The pillbox hat looked carved from a hunk of pure silver—not carved with painstaking skill, but as if the artist had been in a hurry, leaving jagged edges and deep cuts, abandoning his piece unfinished—yet perfect.

A kit fox crept warily around a boulder and stopped at the bottom of the hill to sniff the air before proceeding. He was the hunter not the hunted and moved on with a bold step. Soon he disappeared into the desert, his small form hidden among the tall grasses and creosote bushes.

CHAPTER 8

I awoke with a start. A mountain-sized man loomed above me, staring down. It would have intimidated a woman less accustomed to him.

"What is it with you and this chair?" Barney demanded accusingly. "Tell me you haven't been here all night."

"Okay. I haven't been here all night. Is this night over?"

"It is for us, Ricos. I've been calling your house and cell phone, and this is why you're not answering. The Chili Pepper Café was robbed last night. Don't you have a uniform here?"

"What time is it?"

"It's a little after six. Let's get moving. We need to check it out before they open."

I went into the bathroom, cleaned up a little, and put on the spare uniform I keep in a locker. I didn't have my boots, so running shoes would have to work.

"Did you notice that Luis Garza is in our holding cell?"

Barney looked surprised. "No, I didn't notice. What happened?"

"He broke into my house last night and jumped me, supposedly to warn me that those other perps were going to kill me. I brought him in for questioning."

I walked over to the cell and looked in. "He's still sleeping."

"I remember when I used to sleep like that," said Barney. "I could've slept through a three-alarm fire."

"It's a teen-age thing. No worries, no responsibilities, just hormones raging."

"Speaking of hormones, did Agent Gapes-a-Lot call you last night?"

"Shut up. He's never going to call."

"Don't be stupid. He's taking his time, making a plan."

"What's the story on this robbery?"

"Food and cash have been stolen, but that was all the dispatcher knew. What in the hell is going on in this place?"

* * *

The café owner, Rosita, stepped onto the front porch and dropped to a bench at one of the picnic tables. "They got in through the door," she said.

A glass panel had been knocked out and glass was everywhere, so that much was evident.

She sighed wearily. "I don't need this today."

Barney and I exchanged looks. We didn't need it either.

"I told Pepe that was the wrong kind of door for a business," Rosita said, "but we didn't think much about it after it was installed. There's no crime here."

"What did they take?" I asked.

"They stole my bank bag with about four hundred in cash and a few checks. We had some personal beer and cigarettes—they took that—and frozen burgers, chicken, and fajitas meat, along with burger buns and a restaurant-size jar of mayonnaise. Who is going to eat that much mayonnaise?"

When she stepped back inside, I told Barney we needed to look for someone with big, greasy mayo stains on their shirt, but he didn't laugh. He was already filling out an incident report, frowning at the paper. I took over while he got the fingerprinting kit from the Explorer.

About that time, one of the waitresses arrived. She cursed passionately in Spanish and English, and exclaimed over the door, the broken glass, and pretty much everything else. Then she hurried inside to talk to her boss.

* * *

Barney and I sat together at one of the tables on the porch drinking coffee. Rosita insisted on feeding us, even though we tried to decline because of Sheriff's Office policy against accepting freebies. In the end we let it slide on a technicality. Attorneys and judges do that all the time.

When our food came it was delicious. Rosita put enough jalapeños in my omelet to make the bridge of my nose break out in a sweat. Perfect.

Barney had ordered an omelet *with everything* and in addition, asked for a side order of bacon, extra potatoes, and extra biscuits.

He looked up from his overloaded plate. "Hey, Ricos, shouldn't you be running?"

"I'm dressed in my uniform now, and since we're already here, this seems like the best use of my time. I have to eat to live, you know."

"I see. Well, I hope you aren't going to start getting fat." He stared down at his food, trying not to laugh. "The fatter you get, the harder it is to run."

"Well, I guess you should know."

* * *

Before we interviewed Luis, the sheriff called. "I have a few preliminary reports from the crime lab. They came via the Rangers and I thought you'd be interested. Bill Hayfield died of a massive overdose of cocaine. Of course, that's no surprise."

"Yes sir," we said in unison via speakerphone.

"There was no water in his lungs, indicating he was dead when he was put into the river, also not surprising. A trace of whiskey was found in one lung, aspirated when it was forced down him, and the stain on his t-shirt was the same whiskey. It had also splashed onto the bed, indicative of the scenario you two imagined."

Barney mouthed, "We're good," and I had to stifle a laugh.

"The victim's little finger was broken, which we knew," continued the sheriff. "He put up a struggle trying to save himself. The large amount of cocaine injected into him caused swelling of brain and lung tissue, heart arrhythmias, and complete cardiovascular failure, resulting in a quick death.

"Two sets of fingerprints were consistent with prints found at other scenes the Texas Rangers have been investigating. DNA tests aren't in yet but will be soon."

I informed the sheriff that I had Luis Garza in custody, and one of us would bring him to the county jail later.

"I'm sending you a subpoena in a civil case, so let me send a deputy trainee and he can pick up your prisoner and save you the trip. Does that work for you?"

We agreed that it did.

I reminded him about the feet and said I would include the evidence I had gathered from the fire. It surprised Barney I had spoken with the sheriff about my fire theory. I didn't give him a chance to comment and went home to shower.

* * *

When I returned, Luis was sitting in front of Barney drinking orange juice. His hands were not cuffed, but Barney doesn't have to cuff most people. He can subdue and intimidate without a word if he wants to.

Luis was whining about being flipped to the floor.

"She was defending herself," explained my partner. "You had broken into her house, attacked her from behind, and stuck a gun in her ribs. What did you expect?"

"How did she do that anyway?"

"It's about leverage and surprise," I said.

"Our conversation will be off the record," said Barney, "unless you want me to call your parents and remind them to come."

"No! Don't call them."

I sat next to the boy. Barney laced his hands together and stared at him across the desk. Then he cleared his throat. "I want you to tell me what you know about the murder at the El Dorado."

"I don't know anything about it."

Barney studied him a moment longer. "We have a witness who saw you come from the room several times."

"I wasn't there Friday morning," Luis said with attitude.

"Witnesses say different," roared Barney. "The evidence is going to say different too."

"Your witnesses are *chingado,* man. I was in the room the day before and the day before that but not on Friday morning."

"Where were you?"

"I was at home in my room."

"Your parents say you weren't there. You missed three days of school last week. So where were you Friday morning?"

"I was sleeping; I swear. I came in after my parents were in bed, and I left before they got up."

"I've searched your room, and while I was there, your mother mentioned that you hadn't been home. She was sure because she left a note on your bed. Both the note and the bed were undisturbed."

"You searched my room? Who gave you permission?"

"Cut the crap and tell me the truth."

Luis swallowed and hesitated. His hand was trembling. "I was running around with my cousin from Mexico, showing him stuff. We went fishing one day and played pool. I don't remember what all we did."

"What's your cousin's name?"

"Juan Garza."

"Where is he from in Mexico?"

"He's from Monterrey. I don't get to see him often."

"Why does your cousin have stolen plates?"

"How would I know that?"

"How did he enter this country?"

"I don't know. He called me from Lajitas to tell me he was here."

"If this man named Garza is your cousin, then I would

assume he's the child of one of your father's brothers?"

"Yes, he is."

"And he had no desire to see your father?"

"No."

"Explain that please."

"Well, the last time he was here we went to Ojinaga, and we got in some trouble with—" Luis glanced in my direction. "It was with some prostitutes."

"What sort of trouble?" asked Barney.

"We got drunk and passed out and they stole our money and credit cards, driver's licenses—whatever we carried. I had trouble getting back into the US, and my dad had to bring my birth certificate. He was mad at Juan and blamed him for it because he's older, and he thought he should've known better."

"How old is Juan?"

Luis hesitated too long. "He's twenty-seven." We knew he was lying. Barney and I exchanged looks.

"Okay," said Barney with exaggerated patience, "Please explain to me how you were seen with men in their thirties and forties, but the only man in his twenties was the gringo, now deceased? Are you going to tell me Bill Hayfield is also Juan Garza?"

Luis held Barney's stare a moment then looked away. "Somebody's giving you fucked up information, because I was with my cousin and a friend of his who's older. I think your people are *chingado* for sure."

"Huh." Barney was not impressed. "How does Bill Hayfield figure into all this?"

"He was a friend of my cousin's friend. We were hanging out together. We played pool. You can ask anyone."

"I have, Luis. The word is you were seen with four men, playing pool and riding around. One was Adolfo. There was also a Mexican man about forty, another Mexican man somewhat younger, and Hayfield. He was twenty-seven when he was murdered Friday morning. Where does your twenty-seven-year-old cousin fit in?"

Luis said nothing.

"You pulled him out of your ass!"

"I did not!"

Barney glared; neither spoke.

"Would you like some more orange juice?" I asked sweetly. *Or a heavy dose of truth serum?*

"Yes, please."

"Want something, Barney?"

"I'll have a Dr. Pepper."

I got myself a bottle of water and for a moment we sat around like pals. Except there was an undercurrent you could drown in.

"Where is Adolfo Estevez?" Barney asked after a while.

"I don't know where he is. I swear I don't. I've been looking for him."

"Let's talk about the cocaine."

"What cocaine?"

"You've already admitted to Deputy Ricos that you were involved in that, so don't play innocent. You told her they were going to kill her, didn't you?"

"That's what they're saying."

"So then don't ask me what cocaine."

The boy glared at him. "Okay, well, I did help them move some boxes but if they had cocaine in them I don't know anything about that."

I gave Barney an exasperated look. It would be easier on deputies if liars' pants really did catch fire.

"You know," Barney said, "one of your partners shot two Border Patrol agents. That makes you an accessory to the felony assault of a law officer on duty. That's a serious crime."

"I didn't have anything to do with that."

"You're in over your head, aren't you?"

For a second he had the wild-eyed look of a little boy in deep trouble. "Aren't you supposed to read me my rights?"

"Didn't Deputy Ricos do that when she brought you in last night?"

"Yeah. I guess so."

"Well, you only have to hear it once. Do you have a question about them?"

"No."

"Are you going to let these lies stand?"

"I'm not lying."

"You're afraid of your partners, aren't you?"

"They'll kill me." He began to cry.

"It will go easier for you if you tell the truth, Luis. I promise you that."

"I want to speak to my parents about an attorney."

Those words ended the interview. Barney and I stood. "You can do that when you get to Alpine," he said. "We're finished here." He returned a protesting Luis to the cell to await the deputy trainee.

While Barney served a subpoena to a witness in a civil suit, I made our final report and closed out our part of the murder investigation at El Dorado. I was relieved, in some ways, to pass it on to the Texas Rangers. Fighting drug traffickers and cartel-inspired murderers is something best left to people trained for that. My desire is to keep drugs away from our kids, but breaking up drug cartels? Nah. That's real superhero work.

* * *

"What are you doing in there, Ricos?" yelled Barney when he came crashing back into the office.

"Nothing important, do you need me?"

"Are you looking at naked men on your computer?"

"Not right now."

A fax came in from the Texas Rangers' office with an artist's sketch of Sotol and his sidekick, Ruben Ortiz Villanueva. Sotol's real name was Enrique de Jesus Valdez aka Rudolpho de Jesus Valenzuela aka Juan Francisco Garza and the easier-to-remember nickname of Sotol.

"Señor Sotol de los Cocaine Trafficking Murdering Assholes," said Barney, making me laugh.

"He sure uses Jesus' name a lot."

"He may think of himself as religious in spite of his crimes," Barney said.

"Oh, sure. Killing for Jesus and drugs."

"Maybe that works for him. There's been a lot of murder and other horrors done in Christ's name."

Another fax came in that was a photograph of Sotol eating in an outdoor café in Chihuahua according to the note with it. He looked like the man described by various witnesses in Terlingua.

* * *

The sheriff called for me later. "Do you know a man named Zeke Pacheco?"

"He's my biological father, but I've never met him."

"Are you aware that he's a Texas Ranger?"

"No sir. I didn't know that."

"How do you feel about meeting him?"

"I want to, I guess. Why do you ask?"

"He's been assigned to an old Alpine case so he's coming here. He's a UCIT officer and lives in Austin."

All I heard was *you're going to meet your father.*

"UCIT is Unsolved Crimes Investigative Team," the sheriff explained. "Each Ranger unit has one."

Sheriff Ben continued. "The Midland UCIT guy is out for surgery so Sergeant Pacheco was called in. He mentioned the Hayfield murder, and when I said your name, he said he wanted to meet you."

"Mom said she remembers he was interested in law enforcement. I guess she had that right." I sounded calm, but I was not.

"He doesn't want to put undue pressure on you."

"It'll be all right, Sheriff. I've gotten used to the idea that there is a Zeke Pacheco. I had wondered if this day would come. I want to meet him—and not."

"Should I let him know you're willing or would you rather wait?"

"He isn't going to just show up is he?"

"I doubt it. I think his intention is to contact you by phone before he comes from Austin. I don't think he wants to blindside you, Margarita."

My parents hadn't told me about Zeke Pacheco until recently, and only because they had to. In my heart, the father I had grown up with would always be my father. He agreed to raise me as his own when my mother was only seven weeks pregnant. Miguel Ricos is the father named on my birth certificate and the man I call "Papi." Zeke had known about me, but backed off since Miguel was willing to raise me, and he didn't want to, and my mom was in love with Miguel. It's a long story.

* * *

"Phone's for you," Barney yelled.

I was in my office, staring out the window at my hill, lost out there.

I yanked up the phone. "Deputy Ricos speaking."

"If you don't do something about Crazy Craig, I'm going to do something illegal. I've had it, Margarita. I'm at my wit's end with him."

"What's he doing now, Becky?" I recognized both her voice and her complaint.

"First he was going through the trash behind the restaurant, but now he's set up a camp behind the clay hill in back and I think he might've broken in last night."

"That doesn't sound like Craig. Did you ask him?"

"Ask him? It's like talkin' to a wall. You come and you ask him."

"Okay, I'll be there soon."

"He can't keep living back there."

"Okay, Becky, I'm on my way."

"What's up?" Barney asked when I plopped down in front of him.

"It's Craig again. Becky thinks he broke into her restaurant last night."

"That doesn't seem like him."

"I know, but I'm going to check it out."

"Get prints, okay? Maybe the same culprit robbed both places."

"I was thinking that."

"Agent Romero called when you were talking to Becky," Barney said nonchalantly, as if it was a nondescript call of no importance. "I gave him your cell phone number. I hope that's all right."

"Sure. It's fine." I sounded calm; I was anything but.

"It was something about dinner."

My temperature rose at least a degree. "What about dinner?"

Barney was messing with me, making me wait. "It might have been something about taking you to dinner. Are you going to go out with him?"

I felt as if I had been in the sun too long. "Yes, if he asks me."

"You don't even know him."

"That's the point in going out with someone, to get to know them."

He frowned. "I don't like it."

"It'll be okay, Daddy; it's only dinner. And I hope you're going to mind your own business."

"Where's the fun in that?"

CHAPTER 9

Craig Summers is a Vietnam veteran referred to by some locals as Crazy Craig. They try to say it's an affectionate nickname when I challenge them, but that's a lie. It's mean and shows their ignorance. They don't like him because he's quiet, doesn't attend community functions, and when approached, he will usually run off or remain still and silent.

Craig is in his early sixties and has hung around Terlingua off and on for as long as I can remember. If he's crazy, I never saw that about him. There are a few crazies in my community, but he isn't one of them. He is eccentric, okay, but also bright and caring, not crazy.

I think he suffers from post traumatic stress disorder, made worse by the absence of a caring family, lack of proper medical care, too little money; there is a long list of things he needed and didn't get. To make things worse, some people use him to scare their children. *If you don't straighten up, Crazy Craig will get you during the night,* or *Come in at dark 'cause Crazy Craig comes out.* Craig never moves at night. If it's dark he studies the sky. Always. And he would never hurt a child.

I first ran into Craig in the backcountry when I was eleven. We formed a bond based on a mutual love of exploration, telling tall tales, sharing true stories, and 'claiming' abandoned structures. Being an only child, I often lacked fellow explorers my age. Craig is not childlike mentally—far from it—but he is fun.

He honestly expresses his opinion the way a child does. He loves all natural things and has a special place in his heart for animals. When I was a child, he always thought through my sometimes difficult questions and gave me his honest answers. He has an active imagination and loves to play. He also has an impressive knowledge of the natural world. He taught me to observe with patience, and he paid attention to my opinions in a way most adults never did. So fifteen years later, we are still friends.

During most of my teens, Craig was with a cousin who

tried in his own way to help him. But Craig has a terror of loud noises, a dislike of city life in general, and can't stand a roof over his head. He feels trapped if he can't see the sky. At one low point, his cousin had him committed, but he escaped from the institution and came home to Big Bend. I wouldn't call that crazy.

Becky's little restaurant was not far from the Terlingua Store, so I thought it possible that whoever was breaking and entering had hit both places. There was no way that would be Craig. He knows right from wrong and would never take anything that belongs to someone else. His treasures come from dumpsters, the side of the road, and trash barrels.

I went first into Becky's Grill to speak to her and smooth her ruffled feathers. It seems like half my job is nothing but public relations.

She flew at me in a huff. "He's gone too far this time, Margarita."

"I don't think he would break in, Becky. It's not like him."

"I knew you'd say that."

"What's missing?"

"Food and cash. He took my change bag but it only had about fifty dollars in it. That and sandwich fixin's—oh, and two packs of Marlboro Lights."

"Craig doesn't smoke."

"Maybe he started."

"How did the thief get in?"

"He broke the pane out of the back door. It's not like it would be hard. I never thought about anybody breaking in."

"I'm going to try to get fingerprints and then I'll go talk to him."

"Can't you get him to hang out somewhere else?"

"Yes. I'll do that."

I lifted about a half-dozen prints, for what it was worth. So many people had been in and out that door there was no use trying to get foot impressions. All the tracks were so mixed together they obliterated each other. Craig usually wore combat boots but if the print was there, other shoes had trampled it.

I dragged myself towards the clay hill. I couldn't believe Craig would steal anything. If he had, he was worse. That would be bad news for a lot of reasons.

Craig looked up when I approached and smiled

wistfully. He looked terrible. Some teeth were missing and his gray hair was long and unkept. He needed a shave and a bath. Worse, he sat in the middle of garbage: rusting cans, crumpled packages and bags, fading newspapers, and other peoples' thrown-away things.

There were half a dozen broken boom boxes and radios and bits and pieces of electronic things. Discolored aluminum Christmas tree tinsel glinted from the rubble but it didn't seem festive, nor did the smashed ornaments. There was also discarded clothing, now filthy, and threadbare blankets, orange peels, and things no longer recognizable that stank.

"Hey, Craig."

"Little Boss!" His voice was soft and full of love. He seemed genuinely glad to see me. He calls me "Little Boss" because at age eleven, I proclaimed myself "the boss of the whole Big Bend"; I haven't changed much. We had been arguing about rights to a native rock house we both loved. In the end, we shared it and still do.

I cleared a space with my foot and sat next to him. "How are you, Craig?"

"Fine."

"You don't look too good." He had a black eye and there was crusted blood under his nose and on his shirt. He was filthy and smelled like the garbage. "What happened, Craig?"

"Nothing."

"Craig, I want you to come back from wherever you are in your head. Can you do that for me please?"

He lifted a filthy hand towards his face. "Hurt."

"Who hurt you, Craig?"

"Bad people."

"Someone attacked you?"

"Bad people, bad men."

"Who was it?"

"I told you, bad men."

I took a deep breath. I was getting nowhere with that.

"Craig, I'm going to take you to Mom's clinic and get you checked out."

My mother runs a non-profit medical clinic that provides free or low-cost care to people on both sides of the Rio Grande. She is the only doctor who works full time, but she coordinates others, along with nurses, who volunteer their time in blocks of two weeks to several months.

"No. I'm fine," Craig insisted.

I tried a different tack. "I haven't had lunch. Want to get something to eat?"

"No. I'm too dirty."

"You could take a shower at my house. I'll fix us something and wash and dry your clothes while we eat."

"No. Thanks."

"Come on, Craig. You'll feel better."

"No. I'm too dirty to go to your house."

"Come on. Don't make the Little Boss of the Big Bend beg."

He laughed and rose. "Okay, Little Boss," he said with affection.

He picked up a battered old suitcase and followed me. His camp was a health hazard, and I would have to do something about it before the health department came and shut down Becky's Grill.

"They robbed Becky," he said when we got into the Explorer.

"Who robbed her?"

"Those bad men."

"The men that beat you up?"

"I tried to stop them. They broke the door and I heard them."

"Can you describe them?"

"I think I know them, but I can't remember their names."

"So they're locals?"

"I don't know, but they were once. I haven't seen them in a long time."

"There were two?"

"Yes, two young ones—but not as young as you, Little Boss."

"Thirties?"

"Yes, and one is tall, the other shorter. The tall one pushed me and I fell. They didn't beat me up."

"Do you know where they live?"

"No."

"Are they Mexican? White? Black? Some other color?"

He chuckled. "They're white."

"How were they dressed?"

"I don't know. Nothin' special—blue jeans, t-shirts, jackets. They were getting beer when I came in to see what they were doing there after hours."

"What were they driving?"

"One of those little trucks. It was tan, maybe foreign."

"They broke into the Terlingua Store too, or I think it was the same guys. They took money, beer, and cigarettes."

"I told them to get out of Becky's. She's my friend."

"I know. You did the right thing."

While Craig bathed, I tried to separate his dirty clothes from clean ones and decided to put all of them in my washing machine. Some of the socks and underwear were so bad I stuffed them in a plastic bag and took it out to the dumpster at the end of the road. I made a mental note to replace them.

I had an idea about a place Craig could live. Papi, my dad, owns a house in Mexico across the river from the resort of Lajitas, in the tiny community of Paso Lajitas. It was unoccupied and often misused because it sat empty and defenseless.

I called Papi and begged him to let Craig stay there until I could figure out what to do with him. He tried to say no, but I usually get my way with my papi. I offered to pay him rent, which embarrassed him, and at that point he agreed to let Craig use the house on the condition that I would check on him regularly. I intended to do that.

* * *

Craig sat wrapped in a beach towel and let me hug him, cut his hair, and give him a shave. He looked better except for the black eye. I thought there had been a time when Craig was a fine-looking man, as full of hope and dreams as any young person. Then he had been sent to fight a war I didn't understand that started long before I was born. He had been captured and spent a year as a POW. He had been tortured and God only knew the things that had happened to him. My mother told me that when the soldiers came home from Vietnam, they weren't always made to feel welcome because the war had been vehemently protested; nor was the help they needed always available.

Men like Craig, without family, sometimes fell through the cracks. I thought people in our community should thank him, take care of him, and stand to salute when he passed. A more deserved nickname would be Courageous Craig because even when I was eleven, I knew he was full of courage.

I transferred his clothes to the dryer and gave him a bathrobe to wear. He sat at my kitchen table drinking juice while I made a veggie and cheese omelet, served with hot salsa and tortillas. He ate with so much relish it made me feel guilty. After the meal, we sliced apples and pears for dessert.

"You've got to remember to eat, Craig."

He shrugged.

"You know you can come here anytime and take whatever you want."

"I have money for food."

"Then why aren't you eating? You're starting to look like a skinny old man."

He laughed. "I am a skinny old man, Little Boss."

"Well if you get too skinny you'll get sick, and you'll have to be in a hospital with a roof over your head."

He winced as if I had hit him. "I'll die in the desert first. Please don't put me in a hospital, Margarita. Let me die in the desert."

"Okay, Craig, but you have to eat more or I'll kick your skinny ol' butt."

"I'd like to see you try. I'm strong, and I haven't forgotten the Marine Corps training either."

"Okay. You win, but I still want you to eat. You can't stay strong if you don't feed your muscles. I know Marines believe in eating."

"Yeah, I suppose. I get busy and forget."

"Don't make me get Dr. Ricos on your case. You know how she is."

He chuckled. "She'll aggravate me just like you do."

"Oh no, you haven't seen anything yet." My mom is a pro.

After a while I said, "My father is looking for someone to watch his house in Paso Lajitas." I had to make him think he was doing my papi a favor, not the other way around.

"Are you asking me to help him?"

"Yes. Would you? He has trouble with kids breaking in, and it's not good for a house to sit empty. You could keep it clean for him."

"I'd like to do that because your father's a good man, but you know I don't have much use for buildings with roofs."

"I know, but it would be a big help to him. You could sleep outside if you want. We used to do it all the time when we visited my grandparents."

"You can't see the stars from inside. Or the moon—or anything else important."

"Yes. That's true." I knew that rant by heart.

"I love the stars."

"I do, too."

He watched me a long time while he thought. "Okay, Little Boss. I'll do it for you."

"Thank you, Craig."

"Will you take me back to my camp?"

"Not today. Would you stay here until tomorrow? I feel nervous about the murder and the break-ins going on."

"But you're the law."

"That doesn't make me safe."

"Okay, but only this once, and I'm going to make a camp out back."

"That would be fine, but please come in to use the bathroom. I'll leave the back door open, and you can come in and out as you need to. There's plenty of food if you get hungry, and there's coffee in the cupboard. Help yourself, okay?"

"I could do with some coffee."

I made a pot, folded the clothes, and went back to the office. When I left, Craig was napping on my couch even though there was a roof over his head.

* * *

"I'd like to know what the hell is going on here, Ricos." That was Barney's response to *hey Barn*.

"I could ask you the same thing."

He had the XM radio blasting so loud I didn't see how he could think or answer the phone.

Someone was singing:

If you got a problem, don't care what it is

If you need a hand, I can assure you of this: I can help.

I got two strong arms, I can help.

It would sure do me good to do you good, let me help.

Whoever this guy was, we needed him.

"It sounds like a party." I started dancing. "What is this music?"

"I don't know. It's old rock—sixties stuff." He turned it down.

"Have we had another crime?"

"Yes. More break-ins. This crime spree is starting to piss me off."

"Now what?"

"Two houses have been broken into out on Terlingua Ranch. The thieves took whatever cash they could find, plus liquor, beer, and cigarettes. One old codger is having kittens because he just brought a brand new bottle of Hera Dura Gold in Mexico. They took it and he wants it back. I guess he thinks we can pull tequila out our asses. Everybody wants something from us, and they always want it right now."

"Do you think there's any way these break-ins could have something to do with the men who killed William Hayfield?"

"I don't know. I was thinking that too, but this is so small-time compared to what those guys are into."

"That's true. It's nickels and dimes compared to millions."

"Well, we took their millions away from them," he pointed out.

"Luis thinks they're going to kill me."

"I doubt if they come back since the Texas Rangers are on their case now."

"That would be great."

"What did you do with Crazy Craig?"

"Please don't call him that."

"Sorry."

"Craig is going to stay at my dad's house in Paso Lajitas until I can figure out something better. The problem is he needs someone to watch out for him, but he doesn't need the kind of care he would get in an institution. I can't imagine how much he would hate that kind of place. He likes to be outside, and he loves watching the night sky."

"You have a lot in common with him, don't you?"

I gave him a look, but it was wasted. "You know those two kids who need community service hours? Will you put them on cleaning up the mess behind Becky's Grill? They'll need a lot of tough trash bags. Craig's been camping there, and people dump trash there; it's bad. They should wear gloves."

"When do you want me to put them on it?"

"As soon as possible. I'm going to take Craig to Papi's house tomorrow."

"Where is he now?"

"He's at my house."

"Do you trust him alone there?"

"Of course I trust him, Barney. When I first met him I was eleven. He could have abused me, or stolen from me, or tried to get me to do bad things. All he ever did was treat me with respect and kindness. He played with me. He's not 'normal' by everyone's standards, but he's not a criminal either."

"What about the break-in at Becky's?"

"Seems like the same perps. They took cash, beer, and cigs. Becky thought Craig did it, but he tried to stop them. They pushed him down and he got banged up."

"Did he know them?"

"He says it was two guys about thirty in a small tan truck. They were familiar but he couldn't place them. He said he thought they lived here before—wait a minute. It sounds like Morton and William, doesn't it? Except their truck isn't tan, and they're supposed to be in New Mexico, last I heard."

"Maybe they're back," Barney said.

"They never stole things before."

"That we know of."

Morton and William were small-scale drug peddlers too lazy to work, although the word was they'd gotten jobs in Albuquerque. Barney and I had been on their backs because they sold drugs to kids. We liked to think we ran them off, but in truth we weren't sure why they left. Nobody missed them, or we didn't, anyhow.

"Why don't we go up to their place in the Ghost Town and see if they're back? If they have a tan truck, we can bring them in and Craig will identify them."

"Let's get shakin' then. We still have to take reports from the Terlingua Ranch burglary victims," Barney reminded me.

The hovel in the Ghost Town belonging to Morton and William appeared to be abandoned. The yard was overgrown with cactus and weeds, and no one had seen them. We were still suspicious, but it appeared they hadn't returned.

* * *

The Terlingua Ranch Resort encompasses thousands of acres of rugged and astonishing land that lies alongside Big Bend National Park like a lover. At one time it was a vast cattle ranch, hence the name. Now there are over 4,000 owners of land with parcels of five acres to hundreds.

The main paved route through the ranch is about twenty miles from Terlingua. The first robbery victim lived off that road, down a long and winding trail that was in terrible shape. It was potholed and wash-boarded, but the heavy Explorer made it fine, though our speed was slow.

Before that road turned into another, there was a previously-abandoned rock structure that now appeared occupied. I asked Barney to stop. He gave me his short-on-patience look, and then I made things worse by getting out and looking around. I banged on the door, but it was padlocked and nobody answered.

There was a broken plastic cooler in the yard and trash that looked and smelled recent. The porch had been swept and a broom leaned against the wall. I spotted a faded blue denim shirt slung over a post. The intricate embroidered dragon on the pocket faced me and I recalled—something—but couldn't think why it was familiar. I tried to force the memory by staring at it.

"Ricos!" Barney yelled. "The shirt's not moving and neither are we as long you're standing there."

I headed back to the vehicle. "Have you seen that shirt before?"

"No. It's just some old shirt. Why?"

"I don't know, but it seems familiar. Do you know who lives here?"

"I didn't know anybody lived here. This place has been empty for so long I guess I thought it always would be. Why? Does it matter?"

"I don't know. It's just—peculiar."

As we took the burglary report, I continued to think about the shirt. It meant something, but I couldn't think what.

CHAPTER 10

The next morning I stood with Craig at the river's edge, waiting for the small metal rowboat at the Lajitas Crossing. He was dressed in his nicest pair of dark pants and a white western shirt. Brand new boots and a straw hat purchased at our resale shop, Otra Vez, rounded out his dressed-up cowboy look. Craig clung nervously to his one battered suitcase, a canvas grocery sack full of food, and another that held his other "new" clothes.

I carried a bag with his books and other unleavable treasures and was dressed in civilian clothes so as not to draw suspicion in the pueblito. I know nearly everyone there and some of them for my entire life, but a uniform in Paso Lajitas is usually bad news for somebody; I didn't need any hassling or Mexican policewoman jokes.

Craig insisted on paying, and when he did, we were rowed to the other side by a young Mexican lad who grinned the whole time.

Craig loves Mexico and seemed happy for the opportunity to spend time there. He said he liked the calm pace of life in a rural pueblo, and added that the people were kind and shared whatever they had with generous hearts and without resentment. That was typical in my experience, too.

Dark clouds were gathering, and I hoped the rain would hold off until I could get Craig settled and then haul myself back across the river. The wind was intermittent, blowing dust in gusts and then eerie calm, not a good sign.

We walked together a short way into the settlement. I took Craig by the store and introduced him to the proprietor, Efrain Flores. They shook hands and greeted each other in different languages, but a smile is universal. Then I explained to Sr. Flores in Spanish that if my friend ever came in without enough money, he could put the difference on a tab in my name; I would be in at least twice a week to pay up. I assured him that although Craig was sometimes odd, he was harmless, and I hoped he would look out for him. I knew he would even before he confirmed it.

Adobe and stone dwellings lined the winding dirt road, and there were always mules, burros, and horses everywhere.

Goats played in pens behind houses, or grazed in fenced pastures. Chickens scratched in the dirt in some yards, and most homes had flowers blooming in various containers, none of which were flowerpots. These were people who made do with what they could save, scrounge, or trade. Little was thrown away, and I thought Craig, being a die-hard recycler, would fit in.

Children raced around playing with a ball and squealing. Some were dressed only in underpants and were filthy from the dirt and dust. In some of the houses, mothers stood in doorways calling various things to their children. "Get in here for your bath!" "Come inside and eat." "Have you seen Carlitos?"

Craig expressed his joy at animals running free, like the children. Using English, he greeted the kids who ran past. They grinned at him anyway and returned the greeting spiritedly in Spanish. He said he loved the easy graciousness of the Mexican people, their lack of slavery to clocks, and their generosity. Even the poorest family would offer refreshment to a visitor. He had it exactly right.

My dad's concrete block and adobe house was around the corner, a block or two from the grocery store. The yard is fenced, but the wire was broken down in places. Since my grandparents died, nobody lives there. Papi goes every two weeks to check on it and to water the trees. The shady spot under the big chinaberry was overgrown with weeds, and gone were the flowers and herbs my grandma used to grow. The place had magic when she lived there. Now it's just a sad, empty house, sitting alone on a dusty road.

We went inside using a key I handed over to Craig. It was stuffy in the house, but I could have sworn it still smelled like my grandma: a mixture of vanilla-scented candles, roses, and drying herbs that I always associated with her.

The wind picked up and became steady, and the air smelled of rain. The sun was in hiding and thunder crashed in the distance. We opened all the windows to let in the freshness. I activated the electricity at the box outside as my papi instructed, then turned on the old refrigerator and put Craig's food into it.

He walked around getting acquainted with the surroundings while I explored the familiar house I always loved. Other than a coating of dust, it hadn't changed much since my childhood. My grandparents had added rich layers to my life, and I felt a profound sense of loss at their absence.

When the rain started, Craig and I stood under the roof of the small side porch and watched it pour out of the sky in sheets. After a few moments, hail pounded down as if to drive out the rain, and the temperature dropped by at least twenty degrees.

Craig looked towards the surrounding mountains, hazy in the hailstorm. "I'm going to like it here," he said softly.

We found packages of flower and herb seeds in the kitchen, along with tomato, long green pepper, and squash.

"Maybe I'll put in a little garden," he said.

"Thank you for doing this for my dad, Craig."

"I said I would do it for you Little Boss, but I know you're doing it for me."

So much for the crazy theory.

"I'm not as crazy as everybody thinks," he added with a shy smile.

"Not everybody thinks you're crazy."

"I know you don't, but I'm not talking about you. Anyway, it's okay. I want them to think it so they leave me alone."

"These people will be good to you, Craig. If you need anything, ask. Most of them speak a little English but regardless, you can make yourself understood if you try."

When rain and hail stopped a few minutes later, we walked around outside the house. I showed him a tool shed that still held a few usable tools, and the old chicken coop, long empty. There was a stable where we once kept horses. Craig loved all of it, and said he might trade something for a few chickens.

I made my way back to the river. The children were out again, playing in puddles, splashing and shrieking with delight. The damp air was cool and carried the fragrance of wet earth and creosote bush. One of the joys of rainfall in the desert is the unique aroma released from the waxy leaves of the creosote after a rain.

* * *

I walked into the office, sat, and within minutes, Sheriff Duncan called with some of the crime lab results from the first murder. They had been reported to him by the Texas Rangers. Not surprisingly, Sotol's fingerprints were on the money that came from Luis' room.

Prints at the crime scene matched prints lifted from

Luis' room. His DNA was in the motel room of the victim, in the form of hairs, as well as that of the other three. Luis' DNA was not present under Hayfield's fingernails, but the others were. So Luis was involved, but maybe it was true he hadn't participated in the murder. We could prove he had been in the room, but that was all. Barney and I hoped he hadn't been a part of the killing. It was disappointing enough that one of the local boys had.

Barney asked the sheriff about the fingers I shot off, but that DNA profile hadn't come in yet. He said the fingerprints on the rifle belonged to Ruben Villanueva, so we assumed the fingers did too.

After that call there was another. Barney took it and did more listening than talking. Then he slammed down the phone. "Holy break-ins, Batgirl! Another burglary and it sounds like the same jerks."

"Was it a house?"

"Yep. The residents were out of town for a few days. Somebody broke in and took food, beer, cigarettes, and a new bottle of vodka. We gotta shut these sons-a-bitches down, Ricos."

"Jeez Barney, we're trying."

After ranting and cursing for ten minutes, he volunteered to go. "No reason for both of us to have to suffer. You can go next time."

"I'll cover things here until you get back."

"You do that, and don't let anything happen while I'm gone."

CHAPTER 11

I hate to admit it, but I was seated with my boots propped on the desk when the front door opened. Assuming it was Barney, I did nothing. I was studying my hill and didn't want to be disturbed.

Suddenly a man stood in the doorway to my office staring at me with big brown eyes. He had dark hair in shoulder-length Rasta braids and a wide, wicked-looking scar on his left cheek. He struck me as a stereotypical gangsta, but his sex appeal was undeniable. I stand by my belief that bad men should not be good-looking. It's unfair and—it's just plain wrong.

The goon wore a green muscle shirt that exposed well-developed, tattooed arms. I could live without the tats, but those arms; *aye Dios.* It was as irritating as dust in my eye. Over the shirt were faded denim overalls that were too large, typical cholo. His shoes were dirty blue sneakers, no socks. And he was tall.

I should have felt fear and would have if I'd been paying attention, but I was too busy checking him out. Something about him seemed familiar, but I don't hang with cholos so I couldn't make sense of it.

"*Buenas tardes,* Margarita." He used my name!

I jumped to my feet. *"Buenas tardes."*

He stepped closer. *"No me reconoce?"*

"No, I don't recognize you. Do I know you?"

"Diego Romero. We met a few days ago."

I stared, speechless, mouth open. Standing next to Barney, he had seemed smaller. Also, he'd had normal-length, desert-colored hair and notable turquoise eyes. I still didn't speak, though I wanted to.

"That's the point of my disguise." Small shrug. "I'm working a case undercover. I guess I should've changed before coming."

"Well, I—" was repeated more times than I care to admit while my heart hammered nails into the wall of my chest.

He smiled, and when it became evident that I wouldn't be saying anything noteworthy, he carried the conversation. "I hoped you would go with me to get coffee. Is there a quiet, out-of-the-way place where we could do that?"

"Yes, but—"

"But you don't want to be seen hanging out with a criminal type. I can understand that."

"It's not—" I couldn't even complete a sentence.

"I could change first." He grinned.

"I know a place."

"Where should I change?"

"You don't need to. We're going to the Ghost Town, and it's not like there's a dress code there."

His smile made me weak all over.

Espresso y Poco Más is an outdoor coffee shop with an impressive choice of food and beverages, considering the size of the place and its location in a former ghost town. Their coffee is excellent; their view is worth millions.

Of course it was closed. They close at two in the afternoon. I knew that, but who notices the time of day when they are so smitten?

I lamented that the place wasn't open and started to back away, but Diego put his hand on my arm. "I like this place. Can we sit here anyway?"

I nodded mutely.

First, we walked around the property. The café is adjacent to a bed and breakfast built on the old foundations of original Ghost Town structures. It was recreated by stacking native stone the way they did it during the mining days. I explained that, but it was out of nervousness more than in response to my companion's curiosity about old time architecture.

Gina, the manager, was on duty, and she welcomed us. Her dark eyes swept over my handsome companion, and I thought her appraisal was far less than critical. It occurred to me then that Diego would be more welcome and trusted in Terlingua as a bad boy than as a DEA agent. Rumors would fly either way.

While my mind bounced all over, Gina engaged Diego in a lively conversation about the pastries she was making. In the short story version, we ended up at a table on the patio drinking freshly-brewed coffee and sharing a warm cinnamon roll. Such is the power of tall, dark, and handsome.

We discussed Mule Ears peaks poking up out of distant Big Bend National Park and nearby desert plants. I described hiking in the Chisos Mountains as well as anyone can describe a totally indescribable place. We mostly gazed at each other.

Two guys passed us going in the direction of the old store building. One wore river sandals and stained white coveralls with no shirt. He lifted a ratty cowboy hat to us in greeting. We waved. The other man grinned and saluted but kept up an animated conversation with his friend, using lots of hand-gesturing. His baggie jeans were the comfortable kind with more holes than fabric. A blue plaid flannel shirt was open in front, and he wore combat boots. Both men lugged battered guitar cases. When they reached the Porch, they began to play and sing.

Theirs wasn't the only show. Far off, a storm raged over a bumpy range of Mexican mountains. Distant thunder rumbled like the warning growl of an angry dog, and lightening flashed in showy zigs and zags.

Diego sighed. "This just keeps getting better." He leaned back in the chair, stretched out his legs, and put his hands behind his head in a relaxed pose. "It's hard to take it all in. It's so magical here that even the deputy is beautiful."

I blushed so much that hot sweat broke out on my forehead.

Later, as shadows grew in length, Diego said, "Terlingua is the funkiest place I've ever been. The people are so diverse and talented and—interesting. On a scale of one to ten, the scenery is a fifty, and it's all set in the middle of nowhere. I love it."

If my heart had needed warming, that would have done it.

The troubadours were playing "Poncho and Lefty" to a small audience. Diego sang softly, "Pancho met his match, you know, on the deserts down in Mexico. Nobody heard his dyin' words; ah but that's the way it goes."

Puffy, orange-tinged clouds and a sinking sun played now-you-see-it-now-you-don't with the peaks and stony cliff faces and tortured rock formations. The air temperature was perfect. Then Diego took my hand. It was one of those flawless moments in time you hope you always remember.

"I want to take you to dinner tomorrow evening," he said. "Will you go?"

"I'd love to."

"Could you meet me at the airstrip at five-thirty?"

"The airstrip?"

"Yes, and wear something formal. I want to take you to my favorite restaurant."

"There's no place here where formal wear is required or even appropriate."

"Yes, I know that. We're going to Cuidad Chihuahua."

"Chihuahua? But I can't just take off to Mexico. I'm on call this weekend and it's been so busy I know I'll be called—"

"I'll bring you back the same night, I promise. Do you have a passport?"

"Yes."

"Please bring it. You'll need it at the airport in Chihuahua."

I didn't ask how long it would take to get there, or where he was going to get an airplane, or even if he knew how to fly one. My heart agreed to go, period.

    * * *

Barney had a fit when I told him the next day, and I only told him because I would have to leave work early in order to be ready by five-thirty, and he would be the only one on call that evening.

"Ricos, you can't fly off into the sunset with a man you don't know. You only know his name and nothing else about him."

That was not true, but I hesitated to admit I had spent most of the previous afternoon with Diego while my partner was working. "I know enough. Besides, he's in law enforcement." It was a weak argument, true, but I was going.

"That's all the more reason to wonder about him."

"That's ridiculous. I can tell by looking at him that I'll be safe with him."

"You're crazy. The only thing you can tell by looking at him is that he's a good-looking man. 'Course that's probably the only thing you care about."

"I can take care of myself." I got up and went into my office, as if that would end it. Since I couldn't stop him, Barney followed.

"You've been unwilling to go out with anyone," he remarked from the doorway.

"I know that, but now I'm willing. I told you I'd find my own man."

Barney sank into my overstuffed chair. "What makes Diego Romero special?"

"I don't know, but I'm sure there will be a lot of special

things about him."

"You can't trust a man because you like his looks."

"I know that, Barney. This isn't only about his looks. I can't explain it."

"What do you know about the Drug Enforcement Agency?"

"I don't know the first thing, and this has nothing to do with them. What he does for a job is not who he is."

"What, then?"

"I don't know. I'm as shocked as you are. I can't tell you why I trust him or why I like him. I do, that's all."

"I see you've stopped wearing your wedding ring."

"Barney, none of this is your problem, and yes, I stopped wearing the ring. It's time, don't you think? I took it off the night I ate dinner with your brother."

"Well I hope you aren't going to fall for some guy who lives somewhere else. You'll move away, and Sheriff Ben will have to replace you with somebody I won't like." He got out of the comfortable chair and began to pace. "I won't be able to talk to them about important issues or trust them to follow up on things the way you do. I'll end up retraining some Red Man-chewing good ol' boy with a beer gut, who won't care about this job the way you do."

"Barney, calm down. I'm not moving away. I'm only going to dinner."

"What kind of man flies a woman to a formal dinner in a foreign country on their first damn date?"

"An intriguing man who knows how to fly a plane."

"Oh, shit. I bet you don't come back for a week."

"With any luck." I couldn't stop grinning.

CHAPTER 12

I pulled up next to the airstrip and watched Diego Romero step out of a small tan plane with red and gold markings. It looked new. He walked towards me grinning, even more handsome than I remembered. I had a sudden vicious attack of trembling hands, weak knees, last-minute nausea. What made me think I could fly away with a man I barely knew, and worse, fly away from what I did know?

It's okay, I told myself. *It's okay; it will be okay. You don't have to marry him, but you should be nice to him.*

He opened the door of the Mustang and offered his hand. I was wearing a little black dress of the all-purpose variety, but I had dressed it up with my mother's pearls, hoping I looked formal enough to suit him. It was short and form fitting and when he opened the door I almost panicked. His look was appreciative, but I thought that was only because it was so short. Anyway, it would have to do because I am not a formal type of woman. The last time I dressed like that had been at my wedding. *Do NOT think about your wedding!*

"You look beautiful," Diego said.

"Thank you. So do you."

He was wearing a black tux with long tails, and a blue ruffled shirt that made his eyes look more blue than green. The vest was a lighter shade of blue, as was the bow tie. There was a diamond stud in the shirt. He looked like a prince. His mode of dress was upscale, designer I felt sure. It was nice. He was stunning.

He grinned and kept my hand. I never thought of trying to get it back. We walked towards the plane. He said it was his smallest and newest, which meant he had others, but that fact barely registered. It was a Cessna Skycatcher, he explained. I didn't care if he owned the company or had stolen the aircraft. He gave me other details I didn't hear as he helped me up into it. It had two seats, what he referred to as "deluxe skybox seating for two." It sounded sexy, but I wasn't interested in the plane.

Diego gave a brief safety talk I mostly didn't hear, during which he spent an inordinate amount of time studying my legs. Then he helped me get the seatbelt adjusted to his liking, and smiled at me. "Ready?"

I nodded that I was. He spoke with someone on a radio and we took off. It was a thrill to gather speed so quickly. I'm addicted to fast. The force pushed me back in the seat as we lifted off in a smooth motion. Familiar landmarks became smaller and farther away. We headed straight towards the Chisos Mountains for a few moments then Diego made a sharp turnaround, taking us west and over the Rio Grande.

He spoke again on the radio. I was mesmerized by the tops of mountains in Mexico I had only seen from a distance and couldn't recognize from the air.

"Clear to Chihuahua," Diego said after he signed off.

I was as excited as if we were going to the moon.

"What do you think about flying?" he asked.

We spoke through small earphone contraptions so we could hear each other. Having his rich voice in my ear was intimate and unnerving.

"I love it," I said with enthusiasm. I wasn't sure if I was talking about the flying or the countryside or the voice. I loved all of it.

"I do too, and the better to see the big, beautiful, wild, and rugged landscape." He had captured the essence of it in a few words. "I love working here, and wish I didn't have to spend so much time in Austin."

"Don't you work out of Alpine?"

"I'm there now, but I live in Austin. Of course I have a place in Alpine too, for now. I work wherever I'm sent."

"Is there something extraordinary going on in Terlingua?"

"What do you mean?"

"Well, we've had a drug-related murder for the first time in three or four years. Murder doesn't often happen in Terlingua. Along with that, we have a rash of strange breaking and entering going on. We also pulled a pair of feet out of the river, and we don't know if that's related to the drug murder. I realize this is nothing for a city, but we aren't a city."

"Yes, and that's what's so wonderful about the place."

"An astonishing amount of cocaine has been confiscated. We have a special agent with the DEA relocated to Alpine, and reports of stereotypical Mexican drug dealers hanging around Terlingua. For the first time since I've been a deputy I've met someone with the Drug Enforcement Agency."

"I guess all that would make you suspicious."

"It makes me wonder."

"The truth is it's business as usual for drug trafficking, except for a man called Sotol who seems to be out of control. Normally the people in the drug business don't call attention to themselves."

"Who is he?"

"He works for one of the big Mexican cartels, so he usually isn't the one calling the shots, except that on this he seems to be. He killed William Hayfield, which doesn't make sense. Not only that, but he killed him in a way that drew attention to the murder, which is not the way that's usually done."

"Who is Ruben Villanueva? I shot off two of his fingers."

"He's a cohort of Sotol's—and way to go on the fingers. That's the best thing I've heard this week."

"I don't know much about cartels, but overdosing their victims isn't a normal way of killing them, is it?"

"No, not at all. They shoot them in the head. In killing Hayfield, he murdered his major contact from Texas, which doesn't make sense from a business standpoint but let's don't talk about business."

"That's fine with me."

"Unless you want to tell me about working as a deputy."

"There's not much to tell. It's not like my job is exciting. We have very little crime in south Brewster County as a general rule."

"You make that sound like a negative thing."

I laughed. "It's a good thing, but it makes for boring work. I'm sure it's nothing like what you do."

"I spend a lot of time on stakeouts, also boring."

"You said you were working undercover. Did you mean in Terlingua?"

"I can't talk to you about that. I'm sorry."

"That's all right. I understand the concept of undercover work. You sure fooled me with that homeboy look."

"Did you like my gangsta self?"

"You looked like you were into the part."

"That was the point."

"Do you really have those tattoos?"

"Naw, they were temporary. But if you like them, I could get some."

"No, I don't like them much." *Just as long as those arms are real.* "If you don't get any tats for me, then I won't feel like I have to get any for you."

He laughed. "That's a deal. No tats."

* * *

"I want to get something out of the way," Diego said. "I know you're going to ask because everyone does."

"What makes you think I'm like everyone else?"

"I sense you're not, which is why I'm taking you out in the first place."

"What is it people ask you?"

"They want to know how I afford a plane on a government salary, so before you jump to conclusions I wanted to say that I come from a wealthy Mexican family."

I was expecting almost anything but that. It wasn't even a negative thing. "Are you ashamed of it?"

"No, but other women I've known didn't like it."

"Which part? Being wealthy or being Mexican?"

"I think they had a problem with the money part because they assume I'm on the take or something."

"I would never jump to that conclusion."

"Because that's the first rule in law enforcement?"

"Because it's stupid to jump to conclusions before you know someone."

He looked over at me. "Do you want to know me, Margarita?"

Oh, hell yeah.

"Of course I do or I wouldn't be going to Mexico with you. I don't care if you're rich as a Texas senator or poor as desert dirt. That isn't how I judge people."

"Thank God."

"You don't have to spend a lot of money to entertain me. But if you thought it would make a difference, why not take me to a local restaurant in a normal car until you could see how I am?"

He turned to me with a piercing look. "I like to get the cards on the table right at the start. If my money makes you uncomfortable, I need to know it."

"I can't say, Diego. I never had money. I think it would be nice, in that vague way people dream about having things they don't have. But truthfully I don't care one way or the other about your money."

"Let's have some fun with it then."

"Okay. You're doing great so far."

He laughed and then asked, "What made you get into law enforcement work?"

"Oh, ever since I was little I had this desire to right wrongs and see good triumph over evil. I used to play G.I. Joe or Ninja Turtles, stuff like that. I didn't care what it was as long as I got to be the ass-kicker. That doesn't sound much like a girl, does it?"

"Well, you turned into a lovely one." Diego blushed scarlet.

"Thank you."

"What made you decide to be a deputy?"

"I was in the law enforcement academy in Alpine. I intended to get a degree in criminal justice because I wanted to work as a detective with a large police force somewhere else, like Dallas or San Antonio.

"One day Sheriff Duncan spoke to my class. He described small town law enforcement work and made it sound romantic and important. He stressed that he was looking for the right type of person, someone who cared about the people where they lived, and that appealed to me. I do care about my community."

"That's what makes you good at your job."

"What makes you think I'm good at it?"

"I hear things. I'm in law enforcement too, don't forget."

"Yes, but you're doing big boy work."

"What you do is important and you shouldn't forget it. Who found the cocaine? If you hadn't been vigilant, those men would have passed it through."

"I only happened to be there enjoying the moonlight. I wasn't even working."

"That sounds nice."

"It was until I saw those guys."

"What else do you like to do? Besides hanging out in the moonlight?"

"I like to dance, read, and explore wild country. I like to do almost anything outdoors. I'm a runner, but I also like to raft, canoe, and kayak. I love speeding; anything fast gets my attention, so taking me somewhere in an airplane—that is an extremely good move."

He laughed. "What else?"

"I like to travel, not that I've done much. What do you like to do?"

"All the things you mentioned. I have a motorcycle and I like to ride that. Like you, I'm fond of fast. And I want to say that the place I'm taking you to eat has dancing, all kinds of dancing, and exceptional food."

"It sounds great."

"Would you take me on the Rio Grande sometime?"

"Sure, any time. Have you ever been?"

"I've crossed it my whole life, but I've never rafted or canoed it or seen any of the famous Big Bend canyons."

"I've seen them all. My uncle owned a rafting company when I was growing up. The canyons are so gorgeous and each one is different. They're beyond what I'm capable of describing."

"Which one is your favorite?"

"I can't say. Whichever one I'm in, I guess."

"I've flown over Santa Elena and it looks impressive, but I'm sure it's more so from the perspective of the river."

"That's definitely true."

"So when can we go?

"When we both have a day off, if you're talking about Santa Elena. Also, there has to be enough water to do it in a day."

"What if there's not?"

"Then it has to be done in a multi-day trip or we would have to do a different section of river. Pray for rain."

He laughed. "I will."

* * *

At dinner I noticed that Diego was wearing diamond and gold cufflinks and he wore a gold ring with an emerald in it on his right hand. It wasn't large or gaudy but still, it looked expensive. Maybe he was as rich as Bill Gates, but he was easy to talk to, funny, and one hell of a dancer. I liked him so much I felt like my heart was still flying.

All the things I had stressed about evaporated. Conversation was easy, and when we didn't talk, the silence was comfortable rather than awkward, and we were usually gazing at each other. I felt I was dressed appropriately, except my sexy shoes were killing me. They had three-inch heels, and I hadn't worn them in so long they made my legs ache. I had worried about dancing, being close to a man, being held. That part was wonderful, best of all.

More than anything I had worried about not drinking. It's hard to say *I don't drink*, but when I declined a drink, Diego took it in stride. I asked instead for tonic and lime, and he said he would have the same. He couldn't drink either because of flying us back. So not drinking was nothing, like the other things I had wasted time dreading.

"You're not married, are you?" Diego asked during dinner.

"Isn't that something a person usually asks before a date and not on one?"

"Well yes, but I just happened to notice that there's a white band on your finger where a ring has been. I don't know why I assumed you were single when I met you."

"I'm a widow."

"What I mean is I didn't even look for a wedding band." He turned scarlet. "You took my hand and I was so shaken I couldn't think."

I could've said the same thing. "I assume you're not married, either?"

"I'm divorced."

"I was wearing the ring until a few days ago. I—I— haven't wanted to have a date until you asked me."

"Well, I'm honored." He took my hand. "You felt it too, didn't you?"

"Yes, I felt it."

I thought he was going to kiss me and was about to faint with anticipation.

"Have you been a widow long?"

"About two-and-a-half years."

"When I hear the word 'widow' I think of an old person. You're so young to be a widow."

"I think so, too."

"I'm sorry, Margarita. I don't mean to make you sad."

"It's all right, Diego. You aren't making me sad. You have every right to ask. I think the fact that I'm here instead of hiding out in my house means that I'm ready to get on with my life."

"I'd like to help you with that," he said softly.

"Do you have children?"

"No, do you?"

"No."

"Would it matter to you if I did?" he asked.

"No, not at all; I was only asking."

"What would you think about dancing again?"

After more dancing with him, the life I had known slipped away, and I was a single woman with a single man. I felt like I had a future and wanted one.

We enjoyed one of the best meals I ever ate anywhere

with the kind of service a person could get used to. I thought it must be nice to be wealthy. We talked and laughed and danced until just after one AM. We had to go back sometime, and we both knew it. I know it sounds cliché, but I felt like Cinderella must have felt leaving the ball. I wasn't ready for it to be over. But at least I still had the prince with me.

I thought for a minute he was going to suggest staying at his place in the city, since he said he had an apartment there. I would've gone, but he was so proper and knew how to treat a woman. His slow-moving ways were unbearably seductive.

"Do you mind if I take off my shoes?" I asked while we were waiting for takeoff clearance from the tower.

"No. Take off anything that's bothering you." He gave me a sideways glance and blushed. "I was going to take off my jacket and vest." He did that and asked me to lay them in a storage compartment located in back of his seat.

"May I wear your jacket?"

"Of course."

I set my shoes and his vest into the container and pulled the jacket around me.

"I can turn up the heat."

"I'm fine now that I have this, thank you."

The jacket smelled subtly of the man who had been wearing it. It was more disconcerting than his voice in my ear.

"Won't your feet get cold?"

"My feet will be all right."

"It's not like those straps would keep you warm anyway, I guess." He studied my feet and sighed. "The next time we do this, remind me to bring comfortable clothes for the trip home."

"I will. I don't want to disappoint you, Diego, but I'm more of a blue jean-wearing woman than a get-dressed-up-and-show-off type of woman."

"That suits me fine. I hardly think it would matter what you wear."

* * *

Diego was busy checking instruments and listening to the tower. "Are you ready for take-off?" he asked.

"I'm ready, but are you? You're the pilot."

"I am. We're just waiting on the go-ahead."

He reached over and took my hand and held it until the tower indicated we should move into position. Neither of us said a word. Then it was time to go, and he set my hand on my thigh. "I don't want to let go of you."

"I've had a great time, Diego. If anyone had told me what this evening would be like I wouldn't have believed them."

"I feel the same way."

"That can't be true. You were the one who designed it."

"Well it wouldn't have been so great if you hadn't been here. But somehow I knew it would be like this." He hesitated. "It took me a long time to call you. I tried to talk myself out of seeing you again."

"Why?"

"I don't need to care about someone right now because of my work, and I feel like I will care about you. I think it's already too late to back out."

That was when he unfastened his seatbelt, leaned over, and kissed me. It could have lasted a long time, and would have, except that the tower interrupted to say we were next. Diego pulled back a little, groped around for the radio, responded in the affirmative, and then returned his lips to mine. We didn't need an aircraft to fly.

He checked over the instrument panel one more time, and then before my heart had settled, we were picking up speed. It was thrilling, speeding down the runway and lifting off into the night. I was breathless from the kissing and the speeding and the takeoff and the feel and scent of the jacket and the feel and scent of the man who wore it.

As the lights of Chihuahua became small and the countryside dark, the full moon brought its magic inside the cockpit. Diego and I looked at each other and smiled. He took my hand again. Words would have been excessive.

The sky ahead was bright and shimmering. Wispy clouds dipped in silver skittered by. It seemed like the rest of the world was incidental to the wide night sky and the two of us. We owned the sky. The rest of the planet—who cared?

When the mountains of Big Bend came into view it was breathtaking, but by then my breath had already been taken. Diego's large, warm hand held mine, massaging it lovingly without saying a word. I wanted to ask him a hundred questions but didn't want him to stop making love to my hand. After a while he brought it to his mouth and kissed it. It was almost unbearable. I touched his lips with my fingers. He drew one of them into his mouth causing me to gasp.

"Why don't you unhook that seatbelt and slide over here?" he said.

After that, we were making out in an airplane, a first for me.

"Why do I feel like this about you?" he asked in a hoarse voice after a long time had passed.

"I don't know, but I feel the same way about you."

"I've been looking for you, and I didn't know who I was looking for until the day I met you. Just the touch of your hand—I wasn't expecting it, least of all in Terlingua."

"I wasn't expecting it, either. In fact, I was hiding in my office and had no intention of meeting a DEA agent from anywhere."

"I noticed that."

"Nothing personal."

"I thought Deputy Ricos would be a burly, tobacco-spitting hombre."

"I figured you would think that."

"I could hardly stand to drive away from you."

"I didn't want you to go."

* * *

The airstrip in Terlingua is not lit, or it wasn't, but as we approached I saw blue lights winking below. Diego said he had set them up so he could keep his promise and bring me back that night. They were solar-powered, he explained.

We landed uneventfully, but it was the last—and possibly the only—uneventful thing about that night. The aircraft rolled to a stop and Diego pulled me gently onto his lap.

When making out became serious foreplay, I suggested we go to my house. He seemed to think that was a good idea, but we didn't leave the deluxe skybox seating for two. Diego unzipped my dress, lifted it over my head, and before long his clothes were coming off, too. Fog was so thick on the windows of the Skycatcher that the moon had to force its light in through thin rivulets of moisture. We lost all sense of time, all sense of everything except each other.

When light first began to show itself in the east, we gathered our clothes and went to my house. Diego pulled on his pants and I wore only his tux coat. We tossed the rest of the clothes into the backseat of the Mustang.

At my house we played in a bath until the water got cold, then got into my bed and made love until my phone began ringing. I ignored it at first, but then remembered it was Saturday, and I was on call. I hadn't had one thought about work since Diego asked me about being a deputy.

I fumbled the phone to my ear. It was the dispatcher with news of another body in the river; this one was between Grassy Banks and where the feet had been found. It had been reported by fishermen.

"I have to go," I said. I didn't want to. I was lying on top of Diego and I wanted to stay there until the next full moon.

"What's up?"

"There's another body in the Rio Grande."

"Is it dead?"

"Yes it's dead; that's why they're calling."

He lovingly pushed hair back from my face. "If the guy is already dead, what's the rush?"

"It doesn't work like that, Diego."

"I know. Well, I'd rather stay and play with you all day Margarita Ricos, but if duty calls you, I'll go back to Alpine and see what's going on."

"You can stay here if you want to sleep."

"I'll come back tonight, if you don't have other plans."

"Are we going to fly somewhere?"

"I was hoping you would take me to the moon again."

Yeah; I was thinking about that, too.

I showered and dressed in my uniform. He took a shower and went out to the Mustang with a towel around him to get his clothes. Then I took him, dressed in his wrinkled tuxedo, back to the airstrip. We could hardly stand to part and held each other a long time. He promised to return that evening.

I watched him taxi the plane to the end of the strip, turn it around, and begin picking up speed. Diego grinned and waved as he tore past me and lifted into the air. He flew in a circle above me, tipped a wing, and headed in the direction of Alpine. I stood in a whirlwind of dusty desert and watched until he was a tiny dot in the sky.

Stars had fallen on Texas.

CHAPTER 13

The dust settled. Diego and the Skycatcher were gone. I was not mentally ready for work—what work?—and at that moment I couldn't go. Instead I stood dazzled, looking around as if lost in a place where I had lived my entire life.

The 360 degree panorama of mountains, desert, and boulder-strewn hills shone as if polished. Things stood out. Color I never realized was gone had returned to my life. Things sparkled. It was so beautiful I could have cried, but I also wanted to laugh and dance and sing at the top of my lungs.

I found my way to the Mustang, but I don't know how.

Before I pulled away from the airstrip, Barney called. "Are you coming, Ricos?"

"Yes."

"This week?"

"Keep your shirt on. I'm on my way."

I dreaded what waited at the river; on the other hand, it was difficult to think of anything but Diego. I was so enchanted I went to the scene driving my Mustang.

It was easy to find the location since the ambulance was parked on the road with lights flashing, along with Barney's vehicle, and several others belonging to the ever-present curious onlookers. There was yellow crime scene tape strung through the brush near the body. I wouldn't have come if I'd known Barney was going to respond. I had sent Diego away for nothing, but I was too elated to be mad with anyone.

Barney stood up from what I assumed was the corpse and moved towards me. "Glad you could make it, Deputy Ricos."

"Don't start. I haven't slept yet. What have we got?"

He stood between me and the body. "It's a real floater this time, not a pretty sight. I don't want to tell you this, but it's Adolpho Estevez."

"Oh God; are you sure?"

"Yes, unless his I.D. is on someone else's body. He's not recognizable because fish have picked away his face, and he's bloated, but I'm guessing it's a teenage boy, based on general build and mode of dress."

"How long do you think he's been in the water?"

"At least a week, I'd say, long enough to look revolting. You might not want to look at him, Ricos."

"Well, I'm going to have to."

"How was your date? Did you really fly to Chihuahua City? I saw that his plane was still there this morning. Is the plane his or the DEA's? Hey—I don't think you should look at the body."

Yada, yada, yada; I wasn't listening. I made my way to the river against Barney's protests and endless questions. I was not going to throw up.

The victim's skin was pale and waterlogged. His eyes were gone. There was a gaping, gruesome bullet hole in his forehead. The fleshy areas of his face had been mostly nibbled away. And there was the awful, rotting smell of death. It was enough to make a person vomit. I didn't though.

"Is Sheriff Ben coming?" I asked.

"No. The hearse is on the way and they'll take the body to the crime lab. Mitch is leaving now to speak with Adolpho's parents."

I was glad I wouldn't have to do that. Nobody wants to tell a kid's parents that their son was found floating face down in the river. Mitch was a good man to go because of his calm, empathetic manner. He was fascinated by the state of the corpse, but at the same time understood the seriousness of his mission and the devastating sadness the boy's parents would feel.

"What do we have in the way of evidence?"

Barney shrugged. "Nothing, other than his identification. He was shot in the head. I don't guess you could miss that. The current moved him from wherever he was dumped. This is some bad shit, Ricos."

I couldn't have agreed more.

"This kind of crap never happened here before," he ranted. "Now they're killing kids. We can't sit still for this."

"Of course not, but what are we going to do?"

"Hell if I know. The sheriff said a couple of Texas Rangers would be coming, but since the body is going to their crime lab, I don't know why they're coming here."

"Maybe they want to find the real crime scene," I suggested. "Wherever he was murdered and dumped."

"Think we should look around ourselves?"

"Yes, once the body is picked up we should at least go

to Grassy Banks and any other possible places we see along the way."

"This isn't our case," Barney reminded me in case I still didn't get it.

"Right, but it's our community and our kids. No Texas Ranger will care about it like we do."

"True enough, Ricos. Will you go take a statement from the fishermen who found him? It's that group over there." He indicated two men and a boy who were standing about fifty yards upriver from the body.

I walked up to them and introduced myself. Their story was that they had been out early, fishing up and down the river. They chose that area because of a rocky outcropping that shaded the water and encouraged fish to seek shelter. They had seen something floating at the edge of the rocks and on closer inspection, saw that it was a body.

I got names and addresses and had the adults sign a brief statement. The whole thing reminded me of the feet, found near the same place. I couldn't believe the foot murder was related to Adolpho's, but I tried to keep an open mind.

"Thanks to all of you," I said to the group. We shook hands and they left.

I walked back over to Barney.

He nudged me. "What about your date with the DEA?"

"My date was with a man, not the DEA, and it was wonderful."

"Is that why you were so late?"

"Yes."

"Well." He mulled the implications. "I don't guess you want to talk about it."

"That's right."

My partner scrutinized me. I was too happy to be angry with him or anyone else. At that point I wasn't even tired.

"Have you had breakfast, Ricos?"

"No. I didn't have time."

"Want to go get some later?"

"I'm not hungry."

"Come with me anyway."

"Are you going to fish for details about my date?"

"What kind of partner do you think I am? Of course I will."

"How many times do I have to tell you it's my personal life?"

"As many as it takes, I guess. I don't give up easily."

"I noticed."

The hearse arrived half an hour later. Those guys were not prepared for the state of the body they were transporting. We helped them load it. By the time we got the job done, they were as white as the dead man.

My cell phone rang and the caller was Diego Romero. I walked off to speak in private. I felt more tongue-tied than I had as a teenager whenever a boy I liked called me. After breathless greetings on both our parts, he asked what I was doing.

"We just loaded the dead man into the hearse."

I don't think he heard that. "I'm having a hard time paying attention, Margarita," he said." I want to be there lying naked on your bed with you." His voice went all over me, to the places his hands had been.

"I'd like that, too." In fact, it was difficult to think about anything else.

"Where we are doesn't matter—your bed or mine, your aircraft or mine, your bathtub or mine."

I laughed. "Okay, Diego, I get it."

"I don't think you understand."

"I believe I do. I keep thinking about it, too."

"We need to be together. We *belong* together. I'm eighty miles away and I feel like my oxygen supply has been cut off. Can you pick me up at the airstrip?"

"Of course I will; just tell me what time."

"Forty-five minutes?"

My heart started thudding in my ears. "Yes. I'll be there."

"I only wish that," he said. "I can't get down there until later. I'll call you."

"Listen Diego, the floater was one of the high school kids that were seen with Sotol and Ruben at the time William Hayfield was murdered. He had been shot in the head. This is a Texas Ranger case, but won't it involve you, too?"

"Yes, I'm sure it will. I have to go. I'll call you about picking me up."

"Okay."

"I'm kissing you good-bye now."

"I'm kissing you back."

"Oh God." He cut the call.

* * *

Grassy Banks belongs to the Big Bend Ranch State Park and is an official put-in point for river trips. It is also a campground with outdoor toilets and picnic tables. The site is a wide grassy area at a bend in the river, hence the name. Barney and I split the area in two and perused it for evidence of a murder.

I tried to keep my thoughts on the horrendous crime, but they were also on Diego and went like this: *What should I wear tonight? Is this murder related to the other crimes? What are the chances of having so many different criminals in Terlingua at one time? What about that white lacy see-though thingy? You slut! I wonder when the crime lab will have the results from the bone fragments I found in the burned wreck. He liked that short black dress. Why would someone choose that old truck wreck to dispose of one body but dump the other in the river? You don't even know if there was a body in the wreck. It's not a convenient location to dump a body from either side of the river. Just show up naked and be done with formalities. Maybe somebody was coming down the river and saw it and decided to set fire to it. No, that's stupid. Give me a better explanation. Maybe he'll want to fly somewhere. Flying was great. Why is that flying dragon shirt so familiar? Think! I can't think! You should check out that rock house again. His hands were everywhere and—Stop thinking about him! Criminals are taking over your community, and now they're killing kids, and you just want to wear that lacy thing for a man you just met. It would be—*

"Ricos!" Barney's voice brought me back from wherever I was headed before I had the chance to work up a good sweat and a heart attack. "I got nothing."

"Same here."

After that we scouted every place along the river where there was the slightest access and found nothing. It was frustrating.

"Maybe they killed him somewhere else and brought him to the river and dumped him," said Barney, vocalizing something I was thinking too.

"Or they could have killed him on the Mexican side almost anywhere along here," I said. Then I had a thought. "There's one more place on the American side we should check before we quit."

"Where?"

"Let's drive to the other side of Big Hill."

"What are you thinking?"

"I want to check the beach at the entrance to Dark Canyon."

"Why?"

"Because another crime happened in that vicinity."

"That fire? You think that truck fire is related to this murder?"

"I don't know. It's possible."

"Ricos, it doesn't make sense. Why kill a kid and toss him in the river and then go set fire to an old truck from back in the day? Oh! I forgot you have the fire-to-cover-up-a-murder theory." He was heavy on sarcasm, but it was wasted on me because my head had already made a detour back to Diego.

"If there was a body involved in the truck fire," he continued, "why burn one body and dump the other?"

"There are a lot of possibilities, Barney. They may have been killed in different places and at different times and for different reasons."

"Give me a reason."

"Why burn a dead body?"

"To cover the fact that there is one? Maybe the feet we found belong to the body they burned."

"Right," I agreed. "So if a body was burned in the fire by the same perps what does that say to us?"

"*You*, Ricos, what does it say to *you*?"

"It says they don't care if we know they murdered Adolpho. The body they burned in the truck is someone more important. It's someone they don't want us to know is even missing. So who would that be?"

"The governor of Chihuahua?" he suggested, making fun of my theory. "The president of Mexico? Our president? A cartel kingpin? It doesn't make sense."

"It doesn't make sense because we don't have all the pieces yet."

"Well, duh." He paused but not long. "We need to eat."

"We need pieces."

"We have to eat so we can think," he insisted.

"We have to gather pieces so we can get somewhere with this."

"We should eat and then gather pieces."

"A high school student is dead, Barney. He was only eighteen."

"Okay, okay, you win. We'll eat later."

We found nothing at the place where I was so sure there would be something. It was disheartening. I stood at the river's edge, at the entrance to Dark Canyon. It was short in length as Big Bend canyons go, but steep and rugged—impressive.

There were too many whys and not enough becauses.

"Has Agent Gapes-a-Lot called you yet today?" Barney asked on the way back to our vehicles.

"Yes Daddy, is that okay?"

"Hey, smartass, if I was your dad you wouldn't have flown off anywhere with that guy. I would've forbidden you to go."

"That wouldn't have mattered. I would still have gone."

Barney shook his head sadly. "Your poor parents."

"It wasn't about the flying, or even the dancing and dining. That was wonderful—better than wonderful—but what is so—what am I doing?"

"Don't stop now. You were just getting to the good part."

"Do you agree that Adolpho was probably murdered by the same men who murdered Bill Hayfield?"

"Way to change the subject."

"Somebody had to. Do you agree or not?"

"Yes, I agree with your theory, and it makes me think the feet might be attributed to the same perps."

"We don't have enough information yet even to make educated guesses."

"Luis' life will be in danger when he's released," he said.

"Yes. Definitely. He needs to stay there a while, and there are good reasons to keep him. Do you think they'll come for us, Barney?"

"No. Why would they?"

"We took their drugs, drugs worth millions. And we spoke with Luis. And we're looking for them, and they're bound to know it. We're the only law there is to kill, and they seem to be in a killing mood."

"Now you're scaring me."

"I'm scaring myself."

"They've disappeared into Mexico by now."

"Crap, Barney, I just put Craig over there. Do you think he's safe? Maybe I should bring him back over here."

"Why would he be in danger?"

"They might figure out that he's connected to me."

"But he's a harmless old guy. He has nothing to do with any of this."

"I'm feeling a lot of panic and I don't know why."

"You just need some food, Ricos, that's all. It's already past noon."

Eating is Barney's cure for almost everything—eat, sex, and Dr. Pepper, but not in that order.

* * *

After lunch I changed to blue jeans and old running shoes to cross the river and check on Craig. I left the Mustang in a clump of tamarisk trees near the shore and rolled the jeans up to my knees. Then I hopped from rock to rock at another flat-bottomed crossing point that is near my papi's land. The river is wider there than at other places, which makes it shallower and easier to cross. I never even got damp.

My father's forty-acre field is fenced, but the fencing is easy to climb. I fought through weeds and brushy growth between his land and the neighbor's. The house is across the pueblo's main dirt road, about two blocks from the field. I saw the usual squealing, playing children and women hanging out clothes or hoeing their gardens. There were men plowing with mules, others checking on cattle or feeding goats. No gangsters or suspicious characters were lurking, or if they were, I missed them.

Craig had already repaired the broken-down fence and cleaned the yard of trash and plant debris. He had even cleared the dead vines and weeds from around the rosebushes. It looked almost like the old days, except there was no herb garden under the chinaberry tree in front, and no grandparents to hug and adore me.

The outside chairs on the sliver of porch had been cleaned, too. The kitchen door was open, and I called to Craig through the screen but received no answer. After a few minutes I went in and continued calling his name.

I was happy to see that the place look lived-in again. A bowl of fruit and avocadoes sat in the center of the kitchen table, coffee had been made and drunk, and a mug and plate were still on the table from breakfast. Craig was probably out in the countryside sitting in an abandoned roofless building, or on a bluff overlooking the river, reading or writing poetry.

I left him a brief note of greeting. For a few minutes, I sat on the cement slab that serves as a porch, letting random thoughts come and go. My childhood had been rich, growing up in two countries. I watched my young self run around the yard, dig in the dirt, make up games, and chase chickens through my grandma's garden.

Cuidado, chamaquita! she would call. *Be careful, little girl.* Her underlying message was always *I love you, child. You are precious to me.* You were precious too, Grandma. I miss you so much.

For a while I thought about mafiosos defiling our borderlands. My core belief is that evil people should not be allowed in the desert. If I made the rules, a lot of things would be different. There would be no evildoers allowed anywhere in Mexico, either. I would remove all of them with a great big sweep of my powerful hand.

I laughed at myself and went back to the U.S. by the same route I had come.

CHAPTER 14

I stood by my car, dressed in blue jeans and a red *Texas Rocks* t-shirt, watching Diego land his plane. He touched down at the far end of the runway and raced along it, dust billowing. When the Skycatcher stopped rolling I was standing at the door on the pilot side. The grin he gave me melted my heart to a puddle. He flung open the door and held out his hand.

"Come, Preciosa," he whispered, and I stepped up into his arms. He held me tightly and whispered words of love. Going to Heaven must be like that.

After a long time he said, "I brought you flowers. I hope you like margaritas." He reached to the passenger seat and handed me the largest bunch of them I had ever seen. In Mexico, daisies are called margaritas.

"Oh, they're beautiful. Thank you."

"They're nearly as beautiful as you," he said, "but not quite."

I sighed and fell against him.

"Do you want to learn to fly this plane?"

"Well, sure. Are you offering to teach me?"

"Yes, but let's go to your house first. We'll do that tomorrow. Is that okay?"

Oh yes. It was.

* * *

Later we were sitting on my porch in white wicker rockers, holding hands and waiting for the moon to rise over the Chisos. It was still full, but was coming up later each night, so darkness had already settled. There was a silvery glow behind the mountains that made them stand out. Even though it was dark, there was so much light from the rising moon that the stars were dimmed by it.

I pointed out my personal guardian, Cimarron, and a few other mountains whose outlines I recognized. Diego seemed as amazed by the view as I was. My house is on the slope of a hill, high enough to overlook miles of surrounding desert and to see far into the distance.

I was thinking about those things when he spoke. "Will

you take me to see your sandstone bluff?"

"Sure. Want to go now?"

"Yes. I'd like that."

"I could take you to some places you've never been."

"You've already done that, mi amor, but I'm willing to keep going any and every place you want to take me."

Diego Romero was the sexiest man I'd ever met. He was like the mole sauce used on chicken: spicy hot and sweet at the same time. And he had dropped right out of the sky, meant especially for me.

    * * *

On Monday morning I had to take him to the airstrip early, and again it was hard for us to part. After the takeoff dust settled, I was still standing with his last soft words in my ear. *I love you, Margarita. We have to be together.* I thought so, too.

When I got to work, Barney was speaking with the dispatcher. She had radioed to say a truck had been stolen and she was transferring the male caller to us. We groaned in unison at the news of another crime.

"Put him through," Barney said, and placed the phone on speaker function. Then he informed the caller he was speaking with the Sheriff's Office in Terlingua.

"This is Tom Thomason and my new truck is gone." He sounded as if he was about to cry. "It was taken from my driveway last night."

"Are you sure someone didn't borrow it?" Barney asked.

It was hard to believe we had auto theft in Terlingua. But then, we'd had three murders, far worse, and even more unlikely.

"If someone borrowed it, they took it without my permission. I can't think who would do that. My truck is brand new. It doesn't even have 500 miles on it yet."

Barney assured him we would be right there.

"So much for a boring Monday morning," he said.

"Crime-fighting heroes never get a rest," I declared.

"Hell is bubbling up, Ricos. I don't like it."

"Me either."

"What's going on?"

"I wish I could tell you."

"You look bright and happy today, my partner. Did you get to spend most of the weekend with Mr. Wonderful?"

"Yes I did."

"He has improved your mood."

"You noticed."

When we pulled up at Tom's, he was pacing up and down his driveway. His graying hair was in disarray, his mouth a grim frown.

"Have you ever worked a vehicle theft, Barney?" I had never once worked one and couldn't remember if we had covered it in training.

"Never have. We'll ask some questions and then look around, shake a few trees and see what falls out."

"I doubt if the truck is in a tree."

He gave me an exasperated look.

I jumped out of the vehicle. "Morning, Tom," I said and took his hand.

"How are you going to find who did this?" he demanded to know.

Good question.

"First, we need to ask you for details."

Barney walked up and the men greeted each other.

"Well, start asking," Tom said, "because my truck is farther and farther away from here the longer we stand here jabbering."

"We need a complete description of the truck, including the serial number, so we can get the word out to law enforcement to be on the lookout for it."

"It's a dark blue Ford 4X4 King Cab pick-up. Come on in the house and I'll get the serial number for you."

"When did you last see it?"

"It was right here when I went to bed last night at eleven."

"You're sure it was here?"

"I know because I opened the front door to let the dog in and I saw it there."

"And when did you first notice it missing?"

"My wife noticed when she took the dog out this morning. It was a little after nine o'clock. I thought she was messing with me until I saw how upset she was."

"Have you ever loaned the truck to anyone?"

"Definitely not. I haven't driven it much, and Dora has only driven it once to the grocery store."

He held the door for us. "Go on back to the kitchen."

His wife Dora greeted us and offered fresh coffee, which we accepted.

"Does anyone have a key to your truck?"

"No."

"Are you sure you didn't leave the key in it?" I asked.

Tom looked into his cup as if expecting help to surface and reddened. "I did. I didn't mean to, and I thought of it when we got in bed, but I thought what the hell, this is Terlingua. We hardly ever lock anything."

"Maybe someone saw an opportunity and took it," I suggested. "Can you think of anyone who might do that, a neighbor kid or someone who borrowed a vehicle before? Or someone who has shown a lot of interest in it?"

"The only neighbor I ever loaned my truck to moved away a year ago. I doubt if he'd come back and assume he could take my brand new truck without asking. I'm picky about who drives my stuff and he knows it."

"Yeah," said Dora, "I don't get to drive anything until it's fifteen years old."

"Oh, Honey."

She gave him a look, but it was not a sore point with her.

"Do you have insurance?" I asked.

"Full coverage, thank God."

"I advise you to call the company and notify them that the truck has possibly been stolen," said Barney. "They can call us for the full report, which we'll make after we do some looking around and talking to people."

"Okay, I'll do that. Thank you, but I hope you find it."

"I do too. We'll call you later or come by. Do you have a way to get around?"

"Yeah, we've got an old truck out back that runs fine. Guess we'll be driving that a while longer."

We left Tom and Dora's on foot and spoke to the closest neighbors to see if they had heard or seen anything last night or early that morning. Nobody had.

Since that turned up nothing, we drove through the neighborhood, which consisted of one dirt road about a mile long with houses on either side, then extended into some clay hills near where I'd sat with Diego in the moonlight on the sandstone bluff over the weekend.

Remembering it made me think of flying through the silver-lined sky, and the moonlight on his face. Those thoughts lifted my heart. Since Kevin's death I was unaccustomed to having a sudden happy thought without working for it. While I was driving around with Barney that morning, I felt joy descend on me and I almost started singing.

It took less than thirty minutes to establish that Tom's truck was nowhere in sight. We didn't expect it to be, but had to rule out possibilities.

We stopped at the Chili Pepper Café for breakfast burritos to go and Barney went in to get them. While he was gone, Diego called me to flirt and make me miss him.

"I have to go to a meeting," he said after a few sentences. "I'll call you later. Bye, Beautiful."

"Bye, Diego."

Barney came out with a bag of burritos and two cups of cold orange juice, just in time to save me from myself.

"What's with you?" he asked when he got back in the vehicle.

"Nothing."

"You look like I caught you at something. You've been talking to Lover Boy on the phone, haven't you?"

"Yes I was."

"What did he have to say?"

"Let's go talk to people about that truck."

"Oh sure, now you want to do your job."

"Well if it was my truck, I'd want the deputies to be looking for it."

"If it was yours, we would be," he said. "Let's eat first."

* * *

We visited a few people who always have their ears to the ground. One of them is Sylvia, who has more spies than the CIA. She was as baffled as we were and couldn't believe it had happened if she didn't know about it.

There were a couple of other people Barney and I relied on because they knew things before anyone else. One of them was my papi. He's the Father Confessor of the Hispanic community. People confide in him since he listens and can keep a secret. He owns a convenience store so he sees much of our community on a near-daily basis. Since we had nada from everywhere else, we were forced to visit him.

"Don't mention Diego," I instructed before we got out of the Explorer.

"You forget where you live. I bet he already knows."

"I don't see how he could know about it yet."

"This is Terlingua, Batgirl."

"Stop calling me Batgirl."

We might have continued to bicker, but my father walked over to the vehicle. *"Qué pasa?"* he asked.

"Hola, Papi." I got out and gave him a hug. I couldn't tell by his manner if he knew about Diego or not. Anyhow, I thought my parents would be happy about it, not angry. They knew how sad and heartbroken I had been and had suffered with me. Besides, I am a grown woman with my own life to live.

Barney and my father shook hands, but my partner stayed in the Explorer with the door open. I walked with Papi into the store while I explained what we'd been doing all morning and why. While I spoke he leaned against the sales counter. I pulled up an empty five-gallon paint bucket, turned it over, and sat in front of him.

"You should have come here first," he said in his irritating way. "José Velasco came by early to ask for a job, but he works too slowly for me to pay him by the hour, so I passed on that. He had a thermos of coffee and we shared some."

I tried to be patient while he moved at his own pace. I knew he had a point. It was the getting to it that made me want to yank out my hair.

"He mentioned he was across the river last night visiting his parents. He said some guys passed a new truck across the river at about four o'clock this morning. Those bad characters were driving it—Sotol and them. Earlier in the evening they were drinking beer and bragging that some gringos were bringing them a new Ford. They made it sound like they were buying the truck, not stealing it, so nobody thought much about it."

"Are you sure about this?"

"Margarita, do you doubt me? Of course I'm sure."

"Papi, why didn't you call me? You have my cell number."

"But I don't have a cell phone. You know that."

"How many times do I have to explain that you can call a cell phone from any phone? The phone in your house or store would work fine. You have to call long distance, that's all."

He stared at me blankly even though we'd had this conversation more than once. There were things he refused to understand.

"Did José see them with the truck?"

"He didn't, but his father did. You should ask him about it."

"Were the gringos with Sotol?"

"No. The word is the gringos only brought the truck to the river, at the crossing place down near my field."

"I know the one."

"I would guess the gringos stole the truck and sold it to Sotol. I don't think you're going to find it, and you might get killed trying."

"I have no jurisdiction in Mexico, so I can't even look for it, and I'm sure the truck is long gone anyway. It's the gringos I want. Nobody can buy a stolen truck unless some low-life steals it first."

"Other than a man like Sotol, there's no market here for stolen vehicles. It's too far to anyplace where they could be sold. I think you're looking for some guys who want to make a quick buck, not a ring of car thieves. Still, it could be dangerous." Then he added hopefully, "Maybe they've already left the area."

"Somehow I doubt it."

I thought and he smoked.

"I wonder if the truck thieves are the same ones who are breaking into businesses around here," I said after a few minutes passed.

"Could be. I don't like it. I want you to come run my store—help me learn English and bookkeeping."

"Papi, you've lived here forty years. It seems to me if you wanted to learn English you would've done it by now. Mom tried to teach you, but you wouldn't even try. I want you to find someone else to work with you and help you learn the things you need to know and teach you English if that's what you want."

"But I want it to be you."

"I don't want to do it, Papi. I have a career I like, for now at least. It could lead to other things when I cease to like it."

"If you don't get killed first."

"A few days ago you told me my job was a joke."

"I never said that."

"You didn't use those words, but that's what you were hinting at, that there was nothing for me to do but drive around wasting county money. Now you think I'll be killed. You can't have it both ways."

"I want you to work here with me."

"Papi, I have to go back to work." I stood. "Do you know where I can find José?"

"My guess is he's drinking beer over there where Rudy and Paco and those guys live, unless he found work."

"Doesn't he work at the Motor Inn?"

"Yeah, but he looks for extra work on his days off."

I moved steadily towards the Explorer, but I didn't get away.

My father cleared his throat. "People say you've been flying around with a tall, good-looking Mexican man. Some say he's been staying the nights with you, but I'm sure if that was the case, you'd have told me about him by now."

"I was going to tell you, Papi."

"When? Before or after the children come?"

"Oh, Papi."

"I'm happy for you, Margarita. You know I want you to be happy."

"Yes, Papi, I know."

"But please be careful."

"I will be."

"Who is this man?"

"His name is Diego Romero. He's a special agent with the DEA."

"Is that his airplane?"

"Yes, it's his. He's from a wealthy Mexican family."

"Way to go." His eyes were shining. "Wealthy, you say?"

"Yes, he is. But you know his wealth isn't important to me."

"I know that, but wealth doesn't hurt anything. You look radiant and that's all that matters to me. It's been a long time since you've looked like that."

I hugged him tightly and turned around to leave. He opened the door for me and then stood by the window of the Explorer.

"Thank you for your help with our case, Papi."

"You're welcome, Margarita."

My father is getting old, but his looks haven't left him. "You don't need English, Papi. Just smile at those tourists, and they'll buy whatever you're selling."

He gave me a look of exasperation but was laughing as we pulled away.

I told Barney what I knew and we went to find José,

who was where my father thought he would be. We pulled up to a small group of men drinking beer in the shade of a leaning mesquite. I never know how those guys are going to treat me. Sometimes they act like I'm flesh on parade, uniform or not; at other times they are quiet and respectful and seem to take me seriously.

Since Barney, *"El Grandote,"* was with me, they greeted us with respect and offered cold soda or beer, and invited us to share their lunch, which sizzled on a nearby grill. It smelled wonderful but we passed.

"We're looking for some thieving gringos," I said.

They thought that was hilarious.

"José, my papi says you gave him information this morning about a stolen truck. Would you come back to the office with us to answer a few questions, so we can make a formal report? We'll bring you back here in about thirty minutes."

He hesitated for a second and then said, "Sure. I'll go."

Back at the office we settled ourselves at Barn's desk. José watched us with wide eyes, as if he were in trouble.

"It'll be easier and faster if I record this," Barney said. "Do you mind?"

"No. It's okay, but I don't speak good English."

"No problem. We'll continue to speak Spanish. Please begin by stating your name and address. Then I'll ask you a few questions."

He spoke right to the recorder in a comical way, looking at it as if it would speak back to him.

I told him a short version of what my father related earlier. "Were you present when Sotol was talking about buying a new truck?" I asked.

"Yes, I was there for a while. A bunch of us were drinking beer together and listening to music. We didn't invite him or want him there. He's a narcotraficante and a murderer, and we don't want him hanging around."

"I understand."

"We weren't saying much and hoped he'd go away and take his friends."

"Do you know his friends?"

"No, I don't."

"Does one of them have a scar on his face? He's around forty and has dark hair in a ponytail."

"That one's called Ruben. I never heard a last name.

There was a guy with them they call *"El Gato."* His real name is Socorro Benavidez. He's from Chihuahua now, but he lived in San Carlos a few years back."

"Please tell me what you remember about the truck conversation."

"Sotol wanted us to pay him attention, so we knew he was bragging, and he made the comment he was buying a new truck from a couple of gringos who were going to bring it to the river for him. It never occurred to us they were stealing it."

"Did he say what kind of truck?"

"He said it was a Ford. We didn't pay attention and our party broke up early. He and his friends took away the fun."

"Did you ever see the truck?"

"I went home and never saw it. Truthfully, I didn't care one way or the other about his truck, except for hoping he would leave when he took delivery of it."

"Your father saw it?"

"Yes, he got up during the night and those three guys were driving around in a blue Ford pick-up. They called to him when he was coming back from the outhouse and invited him to go riding with them. He could see them because of the moonlight."

"Did your father go with them, José?"

"No, he didn't care anything about their truck. But he noticed it was still dripping water, so they had just brought it across the river."

"Do you have any idea who the two gringos are?"

"We never heard any names."

Barney gave him his card. "Will you let us know if you hear anything?"

"Sure. I will. Did those guys kill Adolpho?"

"We don't know. You haven't heard anything about that?"

"No, I would've already told you."

We took him back to where we had picked him up. Lunch was being served.

CHAPTER 15

I was in my element: overstuffed chair, boots on desk, focused on my hill. There had to be an explanation for the rash of crime in Terlingua, but no way was I going to figure it out; my head was on Diego and nothing but. I turned on the computer, but only in case he had emailed me.

"Ricos! What are you doing in there?" Barney's voice brought me back from wherever.

"Thinking about the crimes."

"Bullshit! If I had to guess, I'd say you're thinking about Diego Romero."

"Not your concern."

"You're sitting there staring at that hill and you probably haven't had one clean thought you could repeat."

"What's it to you?"

"Come out here and let's put our thoughts together."

I got up and reseated myself in his visitor chair. "Which thoughts?"

"The ones about the crimes—but the others would be more fun. Agent Romero puts the fizz in your soda pop, doesn't he?"

"Oh yeah, he does."

"You look guilty when I mention him."

"Do you think about much besides sex?"

"Not much," he admitted.

"Me either."

"Sometimes I think about food, and now and then about sports or work, but sex overrides the rest of it. Sex I've had, sex I'm going to have, sex I'd like to have, sex I shouldn't have had, sex I'm going to have—oh—I said that already."

I laughed. "What about the crimes?"

"Do you think everything is connected to Sotol?"

"I don't think we can blame him for everything, but on the other hand, it's hard to believe this is all coincidence."

"Yep." Barney leaned back in his chair until it hit the wall. He jumped as if it was a surprise the wall was still there. "Does Mr. Wonderful have any ideas?"

"He doesn't talk to me about his work. He doesn't seem

to be on this case."

"But he was sent for the cocaine."

"Yes, but that's because he was here. I have a feeling he's doing something else but I don't know what."

"So something big is going on."

"I think so."

We had no idea.

Our conversation ended for the time-being because Sheriff Duncan called with news from the crime lab. At every break-in there were the same two sets of prints. This was no surprise and confirmed what we suspected. The bad news was that the prints weren't on file anywhere. That was disappointing.

"You'll have to get them another way," he said, as if that would be a leisurely stroll by the river. He didn't offer any ideas, either. "The fingers belong to Ruben Villanueva," he said, "which we had already assumed."

"It's good to know for sure."

I was submerged in hot sexting with Diego when we got another call from the dispatcher. I wasn't aware of it and didn't hear a thing until Barney started yelling at me that a human head had been found. A head?

"Slow down Barney. Who found a head and where?"

He took a deep breath. "The boys who were cleaning up Craig's campsite behind Becky's found a head buried under all that trash. So we need to bring him in pronto, because it looks like he's finally murdered someone."

"What? You're jumping to conclusions. Just because a head has been found there, why would you think Craig had anything to do with it?"

"Everybody knows he was camped there for weeks. And you refuse to see that he's more and more weird." He slammed around, gathering his things, and he avoided looking at me. "We need to go see about the head. The dispatcher said Mitch would meet us. After that, you better get Craig back over here so we can talk to him."

"I don't understand how anybody could think Craig would kill someone," I said on the way to the scene. "He's a pacifist with a kind heart, and he's gentle."

"He's been to war and he killed people. He's specially trained for it. You go ahead and believe whatever you want, but folks here are afraid of him. All I'm saying is you had better go get him before someone else does."

"What is that supposed to mean?"

"People are upset about this, Ricos."

"How does anyone know about it?"

"The boys were terrified and they told Becky. She's the one who called 911 and has been broadcasting it ever since. No such thing as a secret in Terlingua, Ricos. You know that. Think how much mileage they'll get out of a head."

"Yeah, before long they'll be saying we've already proved it was Craig."

"We will, soon enough."

I stayed quiet. No way had Craig done it.

It's hard to steel yourself against something you've never imagined: a solo head. This one had been buried under garbage and had been dead a week or better, assuming it once owned the feet we pulled from the river. Thinking about it made me want to throw up, but I didn't, not then. I thought Barney was going to, but he didn't either. The rotting head was infinitely more repulsive than the feet.

Mitch handed us surgical masks that didn't help. The stench alone kept most of the onlookers back and another medic assisted with that. Barney strung yellow tape around the area and announced in his booming voice that anyone crossing it would be jailed and prosecuted for interfering in a police investigation.

"I've had it with these nosy locals," he whispered. "I don't want to hear any of their lame suspicions. I already heard mention of the *chupacabra.*" *Chupacabra* means "goat sucker" and is rumored to exist all over North and South America. Some would argue, but it appears to be more of a mythical creature than a real one.

The only comments that bothered me were ones about Craig. We had been there five minutes when I heard someone say, "Margarita will probably screw it up so he can't be prosecuted since she and Craig are tighter than Siamese twins. And isn't there something sick about that since he is so *old?*"

The head had belonged to a male with brown hair and brown eyes that were still open. He was unrecognizable. We only guessed he was male because of the size of the head and stubble on one rotting cheek. The other cheek was no longer there.

After I had taken photos, Mitch closed the eyes. "He doesn't need to see anything here, and we don't want him watching us, either."

A swollen tongue lolled out of the misshaped mouth. Maggots had eaten away a large portion of it, and they crawled through the hair and in and out of every place—wriggling, fat, stinking maggots. That was when I threw up.

"Where is Gil Grissom when you need him?" Barney muttered as he gathered a few of the revolting little creatures for the crime lab. "Go call the sheriff, Ricos. He needs to hear about this from us first."

I gladly stepped away from the scene and called Sheriff Ben.

"You need to take that head straight to the crime lab," he said, "before it becomes any more decomposed than it already is."

"Do you want to see it first?"

"God, no, I don't need to see it." His aversion was comical, considering all the things he had seen in more than forty years in law enforcement.

"Do you care which of us takes it?"

"You should take it, Deputy Ricos. I think you'll enjoy seeing the lab."

You must have me confused with someone else, sir.

"On second thought, put it in the refrigerator and take it in the morning. I don't think there would be anyone there to accept it by the time you could get there tonight, and I know you don't want to spend the night with it in a motel in Midland."

No shit, Sheriff.

I shut my phone and it rang again. When I answered, Sylvia began whispering. "Hey, I have some news that will interest you."

"Are you okay? You're whispering."

"Nosy people are everywhere. I'm on the porch because I don't want anyone to hear what I'm saying. I would've called you earlier but I was the cook today."

"What is it, Sylvia?"

"I thought you ought to know that Morton and William are back."

"Have you seen them?"

"Of course I've seen them or I wouldn't be calling. They came in here, Rita, and they had money. Two things—they never eat here and they never have money. Figure that one out."

"When did they come in?"

"They were waiting this morning when I opened. They told me they'd just pulled into town. Remember the old busted-down pickup they drove?"

"Sure."

"Well, they have a different one now that is better. They're still scroungy, but they have a more prosperous look about them."

"Did they say where they had been or what they'd been doing?"

"You know me, I asked. Morton said they'd been traveling around, working odd jobs, and were arriving from New Mexico."

"That's possible, I guess."

"I have a feeling they have something to do with the theft of the Ford. Morton plus William plus they're back plus no scruples plus they have money equals auto theft."

I laughed. That made a crazy sort of sense. "Barney and I will go talk to them."

"They were talking about cleaning up their place and moving in, so that's probably where they are."

"We'll check it out, Sylvia. Thanks for letting us know."

"Not so fast, Rita. What about the head? Is it true you found one? Did Craig kill someone?"

"Wait a minute, Sylvia. A head has been found, but there's no evidence of wrongdoing on Craig's part. Please stop that rumor. I'm taking the head to the crime lab in the morning, and we'll hope to know something soon."

"Can you at least tell me if the head and the feet go together?"

"We suspect it, but we can't say for sure. The lab will make the determination."

"If Craig didn't do it, then who did?"

"That's what we have to figure out. Jumping to conclusions isn't helpful."

"People say you're hiding Craig in Mexico."

"I took Craig to my dad's house before I knew there was a head. He needed a place to stay. He's been my friend since I was eleven. But if Craig murdered anyone and the evidence proves that, he'll be prosecuted just like anybody else."

"People here don't think so."

"I don't care what they think. Why are they so quick to jump on Craig, and why do they think I would be so prejudiced in his favor?"

"Because you love him and he loves you and you know how people are. They can't stand it that Craig talks to you but won't give them the time of day."

"He doesn't usually know the time of day, unless it's night."

"You know what I mean, Margarita."

"He trusts me because I wormed my way into his heart before he had closed himself off. I've spent a lot of time with him and cared for him. What have any of these gossips ever done for him?"

"Be careful, Rita, we don't want to find your head in a trash heap."

"Or yours," I said and snapped my phone shut.

Barney looked up when I walked up beside him.

"Sylvia says Morton and William are back, and she knew about the head."

"What did the sheriff say?"

I related our conversation.

"So now we have to put a head in our fridge," he said. "How are we supposed to use it after that?"

"I haven't used it since we had the feet in there."
* * *

Morton and William were unloading boxes from their truck and stacking them in front of their small rock house. They were a scruffy duo in their thirties who didn't appear to have the drive even to wash up. It was nearly impossible to think they had gathered the energy to break and enter or steal a truck.

The house lacked upkeep and the yard was littered with trash. It was as much overgrown with weeds as a desert yard could be overgrown.

When we pulled up the men stared blankly, as if they had never seen us before and didn't recognize a Sheriff's Office vehicle.

"Hey guys," said Barney when we got out of the Explorer.

"Hey," they echoed sullenly.

One was tall, one short, and they drove a small tan truck. Craig said the men who robbed Becky had lived here before. If I got Craig to identify them now, nobody would believe it, and it would subject him to the community's prejudice and suspicion.

"When did you get back?" asked Barney.

"Early this morning. We drove all night," answered Morton. He glanced over at William, who rarely spoke. It's harder to get in trouble if you don't open your mouth.

"Where were you coming from?"

"From New Mexico," Morton said. "We been working up there."

"Let's go inside," said Barney. "It drives the nosy people crazy."

"Whatcha want?" asked Morton. "We ain't done nothin' for you to be comin' 'round here talking to us."

"You can invite us in or we can take you to the office for questioning."

"But we ain't done nothin'."

"Then you shouldn't mind speaking to us."

Morton shrugged and opened the door, then stood back so we could enter. The house looked like it had been left in a hurry. Spider webs hung everywhere, and old dishes sat on the table and in the sink, and trash was scattered as if animals had gotten into it. I couldn't see anything related to the thefts, but the refrigerator wasn't even running yet.

"We just got here," Morton said when he saw me looking around. "We didn't have a chance to clean up yet."

"You pulled into town today?"

"That's what I said—"

"What do you say about it, William?"

"It's like Morton says."

We didn't have anything that said different, so we had to go. Barney gave them a stern warning about selling drugs and causing trouble. They swore they would keep their noses clean, but toed the floor and acted guilty. They weren't going to admit to anything. We had to have proof.

That evening I ran, and then went by the store to get something to cook for dinner. I was meeting Diego at the airstrip at eight and we would only have about eleven hours together, so I wanted something easy and quick.

While I waited in line to pay for my selections, Morton and William came in. They had cleaned up, and Morton was wearing the flying dragon shirt that had been driving me crazy. That was where I had seen it—on him a few years ago at a dance.

The two men avoided me, not realizing I already knew they had been lying about the time of their arrival. They had been here a while and now I could prove it.

I should have called Barney and not waited, but I was meeting Diego and had to shower and get ready. We were talking about theft, not murder, and my love life took precedence now that I had one.

CHAPTER 16

I left Diego at his plane on Monday, thinking, *take me with you.*

Suddenly I was at work. I didn't remember getting ready or driving there. I had been thinking about Diego and for some reason, about Zeke. I told Barney about the shirt, hoping he would care because at that moment I didn't.

Barney jumped right on it. "We should go pick them up. That's proof enough for me. Hello, Ricos? Where are you, 'cause you're not here. Are you going to be like this every morning?"

"Do you know that Sheriff Ben spoke with my father?"

"About?"

"I mean Zeke Pacheco, my biological father. He's a Texas Ranger."

"Well." Even Barney seemed stunned. "I guess it's true what they say about the nut not falling far from the tree."

"He's coming to Alpine to work on an old case, and he wants to meet me."

"You don't want to meet him?"

"I do I guess. It's so weird. I feel flustered and nervous. I wonder why he wants to meet me now, after all these years. He never wanted to meet me before."

"You don't know that, Ricos. Maybe he stayed away out of respect for the man who was raising you."

"I'm in love with Diego, Barney, and it scares me half to death."

"Damn, you change subjects faster than anybody I ever knew. Why are you afraid of being in love?"

"It seems like it's too soon to be in so deep. But I don't have any doubts. None. It's like he was made for me. It's scary as hell."

"I know you're not asking for love advice from me, but have you given serious thought to this?"

"This is not a thinking thing."

"Yeah, I hear that." He leaned back until he smacked the wall. "About your father, you should go ahead and meet him and get over it. He's probably an okay guy. About Diego, I can't say. Maybe he's Mr. Right, or maybe he's Mr. Right Now.

Would either thing be bad?"

"No, but everything about it feels right."

"It's good to see you so happy. As for work, let's go talk to those degenerates about the B and Es. You can't sit around here all day with stars in your eyes."

"I bet I could."

"Right. Come on. Just follow my lead and act like you give a shit."

"Barney, I have to take that head to Midland."

"This'll take twenty minutes, tops. I know you want to be part of this, Ricos. That head will still be there. The poor dude is on ice, so to speak."

"Okay, let's get going, then."

"When are you going to talk to Craig?" he asked on the way to Morton and William's place.

"As soon as I have the time."

"This whole community is going to come down on you if you don't treat him like any other suspect."

"Okay, I get it. But what I don't get is why you want to jump on him first thing. Do you really think a quiet man like Craig has suddenly turned into a vicious killer?"

"He's mentally unstable. You need to open your eyes."

"And you need to open your mind," I snapped.

"Truce, okay?"

"Okay."

"To change the subject, that shirt only proves they were here longer than they claim, not that they committed any crimes."

"Do you think they're innocent?" I asked.

"Hell, no, I suspected them all along."

"Let's accuse them and see what happens."

"That's your big plan?"

"Hey—I'm just along for the ride, trying to act like I give a shit, remember?"

"Oh yeah, I guess you're thinking non-stop about Lover Boy."

"Just shut up about it. I'm sorry I said anything."

"Don't start that with me, Ricos. You brought it up, and you still haven't told me anything juicy."

"I'm not going to."

"You almost got into it back at the office."

"Well, you missed your chance by forcing me to work."

We had to pound on the door a long time because the

suspects were still sleeping. Morton came to the door in his jockey shorts, rubbing his eyes and yawning. It was not a sight you want me to describe.

"You and William need to get dressed and come with us," Barney said. "We have some questions for you."

"What the fuck? We ain't done nothin'. How many times I gotta say it?"

"Until I feel satisfied, Morton. Get dressed right now, and we need William, too. Don't make me ask you again."

Barney is intimidating. His size would do it if nothing else, but when he gives a command, only drunk people will argue. Morton scratched his belly, turned around, and yelled at William to get up.

"The goddamned law is here again," we heard him say in a low voice.

Barney grinned at me. That kind of comment will make a deputy's day.

They complained the whole way to our office about disrupting innocent citizens' lives and our callous violation of their rights. Morton called it *police hasslement*. He stopped short of claiming police brutality. William mostly said *yeah, Morton*.

We got them seated and I started the questioning.

"When Barney and I answered a burglary complaint on Terlingua Ranch, we passed a stone house that was abandoned for years. I noticed a blue denim shirt with an embroidered dragon. I recognized it but couldn't place it. Yesterday evening I saw it on you, Morton, and I remembered I had seen you in it at a dance a while back."

"So? That's what this hasslement is about? You have to be kidding. You want my shirt? I'll give it to you."

"The point is that you and William have been living there a while."

"So? We stretched the truth about when we got here; that's all."

"So I think you're guilty of the breaking and entering episodes we've been having."

They shrugged and looked at each other.

"Well?" Barney glared at them.

"We already said it wasn't us."

"We have two sets of the same fingerprints at every scene. Two sets."

"But they're not ours."

Barney slammed open a drawer in his desk and grabbed a fingerprinting kit. He set it on top of the desk. "If you're innocent then let me print you right now."

"Hell no, it wasn't us."

"Let me have your finger, Morton." Barney's look said he would cut it off if he didn't cooperate.

"Hell no; it ain't us."

"If you're innocent you should have no objection to me taking a comparison print. I'll fax it to the crime lab and have the truth in thirty minutes. If you and William didn't do the break-ins, we'll apologize and take you home."

The culprits were backed into a corner. They conferred at length without speaking one word between them and must have come to an agreement.

As usual, Morton was the spokesman. "Okay, look, we did the burglaries 'cause we were hungry, but we were going to pay it back. We have to get on our feet first."

"Did you also steal a new Ford truck?" I asked.

"No, man, I swear we didn't."

"Like you swore you had just rolled into town?"

"I guess we need an attorney," Morton said softly.

"You can call him from the jail in Alpine," said Barney as he rose. "Let's go. You're under arrest for breaking and entering." He proceeded to list the names of the people and places they had robbed, and then recited their rights.

"Why do we have to go to Alpine?" whined William, his first full sentence.

"A deputy is always on duty at the jail. Deputy Ricos and I can't be here 24/7. In Alpine things are different. For one thing, that's where the judge is. And they serve meals. Ricos and I don't feed our prisoners."

That ended his complaining for the time being.

"I can take them on my way to Midland," I volunteered.

"Yeah, I forgot about that. Want me to load the head for you?"

The panicky look that passed between Morton and William was priceless.

* * *

I handed the two bad boys over to the deputy on duty at the county jail, filled in the paperwork, and went to speak with the sheriff. He had been called away, and his secretary didn't know how long he would be gone.

"Will you tell him I'm on my way to the crime lab with

the head?"

"The head?"

"You heard right; I only have a head."

"Yuck. I'm glad I don't have your job."

I was passing the city limit sign when Diego called. He couldn't tell me where he was, only that he couldn't get to Terlingua until tomorrow.

"I'll call you later and sweet talk you," he said. "I gotta go, Mi Preciosa."

"Okay. I would love some of your sweet talk right now."

"Later, Mi Amor, I'm kissing you."

"I'm kissing you back," I said, but he was already gone.

Barney was next to call. "You narrowly escaped an angry call from the sheriff this morning," he said. "He wants me to pick up Craig for questioning."

"Does he realize he's in Mexico? You have no authority there, and Craig is not going to cooperate with you, if you can even find him."

"So you have him hidden or what?"

"What happened to our truce? What do you think of me, Barney? You don't know me at all if you think I would try to protect a murderer."

"I believe you're not thinking clearly on this."

"Really? What do you have that points to Craig?"

"To start with, he lived where the head was found."

"Becky has a business there. People go there to dump trash."

"It's against the law to dump there."

"Did you notice how the law doesn't stop some people?"

"Yeah, I noticed."

"What would be his motive?"

"How can I know that until I know who the victim is?"

"Where would Craig get a saw with a rotating blade? How would he transport a body? He has no vehicle or access to one, and that head was not cut off there. So what did he do with the rest of the body? How would he have gotten the feet to the river?"

"I can't answer those questions yet."

"Are we partners or do you just put up with me because you have to?"

"Ricos—"

"Yes or no."

"Of course we're partners. We—"

"What if a head had been found in a trash dump behind your friend's house? Would you expect me to jump on him without knowing any facts about the case? Wouldn't you expect me to have the tiniest bit of faith in your judgment of him?"

"Stop, Ricos. I get your point."

"You won't find Craig because he's always in the backcountry. He doesn't stay in houses. This is true no matter what country he's in. If you look for him you're only going to scare him. He can be a little paranoid because—because of being a POW. This community hasn't helped by calling him Crazy Craig and teaching their children to be afraid of him. And they sometimes talk about him in front of him, as if he's not there or wouldn't understand. He does understand. He's smart, not crazy. He stays quiet because in his head he's still a marine in enemy territory."

"You have to admit that sounds a little crazy."

"He's eccentric not crazy, and he's not dangerous."

"Okay, I'll tell the sheriff you're going to bring him in."

"Barney, if Craig did this, he'll tell me. I know he will. He's a man of honor. Please let me handle him in my way because nobody gets him but me."

"Everybody is suspicious of him."

"I understand that, but could you stop supporting those suspicions? It makes it look like you don't trust my judgment either, like we're not tight. If that's true then we shouldn't be partners. It would be dangerous. You should talk to the sheriff."

"Ricos, calm down. I already told you I don't want another partner."

"Then please support me in this. I know I'm not wrong."

"Okay, Ricos. I support you all the way."

"Thank you, Barney."

"What is Lover Boy doing today?"

"He couldn't say. He's on some kind of a secret mission."

"So does he work in Terlingua or not?"

"I don't know, Barney. What he does is secret."

"You better hope he isn't married."

"He's not."

"How can you know that for sure?"

"He isn't a liar. I don't think he's the type to cheat."

"I hope you're right. You don't know him very well."

"Yes I do. I know him."

"The sheriff is going to call to congratulate you on your part in solving the robberies. He's impressed the way we did that."

"He should be. We're exemplary deputies."

"Hell, yeah, and we're even good-looking" Barney bragged. "They don't get any better than us."

"And we're so humble."

"Damn straight. When you know you're great you don't have to brag."

"So what you're saying is that *we're* the ones who put the fizz in Dr. Pepper."

I could hear him grinning. "Yeah, that's right. We don't need no stinkin' DEA. Who finds the drugs and the bodies? Who hauls in the criminals? Who kicks ass up and down the county, sideways and backwards?"

"That's us, Batman."

"So we've solved the breaking and entering, but not the truck theft. And now we have the murder of a boy, not to mention Hayfield, and even though neither of them are our cases per se, they're still ours, if you know what I mean. On top of that, we have two feet and a head. That one's totally our case. This shit is multiplying. It didn't use to be like this, Ricos."

"I know. It seems like our raft is sinking."

"It feels like we're trying to hold the wind up with a sail."

* * *

Sheriff Ben called to congratulate me on my part in solving the break-in crimes. That felt good. Then he jumped on me about Craig. That didn't.

"I'm afraid your close relationship to Craig Summers will cloud your good judgment," he said, and I lost it. I told him the things I had told Barney, and with attitude.

He ignored me. "I've already had ten phone calls from people who're afraid of him. "Every one of them mentioned that you would hide and protect him, not that I believe that about you."

"I'm going to do my job. If you don't like the results then fire me. But you should let me do the job first."

"I'm not talking about firing you."

"If I was the sheriff and I had a deputy I didn't trust, I would fire them. You might as well do it now, and I'll bring you back the ice chest with the cold head."

"Deputy Ricos—Margarita—"

"I just had this conversation with Barney. If the two of you don't have any faith in me then why am I here? You should replace me with one of the ten busybodies who called you this morning. I'm sure they would be much more on top of things. They'd be turning in their friends left and right."

"Stop talking for two seconds, please. I have total faith in you. I'm trying to speak with you about the perception of people in the community."

"Fine, I get it. They're often wrong—on a lot of things. There's a faction that think I killed my husband."

"Surely not—"

"Don't confuse them with the fact that a *bull* killed my husband—at a rodeo and in front of a lot of people. I wasn't even there! They think I'm having an affair with Barney because they can't understand that he and Julia are happy or that a man and woman could work together and not have their hands all over each other. They're suspicious of me because I haven't remarried or even dated any of the local men. Maybe I'm a closet lesbian. Maybe I'm a plant from the DEA or the CIA, and I'm not even a woman—or human. Maybe I shimmied down on a moonbeam from some other planet and I'm only here to—"

"Okay Margarita, I get it."

"Sheriff, if I don't bring Craig back in cuffs and beat the crap out of him right in front of them, then I'm a joke. If I did that, I'd be a brutal bitch. Do you see a way to win this? I keep my eyes forward and do my job."

"One of the callers thinks you're Craig's daughter."

"Well I'm not."

"Another thinks that Craig has been sexually abusing you since you were eleven, not that she's ever reported it. Still another says you and Craig are secretly married, so I understand what you're saying."

"I rest my case."

"Carry on, Margarita."

"Thank you, Sheriff Ben. Adios."

On top of everything else, I had a severed head on ice in the back of my vehicle. Who in my community would want my job or even knew what it was?

CHAPTER 17

I had to go by the office of the Texas Rangers to get directions to the crime lab. That was intimidating and made more so by the fact that my birth father was one of them. I didn't ask about him and felt guilty when I gave my name.

At the crime lab I signed in, was issued a mask, gloves, and paper shoes, and was allowed to enter the eerie domain of the medical examiner. There were several covered bodies on shiny stainless steel tables, but he was bent over one.

I introduced myself, and he only glanced up but seemed friendly. "I'm Brent Woodson," he said. "I hope you'll excuse me if I don't shake your hand." His gloved hands were indescribably gory.

I explained why I had come and set the cooler down.

"I'll try to help," Woodson said, "just let me finish up here."

I wasn't going to stop him. I wandered around a little but the entire place was about death and bodies and parts of bodies—and smelled like it. I returned to the doctor's side and stared at the floor with breakfast crawling up my throat.

"This takes some getting used to, I know," he said. He covered the body with a plastic sheet and returned it to a refrigerated unit. "Now then, let's get to the head."

"Could I leave it with you?"

He disposed of the gloves, washed his hands, and pulled on new ones. He set the ice chest on a different stainless steel table and took out the head. "Of course you can leave it, but maybe I can tell you something right away."

He studied it intently. "One thing I know right off is that this neck was severed by the same instrument that severed the feet, so without comparing the DNA we can be fairly sure this is the same victim. Of course to be certain I do have to make the DNA comparison." He walked over to the refrigerated compartments and took out the feet and laid them next to the head. "Look at this," he said.

I didn't see how I could get out of it.

"See these marks? I think they were made by a saw with a moving blade, like a chainsaw. Do you see how the marks are the same on both body parts?"

"Yes, I see that."

"Unless you have someone down there killing and cutting people up, then this head most likely belongs to these feet or vice versa."

"We want to assume that. Nobody wants to think we have a serial killer."

"It takes a special kind of—focus—to cut up a human body this way. Most people couldn't do it. You're looking for a sociopath or someone so consumed with anger that they didn't have the usual aversion to handling a dead body—and being sprayed with bone matter and blood. The crime scene will be obvious."

"Once I find it. I cover a county that is made up of more than six thousand square miles, so it'll be hard to locate a lone crime scene, no matter how bloody it is."

"True, and I suppose these body parts could've been transported from far away."

"Yes, but they probably weren't."

Another man entered the room and both of us looked up. I knew him and didn't. It was Zeke Pacheco. He was older than he'd been in the photos I studied, but there was no doubt about his identity. His hair was still black and his eyes—his black eyes were amazing.

"I'm Zeke Pacheco," he announced.

"Hey Zeke," said the doctor, who appeared to know him.

I was speechless and probably gaping. The doctor looked back and forth between us, and it dawned on him.

"I apologize for interrupting," Zeke said.

I took him in all at once, trying to memorize details: his hair, his face, his eyes, his size, and even his clothes. He studied me the same way I studied him.

He wore tailored brown pants, a white shirt with a bolo tie, a Silver Star badge on his chest, and a tan cowboy hat. His belt was brown leather and a pistol rode high on the side of it. The boots matched the belt.

He walked forward into the room. "They told me you were here, Margarita. Excuse me Doc, but I came to meet my daughter."

The doctor didn't comment because he had already figured it out.

I didn't know the proper etiquette for meeting someone I should've known a long time ago, someone who had given me life without taking credit or responsibility. I approached him offering my hand. He took it and pulled me towards him, and his eyes filled with tears. Then we were hugging.

"I can hardly believe it," he said. "Margarita, Margarita." He used the soft Spanish pronunciation of my name and squashed me against his chest. He smelled nice, my stranger-father.

I didn't know what to say or do. I had imagined a more reserved meeting and no hugging, but he disarmed me with his warmth and his paralyzing eyes and the tender way he spoke to me.

He took my hand after the hug and turned to the doc. "May I take her away for a while?" Then in practically the same breath he asked me, "May I take you away?"

The doctor and I agreed that he could.

So I walked with my father a few blocks to a nice restaurant. He held my hand as if I was six and not twenty-six, but I had no objection. He didn't say much and was wiping away tears with his free hand as we walked.

Then I was sitting across from him at a table for two. I couldn't tell you much about the place, but I took in every detail about him. In the photos I had seen he was cocky, a young man who knew what a looker he was. He had lost that youthful arrogance, which made him more attractive. The years had danced across his face and made it less movie-star-perfect, and yet more interesting. I got it why my mother had fallen for him. She probably didn't have a chance once he smiled at her.

His shirt was expensive, white cotton, western in style but fancy, upscale western, not regular cowboy western. I don't know why I noticed that detail except that I took in all the details.

He spoke with the waitress in a low voice, charming her without trying to. I was so interested in him that I forgot about the head and murders and the truck theft, and even Diego, all of it, except the man in front of me.

He asked the waitress to give us a few minutes.

"I don't even know if you want to eat," he said, "but I wanted to get you out of the lab where we could talk in private."

"I'll have some iced tea."

He ordered tea for both of us and a plate of nachos.

"There is so much I want to say I don't know where to start." He smiled at me and the sincerity of it made me sorry I hadn't known him before.

He took a deep breath. "Perhaps you think you never mattered to me, that you weren't important. It might look like that, Margarita, but it's far from true. I bowed out of your life because Miguel Ricos won your mother and wanted to raise you as his own. I was young and—"

"I don't judge you for what you did," I interrupted.

"But you must."

"Papi more or less explained. Since I grew up with a great man as my father, it's hard for me to imagine it any other way."

"So I did the right thing?"

"Yes, I think you did, but I'm sorry I never knew you."

"Could we start from here and move forward? Now that you're an adult, maybe you can appreciate the fact that you have two fathers who love you." He paused and was watching me. "I have always cared about you."

"I would like to hear about you, anything you're willing to share."

"What do you want to know?"

"Do I have brothers and sisters?"

"No, I'm sorry to say you don't. You look disappointed."

"Well, I thought I would like having a brother or sister or both."

"I was married once for a few years, but it's hard to stay married when you're off chasing criminals all the time and spend more time with them than the person you love. My work was never suited to the married life. I gave up one thing in order to have the other."

"Are you sorry?"

"Sometimes. I can't judge because I chose this path instead of another and have made the best of it. I enjoy my life. If I had taken the other path—who knows?"

The waitress came with the nachos, refilled our tea, smiled at Zeke, and left.

"Please," he said, indicating the mound of food, "have some."

"My mom thinks I inherited my save-the-world, right-all-the-wrongs genes from you."

He laughed. "Could be, but your mom had a few of those genes, too."

"Yes. She wants everyone to be healthy, even if she has to hound them to death."

He laughed. "She got that about me, even though we were young. Looking at you, I see her, but I also see myself. You're a beautiful combination of the two of us."

I put a few nachos dripping with beans, cheese, and jalapeños on my plate. "All my life people have said I look like my papi."

"You do; that's true, but have you noticed how he and I could be brothers?"

"Are you brothers?"

"No, that's not possible."

"Good. I've had enough surprises along those lines."

"Were you upset when you learned about me?"

"No. Maybe I would have a different opinion if I'd had a hard life, but I had a great childhood and never suspected anything. I was more surprised than upset. At first I didn't want to know you or know anything about you because it seemed disloyal to Papi. I changed my mind, though. Knowing you won't take anything away from him."

Zeke took out his wallet and opened it. "When you were first born, and for the next eight years, your mom sent me photos of you." I was stunned to see baby, toddler, and little girl photos of me.

"She wrote letters about you," Zeke continued. "Sometimes she sent me pictures you had drawn. When you go to my house someday, you'll see them."

I was so touched by that surprising detail I nearly burst into tears.

"As time went by she sent less and less. I'm sure that's because she was busy and life moves on. I couldn't write her because I didn't think Miguel would appreciate it. For a while I sent Christmas cards, but then I stopped doing even that regularly. I think it gave your mother the impression I didn't care about you, but if so she was wrong. I cared very much, but I was in a terrible position. I agreed to let Miguel take responsibility for you, so I couldn't go crying to him."

He paused and ate a few bites but then continued. "As so often happens when you truly want something, the universe played its hand and here we are. I know it upset Miguel to have to tell you his long-kept secret. He is your papi, and that will never change. I would like to experience a small part of what that's like—to be a papi to someone. Would you object to that?"

"No. I don't object at all, but you can't be Papi. I could

call you—something else."

"You can call me Zeke for now. Later, when you get to know me, maybe you could call me Dad. It's up to you. I've known about you all along. You're the one who has to get used to it. I've waited all of your life and nearly half of mine for this day."

The sadness and hope—and love—in his voice made me tearful. I thought this stranger who was not a stranger after all would be a blessing to me.

Zeke handed me his handkerchief. "Please don't cry. I didn't mean to make you cry." He took my hand across the table and squeezed it.

"I'm okay. In all my wondering about you, it never occurred to me that you would love me."

"That's the thing I want you to understand. I always have."

For a while we talked about my work and what it was like to grow up in Terlingua. He explained that he was a UCIT officer working on unsolved crimes, which is how he came to know Sheriff Duncan. We talked a long time but it wasn't long enough. You can't catch up twenty-six years in little more than an hour and a half.

When he returned me to the medical examiner's lab, he hugged me a long time at the door. I thought I was going to like having two fathers.

"I'll be in touch soon." He touched my cheek. "Be careful, Margarita. It's becoming more and more dangerous to be in law enforcement on the border."

"It's dangerous everywhere."

"True, but the border is volatile. I guess I don't need to tell you that."

"I've never felt fear there."

"Keep your eyes open, that's all I'm saying. The murders you've had probably won't be the last."

"What makes you say that?"

"Hayfield was aligned with a powerful Mexican cartel. Nobody understands why they eliminated one of their major U.S. contacts, but if I find out anything I'll let you know. In the meantime I want you to watch your back."

"I will, Zeke."

When I went in, the doc said he sent DNA evidence from the head to be evaluated and matched to the feet. Someone else was studying the maggots, but his estimation of time of death was about a week to ten days ago. He pointed out needlessly that when the head died, so did the feet.

"I found something interesting in his throat," he said. "Your victim bit somebody, probably his attacker. He took out a chunk that lodged in his throat about the time he died. I believe it came from a forearm, so somebody has a serious bite wound on their arm. If you can find the wound, we can match it to the teeth. Failing that, the DNA might turn up somebody if it's in the system."

"How long will that take?"

"About two weeks. Find somebody with a wound and we'll compare it."

Easy for him to say.

"One more thing about the head," he added. "This man's life was ended by blunt force trauma to the back of the skull with a hammer or something similar."

* * *

"It's going to rain," Barney said during our phone conversation on my way home. I had already told him what I learned from the medical examiner. "Dark clouds are storming the mountains to the west," he said.

Those were the mountains Diego and I had flown over Friday night. If it rained enough I could take him on a trip through Santa Elena Canyon.

"Ricos, I'm talking to you."

"Sorry, Barney, I was thinking about something."

"Surely you haven't gone straight back to sex."

"Well, I was thinking about rain, and that led to it."

"Sure. Easy to see how that would happen."

"What were you saying?"

"Diego Romero is a threat to the status quo, isn't he?"

"He could be."

"Are you going to run off with him?"

"Maybe. I don't know. He hasn't asked me."

"If he asked you, would you?"

"Yes, probably so. Definitely I would."

"Wow, you gave that a lot of thought."

"I think it was love at first sight."

"I was there," he said. "I think it was too."

"I never believed in that. Now I do. A little over a week ago, I thought I'd never be in love again. Life is so amazing, Barney."

"Yes, it is. It's great to see you so happy."

"Thank you for caring and for cutting me slack when I wasn't functioning after Kevin died."

"Well don't get too worked up about it," he said, flustered.

"I met my birth father today."

"What did you think?"

"He seems great. I'm glad to know him. Barney, he has photos of me in his wallet. He says he's loved me all these years. How amazing is that?"

"It's wonderful."

"All these incredible things are happening to me. I can hardly take it in."

CHAPTER 18

By the time I got to the river, it was twilight plus an extra degree of darkness tacked on by storm clouds. No rain had fallen, but it still threatened. I had changed into flannel-lined jeans and a warm jacket since the wind had begun to blow from the north and was cold. I caught the rowboat, which is quicker and drier than walking. It was the last run of the day.

The word from the hang-arounds at the boat launch was that the evildoers had not returned. The local guys usually know up-to-date goings-on in the pueblo, or that's what they claim. I was about to learn that they didn't always.

I stopped at the little grocery to see if I owed money on Craig's account. I didn't. The owner said he had been in a few hours earlier and paid cash for his purchases. According to him, Craig seemed fine and had made friends. Whoa. He explained with a wink that a couple of widowed ladies were interested in him. They made him food and helped him with things. I couldn't hide a smile at that news.

Thunder crashed as I ran to Papi's house. The wind was gusting and blowing dust and bits of trash past me on the road. In the distance, streaks of lightening sizzled in wide zigzags over the mountains.

Craig wasn't home, which didn't surprise me. He might not return even if it rained, but I intended to wait. Instead of going inside, I looked around in the yard and ended up in back of the house. There was an old stable that had been fenced at one time, but the fencing was dilapidated. It had been a long time since my papi had any kind of animal in Mexico.

I flipped on an outdoor light and was amazed it still worked. I wasn't worried about Craig until I saw the blood. The stable was a crime scene, but it took a moment to figure out what crime had been committed there. At first I thought Craig, but the blood was pooled and dried and too discolored to be recent. It had been there a few days at least.

A gold shirt crumpled near the back of the stall caught my attention. I ran into the house, found a box of gallon-sized plastic bags, and took it outside with me. With a bag on each hand I picked up the shirt. When I unfolded it, I knew I was looking at where Adolpho had been shot. It was a Paisanos basketball t-shirt. I didn't know for sure it was his, but he was on the high school team. He had been missing until his body was found in the river. What didn't make sense was killing him here and transporting his corpse upriver to dump it. Maybe they hadn't intended for it to happen here but had to do it for some reason. They had taken a big risk shooting him with neighbors so close. And how did Craig figure in? Had he witnessed it? Or figured it out? Had they killed him too?

Craig had been seen a few hours earlier, so no. What had he seen though, and was he hiding because of it? Had he been taken away or was he busy enjoying the backcountry? My head began its usual run-through of worst case scenarios. Sinister clouds, jagged lightning, and crashing thunder seemed the perfect backdrop to my dark thoughts.

I stuffed the shirt into a plastic bag and was so intent on my morbid suppositions, that I didn't hear the men approach until it was too late to save myself. I couldn't have saved myself anyway. They were armed and I wasn't. They had the advantage of surprise, weapons, and numbers.

Two men grabbed my arms and pinned them against my back. The makeshift evidence bag dropped to the ground, along with the t-shirt. The impromptu plastic bag exam gloves were yanked off my hands and thrown to the ground. They began blowing towards the desert, not that I was going to lecture these guys about littering. That was probably the least of their crimes.

Sotol and Ruben walked around to face me while the others held me. Ruben's hand was bandaged.

"Here's that nosy bitch that shot your fingers off, Ruben," growled Sotol.

Ruben's mouth was a snarl. "Can I hurt her?"

"Not yet, Ruben. Soon, but not yet."

"Let's take her back to San Carlos," Ruben said with a look that practically made my hair stand on end. He looked into my eyes. "How would you like for me to take two of your fingers?"

Well hell, I thought it went without saying. Anyway, I was silenced by terror.

Sotol was as he had been described: mid-thirties, big droopy mustache that made him appear to be frowning, short, stocky, sunglasses, lots of bling. When it came to gold and diamond jewelry the man was over the top. If he ever ended up in the water, he would sink right to the bottom where he belonged. He had it all when it came to flash: a gaudy diamond earring in one ear, a gold and diamond ring, gold chain bracelets, and not just a few. He also wore big, heavy chains around his neck. One had diamonds inlaid in a medallion so large I don't know how his neck held it up. One chain had a gold saint hanging from it. That was only the beginning of the chains, but I was amazed by the saint. Surely there is no saint for evil villains.

Ruben was taller than Sotol and thinner. His jagged scar added an exclamation to what was already a cruel, brooding look. Now he had two missing fingers to make him look even tougher.

"We will, Ruben. Just try to be patient," Sotol said regarding taking me to San Carlos or taking my fingers or both. "I have to think."

He was so stereotypical it was laughable, except I was a hair from crying with panic, fear, and the painful position of my arms. I couldn't think of a single thing I could do to get myself out of the mess I was in.

"What are you doing here?" Sotol demanded.

"This house belongs to my father. My grandparents lived here."

"Where are they now?"

"They died."

One of the men behind me snickered. "You're going to join them in Hell."

"Shut up, Alfredo."

That was a new name. I wanted to tell him my abuelos were not in Hell, but I didn't think he would appreciate that input.

"Who is the man that stays here?"

"I didn't know there was a man staying here."

In a flash, Sotol stepped up and backhanded me across the face so hard blood gushed from my nose into my mouth and dripped down my chin. My mouth was bleeding too, or I thought so. Blurry, wavy lines replaced my vision and I was sure I would pass out.

"Who is he?" Sotol demanded again.

I didn't want to tell him, but I didn't want him to beat me to death, either. "He's a friend of mine."

"Don't fuck with me again."

"I won't."

"Make sure she doesn't have a cell phone," he commanded.

A rough hand went into the pocket of my jeans, felt around, and pulled out the phone. Then it went into my other pocket and felt around way too long. I wasn't in a position to complain, but I wanted to kick his teeth out.

"We're going to fuck you so much," breathed a man behind me. His hand snaked under the jacket and touched my right breast.

Terror rose so fast I only thought I was scared before. There were four of them. They could do anything.

"I said to shut up," Sotol growled.

His jewelry glinted when lightning blazed behind us. I hoped he would be struck dead on the spot, but the storm was moving away, not coming closer.

"Why are you here?" Sotol asked.

"I came to see my friend, but he's not here. I was waiting for him."

He stepped towards me and lifted his gold-weighted hand in a threat. "The truth this time."

"That is the truth. I was checking on my friend."

"We killed the little crybaby boy," said Ruben to a question I hadn't needed to ask. "He cried for his mama."

Damn. I wanted to kill him.

Sotol turned his wrath on Ruben. "Shut up!" he screamed. "How many times do I have to say it? I have to figure out what to do about this woman."

"We have an opportunity here," said Ruben, evidently unafraid of his partner. "We could get money for her. We could get a lot from Emilio, or we could kill her after we have some fun with her."

Who in the hell was Emilio? That gave me hope. Maybe they would ask for money from whoever he was. If they didn't kill me right away, I would figure out a way to free myself. Barney would come for me. My papi would tear up the entire country looking for me. Diego would rescue me. Goons and gangsters didn't faze him. They wouldn't faze Papi either, not if bad men had his daughter.

"Tie her up," said the gold-spangled boss of the goons.

They did that but before they did, they hit me hard with something. As I went down I thought I saw my father's old horse, Gringo, standing in the corral, and I tried calling to him for help.

* * *

When I came to it was dark, and the pounding in my head was so painful I couldn't think. I wiggled my hands, but they were tied behind my back, making my shoulders ache. My face stung and throbbed, and the lingering taste of blood made me gag. I needed to scream. My mouth was parched and stuffed full of something so I couldn't. I needed to pee. I needed to figure out where I was. What I needed most was to get away from where I was.

I could tell it hadn't rained because the air was as dry as my mouth and dusty. It made me want to sneeze. Maybe it hadn't rained because I was in a different part of the country. I didn't know how much time had passed or what had been done to me.

It didn't help when the first clear thought I had was that Emilio was a traficante in humans. Maybe he was going to buy me to sell me to some twisted pervert. *Shut up! Don't think like that.* The last thing I needed was to throw up. The ball of whatever was blocking my mouth would cause a miserable choking death.

I tried to determine where I was but didn't have a clue at first. I couldn't know if it was dark out or only dark where I was. How long had I been there?

When I settled my nightmare thoughts, I realized I could hear the faint evening sounds of the pueblo: men laughing and gossiping together, mothers calling their children inside, a donkey braying, trucks moving up and down. I wasn't far from the road but I wasn't next to it, either. I had to be in an unoccupied house or shed or a room. Or any damn place.

There was a dominant smell of vanilla, dust, and herbs, or something spicy. After a little time passed, I realized it must be the old adobe church. It was used so irregularly that it looked abandoned. Rarely would a priest come to remote Paso Lajitas, and the windows were kept boarded most of the time. What I smelled was the fragrance of candles and the lingering aroma of incense from past services. It seemed ironic that men without souls were holding me in a church.

"Are you seeing this?" I thought towards Christ, who was hanging from a cross somewhere close. His predicament was worse than mine. A statue of Mary would be there too, as the beloved Virgin de Guadalupe—maybe two or three of them and several paintings besides. Mementos, dried flowers, and small photos of loved ones would be sitting at their feet. Touching, but none of that helped me.

We're going to fuck you so much.

Can I hurt her now?

Emilio will pay a lot for her.

How would you like it if I took two of your fingers?

I had to get myself out of there before they returned. It was cold on the floor and desperately lonely, and the bonds were so tight I had no hope of getting out of them without a savior. One was hanging on the wall—but he was in no position to help me. I needed to cry, but I was so terrified of choking to death I couldn't risk a tear.

Was it too early for people to look for me? I thought it was, and if my captors had a brain between them they would move me before anyone could. I struggled against the ropes that bound my hands and feet, but all I got for my trouble was exhausted. And more pain.

Before long I heard the crunching of footsteps near the church. Terror returned its cold hand to my heart. It was hard to breathe, impossible to think. Two men were speaking, too low to understand. Then they sat against the wall of the church and I could hear their banter. That didn't help my terror level.

"I still think we should fuck her," one of them said.

"Sotol said to leave her alone until he gets back."

"He just wants to go first—before he gives her back to Emilio."

"You mean before he sells her back to him."

Who was Emilio? What did they mean *give her back, sell her back*? I thought I had misunderstood. Their voices were muffled, and my heart was jack hammering in my ears, so maybe I had it wrong.

"Go get those beers from the truck."

"We should fuck her first and drink beer after."

No, no, no you should drink beer first, a lot of beer.

"Stop thinking about fucking her, hombre."

Please stop thinking about it.

"I can't. She's a sweet piece, don't you think?"

"Sure, but you know what Sotol said. Now go get the beer."

"Shit, hombre, the truck is parked way back there."

"Go on, and bring some water to throw on her face. I

want her awake when I do her, so she can enjoy it."

"Shut up. You said we weren't going to."

"Hell if I'm not. That asshole Sotol can't tell me what to do."

"Don't do anything with her until I come back."

"Why, you want to watch or what?"

"I want my turn."

There was the sound of footsteps walking away. I heard movement against the side of the building. Suddenly there was a struggle, not far. Gravel pinged against the side of the church. There were ughs and ahs, breathless grunts, and then silence.

A few minutes passed, maybe ten or not that long. I heard the scuffling sounds again but no grunts, just one ugh that sounded like a dying breath and then nothing but heavy breathing and crunching, someone walking. I pictured Barney killing thugs with his gigantic hands, but I didn't think it could be that; not yet. If Barney didn't know I was missing, then my papi wouldn't know either, or Diego, or anyone else.

It's impossible to accurately gauge the passage of time when you're alone in pitch black darkness, lying tied up on a cold, hard floor, throbbing with pain everywhere, scared shitless, and waiting for merciless traficantes to do what they want. I guessed that about five minutes had passed when the heavy wooden door creaked open and someone shined a flashlight on me for a split-second. Then it clicked off. Heavy boots trudged towards me. If my mouth hadn't been stuffed full I would've screamed loud enough to be heard in South American countries. Again the light flashed on me a few seconds, then nothing.

The next thing I heard was close and whispered. "Little Boss, I'm here."

I began to cry. I have never felt such relief. My ex-Marine hero had come to save me. His trembling hands reached around my head and untied the cloth stuffed in my mouth.

"Craig!" I sobbed.

"Shh, Margarita, I only killed two of them," he whispered. "I don't know where the others are, but they'll be back."

"How did you find me?"

He cut the rope binding my wrists, and then whatever was holding my feet. "I'll explain later. Don't talk now."

Within seconds I was free. Craig pulled me to my unsteady feet. I don't know which one of us was shaking more, but we held each other a moment in the darkness of the old adobe church. I said a silent but heartfelt thank you to whoever was listening in case someone was. Then I sob-whispered it to Craig as I hugged him tightly, clinging to him.

"Come on," he said, embarrassed by my emotional outburst. "I'll go first. Stay close behind me."

He didn't need to worry about that. If I stayed any closer, he'd be wearing me.

We crept out of the church. He listened a while before he indicated that we would move on, guiding me through the shadows almost to the road.

"Wait here while I look."

"Stay over there while I pee," I said.

Afterward I collapsed against the building, an empty adobe that was melting back into the desert. After less than a minute, Craig motioned for me to come on. We ran across the road into the shadow of an old barn and from there onto my father's field. Halfway across it was an ancient, tilting mesquite. He leaned against the rough trunk to catch his breath. I cradled my pounding head in my hands.

"I'm getting too old for this, Little Boss," Craig said when he got his breath. He dug around in his pocket and pulled out my cell phone and handed it to me. "I think it's yours. I took it out of a dead man's pocket."

That wouldn't stop me from using it. Besides, it was mine. I thanked him and called Barney. He was at home and hadn't realized I had never returned. He said he would pick us up, and I explained where we'd be waiting. If Craig hadn't come for me, I might not have been rescued. Nobody had missed me except Diego. He had called a half dozen times, but had no reason to think I needed help; nor could he have known where I was.

Wading across the Rio Grande in the dark is eerie even on the best nights, and we got our feet and legs wet. Once we were on the American side, we sat shivering in a thicket of mesquite, tamarisk, and weeds. It didn't occur to me that my Mustang was less than two hundred yards away.

I returned Diego's calls. "I'm waiting for you at the plane," he said. "I was about to start walking to your house. It turns out I'm free after all."

"Oh, that's great. I ran into some trouble. I'll explain

139

later."

"Are you all right?"

"I am now. We'll pick you up in about thirty minutes."

"We?"

"Barney and my friend Craig will be with me. I'll explain when I see you."

"I can't go with you," Craig said when I hung up. "I left the house open."

"Forget the house."

"But your father—"

"When my father hears you saved my life he'll give you the house. You have to come with me Craig, or they'll kill you."

"But I have a kitten."

"We'll get it later, I promise."

"But he won't know that. He was starving when I found him, Margarita. I'll run get him and be right back."

I tried, but there was no talking him out of it. His argument was that he was a Marine. He had completed harder missions; nobody would see him. He would be in and out of enemy territory and back before I had time to worry. I was too weak to physically stop him or even put up a good argument, so he left.

He was back before Barney arrived, which was fast moving for an old guy. For the first time, I noticed he was dressed in desert-colored clothes, including a tan cap and boots. Blood spotted his shirt, but otherwise it was clean and looked like it had been ironed. It was hard to imagine Craig ironing. Other than fresh mud and a few smudges, he was clean. He looked more like the man I had first known, and not so much like the wild-eyed, starving homeless man I had moved to my father's house.

The kitten's name was Marine. He was skinny and his gray fur stuck straight out from his emaciated little body, but his eyes were blue and bright and he purred with enthusiasm from his snug seat inside Craig's jacket. Craig let me hold him for five seconds, then took him back and returned him to his cradle.

When the kitten poked its head out, Craig saw me watching it. "He looks like a few prisoners of war I've known. I couldn't leave him behind. That would be wrong."

It was so like him to go back for an animal that I wasn't even surprised. It caused me to wonder how many lives he had saved during the war. I knew better than to ask or even mention it. I also knew and was even surer, that he had nothing to do with the head and feet we had found.

"Tell me how you knew where I was," I said.

"I saw them take you, Little Boss."

"How? Where were you?"

"I was hiding on the hill behind the stable."

"But there's no place to hide." It was a clay hill and the tallest thing growing on it was prickly pear cactus maybe three feet high at most.

"There's a place to hide if you can be still," he said. "And you know I can. Also, I dressed for camouflage in the desert."

"You're amazing."

"Nah, I'm not. I'm just an old marine who loves you."

"You saved my life, Old Marine. How can I ever thank you for that?"

"You don't have to thank me for anything. How many times have you saved mine? Stop thanking me. This makes us even."

"No it doesn't, but I'm not going to argue with you. Tell me what happened."

"I saw them, but there were four of them and one of me, and they had rifles and pistols, and all I had was my knife. So I followed when they took you and I waited. Two of them left to talk to someone named Emilio, so that improved the odds. I kept waiting. One of the men went to get beer, so I crept up on the lone sentry and slit his throat. Then I waited for the other one to come back and killed him, too. They were going to rape you before the boss came back. I couldn't let that happen on my watch. They won't be raping or hurting you now, will they? They were planning to kill you after using you or else sell you."

That was more talking at one time than I had ever heard out of him.

"Do you know who Emilio is?"

"No, but I heard them talk about him before on some of my reconnaissance missions. I thought he was their boss, but I guess that's wrong."

Marine poked his head out of the jacket and mewed once. Craig stroked his head as he spoke. "I saw them kill that youngster, Margarita. I wanted to stop them, but I needed more troops. I was going to come tell you afterward, but they started looking for me, and I had to hide."

"I understand. I'm just glad they didn't find you."

"Me, too."

My community claimed my old friend was crazy and dangerous but he was exactly the hero I always suspected he was. He had the love, patience, and presence of mind to save my life right under the noses of the traficantes.

I needed to cry. I hurt all over and my head was still pounding. And there was residual terror from facing rape, torture, murder, or all three. I laid my head against the chest of my hero and let the tears come. His new kitty Marine was like a tiny, warm buzz saw in my ear.

Craig put his arms around me. "You're safe now, Little Boss," he said softly. "I will keep you safe. I will always keep you safe."

Our ragtag regiment stayed huddled together until Barney came.

CHAPTER 19

Diego was practically biting himself as he listened to what I had been through. I thought he would have a heart attack if he didn't slow down and take a breath. He wanted to fly me to the hospital, take me to his home in Austin, find and kill the culprits, and he wanted to do it all right now. He paced and gestured like a wild man, ranting in a jumbled mishmash of Spanish and English while Barney, Craig, Marine, and I watched him.

Craig gave Diego a fierce Marine-commando glare. "Look here, young man," he broke in when Diego took a breath, "Margarita's head is still oozing blood. They split it open with a rifle, and before that she took a hard punch to the face. Then she was lying in the cold in terror. I think you should take her to the hospital and then go kill people. When you tell me they say she's all right, I'll help you."

Diego turned to him as if he had never seen him before. "Who are you again?" It was rude and uncalled for, stress talking I thought.

I intervened. "This is Craig Summers, an old friend. He saved my *life*, Diego." *Be nice to him for cryin' out loud* was the underlying message.

I needed to lie down and try to forget what had happened so I could quit shaking and wanting to cry.

"I'm calling the ambulance," Barney announced in a loud, bossy tone.

"Let's get in the plane, Margarita." Diego took me by the arm. "I'll take you to the hospital right now."

"Hold on there, Sky King. First, a medic is going to look at her. They're on the way now. If he says it's okay, then you can take her."

"You can kiss my ass," Diego growled through clenched teeth. He kept moving me steadily towards the Skycatcher.

I was hurting and bleeding and had practically had the life scared out of me. I needed to lie down, and the men were having a pissing contest.

The world began spinning. "I need to sit," I said.

The Explorer was the closest seat, but as I got in I

passed out. Diego caught me before I hit the dirt. I felt his arms go around me, then nothing.

When I woke up I was lying sandwiched between stacks of blankets. Three men and one little kitty stared down at me with somber expressions. An ambulance siren wailed in the distance.

"What's going on?"

"You passed out," Barney said.

Diego knelt beside me and took my hand. "How do you feel, Mi Amor?"

"Not so great."

Mitch arrived with Galveston, and one more man entered the contest. Galveston stayed in the background, but Mitch took over, which nobody seemed to appreciate but me. Then he adamantly insisted on transporting me himself.

Diego argued, saying that the plane would be faster.

"Yeah, well," Mitch said, "the ambulance will be safer. I'm going to start an IV and put her on oxygen as a safety precaution."

"I don't see why you can't ride along with us in the Skycatcher and do those things on the way," Diego said.

"Your plane is not an approved medical transport vehicle, is it? I know it's not, so that won't work. You can ride in the back of the ambulance with us if Margarita wants you to, or you can take your plane and meet us up there; it's your call."

He and Galveston were loading me onto a stretcher.

"Barney, would you take Craig to my house?" I asked.

"Sure."

"Craig, there's food in the fridge and cabinets, and you know where I keep the coffee. Make yourself at home."

"I can't stay at your house."

"Yes you can, and you're going to. Please don't make me argue. My head is killing me. When I get back we'll find you a new place to live."

"Those men were using your father's house before I moved in. They weren't staying there, but they came and went from it and sometimes left things. They'll take over again if I'm not present."

"I doubt that," said Diego. "What they've done is incredibly stupid and they'll go back to Monterrey now—or to somewhere else. If they were smart they'd go to another country and hide, but they're not smart."

"What do you know about this that you aren't telling us?" Barney asked in a voice heavy with accusation.

"I've run into these thugs before. They work for the Martez cartel out of Monterrey. Are you familiar with them?"

Mitch interrupted. "We're leaving. If you want to ride along, get in."

"I don't know anything about a Martez cartel," said Barney. "We don't deal with drug cartels. This is Terlingua for Christ's sake. Small amounts of drugs pass through but—wait a minute—you're DEA. You should know this already. I want you to tell me what's going on."

"You've had them here. You didn't know it before because they didn't call attention to themselves."

"That's not right," insisted Barney. "We would know about that much cocaine. This is Terlingua."

I didn't think *this is Terlingua* meant anything to Diego. Barney meant that what happens in our community comes to light, usually sooner rather than later. Nothing is secret for long, and everything is everybody's business. I didn't feel like explaining it and shut my eyes.

"We're out of here," Mitch proclaimed as they lifted the stretcher into the back of the ambulance.

Diego rushed up to the doors. "I'll be right behind you." He jumped inside and kissed me before anyone could stop him. "I'll meet you there, okay Preciosa?"

"Okay."

When Diego jumped down, Galveston slammed the doors shut.

"I'm going to start an IV now, Margarita," Mitch said. While doing that he asked, "Who is that man?"

"He's Diego Romero with the DEA. I'm sorry I didn't introduce you."

"He kissed you."

"Yes, he did."

"He called you Preciosa."

"That's true."

Mitch had been Kevin's best friend and rodeo buddy. In fact Mitch had been with him the day he died. Kevin was a champion bull rider and Mitch a skilled roper, but they shared a love of rodeo and had served on each others' teams when possible.

"So you're dating him."

"Yes, Mitch. I have to move on. Does it bother you?"

"It seems weird to see you with another man."

"I know. I'll tell you about Diego, but not right now."

"It's all right. It's not my business anyway."

"I want to tell you—it isn't that—but I feel like I'm going to throw up."

"I think you have a concussion. Did those men inject you with anything?"

"No, I don't think so."

"Then it's probably a concussion." He patted my shoulder. "I want you to try to rest."

"Then quit talking to me."

"Rest, but don't go to sleep yet."

"I want to sleep."

"I need to make sure you're okay. Tell me about this Diego Romero. Is he a rodeo man?"

"Oh God, I hope not. No offense, Mitch."

"He doesn't seem like a cowboy."

"I don't think he is."

"Is that his plane or the government's?"

"It's his."

"I was hoping you'd go out with me when you felt ready to date."

"You never once indicated anything like that, Mitch."

"I know, but I was going to."

"How is a woman supposed to know what a man is planning to do possibly, maybe, sometime in the future?"

"I don't have an airplane, though," he said sadly.

What is wrong with men?

* * *

It took eight stitches to close the back of my head. The doctor wanted to keep me overnight for observation, and I didn't argue because it meant I could sleep. Diego did not come, but called me later to say he would take me to his villa on the Pacific coast of Mexico south of Mazatlán as soon as I was released.

"What are you doing, Diego?" I asked, even though I felt sure I knew.

"I have critical business."

"Please don't go looking for those men."

"They've gone too far this time."

"Where are you? Are you in Mexico?"

"You rest, and I'll be there soon."

"Answer my question."

"Okay, yes. I'm in Mexico. I'll be back tomorrow."

"What if they kill you?"

"How about having a little faith in me?"

"Please don't do something stupid."

"I didn't come this far as a stupid man."

"I know that, but please be careful. I don't want to lose you. I just found you."

"I found *you* Margarita, and I don't intend to ever let you go."

That ended the argument.

Fifteen minutes later, José Velasco called me speaking Spanish so fast it was a wonder I recognized the language. I made him slow down. "Did you kill those two men at the church?" he wanted to know.

"No. Why?"

"Sotol and Ruben are looking for you. They're going through all the buildings and houses searching for you and that man living in your house. What is going on?"

"Did they hurt anyone?"

"No, just pushed people around and scared our wives and kids."

"I'm sorry, José. I was over there checking on Craig and those guys grabbed me and tied me up and put me in the church. Craig saved my life."

"So he killed them?"

"Yes."

"Another man came and they took off running like Satan was after them."

That was probably Diego. *Hell.*

"Are you all right?"

"Yes, I'm fine. Was anyone else hurt?"

"No. There was shooting, but nobody's dead far as I know. Where are you?"

"I'm where they can't find me."

"What about the old man?"

"He's not there, either."

"I think they figured that out. Anyway, the man that came ran them off."

"Have they been driving the new Ford?"

"Yes, of course. Sotol loves to show it off. What are you going to do, Margarita?"

"I don't know." *My head is killing me.*

"Who is that man?"

"He's with the Drug Enforcement Agency."

"He can't work in Mexico, can he?"

"No, but that doesn't stop him."

"What did you do to those guys to make them tie you up?"

"I interfered in their business."

"Shit, Margarita, everybody knows not to do that. That's a sure way to get killed. These guys aren't in it for fun."

"Neither am I, José. When they bring drugs into my country it's my job to stop them. And they killed a teenager. I can't turn my head the other way."

"The teenager was helping them move the drugs. He was part of it."

"I know that, José, but he didn't deserve to die. He was just a kid."

"You better be careful."

"I will."

"Vaya con Dios, mi amiga."

After that exchange, I called Barney, even though it was late, to ask him to check on Craig. He was grumpy because I woke him out of a dead sleep, but I was grumpier because of pain and exhaustion. I won.

* * *

The following day I was released. I wanted to go to Diego's villa—would've gone anywhere with him—but a local teen had been murdered, a man's head and feet were in Midland, an incredible amount of drugs were coming through Terlingua, a new truck had been stolen, we had two men in jail for breaking and entering, and I had to be there to speak to the judge. And who knew what else would happen. Diego seemed to understand and took me home without much argument.

Craig had made a camp in back of my house. We invited him to come in and talk to us while I rested. The weather had turned cold and somber so the men made a roaring fire in the fireplace. I lay on the sofa with Marine cuddled next to me buzzing at high volume. We were the picture of contentment, except that one of us had a painful head, a messed-up face, and ugly things on her mind.

Craig told us the whole story, from first seeing the men in the village to rescuing me from the church. He vowed to help Diego in any way he could. I asked him about the stolen truck. He had seen it but hadn't seen the gringos who brought it to the river. Nor had he heard any useful names.

I asked about Adolpho's murder, which sucked the coziness from the room.

"They brought him to your dad's house and left him at the stable. I think they were going to take him to the river to kill him. He was tied up and blindfolded. I was trying to get to him, but they came back too soon and I didn't have the chance. I'm so sorry about that. He was just a boy."

"That isn't your fault, Craig."

"I know, but it makes me sad."

"It makes me sad, too."

"One of the men removed the gag from his mouth and they exchanged a few words. Whatever the boy said infuriated Sotol, and he pulled out a pistol and shot him. When it got dark, they put his body in the back of a pick-up and left with it." Craig paused and looked from me to Diego. "If I don't do anything else in this life, I'd like to kill the man who murdered that boy."

"You can leave him and Ruben to me," Diego said.

"But you work for the government, man. I know you're not as free to do what you want as I am. The government mostly forgot about me. I don't punch a clock or take orders from anyone."

"I think you should avoid Mexico for a while, Craig," I said.

"I'm not afraid of those assholes. They don't operate with a plan, or it seems that way. They preen and strut and drink too much beer. They bicker and can't seem to agree on anything. They need a sergeant. They kill as if they don't have to answer to anyone. I never saw anything like it. Who are they?"

Craig and I looked at Diego for the answer.

"They work for the Martez family, or did," he said. "They seem to be renegades now. I don't think they're taking orders from anyone."

"Do you know a man named Emilio?" I asked.

"Why?"

"They talked about selling me to him."

"They're probably talking about Emilio Martez. He's one of five sons of Emanuel Martez, head of the Martez family."

"Are they human traffickers?"

"No, just drugs, as far as I know."

"Then why would those guys think they could sell me to

him?"

"Maybe because you're so irresistible," he said and pulled me close. "Those men had never seen such a beautiful woman."

"Oh, Diego, you're crazy."

"Maybe they thought he'd have some use for you, since he's young and horny. I can think of a few things myself. Oh. Sorry Craig."

"Don't mind me. I'm going to take Marine and go back to my camp so you two can be alone."

"But it's cold out," I protested.

"You forget you're talking to a Marine, Margarita."

"So Marines don't feel the cold?"

"We feel it. We don't whine about it."

"Craig—"

"It isn't half cold yet, and I have warm clothes. I'm accustomed to living outdoors, and don't forget, I have my cat now. He's like a little heater."

"Okay but if you get cold, tap on the bedroom window. We'll let you in."

Craig had his hand on the door when he turned and addressed Diego. "You seem all right to this old Marine, but I want to tell you something, young man. You'd better treat her right. I hope you know what a blessing you have here."

"Yes sir. I know." Diego looked so dead serious I almost laughed.

"She's the most special woman you'll ever have the honor to know."

"Yes sir. I agree."

"All right, then. Good afternoon." He saluted us, and we returned the salute.

* * *

Diego asked me to marry him. My head said it was too soon, I hadn't known him long; I was too busy driving crime from Brewster County, on and on. While my head spun my heart caused my lips to say yes, I would marry him.

"Tomorrow I'm going to buy you a diamond ring," he said. "Do you like big ones or little ones or lots of them grouped together?"

"I don't care. I don't care anything about diamonds, Diego. I know I'll like anything you give me, but a diamond ring isn't necessary."

"I want you to have one, while I still have money to buy

one."

"What do you mean?"

"In order to marry you—and for us to be happy—for us to be free—I may have to give up my family's money."

"You don't think they would approve of me?"

"It isn't that. I think they'd love you if they knew you, but my family situation is complicated."

"All families are complicated. I recently discovered that my papi is not my papi by blood. I have another father that I just met."

"Does that upset you?"

"Not much. It would be different if Papi didn't love me, but he does, and I love him, but it's still weird that I'm not his. For twenty-five years I assumed he was my birth father and he's not."

"I could tell you worse things about my family. See, my father calls all the shots and he can be difficult. He's old school Mexican and patriarchal 'til it makes you want to shoot yourself. He thinks his word is law."

"Sounds a little like my own papi."

"No, Margarita, I assure you, they aren't even similar."

"But you haven't met Papi yet. By the way, you'll have to meet my parents before long."

"I'd be delighted to meet them. I just don't think you'll want to meet mine."

"Of course I do."

"I'm not allowed to call my father 'papi'. I have to say 'Padre.' It's formal and stupid. All my life I wanted him to love me. I wanted him to take me on his lap and read to me, or tell me stories and put me to bed, and say that he was proud of me. Just once I wanted to make him proud."

"Maybe he's a man who can't show his love. He was probably raised the way he raised you. I'm sure he loves you, Diego. How could he not?"

"You say that because you love me, but I'll never be the man my father wants me to be."

"I'm sorry, but I can't see how you could be failing him."

"What I want to know is if I was poor and had to sell the Skycatcher, would you still love me?"

"I can't believe you're asking me that question."

"I want to hear you say it."

"I'm not in love with your money. I don't want a diamond, and I don't care about your airplane. All I care about is you. I have an income, and so do you."

"Yes, but I'm talking about more money than you can imagine."

"I'm in love with you, Diego, and it has nothing at all to do with your money. I loved you the first time I saw you, and I didn't know anything about your money. It was your idea to fly to Chihuahua and spend a fortune, not mine."

"I wanted to give you the best, and I still do."

"But you do that when you give me you. Why can't you understand that?"

"In my father's world, everything is judged by money and power. The more the better—and power is his favorite. Money is power. More money is more power. I used to think that, and then I met you. You've changed how I see the world."

"If money and power aren't what you want, then maybe you should tell him you love him, but you don't want to live his way anymore. Do whatever you need to do, and I'll support you. I promise you that."

"Okay, I'm going to talk to him."

"Maybe he'll be proud of you for living your own life."

"He's more likely to kill me."

"You're his son."

"He has four others."

"Diego, that's not how it works with parents."

"You don't know my father. My older brothers are more pleasing to him. They're more like him and he dotes on them. I, on the other hand, displease him."

"He doesn't want you to work for the DEA?"

"He thinks I'm soft and dimwitted. Let's don't talk about him."

"You're not making me want to know him."

"Good because truthfully, I don't want him to meet you. It'd be putting something beautiful, innocent, and real next to something sinister and twisted. Next to you, he will look even worse than he is."

"Okay. Well then, I'll leave him off the guest list."

He laughed. "Do you want to have a big wedding?"

"No, I was kidding about a guest list. I'd be happy to be married by a justice of the peace or a minister, but in a private ceremony. I guess my parents would prefer the minister, but they'll understand whatever we do as long as they meet you first. My papi asked if he could meet you before we have children."

"I think I'm going to like your papi."

CHAPTER 20

The next day I drove to Alpine to appear before the judge in the case of Morton and William, the B & E Kings of South Brewster County. Judge Samuels was going to set bail, and I wanted to be sure he set it high enough to keep them in the county jail until their court date. I was pulling up to the courthouse when my cell phone rang.

"Margarita?" a male voice asked in the Spanish pronunciation of my name.

"Diego?"

"No, José Velasco." He began speaking so rapidly it was hard to follow.

"José, calm down or I can't understand you."

"Those men are offering a fifty thousand peso reward for you, dead or alive. And it's the same offer for your friend Craig, too."

I felt chilled. "How do you know this?"

"Some guy—we don't know who he is—he came and put up notices with your photograph and your friend's. Where are you? Are you safe?"

"Yes José. Thank you for calling me. What did the man look like?"

"He's like those others, surly and full of himself. He has a pock-marked face, and he's short but beefed up like a knee-breaking goon. He smokes big, stinking cigars, and his teeth and fingers are stained with them. He was carrying an automatic rifle and didn't care who saw. In fact, he wanted us to see it. You don't want that man to get hold of you, Margarita."

No shit.

"Have Sotol and Ruben been back?" I asked.

"No, but who do you think sent the goon?"

"Is he still there?"

"I don't know. It's hard to know from one minute to the next what any of those men are doing. We need that big man with the pistol to come back and chase these bad people away. He had those men running for their lives."

Oh, crap.

"Send him if you can, but don't come back and don't let Craig come back."

"Okay José; we won't be back anytime soon. Could you take one of those fliers to Deputy George at my office in Terlingua?"

"Sure. I'll do that when I go to work. Watch your back, Margarita."

"I will. Thank you, José."

Paso Lajitas is unprotected when it comes to law enforcement. Technically it's an *ejido,* not a pueblo. An *ejido* is communal land, normally used for homes and agriculture. The land is owned by Mexico and used with permission. This system has been around since the Aztecs ruled Mexico but is now being discontinued.

About twenty families live in Paso Lajitas, and while there is a mayor, he isn't armed, and his duties don't include providing protection or the enforcement of laws. Mexico's citizens aren't allowed to bear arms, so besides the army and various police-type organizations, only criminals have them.

I tried to call Diego, not to ask him to return to Paso, but for advice. I thought he could call Mexican authorities to settle things there. The recording said he wasn't available, and I didn't leave a message because I thought I shouldn't tell him about the bounty through a voicemail. That kind of news needs a conversation.

I called the sheriff and told him about the bounty on my head and Craig's. He was horrified and said he would call Border Patrol and see what they said. I didn't think they would care unless the men came onto U.S. soil. He asked if I could get him a copy of one of the fliers, and I told him José was taking one to Barney.

"Good, he can fax it to me," Sheriff Ben said. "I want to see who's offering a reward. Maybe we could get them that way."

I doubted it.

Then he shocked me with, "Have you seen Diego Romero?"

"I saw him this morning."

"It seems he's missing."

"What do you mean he's missing?" I couldn't keep the panic out of my voice.

"I mean that his office in Austin hasn't seen him in two weeks. He was on an undercover mission in the Terlingua area, and now he's gone."

"But he's not gone, Sheriff. I speak with him many times every day."

"Something is wrong, Margarita."

"Have they called his office in Alpine?"

"No one works there but him, and he hasn't been there in quite a while. The Austin office called me this morning and asked me to check, so I went there myself. Do you know what he's doing or where he is right now?"

"No sir. What he does is secret. I think he might be in Mexico."

"I don't want to alarm you," he said in the kind of voice that alarms a person, "but I don't think the man you know as Diego Romero is Special Agent Diego Romero with the DEA."

"That's impossible, Sheriff, of course he is."

"Maybe he's a different Diego Romero."

"Sheriff, he works for the DEA and has a home in Austin and an apartment in Alpine. He came to pick up the cocaine and he—" *No. Oh no, no, no, no no.*

"Okay, Deputy, but if you hear from him, will you ask him to check in with his Austin office? His wife is terrified that something has happened to him and reported him as a missing person."

His wife?

"Diego isn't married, Sheriff."

Diego is not a liar.

"Diego Romero of the DEA is married, Margarita. He has two children."

No, no. It can't be.

It happens all the time.

But I know his heart. I know I'm not wrong about his heart.

"Margarita, are you all right?"

"Yes. There must be an explanation, Sheriff."

"I'm sure there is. Please have him call in when you hear from him."

"Okay, will do."

"Are you about to see the judge?"

"Yes sir, I'm on my way."

"All right. Good luck. Come by my office when you're finished."

I no longer cared about petty criminals. I opened the door of the Explorer, sure I was going to vomit, but sat there with the door open.

It was not as much what Diego said but the way he said it. He had been forced by his father to marry at age twenty-one to a woman he did not know well. Somehow he had stayed married for five years, even though love was never part of it. Then, in spite of the fierce objections of his father, his wife, her parents, and even the Roman Catholic Church, he had obtained a divorce and moved to Austin to find his own way. At that point he went to work for the DEA.

If any part of what he said was a lie, it was the part about working for the DEA. The rest of it was true; I knew it. He was not married and had never been in love before. It was clear in all that he did and little things he said.

I entered the courthouse but my head was not on my job. I testified about the shirt and the fingerprints. The judge set bail, and I never argued for it to be higher or even heard what Judge Samuels said.

I was thinking that Diego, or the man I knew as Diego, was a member of a drug cartel. *An alliance of powerful families,* he had said of his forced marriage. *Oh, God.*

More money than you could ever imagine, he said of his family's wealth. *We might have to give it up—to be happy—to be free.*

* * *

I flew out of the courthouse and drove to the library. Using their computers, I searched the richest families in Mexico. There was no "Romero" listed. And there, in plain English, it said cartel bosses did not disclose their wealth and therefore could not be counted, meaning they would qualify for the list. But it was a list of billionaires. Maybe Diego's family was millionaire in status. I couldn't find a list of millionaires in Mexico, but I didn't spend a lot of time on that.

I searched "Diego Romero" and got thousands of hits, from a famous potter in New Mexico to high school football heroes, to MySpace and Facebook references. On the fifth page was a news article from the *Austin American Statesman* about a large drug bust by DEA Special Agent Diego Romero, dated one year earlier. He was cited as being forty years old. Nothing was said about his family, nor was he pictured, but he didn't have to be for the truth to sink in. My Diego was thirty.

I had never seen his driver's license or any other form of identification. I didn't have his business card and hadn't asked for one. Why would I? I was trusting, naïve, pathetic. I had looked into those jewel-colored eyes and fallen in. Now I was drowning and doubted that I would, or could, be rescued.

    * * *

When I got to the sheriff's office, my Zeke-father was there. Both men looked at me with tragic faces. Zeke hugged me and invited me to sit.

"I don't want to do this," he said, "but we need to talk about the man you've been dating, Diego Romero."

My heart went into overdrive at the mention of his name. I couldn't even pretend to play it cool. Nor could I speak.

Zeke pulled a folded piece of paper from the pocket of his shirt and slid it across the table to me. "Is this the man you know as Diego Romero?"

The man I know as Diego Romero?

The paper was a faxed copy of a photo of Diego, grinning, his eyes dazzling.

"Yes, that's him," I said, hoping Zeke wouldn't notice the flush overtaking me. Somehow I knew what I was going to hear next would change my life. I wanted to beg him to keep it to himself, never tell me. I would run away with Diego, no matter his name. What's in a name, right?

Zeke took a deep breath. His eyes were so somber the sparkle had left them. "This man is not DEA Special Agent Diego Romero."

"Please," I begged, "I love him."

"I'm so sorry, Margarita. I didn't want to be the one to tell you, but somebody has to tell you because we fear you're in grave danger."

"No."

"Margarita, this man is Emilio Martez. He's a wanted criminal, a drug trafficker, and vicious murderer. He's the youngest son of Emanuel Martez, the head of one of the largest of the Mexican cartels."

"That's not possible. I'm going to marry him."

"I wish it weren't true. I wouldn't break your heart for anything."

"But he's a wonderful man. He's so warm and—" I stopped talking because it sounded so pathetic. How could I have been so wrong about someone? I felt sad, unbelievably sad, and yet no tears came. *I'm not wrong. I couldn't be wrong about something like this.* But at the same time, it occurred to me that this was what the thugs meant when they said they were going to sell me back to Emilio.

Still not wanting it to be real, I said, "There has to be an explanation."

My newfound father watched me with sorrowful eyes. He reached over and took my hand. "Listen, there's something else. You know the burned evidence you sent to our lab?"

"Yes."

"You were right that it's a human bone fragment."

No. Don't say it. Do NOT say it.

"It belonged to Diego Romero—the real Diego Romero."

No. You're wrong. This is a trick. I'm dreaming.

"He was murdered and then burned in that old wreck to hide the fact."

Stop talking!

"Then Emilio Martez assumed his identity for reasons we can only guess at this point. He is similar in looks, though younger, and Diego Romero had brown eyes and Emilio has—those memorable eyes."

My God, what have I done?

"Several DEA agents have gone to Terlingua, and they'd like to meet with you there. Emilio is on the F.B.I.'s Most Wanted List. Everyone in law enforcement has received notification, and we fear for your life. He's a man used to getting what he wants, and he's not going to let you go."

"I don't fear him, Zeke. He loves me."

"Perhaps he does. Maybe he would never hurt you, but he'll be desperate soon if he isn't already. It's impossible to say what a desperate man will do when pushed or threatened."

"He asked me to marry him."

"I'm so sorry."

The sheriff's hands raked through his mass of hair, back and forth. He had heard what Zeke said and watched me with sad eyes.

"I know someone so different. The man I know is not a killer. This doesn't make sense." Jeez, I sounded so lame.

"I think you should head back."

"Diego was using me." *No! He wouldn't.*

This man I didn't know well, but saw a vague resemblance to in the mirror every day of my life, watched me with a look I had seen many times on my papi. It was love and concern.

"Maybe at first he was," he said, "but sitting here with you, watching you and talking to you, I think he fell in love.

He couldn't help himself. The poor man didn't have a chance."

"Thank you for that."

"Listen. He may try to get you to go away with him. Please don't do that unless you think you could live the life of a drug lord's wife. You would have to be blind to the killing and suffering they cause. I think it would wear on you."

"You know it would. I'm your right-all-the-world's-wrongs daughter, remember? I could never be blind to that."

"I know you'll do the right thing even if it breaks your heart."

There was silence and then Zeke rose. "I'll wait out there. The sheriff wants to speak with you."

"I encouraged those men to go on to Terlingua," Sheriff Ben said. "They wanted to wait for you here, but I wanted to speak with you myself."

"Sheriff Ben—"

"I know you thought you were seeing Diego Romero. I spoke with Barney. Please don't be mad at him. I—I told him it was life or death. I had to know what was going on. He told me everything he knew, which was enough for me to understand how difficult this is for you."

"I'm in love with him," I sobbed.

"I know."

"What can they do to me?"

"If you mean government agencies, they can't do anything to you. It's not against the law to be in love with the wrong person. It is against the law to aid and abet a criminal."

"Yes sir. I know that."

"It looks like Emilio murdered the DEA agent in order to assume his identity."

"Yes, I know that's what's assumed."

"Do you know something different?"

"I know the man I love isn't a murderer." That seemed a weak argument, especially coming as it did on the heels of being questioned about Craig. The fact that I had no judgment about Diego made Craig look guilty.

The sheriff heaved a weary sigh. "They're going to try to get you to help them trap him on U.S. soil."

"I won't. You don't expect me to do that do you, Sheriff?"

"No. I can't give you orders like that. I want you to do what your conscience tells you. Don't let those feds strong-arm you. I already tried to forbid them from involving you because of the danger. Of course that didn't work. They want him, dead or alive, and they don't care how they do it or who they hurt."

"I won't help them. I don't care what they do to me."

"There is nothing they can do to you. However, you can't let anything you do be construed as aiding and abetting. You shouldn't even talk to him until they back off some. I don't know what else to tell you. Tell them what you've told me. They'll laugh you off, probably, but still tell them."

"I will."

"They're tricky and do what they feel they have to. It's bad that he's on the Most Wanted list. They'll kill him and ask questions later. You're a professional officer of the law. Go back to Terlingua, hold your head up, and take them to the site of the fire; that's one thing they want. Other than that, all I can say is call if you need me. Barney is standing by. I guess you know he'd face the fires of Hell and all its demons for you."

"Yes sir. I do know that."

"Sergeant Pacheco is standing by, too. He's upset about this, Margarita, from every angle. More than anything, he doesn't want you to get hurt, and neither do I." He took his hands out of his hair. "Did you get anything that helps with the head you delivered to Midland?"

"A few things, but I can't think to tell you right now."

"I understand. You go on and we'll talk later."

"Thank you, Sheriff."

"Life is never dull. It might break your heart every which way from Sunday, but it's never dull."

When I didn't move, he added, "I'm sorry for the pain this brings you, truly sorry. I wish with all my heart it was happening to somebody else."

* * *

I drove back to Terlingua but had to stop twice to vomit. My emotions go right to my stomach and twist it upside down.

Just when I thought things couldn't get worse Diego or Emilio or whoever he was called. I didn't know what to do, but I had the same reaction to his voice I always had. It was pitiful. I listened to him go on about the engagement ring he bought. I let him call me *mi amor, mi preciosa, mi corazón,* soaking in his love while I still could. How would I live without it?

"You're not saying much," he said when he noticed my

silence.

"Diego, are you Emilio Martez?"

At first there was dead air. I thought he had disconnected.

"I was trying to tell you. I—I—just couldn't. How can I make you understand?"

"Did you murder Diego Romero?"

"No! I've never killed anyone. That's why my father can't stomach me."

"Were you going to tell me who you are before we got married?"

"Yes. I knew I had to. First I came to Monterrey to speak with my father about getting out of the business. I decided not to do it because I've seen men try to get out before. He has them killed.

"You're his flesh and blood, Diego."

"He will never let me go."

"Who killed the D.E.A. agent?"

"Sotol and Ruben did it for my father before they broke away from his organization. My father ordered me to take Romero's identity and get our drugs back. I never counted on falling in love with the deputy who took them. I thought it would be a matter of going in, getting the drugs turned over to me, and moving them on. I wasn't supposed to fall in love. I've never felt like this in my whole life, Margarita."

"Sotol and Ruben were going to rape and kill me. Who gave those orders?"

"They're acting separate of my father's organization now. He wants them eliminated. The drugs you saw them putting into that house—they had stolen them for themselves. For whatever reason, fate put you there that night or they would've sold them and made off to who-knows-where, and I would never have gone to Terlingua and met you."

I no longer knew if that was a good or bad thing.

"Do you know there's a fifty-thousand peso bounty on my head?"

"Of course I don't know that! It has to be Sotol. My father doesn't know anything about you or where you live, so it couldn't be him and besides, public wanted notices are not the Martez style."

"You're on the F.B.I.'s Most Wanted list as of this morning, for killing Diego Romero and for drug trafficking. My phone is probably already wired."

"I don't think even the F.B.I. can move that fast. Besides, let them hear me say I've never killed anyone."

"I don't know if anything you say is true."

"Oh Margarita, how can I convince you? I've done bad things, yes, but I've never killed anyone. I grew up surrounded by the drug trade and oblivious to the fact that it's wrong until I was old enough to figure it out for myself. My whole family is into it. To us it's about moving product, same as if we were selling and transporting televisions." He took a deep breath and was quick to add, "But I know what you think about it. I'd never ask you to live that life. I want to take you away somewhere and love you for the rest of our lives. That's why I said we'd have to give up my family's money. We'll disappear, and they'll never find us."

"I can't do that. What about my family?"

"Could we meet somewhere and talk?"

"Not now. Terlingua is crawling with law looking for you. They want to talk to me."

"I'm so sorry, Margarita. Why do they think I killed Agent Romero? There's not supposed to be a body."

"So you do know about it."

"I only know what my father told me. He said Sotol and Ruben had eliminated the agent and disposed of his body. My job was to go to Terlingua and pretend to be him. Were his remains found?"

"They burned the body in a fire in a place that should never have caught on fire. It's a remote place they thought we'd ignore. I questioned it because the fire had been set. There had to be a reason, so I dug through the ashes and found a twisted belt buckle and some charred bone fragments that I sent to the crime lab."

"It's just my luck to fall in love with a woman in law enforcement, and not just in it but who kicks ass at it. It's impossible to miss that irony."

"I get it, but I'm in deep shit here."

"Please tell me you still love me."

"I do love you, Diego—whatever your name is. That's the pitiful thing. I wish I could stop."

"Please don't. Please believe in me. We'll work this out somehow. I'll call you later. *Te amo con todo mi corazón.* I'm kissing you now. *Adiós, Mi Amor.*"

"I'm kissing you back," I said to dead air, or probably right into an F.B.I. agent's tape recorder. They couldn't put a woman in prison for loving a criminal. But they could make her life hell. I didn't need help with that. I had done it to myself and there was no way out that made sense. My heart said I would go with him anywhere he wanted to go, even if it was to another planet. Love would make all things right.

My brain sneered and said it had never known a bigger idiot.

CHAPTER 21

I continued to Terlingua, lights flashing, flirting with suicide speeds. I felt as if there were a sword in my heart.

Barney called on the satellite phone when I was about halfway there. "Ricos?" he asked even though I answered with my name.

"Who wants to know?"

"Man, have you got some suits waiting on you."

"Are they there now?"

"No. They left to get iced tea at the café. But they're waiting for you to take them to the site of the fire. And they want to talk to you about your boyfriend. My God, Ricos, I only thought he was married."

"I wish it was something that simple."

"It's seriously bad when you have to wish your boyfriend was married and not a major player in a drug car— well, what are you going to do?"

"I don't know. I don't know what to do."

"Get on back here and we'll figure it out."

"Barney, I know I'm in a mess, and I can only blame myself, but I want you to trust me. I'm not going to help those men kill Diego. I'll tell them what I know, but that's all I'm going to do. I hope you understand."

"For Chrissakes, of course I understand. I wouldn't help them either if it was me. It's wrong for them to ask you to do something like that."

"They haven't asked me yet, but Sheriff Ben says that's coming."

"We'll stand up to them together. Those government types will never get past the toughest ass-kickers in the West."

Barney can always make me laugh, even when all the sunshine has been sucked from the planet.

* * *

When I pulled into our parking lot, there was a plain white government van like Diego had used when he came for the cocaine. The sword in my heart made a searing twist, reminding me it was still there. I sucked in a slow, deep breath, and checked my face in the mirror. I looked like crap. Somehow my braid had made it through the day. Good hair is better than nothing. You have to go with what you've got, so I adjusted my hat until it was perfect, and pulled my invisible bulletproof shield over me. Then I strolled inside as if I owned the place.

Three men in dark suits sat in front of Barney's desk, and all of them looked up when I came in.

"Here she is now," my partner said. "Gentlemen, this is Deputy Ricos."

I offered my hand to the one closest to the door. He said he was Agent Fillmore with the Federal Bureau of Investigation. He then introduced Special Agent David Small and Special Agent Bart Huddleston with the Drug Enforcement Agency. One of them politely pulled up another chair and invited me to sit as if I had a choice. Every one of them was staring at my bruised face.

"Deputy Ricos, it's our understanding that you have a relationship with Emilio Martez," said FBI Agent Fillmore. "Would you tell us about that, please?"

"That's none of your business. My relationship to him is a personal one."

Barney gave me an *atta girl* look but stayed quiet.

"Ms. Ricos, I can get a court order that will force you to tell us what you know. Emilio Martez is a wanted criminal on both sides of the river."

"I don't know anything that will interest you, and getting a court order won't change that. I thought he was Diego Romero, and I had a relationship with him under that assumption. We didn't talk about business, his or mine or anybody else's."

"I'm having a little trouble believing that."

"Well believe it or not, that's the truth."

"How can that be?"

"We were preoccupied by other things."

"Do you know where he is right now?"

"No. I don't know."

"When did you last speak with him?"

"About an hour ago."

"Didn't he tell you where he was?" asked Special Agent David Small.

"He was in Monterrey, but he was leaving."

"Did he say what he was doing there?"

"He'd gone to speak with his father about getting out of the business, but he lost his nerve. He said his father would never let him go, that he kills the people who try to get away."

"Did you make arrangements to meet him?" This was the FBI agent again.

"No, we didn't make any arrangements."

"Ms. Ricos, do you understand it's against the law to aid a wanted criminal?"

"Yes, I understand the law. I've never aided him in any way, unless you want to consider loving him aiding and abetting. I don't see how that will work, since I thought he was a DEA agent until a few hours ago."

"You thought he was Diego Romero until a few hours ago?"

"Yes, that's what I just said."

"Did Emilio Martez hit you?"

"No; he would never hit me."

"You never had any indication that the man you thought was Diego Romero was someone else?"

"No. Of course not. How many times do I have to say it?"

"How do you feel about the fact that he's a murderer and drug trafficker?"

"How do you think I feel? Among other things, I can't believe it."

"Do you intend to continue your relationship with Emilio Martez?"

"I can't give you an honest answer to that question. I can't think."

"This is not the time to stand by your man."

Maybe he thought that was clever, but one look at my expression and he changed the subject. "Ms. Ricos, would you take us to the site of Diego Romero's murder?"

"I can take you to where I discovered fragments of his bones. He wasn't murdered there, and I have no idea where that crime scene is, but probably not far."

"What makes you think he wasn't murdered where you found his remains?"

"Barney and I found no evidence of it. No blood, no bullet casings or fragments. It's possible, but unlikely. How would someone get him to go there?"

"Maybe he was lured. It happens sometimes. At any rate, we'd like for you to take us to the scene you know about."

"Of course; I'll be glad to."

"We'll go in our van unless we need four-wheel drive."

"Your van will work fine. We'll have to hike to the site no matter what we drive."

Everyone stood. I got a few bottles of water out of the refrigerator to take along.

"Barney," I started to ask him to join us, but he was already standing and had grabbed his hat. He was getting investigation gloves out of a desk drawer. He looked up at me and raised one eyebrow.

"We have plenty of those," said Agent Fillmore, "and evidence bags."

My partner said nothing and shoved the gloves back in the drawer.

We followed the men out the door to the parking lot. Barney nudged me. I looked up at him and he smiled a reassuring smile.

The FBI guy drove and one DEA agent sat in front next to him. We were asked to sit on the bench seat behind them, and then the other DEA man sat behind us. Barney gave me a wide-eyed look but stayed quiet. I got it. We were surrounded.

* * *

It was twenty-some miles to the site of the fire, and even though I explained that, I believe the agents thought I was trying to pull something. They were unused to such wide-open spaces, and long, unpopulated distances between places. Desolate, they called it. Unpopulated is not the same as desolate, I pointed out.

Special Agent Small commented that it was beautiful but sounded both frightened and awestruck. The others murmured their agreement. I wondered what they would think when we got to the site.

"There's the Rio Grande," I pointed out when we began to see it, though they probably already knew that. The low adobe buildings, placidly grazing animals, and Mexican men with sombreros riding burros and horses on the other side of the river would've been the first clues.

"No wonder they can get drugs across with little effort," said one of the DEA agents. "The river doesn't look deep or dangerous."

"And it's not like anyone is going to stop them," said another.

Barney and I took immediate offense at that comment and looked at each other in silent solidarity. The no-longer-formidable river and the miles of unpopulated land adjacent to it is part of Law Enforcement 101, covered the first day of class anywhere within five hundred miles of the border.

At times, the Rio runs deep and dangerous, but I didn't bother to mention the obvious: that traficantes can and do use boats like anybody else. Nor did I explain the effects of rainfall and dam releases on the river's flow since these guys weren't staying.

"This is incredible," said the FBI agent when he saw the approach to Big Hill. The subtle jokes they had been making about us being remote and Godforsaken and "easy for traffickers" were quieted by the enormity and unspoiled beauty of the landscape. They had the "civilization" and city conveniences. Our scenery trumped it.

"You can't have much in the way of scenery in cities," commented Barney to no one in particular.

"Nobody can argue about the beauty of this area," said the man behind us.

"The site is on the left," I said, "not far, but you should park on the right. You'll see a pullout in just a second. Look—right there." He was expecting a paved parking area, probably, not a rocky half-circle of ground intended for emergency use.

After Agent Fillmore parked, he jumped out and stretched—and froze as his eyes moved up to the imposing boulder-infested hill beside the van. "Do you think those things will hold?" he wondered.

"I think so," Barney said as we piled out the side doors. "If it rains, it'd be best to move the van. Those boulders loosen up sometimes and come down." The boulders he was referring to were about the size of Volkswagens.

I headed across the road and stood by the thick, two-foot high rock wall that serves as a guardrail. The youngest of the three men hurried to catch up. "Do you like living here, Deputy Ricos?"

"Yes I do."

"What is there to do—on a date, I mean?"

I was speechless a moment because what came to mind was flying to Chihuahua in a silvery sky, riding an ATV by the light of the moon, and counting the stars with a man who made love to my hand.

"We have bars and restaurants and dances," I said. "Or people gather for parties around a bonfire in somebody's backyard. There are lots of outdoor things to do if you like hiking, rafting, canoeing, biking, or camping. Have you ever visited Big Bend National Park?"

"No. Would you show me around sometime?" As the other men came up, he turned serious. "Is it true you discovered the boxes of Martez cocaine?" he asked, as if he was all business and hadn't been flirting with me.

"It was a lucky break. I happened to be in the right place at the right time."

"You seem to have pissed off the Martez family."

"The men behind this are not the Martez family. They are Sotol Valenzuela and Ruben Villanueva," I said. "They worked for the Martez cartel until they were handed three or four million dollars worth of cocaine to move through here. At that point, it seems they broke away to sell the drugs for personal gain. So they're the ones angry with me."

Before anyone else mentioned the Martez name in vain, I pointed down the hillside to the charred wreck. "Shall we go down?"

"We'll follow you," said Agent Fillmore. "But I want to know how you know so much about this."

"I heard it from Emilio, speaking as DEA agent Romero."

I hopped up on the wall while Barney stepped over it, offered his hand, and then did the same for the men. "Watch your footing," he said to them.

As we picked our way towards the burned-out wreckage I felt pity for the men following us. They were wearing nice shoes and suits, and it became evident they were management, not men from the front lines. Diego Romero had been front line. That led me to consider his death at the hands of criminals. It made me sad. He was one of us, doing the best he could to stem crime along the border, and he had given his life for the cause. The sword in my heart gave another stab.

Men had been murdered for less, but it still seemed an unspeakable waste to die trying to stop drugs from coming into a country that is consumed by the desire for them.

My whole family is into it. To us, it's about moving product, same as if we were selling and transporting televisions.

Why did I think I could run away with the son of a drug lord and live happily ever-after in a foreign land? How would that work? I was raised by a man who had seen his cousins, uncles, and friends go to prison or get murdered over drugs.

He had heatedly warned me away from them my whole life, not because of immorality or law or even health issues, but because of the misery inflicted on the good people of Mexico by the illegal drug trade.

Barney took my elbow and pulled me close. "Whatever you're thinking," he whispered, "please stop or we're all gonna bust into tears."

I started to speak but he interrupted. "We'll talk about it later, Ricos."

So now he was reading my mind.

As we came closer to Dark Canyon, one of the men said, "This is extraordinary scenery. It's so damn *big* and—well, it's just extraordinary."

All of us agreed.

"Over there," he said, indicating the Mexican side, "it looks like no human has ever set foot."

We all agreed to that, too.

"Hey—look up there. I saw a bighorn sheep." One of the DEA agents pointed to the cliff towering behind us, the top of the other side of the mountain that forms Big Hill.

"It's an aoudad," explained Barney, "a goat-antelope crossbreed that is native to rocky North Africa. There's a small wild herd of them in this area."

Suddenly we arrived at the charred spot and all talk stopped. We surrounded and stared down at what was now a misshaped, buckled hunk of junk sitting on top of blackened earth. The place looked even more somber now that I knew for certain why it had been burned, and that the victim had been one of us.

"How did you discover the fire?" asked one of the men.

"It was called in by a motorist."

"Not one car has passed since we got here."

"One happened to be passing that day," Barney said. "Traffic through here is sparse but this road is used. It's Farm and Market Road 170, better known as the River Road."

"Where does it go?"

"It goes to Presidio, but people come through here to visit Big Bend Ranch State Park and for river trips, or to cross into Mexico at Presidio."

"It seems like we're standing at the end of the earth," said Agent Small, looking around with wide eyes.

"Aren't we on state park soil now?" asked Agent Fillmore.

"Yes, but this area is not a tourist destination per se. The headquarters is close to Presidio, and some camping areas, river put-in points, and other sites of interest."

"So the fire was reported by a tourist; then what happened?"

"We were called to the scene," I said.

"Isn't this Presidio County?"

I thought he knew more than he let on. "Yes, but we're usually called to accidents or other emergencies that are this close to Brewster County since we can respond faster than their personnel."

"Was your fire department called too? Do you have a fire department?"

"Yes, we do and yes, they were."

"We arrived before they did," Barney added, "and it was obvious there was no way to stop a fire in this location that was burning with such intensity. An accelerant had been used."

"What did you do?"

"First, we looked for bodies that might have been thrown from the vehicle. That was before Deputy Ricos pointed out that no vehicle had come through this area since this old truck ran off the road thirty-odd years ago."

The men turned to me. "How did you come to that conclusion?" one asked.

I pointed back up the hill. "There are no crushed plants, no disturbed dirt, or path of any kind. Nor is there any place where the wall or the guardrail is damaged. Then I remembered there had been an old truck body here since I was a child."

"So you had seen it there before?"

"Yes, I had seen it from the road and from the river. I'd even hiked to it before."

"Have you been on the river a lot?"

"Yes, more than most people, probably. My uncle owned a rafting company when I was growing up, and I did some exploring on my own and still do."

"Have you ever brought anything illegal from Mexico?" asked Agent Fillmore with the calm, detached look he would use in questioning terrorism suspects.

"Well sure. I've brought avocadoes, fruit, and other banned food from the little store in Paso Lajitas, as most people around here have. Since the aftermath of 9-11, we can't do that anymore. But if you're talking about drugs, no, I don't have anything to do with drugs and never have, and I resent your implication."

"I didn't mean to offend you."

"The hell you didn't," said Barney, my personal Superman.

The agent ignored him and addressed me. "Didn't your mother ever tell you that people will judge you by the company you keep?"

"You sonofabitch," growled Barney and stepped towards him.

The agent took a few steps backward.

I continued to study the ground. Tears clouded my eyes and my bottom lip was trembling. At my feet were tiny shoots of green beginning to emerge from the charred hardpan. There was the definition of determination: life persevering after total annihilation. I couldn't be too sure about my own life, though. My future seemed darker than black.

I didn't want those men to see how upset and vulnerable I was. At the same time, I wanted to help Barney beat Agent Fillmore's face in.

"Don't you dare touch me," the FBI man said to Superman. "I was stating the obvious, nothing more."

"Now you look here," Barney said, and steadily backed him away from me. "She thought he was Agent Romero and made a date with him based on that. They fell in love. Nobody but the FBI would turn that into something sinister."

One of the DEA guys decided to get off the sidelines. "When Martez showed up for the drugs, did you ask for his I.D.?" He addressed Barney.

"He was driving a government van, for Chrissakes. We had spoken to the Austin office about the drugs, and they said they were sending someone to get them. It was an honest mistake. We had a lot more going on than turning over drugs to the feds."

"Such as?"

"Are we about through here?" I interrupted, hoping to stop Barney from assaulting a federal officer. I didn't want them to shoot or pummel him or make him disappear to someplace like Guantanamo.

"Why would they bring him here?" asked Special Agent Huddleston.

"To dispose of the body," I said, "We assume they

destroyed it so nobody would miss him for a few days. I thought it was peculiar to burn a thirty-year-old wreck in this remote location, so after the fire I sifted through what was left and sent what I found to the crime lab. I'm sorry that Diego Romero was murdered, but I think it's disrespectful to his memory to stand around here bickering about mistakes nobody can change. Barney and I acted in good faith. We have work to do. If you want to look around here a while, that's fine. We understand. We'll wait by the van." I gave my partner a let's-go nod of my head. He looked speechless.

"Not so fast," said Fillmore. "We have some questions for you, Ms. Ricos. You can either answer them here or we can—"

"Ask them."

"At any time did you figure out that Diego Romero was Emilio Martez?"

"You've already asked that. No. I know him one way, you know him another." I tried to step back from it and pretend this was happening to someone else. I took a deep breath. "I only want to say this once, so take notes if you need to. The man I know as Diego Romero is charming, sweet, and thoughtful."

The three men exchanged knowing smirks, but I didn't even slow down. "Maybe he has a vicious, cruel side, but I never saw a glint of it. We seldom spoke about jobs, his or mine. I flew to Chihuahua with him in his plane for dinner and dancing. I flew all over the Big Bend with him. I fell in love with him. I slept with him. He never asked me to do anything I didn't want to do, so no, he never hinted that I should move drugs for him. And he never said a word about what he does. I assumed it was secret, that he was watching the drug activity along the border. I totally get the irony of that, so there's no need to point it out to me."

I took a deep breath but didn't give anyone a chance to speak. "I see your contempt, but you weren't there. I think you should try to see this from my point of view. I am not some stupid little redneck from Nowheresville. I'm just as educated, smart, brave, and capable as you are. I don't give a shit if you agree with me or not. Deputy George knows who I am, and so does Sheriff Duncan.

"I know Emilio Martez as a lover, not a killer. He was trying to tell me the truth of his life, but hadn't gotten to all of it yet. His father despises him because he won't kill. He's never murdered anyone or ordered it done. His father, the patriarch from Hell, does all that. Emilio did not kill Diego Romero, but he did come to get the drugs, as ordered by his father. The son is a drug trafficker, granted, but not a murderer. His father is the murderer."

"How do you know the son isn't a cold-blooded killer, too?"

"I know him."

"Excuse me for stepping on your toes, but you don't know him or you would have—"

"I know his *heart*, Agent Fillmore." I said it with such conviction, not one of them dared to challenge me.

"I know you think you know him," I added, "but you don't."

As Sheriff Ben says: *when you've made your case to the judge, stop talking.* They were going to think what they wanted anyway, and I would never change that.

Nobody stopped me when I began the uphill climb to the van.

"Alrighty then," said Barney and then he followed me.

We sat on the low rock wall with our backs to the men. They continued to study the wreckage and speak in low tones. The sun was setting, making red rocks blaze. From where we sat, halfway up a mountain, the river looked like it was on fire where it flowed out of faraway Colorado Canyon. I tried to take comfort from the scenery I love. Sometimes the sheer size and age and the enduring grandeur of it will put human problems into perspective; sometimes it doesn't.

"At least they haven't asked you to help them get him," Barney said.

"They haven't gotten around to it. They've been too busy questioning my morals and intelligence and my dedication to my job."

"I think they might be afraid to rile you again," he said.

"Those assholes aren't upset by anything a woman says."

"Yeah, that's what you think because you're never on the receiving end. Ricos, you get a look in your eye that could melt cold steel."

I laughed and leaned into him. For a minute I rested against his strength, and he was my friend, not my deputy partner. Crime and heartache stepped back.

"Sometimes it's hard to remember we're on the same

side as them," he said.

Soon a white and green Border Patrol vehicle sped past and the guys waved. We waved back. Barney laughed.

"What?"

"Aww, nothin'."

"Why are you laughing?"

"I was just thinkin' about you trying to get that guy to go into the backcountry with you the night you discovered the cocaine. You called him 'Agent B.P. Pussy.' I always think of that when I see those guys now."

We enjoy a chuckle about them now and then since they consider themselves so superior to deputies.

For a while, we watched the feds talk and look around the burned-out chunk of metal below. We had a few laughs at their expense, too.

* * *

"How is it I find a man who is perfect for me in every way except for one detail that ruins every other thing?"

Barney sighed. "Well, I did try to get you interested in my brother."

"That's not funny."

"I'm sorry, Ricos, I know it's not. I wanted to make you laugh. None of this is funny and someday when we look back on it, it still won't be funny."

I leaned against him again. He sighed and put his arm around me.

"What are they looking for down there?" I asked in exasperation.

"I don't know, but I hope they find a shred of decency."

CHAPTER 22

When the men returned from whatever they were doing, they had no evidence bags. They hadn't picked up one thing. I thought they would take their own evidence in case I had faked it or burned their man's body myself. They were out of breath and out of their element. I decided to cut them some slack. Besides, I had nothing to prove. My mom says *who you are speaks louder than what you say.* Sometimes I had to admit she was right. That is how I could claim to know Emilio Martez. It had never been about what he said.

Once my mind went to him it was impossible to tear it away. Barney was talking with the agents, and I tried to look like I was paying attention. He offered to drive because it was dark, and he knows the roads.

Agent Fillmore relented. "When it gets dark here it's not kidding around." Then he smiled at me as he held the door open. "You sit up here with your partner," he said as cordially as if we were on a first date. It was a tiny olive branch, but I accepted it and tried to return the smile.

On the way back, we spoke about living in Terlingua, the national park, the state park—anything but drugs and drug dealers. Barney did most of the talking with the men because I was somewhere else for most of the trip. I had given them the opinions they needed to hear from me. How I felt about my community, the stark beauty of the land, what I did in my job—they didn't care about any of that.

We got out of the van at the office.

"Look at those stars," Agent Small said in a voice filled with wonder. They were hanging so close to Cactus Hill that some appeared to have snagged themselves on the rugged hunk of rock at the top.

Everyone agreed it was a spectacular display never seen in cities. We stood around a bit trying to be friendly, but were dismayed when they followed us inside.

Agent Fillmore didn't look at me, but he spoke to me. "I believe we got off on the wrong foot. I apologize for that. It—it was horrifying to be in that remote, dark place looking at the charred ruins of where Agent Romero's body was destroyed. It's one thing to hear about it, but seeing it is indescribably

Barney and I agreed with him.

"There's something about that location, too. It's so wild and vast—" He didn't seem able to finish the sentence.

"We understand," I said, "our wide open spaces take some getting used to."

A few wordless beats passed and then Agent Fillmore said, "I already spoke with your sheriff and he holds both of you in high regard. He says you're dedicated to law enforcement and take your jobs seriously."

Barney and I watched him, silent, expecting the other shoe to drop.

We didn't have to wait long because Barney dropped it for him. "Are you gonna tell us what you want or blow smoke up our asses all night?"

The agent shifted in the chair and coughed. "We came here to ask you to help us bring to justice the men who killed Special Agent Romero."

"We would like to do that," said Barney. "We don't have jurisdiction in Mexico and it seems a slim chance that they'll come here now. Their dirty work is done. Don't you think they've moved on?"

"The Martez cartel is never going to move on, Deputy. They're going to continue moving millions of dollars worth of drugs through here unless we stop them." Then he turned to me. "We find some discrepancies in what you've told us, Deputy Ricos, and I'd like to ask you about them."

"Okay. Ask."

"You claim you and Martez never talked business, yet you know some details you have no way of knowing. You know the names Sotol Valenzuela and Ruben Villanueva, and somehow you know that they broke away from the Martez family."

"We knew the names before I met the man I thought was a DEA agent. There was a murder here, remember? William Hayfield? Your office faxed information to the sheriff. We know they murdered Adolpho Estevez, too."

"How can you be sure of that?"

"Because they admitted it to me after I found the crime scene in Mexico."

"What made you look in Mexico? You don't have jurisdiction in Mexico. You shouldn't even be in Mexico." He was determined to catch me at something.

"My father has a house there, and I was checking on it. They caught me there and abducted me and were going to kill me. They're the ones who messed up my face. A friend rescued me when the men holding me went for beer."

"So a friend just happened to come along and rescue you from two diabolical drug dealers? He must be some friend."

"Yes. He's quite amazing." I didn't think I should mention that there had been four diabolical drug dealers or that Craig had killed two of them.

"Look, I'm trying to help you," I said.

"Please continue."

"My friend witnessed the murder of Adolpho and later, my abduction. I made a report to the sheriff, and I know he faxed your office about it."

Fillmore watched me with a face that showed no emotion, and he didn't admit or deny anything about the fax.

"Sotol and Ruben are offering a fifty-thousand peso reward for me dead or alive," I continued. "Everything that's happened here has nothing to do with Emilio Martez except that he came to get the drugs, and when he did, he met me. Since I believed he worked for the Drug Enforcement Agency, I asked him about Sotol and Ruben and he told me. It seems logical that a DEA agent would know about this, right?"

I didn't give him a chance to agree or disagree. "So I'm not lying when I say we didn't talk about business. He was reluctant to tell me anything, but he did confirm what I had figured out on my own. I was taught that if you put two and two together you get four."

"So you spent time with him but never spoke about business, other than to confirm what you knew?"

"That's what I've said a hundred times. You can keep asking me, but I have to keep giving you the same answer. Agent Fillmore, we had more compelling things to occupy our time. When we're together business doesn't usually come up. If you want me to spell it out, I will."

"That won't be necessary, but listen, Ms. Ricos, you're in a position to provide us with crucial intelligence we need."

I didn't dare look at Barney. He coughed in an attempt not to laugh and then took a breath, coughed again. "We'll support you every way we can, but you people are the experts on drug cartels. What Deputy Ricos just told you is all we know about it."

He paid no attention to Barney and was looking right at me. "You could gather information from Emilio Martez that would be crucial to us."

"It would be a great service to your country—and to Mexico. They want these men as much as we do," he added when I didn't respond.

"Agent Fillmore, I love my country and I abide by the law, but I'm not going to help you by ratting out a man I love."

"Surely your feelings have changed since—"

"My feelings haven't changed."

"We want you to help us lure him here. He's an American citizen, so—"

"No. I won't aid and abet him, but I'm not going to stab him in the back."

"But you'd be bringing in a wanted man, a murderer. You won't be able to see him again anyway without breaking the law."

"If I never see him again I'll have to live with that. I couldn't live with myself if I did what you ask. I won't do it, so stop asking."

"We're going to spend the night here tonight, so I'll check with you again in the morning. I'm just asking that you think about it, okay? Will you do that?"

"Sure, I'll think about it, but I won't change my mind tomorrow or the next day or the next. Haven't you ever been in love?"

"Of course, I'm a married man. Perhaps things will look different to you after some thought, now that you know who he is."

"I've always known who he is—not his name—but who he is in his heart. It's the reason I love him. You're the one who should think about what you're asking of me. What if you found out that your wife was known by another name in her past and did some things that were wrong—some things she didn't want to do but had to? Maybe you'd be disappointed, but would you stop loving her?"

Instead of answering my question he changed the subject. "We're going to release Luis Garza. He refuses to talk and we have no proof about his involvement in the murder, other than witnesses who saw him with the men. Being seen with criminals doesn't make him one in our opinion."

"Can you hear yourself?" Barney was practically yelling. "You hinted that Deputy Ricos is a drug trafficker because she knows one. Now Luis Garza should get a break because being with a criminal doesn't make him one? There are some serious discrepancies in your theories, Agent Fillmore."

"Luis Garza is a child. Deputy Ricos is a grown woman in law enforcement."

Barney threw up his hands. "So if I use your reasoning, grown women in law enforcement who are seen with criminals are probably criminals. There are a lot of women in law enforcement positions who would take issue with that theory. Prison guards, policewomen, detectives, deputies, Border Patrol agents—"

"All right Deputy George, point taken. Perhaps I was hard on Deputy Ricos. I did apologize to her."

"What else do you have for us?" Barney asked.

"I have one more thing," I said. "If you release Luis Garza, he will most likely be killed, the same way Adolpho Estevez was killed. The thing that has saved him so far is that he's being held in a safe place."

"If he's innocent, as he maintains, then why would he be killed?"

"He's not innocent, Agent Fillmore. He's lying because he's afraid. He was there when Hayfield was murdered. He was an accomplice. He came to see me, to warn that they were going to kill me. When I arrested him, he cried and said they were going to kill him, too."

"Why would they want to kill you?"

"I'm the one who saw them with the drugs. They lost their fortune because of me. They're hateful and vindictive and scorn women. They like to kill. I don't know all the reasons, but I know they'll kill me if they have the opportunity."

"If you cooperate with us they'll be behind bars until they get the needle."

"We are ready to cooperate with you in every way if you're speaking of Sotol and Ruben. If you're still talking about Emilio Martez, then no is my answer."

"You are an extraordinarily difficult woman."

I looked at Barney, who was studying his hands and trying not to laugh.

The men in suits left soon after that.

"Those guys couldn't put two and two together and get four," said Barney.

"They're trying to do a difficult job. I feel kind of sorry for them."

"Why?"

"Well, they're out here in the big ol' scary wide-open spaces. And they've run up against two deputies who don't roll over on command."

"They don't know what to think about you, Ricos."

"Do you think they'll tap my phones—and what about the office phone?"

"I don't know. I'm sure they can get permission because of the Martez name. All they have to do is mention that with his cartel's millions he might fund a terrorist organization, and they can watch every single thing you do. You'd better be careful for a while."

"I'm going to go home. If the FBI wants to follow me it's just going to be boring."

"Shut your drapes and keep your door locked."

"Don't worry."

"You don't want those guys watching you undress."

"God no, that's perverted. Surely they wouldn't do that."

"They're men, Ricos."

"Well, there's that."

"They'd only do it if they had a chance," he said. "There're not just men, but men with a license to spy."

"I'll stay with my mom."

Instead of going to Mom's, I went home and found Craig in back of my house making dinner over a small campfire. I begged him to bring the food, his kitten, and whatever else he needed and come inside so I could talk to him.

"But the food's not done yet."

"I have a stove, Craig. Now please come inside. I think we're being watched."

That got him. He came in with no more argument. I carried a bubbling pot of beans and a skillet of sizzling potatoes while he brought Marine and the rest of the things. His food smelled so good I asked if he would share if I added a few things. He would've given me his last crumb, so it was a question of manners, not wondering if he would share. He answered me with a look.

Craig tended the food on the stove while I put a salad together. I also got out salsa, tortillas, and slices of cheese. I realized that I hadn't eaten anything in that entire day. We had a feast.

"I'm worried about Marine," he said. "He doesn't understand being inside."

"I'll make him a litter box when we finish eating."

"So you want us to sleep indoors?"

"Please, Craig. I feel safe with you here."

"Okay, Little Boss. Can you tell me who's watching us?"

"It's the FBI."

"Oh, shit. What have you done? Or is it me?"

"It's me. Could we talk about it after we eat?"

"Sure, whenever you want. I could make a fire later if you'd like."

"That would be great."

"Is Diego coming?"

"No, he can't be here tonight."

* * *

Craig cleaned up the kitchen while I made an impromptu litter box and showed it to Marine. He seemed to understand what it was for right away. Then I took over in the kitchen and Craig went to make a fire. When we sat down together, he was the first to speak.

"There was a man here earlier this afternoon asking about you."

That was alarming. "Did he say who he was?"

"He's with the Drug Enforcement Agency. He knows Diego. He asked who I was, and I told him I'm your friend. He didn't believe me at first, asked if you knew I was camping here. Stupid man. He asked if I know Diego, and I said of course I know him, and then he wanted to know what I think of him."

"And you said?"

"I said I like him, of course."

"What else?"

"He started asking personal things, like if he stays here with you and how long you've known him—things like that. I told him I wasn't going to tell him those things unless you said it was okay."

"Thank you, Craig."

"Then he asked if I'd ever seen any other men here. Can you imagine? I said only me, and I've been her friend since she was a little girl. Then he asked if I'd ever seen unusual or suspicious activity. I told him I reckoned the most suspicious thing here was me. He laughed when I said that. I didn't have a good feeling about him. He was too nosy and disrespectful, asking me about men coming here. It's nobody's business but yours who comes here or sleeps here."

"I have a long story to tell you, Craig."

"Well I don't have another place to be, Little Boss. Take your time."

I told him about Diego not being Diego. He listened patiently and asked questions when I babbled and failed to explain. He didn't seem horrified and didn't offer advice. Nor did he warn me away from the man I loved. Marine sat on Craig's lap, watching me with wide eyes, as if my story fascinated him.

When I finished, Craig stroked the kitten thoughtfully. "How can I help you?"

"I don't know. I need to be with Diego; that's all I know."

"Yes, I know that. Let me think about it. Right offhand, I think you should run away with him. But his people will look for him and what about your parents? I don't think you'd be able to turn your back on your parents."

"No. I wouldn't do that."

"Well, we'll think of something."

"Do you think my house is bugged?"

"I doubt it. Could they move that fast? Anyway, I've been here all day and only that one man came by and I watched him every minute."

"Craig, do you still have that cell phone I bought for you?"

"Sure. I have it, but I don't use it."

"May I borrow it?"

"I'll get it." He handed Marine to me. "Be right back."

* * *

Later, I was making a bed for Craig on the sofa. "I'm going to leave for a little while." I held up the phone as explanation, feeling paranoid.

"I should go with you in case you need me."

I thought it would feel good to have company, his most of all. I wasn't afraid of the dark, but the thought of spies lurking made the hairs on the back of my neck stand up. Not to mention the bounty on my head. Anybody could be looking for me, good guys or bad, and I was easy to find.

"Okay then; come on, Craig."

"Just let me get my jacket on."

We got into my Mustang. I took my personal Beretta from the glove compartment. Wordlessly, Craig watched me check it and shove it back in.

"You could call him right here," he suggested. "Nobody

can hear you. I'll wait outside the car."

"Let's drive to the entrance of the park."

"Okay, but I think you'd be fine right here."

"I want to see if anyone follows me."

"Oh. Now you're thinking like a Marine."

"I've had lessons from the best."

There is a solar-powered light at the entrance station. After that, the national park is so dark you can see lights coming for miles. I parked in a pullout a mile or so from the entrance.

"Before you get out, I want to ask you about something, Craig."

"Sure, what is it?"

"When you were living behind Becky's did you ever see anything suspicious?"

"Well, I saw those guys breaking in at her restaurant."

"I'm talking about the area where you were living. Did anyone ever come there to dump something while you were there?"

"People came now and then and dumped stuff, yes."

"I'm thinking it would've been at night and the person or people might have been acting strangely or guilty, sneaking around. You know."

"Oh." He thought about it. "One time I was asleep and lights woke me up. There was somebody dumping something, but what was weird was that afterward she was raking up some of the garbage."

"She?"

"It was a woman, Little Boss."

"Could you see her?"

"No. She was in the shadows, acting guilty. When I called out *who's there* she said *go back to sleep, old man. This is none of your concern.* I was going to look around in the morning, but I forgot about it."

"How long ago was this?"

"About a week, maybe ten days, I guess. Is it important?"

"Yes, it could be. Craig, a head was found there after you moved to Mexico."

"A head? Whose?"

"We don't know yet. The head is at the crime lab."

A few seconds passed and Craig asked, "Are people saying I did it?"

It hurt my heart that he knew what our community thought of him. "A few people, yes. I might have to take a statement from you at the office, okay?"

"You aren't going to put me in jail, are you?"

"I would never do that, Craig. A formal statement is a far cry from jail. Can you remember anything else about the woman?"

"I don't want to go to jail."

"Craig, I would die to keep you out of jail. Is that clear enough for you?"

He smiled the sweetest smile I ever saw on him. "I guess you know I would die for you, too, Little Boss."

"I know that, Craig. I've known it since I was eleven."

"The woman I saw was driving a truck. It was too dark to tell what kind, but when she left I was sitting up. When the door opened a light came on, and I could see she was a tall woman and had her hair pulled back. But the important thing might be that there was a little child standing in the seat."

"Like a toddler?"

"Yes, a little one that was crying. He had one of those things in his mouth."

"A pacifier?"

"Yes, that's it."

"That helps me, Craig. Thanks. Please tell me if you think of anything else."

He got out, insisting he would be plenty warm with Marine stuffed in his jacket. He also said, "Talk as long as you want, and don't worry. Marine and I are going to have a look at the stars, but I've got your back—or your front, in this case."

The phone number Diego had used was no longer in service.

I began to cry. Craig was leaning against the front bumper, his back to me. I didn't want him to see how upset I was, but I couldn't stop.

I had given my heart to a drug dealer, and he still had it.

CHAPTER 23

Feet on the desk, butt in my favorite chair, gazing at my hill. I had been watching the effect of sunrise's pink glow and thinking about Diego Romero, the one I knew, not the other one. By the time Agent Fillmore came in, the sun was up shining brightly, in diametric opposition to my mood. Having my feet on the desk, staring out the window, presumably doing nothing, might have given him the wrong impression when he walked in on me.

He shot me a big, sarcastic grin. "Busy this morning?"

He was like a dog that approached wagging its tail and then bit you when you reached out a hand. Maybe I was just feeling touchy because I didn't like him.

Fillmore was wearing a different dark suit. Seeing a dark suit in Terlingua is so unusual people will say it's the IRS, Mormons, or Amway salesmen. He wouldn't have stood out as much dressed as a clown with oversized shoes.

"I was doing some thinking," I said, accustomed to defending my feet-on-the-desk stance to my partner, who also liked to accuse me of doing nothing.

"I hope you're thinking about helping me."

I got out of the chair. "Let's move out here." I indicated the main office. I didn't want him looking out my window at my scenery.

Barney pulled up out front, so I sat in one of the visitor chairs, and Fillmore sat next to me. "Did you think about what I said?" he asked.

"Yes. I thought about it." I hadn't, not much, but what could I say? "I'm not going to do what you ask. I won't help you trap him."

"I think you're making a big mistake."

"Maybe I am, but I can't stab him in the back."

Barney came in, greeted me and Agent Fillmore, and then sat at his desk.

"I'm going to need you to turn over your cell phone," the agent said in his usual abrupt way.

"Why? I need it."

"I'm asking you to cooperate, Ms. Ricos. I can call my Austin office and get a court order faxed here, no questions asked. All I have to do is mention the Martez name. So you can cooperate willingly or you'll be forced to cooperate."

Barney turned crimson and started to speak. I thought he was about to go for the agent's throat. I discouraged him with a slight shake of my head.

"My phone is personal. I have photos and things on there for my eyes only. Why do you want it? Oh, I know. You want Diego's number."

Agent Fillmore did not confirm or deny that.

"You're going to try to trace him."

"Your phone will be returned to you unharmed."

"Yeah, except for the little device you plant in there." I handed him the phone. There was no point in fighting him. "Knock yourself out."

"Thank you. I appreciate your cooperation. The phone will be returned tomorrow or the next day via courier, unless we have to keep it."

"Why would you have to keep it?"

He didn't answer my question. Instead he said, "We're going to get him with or without your help."

"A man shouldn't be killed for being in love." I felt outraged that they would want to use his trust of me to bring him down.

I had never contacted any terrorist groups or other drug cartels, so I thought I'd get my phone back. There was a lot of practically pornographic texting on there, but it proved nothing except what they already knew about my relationship with him.

Diego had a phone full of photos of me, and I wasn't wearing clothes in most of them. Sometimes I fail to use even one whole cell of my brain. But it seemed like he had ditched that phone. Hopefully he disabled it first, and my photos wouldn't turn up online.

* * *

"Well," said Barney when the feds left, "Agent Fillmore sure is a lot of fun. I kinda hate to see him go. You and I could get a lot of mileage out of that guy laughs-wise." That would've been true on a different day. He leaned back in his chair until it smacked the wall. "You don't seem to be in a laughing mood."

"There's nothing funny. Just when I thought things were going my way I find out I'm in love with a cartel kingpin. There's a bounty on my head, and he might have put it there for all I know, and I have a new father in my life who said, 'the man you're seeing isn't Special Agent Diego Romero,' so imagine what he thinks of me. Now I'm worried about what Fillmore will do. I don't want to go to prison because they won't let me run anywhere that's beautiful. The thought of running circles in a grassless yard makes me want to cry."

"Slow down there, Pard. Take a breath. What can Fillmore do to you?"

"He isn't going to walk away because I said no. He sees me as an in to Diego. I'm terrified I'll slip up, and he'll have something to hold over me. He could make me disappear to someplace and torture me, and I don't even know anything."

"You're getting carried away again."

"You're not the one in love with a drug lord."

"You won't slip up. Don't let them catch you talking to him or seeing him. You wouldn't try to see him, would you?" Barney put his face in his hands. "Of course you would. You're thinking about it right now, aren't you?"

Later I told Barney about my conversation with Craig regarding the head. He agreed that Craig had possibly seen whoever left it there, or that's what he said he thought.

"So now we know it was a woman. Hell, Ricos, a *woman* did that?"

"She must have been hopping mad. I wonder if it was her husband."

"I hope Julia never gets that mad at me."

"Don't make her mad."

"How will that happen? She's a woman and I'm a man. We fight."

"The point is not to make her so mad she wants to cut you into little pieces. If it makes you feel any better, there's no way Julia would have the size or strength to cut you up, even if I helped her."

"You would *help* her?"

"Calm down, Barney. We're talking hypothetically."

"You women always stick together."

"And men don't?"

"Okay. Let's get our act together. We need a formal statement from Craig so we can tell the sheriff we have one."

"Right. I explained that to Craig already."

"Then we need to look for a woman with long hair and a bandaged arm that drives a truck with a baby on board. How hard can it be?"

"Let's take the tape recorder and go to my house. Craig will be more comfortable, and it doesn't matter where we do it, does it?"

"No. That'll work."

When we pulled up, Craig was sitting on the porch with Marine on his lap.

"Does he look like a killer to you, Barney?"

"No. He looks like an old man with a kitten. He's looking better since you started taking care of him. And I think the kitten is helping."

"I think so, too. I've got to figure out where to put him so I can look out for him without him realizing what I'm doing."

"Good luck with that, Ricos."

"Get out and try not to look too intimidating."

He laughed.

"Hey, Craig. Do you remember Barney?"

"He'd be hard to forget," Craig said in his dry way.

"We're here to take a statement from you about the woman you saw dumping something. We're going to record it, okay?"

"Okay."

I took him through the same questions and got the same answers, except he had remembered one more detail. This is often the case with witnesses, which is why it pays to interview them more than once.

"I forgot about this until today," he said. "She stuttered. She said, 'g-g-go b-b-back to sleep, old man. This is none of your c-c-concern.' I'm sorry I didn't remember it before, but in my head I knew what she was saying. I just forgot how she said it."

Barney and I looked at each other. "That is going to narrow down our search." My partner couldn't keep the excitement out of his voice. "Thank you Mr. Summers, this helps a lot."

"You're welcome, young man, but you realize she might not have been discarding a head, right? She may have been there throwing trash."

"Yes. We know that, but it's a place to start," I said. "Thank you, Craig. I'll see you tonight, okay?"

"I'll be here."

"Do you know who she is?" Barney asked when we got back in the Explorer.

"I don't know anyone who stutters. Maybe she was stuttering because she was panicked and feeling guilty."

"Maybe, but to stutter so much seems unlikely."

"Yeah; so if she stutters, somebody here has to know her."

"Let's go to the grocery store. She has a small child, so you know she goes there."

Before long we had a name, Margie Frederickson, married to "that asshole."

"She stutters a little," said the clerk, a short round woman whose name is Mabel. "Her stuttering is only noticeable when she gets upset or flustered. One day she was in here with That Asshole and he started riding her. She began stuttering; that's why I noticed."

"Do you know where she lives?" I asked.

"Is she in trouble?"

"We don't know, but we'd like to speak with her."

"About?"

"Do you know where she lives or not?"

"That Asshole keeps her way out there on the ranch where nobody knows what he does or can help her."

"Do you mean Terlingua Ranch Resort?" Barney asked.

"Yeah, they don't even have a phone."

"Does he have a name?" I asked.

"I guess so, but everyone who knows him calls him That Asshole. Hey—his name might be Darrell."

"Do you know for a fact that he abuses her or do you only suspect it?"

"Everybody says he does. She comes in here with black eyes and bruises."

"Why hasn't anybody reported it to us?" I asked.

"What can you do about it?"

"We could take him to jail and put her in a safe house."

"Nobody wants to interfere in other peoples' personal business."

It was all I could do not to laugh, cry, or rip her into tiny pieces—I couldn't decide which. Before I picked one, Barney dragged me away from there.

"Do people even hear what they're saying?" he complained when we were out in the parking lot. "I've never lived anywhere where people were so embroiled in each others' personal lives."

"Yep. That Clerk is already on the phone with Another

Asshole."

"Now you're doing it, Ricos."

"This is jumping to conclusions, but what I think is that Margie had enough, and she turned That Asshole into That Head and Those Feet and Those Other Parts we haven't found."

"Right, and when That Clerk calls, That Asshole won't answer."

"They don't have a phone," I reminded him.

"We're assuming a lot of things."

"Sure we are, but That's Terlingua."

It was easy to joke about it until we found the house, which was a mobile home with an attached shed. It looked normal, more or less, for a remote, rundown place. Faced with going in, the whole thing seemed way less than funny.

"Ricos," Barney said as we approached, "I'll buy you lunch if she didn't do it."

"If she did it, I won't want lunch."

We banged on the door. A baby was crying and the door was open, so we went in. A toddler in a playpen was making a fuss. He pointed to a bottle lying on its side out of his reach, the nipple dripping milk onto the carpet. "Ba-ba."

I picked him up, ran the nipple under the faucet, and handed him the bottle. He stopped screaming and began sucking, watching me with wide eyes. Barney went through the house calling Margie's name. I set the baby back in his playpen with the bottle, and he settled down contentedly.

"She has to be here, right?" Barney asked when he came back to the room.

"I doubt if she left her son behind."

"I'm going to check the shed." He stared at what we assumed was the door to it. "But for the record, I don't want to." He had his hand on his pistol.

"I'm with you," I said, and my hand was also on mine.

When we entered, Margie looked up, surprised. The scene was right out of a B-grade slasher movie. Dried blood and goo were everywhere. There was nothing that wasn't spattered, but it was the smell that made it real.

In the middle of the nightmare stood a tall, young woman with dark hair pulled back in a ponytail. She looked impossibly young, and at the same time, so old. She held up a mop dripping reconstituted gore.

A chainsaw had been discarded on top of a chest freezer

and had dripped what looked like a mix of bone matter and blood until it ran down the side to the floor and pooled where it dried.

"It ran out of gas," Margie said when she saw me looking at it.

"We knocked but nobody answered, and the door was open," explained Barney. "The baby was crying, so we came in. What happened here, Margie?"

She pushed escaped hair back from her face, leaving a rust-colored swipe on her cheek. "I was just t-t-trying to c-c-clean up this mess. I didn't know I had c-company. Want a soda?"

"No Margie," I said gently, "we need for you to tell us what happened."

"I n-n-never thought it would be so m-m-messy." Her left arm was wrapped with gauze that had dried seepage on it.

"Can you tell us what happened?"

"If you're looking for D-D-Darrell, he d-doesn't live here anymore, he d-d-died."

"What happened to him?"

"He b-beat me up for the l-l-last time." She still had fading bruises on her face. "And he b-bit me." She sobbed and extended her arm towards us as proof. Without warning, she pulled her blouse over her head. "L-l-look at this." Yellowing bruises covered her chest. "If y-you want, I'll t-t-take off all my clothes. There's more."

"That won't be necessary," I said. "We can see that he hurt you. What did you do? You put a stop to it, didn't you?"

"Yes. I did. He was going to hit Abe, and I picked up the hammer and stopped him. He was h-hanging a picture in the living room so it was h-h-handy. N-n-nobody hits my son." She collapsed as if her legs wouldn't hold her any longer. "I didn't mean to k-k-kill him but he just lay there, and I said 'g-g-get up you sonofabitch' but he didn't. He never did anything I asked him to."

"So you cut him up?"

"Wouldn't you? He was h-heavy and it t-t-took hours to get him into the shed. I didn't see how I could b-b-bury him. So I was thinking that if he was s-s-smaller it would be easier to m-m-move him. So I took the c-c-chainsaw to him."

"Did you bury his head in the trash behind Becky's restaurant?"

"Did you find it?"

"It was found, yes."

"So you knew it was him?"

"No. Not at first."

"I put the r-rest of him into the river, but his h-h-head—his *face*—was l-laughing at me. So I put him in the t-t-trash where he belongs. I b-bet he's n-not l-l-laughing n-now."

"We have to take you in, Margie."

"I know. I knew I shouldn't-a cut him up."

"Is there somebody I can call to take care of your baby?"

"C-c-call my m-mom, she'll t-t-take good care of him."

Margie's mother lived about twenty minutes away. I called her and asked her to come. When she arrived, I spoke to her while Barney escorted Margie to the vehicle. She didn't seem surprised that her daughter had ended That Asshole's life, but she was horrified at the details.

"Margie has never been what you'd call stable," she said. "She'd just gotten out of a mental health facility when she met Darrell. She seemed to be doing better. She's a good mom, but I was afraid That Asshole would put her over the edge again."

"What was his name?"

"His name was Darrell Simons. They never married, but the baby is his."

"Why didn't you report his abuse of Margie to the law?" I couldn't help but ask.

"Oh, because he always swore he was trying and that he'd do better."

I thought she was an idiot, but she obviously adored her grandson.

"We're going to take Margie to Alpine where she'll receive help."

"Do you think she'll be prosecuted?"

"I can't say. That's not my call."

"I'll take Abe home with me," she said, "and care for him as long as I'm needed, even if that means raising him."

When I asked, she said she was thirty-five and had Margie when she was seventeen, which I calculated made her daughter eighteen.

I explained that Child Protective Services would contact her soon. I wrote down her phone number and address and gave her my card.

As we drove Margie to Alpine, she spoke of the scenery with the enthusiasm of a child, *what great big mountains—oh!*

The cows!—and clapped her hands with glee over a jackrabbit crossing the road. Margie was the saddest arrest we ever made, and neither Barney nor I said much.

He had already called Sheriff Ben to explain the situation and asked him to have a caseworker from the Family Crisis Center meet us at the jail. There was a soft-spoken woman waiting for us when we arrived. She stayed with Margie while we filled out the paperwork and spoke with the sheriff.

    * * *

On the ride home, Barney smacked the steering wheel so hard it startled me. "I gotta say this, or I'm gonna bust."

"Well say it."

"If anybody, just one person, one damn person, would've had the decency to report the violence going on in Margie's house, none of this would've happened."

"Yeah, Barney, I know."

"These people knew it, Ricos. It makes me crazy. It makes me want to take a chainsaw to somebody, like That Clerk, for starters."

"Yep. People yap about each other day and night but to lift a finger? Hell, no."

"Let's get us a couple of chainsaws and go to town."

The whole thing was too sad and frustrating to laugh.

"I want to drink," I admitted out of the blue. "I'm so desperate you can't imagine it, Beer Boy. Tequila straight up would be best, but rum would be all right, or vodka—even beer."

"Whoa there Ricos, I'd love to have a beer with you, but I think that's a bad idea, don't you?"

"It is, every way you can look at it. That makes it all the more tempting. If it's a bad idea, I'm on it double."

"Forget it."

"Just a few beers?"

"No, Pard. Don't make me take a chainsaw to you."

When he finally made me laugh, I felt a couple of degrees less desperate.

CHAPTER 24

"Morton and William made bail," Barney said, "but I guess you were there."

"Yep." I had been there, sort of.

"There are two things about that, Ricos. One, where did they get money for an attorney? Did you know they had an attorney?" He didn't give me time to say I knew. "Number Two, they made bail. Those guys couldn't have made bail before so what does that say?"

I gave him a blank stare. My focus was you-know-where.

"It says they stole that truck for Sotol, that's what it says. Where else would they get four thousand dollars and another two or more for an attorney?"

"You're saying their bail was twenty thousand each?"

"Yeah, is that some stupid shit or what? You were there, weren't you?"

"I was, but I wasn't paying attention. What is wrong with our judge?"

"You aren't asking me for a list, are you?"

"No. I already know ten or twelve things wrong."

Our judge is sharp as an eagle's talon and at the same time, feeble-minded. He knows the law well, but often seems to resent it or will put his own weird spin on it. He is in his late sixties and nearly always crotchety, but sometimes he shows so much heart it moves a person to tears. He appears to detest all law enforcement personnel, with a special dislike of deputies. If he can do the smallest thing to make life easier for us, he won't.

"I think we should keep an eye on Morton and William," Barney said. "Now they need money like never before. I bet they plan to steal another truck."

"We don't know for sure they stole the first one."

"True, but what does your gut tell you?"

"They stole it."

"Exactly."

"When you say 'keep an eye on them,' what are you thinking?" I asked.

"Spying. Just like your new pal, Agent Fillmore."

"It would be convenient for us if he'd keep an eye out for them too, while he's waiting for Diego to cross the river."

"Sure, that would be nice, but he doesn't care about our problems."

"Look Barney, Fillmore is doing his thing, if he's doing anything. We have to keep doing ours. Let's take a drive over to the river to see who's in Paso."

"Isn't there a bounty on your head? Should you be anywhere near Paso Lajitas?"

"I want to know if Diego is there."

"Ah, truth. You don't care if lowlifes steal every truck in Terlingua, do you?"

"Right now I don't. I'm going. You're coming with me, aren't you?"

"Since you have that ready-to-smelt-steel look on your face, sure, of course I'm coming. I wouldn't think of missing it."

"Don't even start."

"Okay, okay. I'm with you, Batgirl."

When we passed my father's store I groaned. "What is my papi going to say?"

"He'll see you as his little girl in trouble. I doubt he blames you for any of it."

"He'll think I used bad judgment and start lecturing me. He has a way of saying the same thing a hundred different ways."

Barney said nothing.

"I know. You're thinking I used bad judgment too. You'd better not lecture me because I'll jump out of this vehicle."

"You can't do that. You're driving."

"Keep that in mind."

We sat on the rock wall by the highway, looking across the river and passing binoculars back and forth. It was getting dark, and a few men were checking animals in pastures or taking them hay. Others on horseback, or on foot, stopped to chat. Kids were running in the road, chasing a ball and raising dust. People went in and out of the little store but no one we pegged as a criminal.

"Ricos, you never said what you thought of your surplus father."

"I like him. He seems intelligent and better than that, he wants to know me. 'Course maybe not, now that he knows what an idiot I am."

"You're not an idiot."

"Oh yes I am, and it's worse than you imagined."

Barney's brow furrowed. "You know, it's weird. I can call you an idiot, but when you do it I want to defend you. Don't say that again or I'll have to hurt you."

I laughed.

"Huh. I don't see a tall man with braids, do you?" I asked a few minutes later.

"No. What's that about?"

"It's a disguise Diego uses. I thought he was working undercover as a DEA agent. Instead, he was opening up trade routes like frickin' Marco Polo."

"Ricos, you don't know what he was doing."

"I have a pretty good idea."

"Which is?"

"He was using me, and it hurts like hell. In fact, part of me can't believe it."

I was going to say more, but Morton and William pulled up to the crossing in their truck and sat there.

"Things are about to get interesting at the border," Barney murmured.

The boatman waited to see if he had another fare, but when nobody exited the truck, he called it a day, beached his johnboat, and walked towards his house.

Fifteen minutes more and it was dark. Fifteen more and a large truck approached the crossing on the other side. It was too dark to see the color, but we knew what it would be if we could see it. Within seconds, two men got out and came to the bank. One lit a cigarette and his bling flashed in the blaze of a match. I was shocked by the intensity of the hatred I felt for that man.

"I guess you know what this means," Barney said.

"They've come to make a deal on another truck."

"That's what I'm thinking."

A flashlight came on and then we saw Morton and William fording the river for their rendezvous. It was bad boys joining forces with much badder boys—mean monsters that could eat them alive.

"Once our guys cross the center of the Rio, they've violated their bail agreement."

"Yes," I said, "but do we care? I'd like to get them on something big. I don't think the judge will like it much that they're stealing trucks for a Mexican drug dealer who so far has killed three people here, including a teenager."

"Yeah, combined with all those B and Es, they'll do a lot of time."

"I wonder if they know how much danger they're in dealing with a man like Sotol," I said.

"Knowing those two, I'd say they've been too lazy to think it through."

After ten minutes, Sotol drove away from the river. Morton and William came towards our side, flashlight bobbing erratically. They made it back to the U.S., got in their truck, and left.

Barney stood and stretched. "Let's go home. Haven't you had enough criminal activity for one day?"

I agreed that I had.

Before we left, I looked up. There, the stars ruled the night, not the criminals.

* * *

I sat on my porch watching a dark desert and listening to the sound of my phone not ringing. The weather had warmed again, typical of October, but I had to wear jeans instead of shorts, and a jacket was needed at night.

Craig and Marine silently joined me. He sighed, as if he knew what was on my mind, but he had a way of being there without being intrusive. Maybe he was waiting for me to give him the nod to go back to Paso Lajitas and kill bad guys. In theory, it seemed like a great idea, but there were too many ways it could go wrong.

I needed to run, but I would have to use a flashlight, and it felt like that would make me a moving target. I resented being made to feel afraid in a place I had never felt fear, dark or not. I willed my phone to ring, but wondered if it did what I would say. What was there to say?

My phone remained ominously silent.

CHAPTER 25

On Monday, Barney was on a tear about Morton and William. I thought it was wrong to steal and worse to do it to benefit a lowlife like Sotol, but it was hard for me to get worked up about it since I was worked up about so many other things.

He was convinced the duo would try to steal another truck soon and wanted to watch them. That's how we came to be sneaking around on a hill overlooking the Terlingua Ghost Town Monday night.

Dressed in plain clothes, we parked a good distance away and approached from the rear. Climbing cactus-covered hillsides in the dark is no fun, but we were rewarded with a good view of Morton and William's home and just about everything else. It's interesting the things you see when people don't know you're watching.

For about an hour, all we did was observe people come and go from the Starlight Theatre and from the houses scattered around. In the light spilling from The Porch, we saw a couple kissing behind a van. Not only are they an unlikely match, they're married to other people.

William came out, walked a short distance, and looked around as if he'd lost something. Then he surprised and made us ill at the same time.

"Jeez," groaned Barney, "what's he doing? He's takin' a piss in plain view."

"Yep, I believe he is."

"Decent people shouldn't have to watch this, Ricos. We aren't paid enough."

"Hey—this was your big idea, not mine."

"You want these guys as much as I do."

That wasn't technically true. Who I wanted was Sotol and his sidekick, Ruben. Who I wanted, above and beyond everyone else in the world, was Diego. My brain laughed and belittled me but my heart was sure. My heart had never been anything but sure of him from the first time he touched me. Was my heart defective?

"We could use Morton and William to lure Sotol onto American soil," I said.

"Are you nuts? The man is a murderer, and besides, he has a bounty on you."

"That's why I want him. Don't you want to bring his reign of terror to an end?"

"I was hoping the Texas Rangers would get him. He would chew us up and spit us out. The Rangers are more equipped to deal with criminals of his magnitude."

I didn't say anything, but I disagreed.

Barney wouldn't let it rest. "Aren't you afraid to have another run-in with him?"

"Well sure, but I'd be prepared this time. Last time I was unarmed."

"So you'd shoot him or what?"

"I'd arrest him. But if I had to, I'd shoot him. You should give us some credit, Barney. We're trained. We're brave."

"Do you think I'm brave?"

"Yes, I know you are."

At that moment Morton and William came out and got into their truck.

"Holy crap! This is all wrong." I couldn't believe it. "We're here and our vehicle is way back there. One of us should be here and the other should be waiting at the road. How could we be so stupid?"

"We aren't stupid—maybe a little over-zealous is all."

We hurried down the hill, jumping and stumbling over low-growing cactus.

"I do feel like Barney Fife right now," Barney admitted.

"At least you aren't called Barney for nothing."

He swiped at me and yelled, "Gomer Pyle!"

When we reached the bottom, we broke into a dead run. We threw ourselves into the Explorer, laughing and gulping for air.

"I hope nobody saw us," he gasped.

I tried to whistle the Andy Griffith Show theme, but I was laughing too hard.

We wound around the back roads with Barney driving as fast as he dared. When we reached the highway he turned to me. "Now what?

"Let's see if they went to La Kiva."

"Do you think they'll try to steal something there?"

"I don't know, but they'll need a drink for courage before they steal anything."

I guessed correctly; their truck was there.

"Nice going, Ricos. What now?"

"Now we wait and watch."

It hadn't been difficult to figure where they'd go. Once they left the Ghost Town there wasn't another bar, and I couldn't think of any other place they would go. Bars were the only businesses open past nine.

Barn parked the Explorer in the shadow of a storage shed across the parking lot from the bar.

"We lucked out this time," he said, "but we'd better get our shit together."

"Yep. I agree." He didn't know how badly I needed to do that. If I didn't, I would be drinking again and not just a little.

"Next time one of us will watch their place, and one of us can wait below."

"We should use our own vehicles so they don't recognize us," I said. "If one of them sees a Sheriff's Office Explorer, they'll get a heads up. Not to mention other people yapping."

* * *

In about an hour, Morton and William came out of the bar. They looked in vehicles and tried doors. When someone else came out, they acted like they were talking, but when the person drove off, they went back to it.

After another five minutes they left together, either having not found what they were looking for or losing the nerve to take it.

We followed them at a discreet distance until they turned into the Ghost Town. We waited a while at the entrance, and then drove up to and past their place. The lights were on inside, the truck was parked in front, and it appeared they were home for the night. We waited another thirty minutes until their lights went off.

"Do you think they're gay?" Barney wondered. "They're always together and they live together. They do everything together. I never see them with women."

"If you were a woman, would you go out with either of them?"

"Nah."

"There's your reason. Women aren't interested in them. They're dirty. They're dull. They're losers with a capital 'L'. My take is that they formed a friendship based on mutual laziness and a desire to have something for nothing. Kind of an 'I'm going nowhere, do you wanna go with?' sort of deal, you know?"

Barney laughed. "You kill me, Ricos. You have a take on everybody, don't you?"

"Well, you asked. I'm giving you my opinion."

"And what do you think makes us friends?"

"It's the same thing, but in reverse. We're cool. We're capable. We're going places. If I say, 'I'm gonna kick ass' you beg to come with."

* * *

The next night Barney waited on the nameless Ghost Town hill and I waited by the highway in my papi's truck, which he had loaned me for the mission. At nine-thirty my new cell phone rang. It seemed a lifeless thing without the hot text messages and constant calls from Diego.

"They're on the move," Barney said. He was breathing heavily, so I assumed he was scrambling back to his truck.

"They're headed towards Lajitas."

"I'll be behind you, but I don't want them to see my truck," he said. "They'll recognize it, and that might make them suspicious."

"Want to go with me in Papi's truck?"

"No, go ahead. I'll call you when I hit the highway."

He called me again ten minutes later. I was a mile or two from Lajitas.

"Listen Ricos, don't do anything but observe. You got that?"

"Right. Where do we meet up?"

"Watch where they go because they are up to something. I'm sure they aren't headed over there to eat at the Ocotillo." That is the resort's expensive gourmet restaurant.

"Maybe they have hot dates since they started flashing money around."

"Yeah, right."

"I know. Forget it. Until those guys clean up and develop personalities, even money can't buy them love."

He laughed and then said, "Don't hang up."

"Are you nervous?"

"Hell no, I just want to talk to you."

* * *

"I see their truck, Barney. They're perusing the vehicles parked at the hotel. I'm in the lot beside the spa. They won't see me. Even if they recognize the truck, they'll associate it with my dad and not with me. I hope."

"What are they doing?"

"They're driving up and down the parking rows behind the hotel. You should see some of these rides. There's a Porsche I'd like to have and several Mercedes sports models. There are SUVs and great big trucks you wouldn't believe. Uh-oh, they just spotted a shiny new truck."

"They're going to steal a truck since they have to pass whatever they steal across the river," Barney surmised.

"That makes sense. If they put that Porsche in the water, I'll have to shoot them on the spot."

"What are they doing now?"

"Checking out the truck. Morton is standing beside it as if it's his. It'd be great if the alarm went off. I know it has one. It's a beautiful King Ranch Ford 4x4 dual cab. People from the city use their alarms, I hope."

"I'm about five miles away."

"Good. Someone is coming across the lot. Oh."

"What? Speak to me, Ricos. What do you mean by that?"

"A woman is getting into the Porsche. My God, that's the shortest skirt I've ever seen in my life."

"It figures I'd miss this."

"I thought I had short skirts, but I guess I don't. Morton has noticed her, too. He's acting like he's looking for his keys. What a riot. I wonder what she thinks about this ratty-looking guy looking for keys in the parking lot of this high-priced resort."

"She'll think he's some eccentric rich guy."

"She probably isn't thinking about him one way or the other. She's heading your way, Barney."

"Maybe she'll break down and need my help."

"Sure. You can hope. The guys are moving. I'm going to pull out of here as soon as I see where they're going."

I started the engine and waited. "Okay, they've turned towards the Trading Post. Why don't I come pick you up?"

"Meet me at the water plant, on the dark side of it."

"I'll be right there."

"There goes the Porsche," he said. "That woman flat out moves. I should stop her. She's speeding and I'm a deputy."

"Of course she's speeding. Why else would a person have a car like that? Could you try to stay focused on what we're doing?"

He made a smart retort, but I picked him up anyway and we headed towards the Trading Post with our caps pulled low, as if that would confuse anyone. Barney sat as far down in the seat as he could, which made me laugh even more, and I said, "A man as long as you needs to fold in more places," but he just gave me an angry look.

We drove by the Post, saw that their truck was there, and kept moving. For a while we waited in the parking lot of the Ocotillo. We couldn't see the front door of the store, but we would see when they got in their truck. When they did, they headed down a steep dirt road that goes to the river by a rough, seldom-used back way.

"They're going to meet with Sotol again," Barney said.

"Let's do a drive-by," I suggested, but I knew he wouldn't go for it.

Rather than kill people, we went to the rock wall to observe. On the Mexican side of the river, three men got out of Tom Thomason's truck. We heard bits and pieces of conversation, but it was too broken up to understand anything. Soon there was clanking and banging, and we thought—well I thought for a heart-pounding moment—that we were going to catch Sotol on the U.S. side. Of course it wasn't him, but sometimes you believe something is happening because you want it to, like hearing your phone ring.

Barney reminded me that the third man was the boatman getting the rowboat from its mooring. After a string of loud, colorful cursing, there was a big splash and then more metallic clattering. For a split-second headlights flashed, illuminating a figure as he stepped into the boat.

A flashlight bounced onto the river from the American side, then the beam held steady; Morton and William were guiding the boat to shore. Sotol was a cold-blooded murderer and a crass, cruel man, but he wasn't stupid enough to get caught on American soil. He might return, but it would be later, secretively, if he ever did.

Morton and William got into the boat and were rowed across. When the doors of Tom's stolen truck opened again, they got in. There was the flash of light inside the truck and then a match or lighter and the now-familiar gleam of jewelry. It went back to being dark except for the red glow of several cigarettes.

"He has more bling than a rap star," Barney

commented.

"This waiting makes me crazy."

"Quit fidgeting."

"I can't help it. It's hard to sit here while those guys are plotting."

"Patience, Ricos, at least we know they're plotting. We'll be ready for them."

"I wish I could hear what they're saying."

After what seemed like most of the night, our suspects were rowed back, got in their truck, and pulled away. Twenty minutes had passed.

We didn't move until we saw the taillights of Sotol's stolen truck disappear on the road to San Carlos. If he was going back tonight, then Morton and William would not steal anything now. It could've meant 'no deal' and there would be no more truck thefts, but we didn't believe that.

I drove Barney by the Ford to show him what Morton and William coveted, back to his own truck, and then we headed home.

As I pulled back onto the highway, Barney called. "What do you think, Ricos?"

"I think they got their instructions from Sotol, and now we'd better be on the ball. Or maybe Sotol has what he wants and doesn't want to deal with them anymore. I'm sure they frustrate him."

"What does your gut tell you?"

"I don't trust my gut anymore. It has seriously failed me."

"If it was working again, what would it say?"

"That they're going to get him another truck."

"Do you think they'll try anything tonight?"

"I don't know. I sure would like to go to bed."

He yawned. "Yeah, me too."

"I don't think it'll be tonight because Sotol headed back to San Carlos. Maybe he left the job to someone else, but I doubt it. We could waste a lot of time thinking of different scenarios, but I think we should go home."

CHAPTER 26

The next morning I picked up my phone to see if it was working. It was.

I arrived at work early and started coffee for Barney, took a bottle of orange juice out of the fridge, and went into my office to study my hill.

By the time the visitor came, I was sitting at my desk. I checked my e-mail for a message from Diego. Probably the FBI already knew I didn't have one. The front door opened and soft footsteps approached.

"Hello?" I called.

A high school student, Beto Valdez, appeared in the doorway to my office.

"Hi Beto!"

"Hey."

"Have a seat. Why aren't you in school?"

He sat and stared at the floor. "I didn't go to school because I needed to talk to you. I don't want anyone else to know what I'm going to tell you."

"Okay, but realize that depending on what it is, I may be bound by law to tell."

"I don't care if *you* tell people, but I don't want to."

"What is it?"

He fidgeted and kept glancing at me out of the corner of his eye. "Well, uh, um, I saw Luis last night. They released him from jail; I guess you know. He came to the window of my bedroom around midnight and wanted me to help him break into his room. He thought I was small enough to get through the window."

He paused and I had to encourage him to go on.

"My ma was drunk and passed out, and my dad is away. Everybody was sleeping except me."

"What happened?"

"He wanted me to get his clothes for him and a book he'd hidden money in."

"Did you go?"

"Yes, and I got the stuff he wanted and we came back to my house. I told him he could sleep there, and he started to cry. He said he's afraid because he knows about the murder, and those men will kill him like they did Adolpho.

Beto wrung his hands and looked back and forth between them and me. "The truth is he helped kill that man."

He looked up at me with a desperate expression. "He had to. He had to or they would've killed him, too. I told Luis we should call you, but he's afraid. I told him you would understand and protect him, but he wants to run away to someplace they won't find him."

"Do you know where he's going?"

"No. I don't think he knows yet. He said he has to go where people won't know him. But he wanted me to tell you some things. First, he asked if you'd explain things to his mother. He'll try to call her when he gets wherever he's going. The important thing to tell her is that he didn't want to kill the man. Also, he asked me to tell you that Sotol killed him because he didn't want to do business with him anymore."

"Do you mean the man didn't want to do business with Sotol or Sotol didn't want to do business with the man who was killed?"

"The man from Austin didn't want to have anything to do with Sotol anymore. He told him he wasn't buying again, that he was done. Sotol is too sloppy and takes chances, and he said Sotol was ruining the business they had worked for by stabbing the Martez family in the back."

"I see."

"Rita, do you think they'll kill me for talking to you?"

"No. First of all, they don't know you, and they don't know Luis talked to you unless you start telling people. Nobody knows you're here, and you should be careful not to tell anyone. I won't say your name to anyone except Barney unless I have to. We're trying to catch these guys and when we do, Luis will be out of danger, and you can both quit being afraid."

"Will Luis have to go to jail if he comes back and tells the truth?"

"I can't answer that. There are mitigating circumstances, and I'm sure those will be taken into consideration. He might have to go for a while, but it wouldn't be for a long time in my opinion."

"What about me?"

"What about you?"

"Would I have to go jail for talking to him?"

"Who says you talked to him? And anyway, you won't

go to jail for being the friend of someone who does wrong."

"Okay." He seemed relieved. "I gotta go. Oh—one more thing. Sotol is an American citizen. Luis told me to be sure I told you, but he doesn't know his American name if it's different."

"If he's an American citizen he can be extradited. It's good to know."

I stood and hugged him. "If you think of something else to tell me, be careful how you do it. E-mail me and tell me when and where to meet you. Don't tell me anything important in an e-mail because it's not secure."

"Okay. Bye."

"Thank you for coming to me, Beto."

"Sure. See ya."

About ten minutes later Barney came dragging in and went to the coffee. "Sorry I'm late, Ricos. It was a hard night with our children. Is anything happening?"

I took my usual position in his visitors' chair and related what Beto had told me. We were talking about that when an attractive woman about my age came in and introduced herself as Debbie Whitson. She was the woman from the Porsche.

"I was engaged to be married to Bill Hayfield," she explained.

"Ms. Whitson," Barney said, "we're so sorry for your loss. Please sit down." He shook her hand, introduced himself and then me.

"How can we help you, Ms. Whitson?"

"Please call me Debbie. I came to see what I could find out about Bill's death. I thought maybe if I could see where he was when he died I could get a grip on it."

She began to choke up and a few large tears rolled down her cheeks. She wiped them away with the back of her hand until Barney handed her a tissue.

"I spoke with Sheriff Duncan, and he said he would let you know I was coming. Maybe you'd take me to see where Bill died, and tell me what you know."

"Yes, we can do that," I said.

"I have a lot of questions that haven't been answered. I've tried talking to the Texas Rangers, but they won't tell me anything. They say they don't know much yet. I don't know how true that is."

"What do you want to know? We'll tell you what we

can," said Barney.

"Were you there w-when he was found dead?"

"Yes, we were called to the scene."

"They said he was found in the river but not drowned."

"That's true," I said. "He died of a massive overdose of cocaine."

"Was he in pain, do you think? Was he dressed?"

"I don't think he felt any pain. He'd been running, we believe, and was dressed in shorts and a t-shirt, running shoes and socks."

"But they said he had broken bones."

"It looked like the murderers tried to force whiskey down him, and he fought back," I explained. "His little finger was broken in the fight."

She was crying softly.

"It was over in a short time," Barney said. "He struggled too hard for them to make the whiskey and drugs accidental death idea work, so they gave up and injected the cocaine. He was killed instantly."

I could see that she was suffering at the thought of his pain. "Debbie, if it helps, he looked peaceful, as if resting from his run."

She recovered a little, enough to speak again. "I looked for the place last night, but it was so dark, and I don't know my way around. I had instructions but when I got to the motel, I thought I had it wrong. Even if it was right, I didn't know what to say to them. I looked at it a while, and then I went back to my room."

"If you want to go there, we can take you."

"I don't think I can accept it until I see how it was. Does that sound crazy?"

"No," we assured her; it didn't.

Barney called the motel and got permission to enter the room. They were willing, and informed him it had been cleaned and looked like the others now.

When we stood with her in room six, we told her about the things he had purchased that would be turned over to her when the investigation ended. She sat in a chair at the small table and closed her eyes, tears rolling down her face. She didn't move for a long time.

"I don't guess he's here any longer," she said at last.

"I think if he was going to hang around, it'd be with you in Austin, not here," I said. "There'd be no reason for him to stay. He was in love with you. Why would he stay in a motel room far from the love of his life?"

That seemed to satisfy her, and she said she was ready to leave. "I just wanted to see," she sobbed, "where he died."

We left the key at the office and led her back to the Explorer. When we returned to our office, she came in with us.

"Do you think the murderers will ever be caught?"

"We can't promise that," I said, "but many people are working on this case. I know the Rangers aren't forthcoming with answers, but it's the way they work. Keep in mind that they have a good rate of success in solving murders and bringing killers to justice. Give them time. They're putting the case together on a lot of levels. He's murdered others, too."

"You mean Sotol?"

"So you know his name."

"Yes, I know all about him. Bill didn't want to do business with him since he'd broken away from the Martez family. Being associated with a renegade is risky. He told Sotol he didn't want any part of it, but Sotol wasn't going to let it go that easily. He had all that stolen cocaine, and he was counting on Bill to buy it. Bill was loyal to the Martez family, and he didn't want to deal with Sotol except as their emissary."

She stopped to wipe her eyes and blow her nose and then continued. "Bill was naïve in some ways. He should've left in the night and never looked back."

"Debbie, do you know Emilio Martez?"

Barney shot me a look, but I was undaunted. I wanted to find out what I could.

"Sure. He's a friend of ours. He's professional and a man of his word. Bill let him know what was going on, but Emilio couldn't move fast enough to stop Bill's murder."

"So he didn't order Bill's murder?" I asked.

"Oh no. He and Bill have done business together a long time and trust each other. He helped me arrange Bill's funeral, and he's paying for it. Emilio has been looking for Sotol. If he finds him before you do, you won't need to."

"So Emilio would eliminate him?"

"Yes, and his partner, Ruben Villanueva."

"So Emilio is a murderer."

"Ricos—" Barney tried to save me from myself, but it was too late for that.

"Well, he's a member of a large drug cartel, so yes, he

is. Sometimes people have to be dealt with. Bill did it too when he had to."

A lump the size of Cimarron Mountain stuck in my throat and silenced me.

"You two have been so kind," she said. "I can't thank you enough. I guess I'd better be going."

We walked her to her fabulous car, being cool, as if we saw Porsches every day. I was anything but cool. My life would never be the same. It felt over. Barney told her to take care and promised to call if we found out anything more.

"It's a small world," Barney commented as we walked back into our office. "Who would have guessed we'd meet the beautiful Porsche woman? Now I feel guilty for wanting to see up her skirt."

On a different day that would've gotten a rise out of me, but I couldn't even manage a smile. I plopped into his visitors' chair.

"He lied to me, Barney. I guess he lied about everything."

He didn't need to ask who.

"He came to get his drugs and then he looked around for a gullible hick from the edge of Texas which it turns out I am. He found out how I discovered the drugs, and he knows we're watching, but he knows how vulnerable this area is—how remote and defenseless. And he knows we can't sit at the river and in fact are almost never at the river. He knows that when we're off, there's nobody on duty, just one of us on call. He knows our backup is eighty miles away, and he knows where I live and even where you live. We talked about some places where it'd be easy to cross tons of drugs, which is exactly what he intends to do. So I helped him, Barney, that's what I'm sayin'. I hope he's having a laugh over that, because the way I feel about it, I might shoot him myself."

"Well, damn. What changed?"

"I've been thinking about nothing else and remembering innocent little things we said in passing—or my part was innocent. I thought I was helping a good lawman figure out where lowlifes might be crossing, and instead I was helping a lowlife. So yes, I feel like an idiot and my heart is broken, and my life is over."

"I'm sorry, Ricos. I thought you had found somebody special."

"And you know what the worst thing is? He flew me

around and wined and dined me and all with money earned from drugs. And he knows how I feel about them, how much I resent what the cartels have done to Mexico. God, I'm so pissed." I began to pace. "I'm still not going to help the FBI kill him."

I paused, but not for long. "In spite of everything I just said I'm in love with him. I can't turn it off like he's a faucet I left running. And I can't believe he's evil. The man I know is so different. I think about how it was between us, and I just don't see how he can be the same man."

"Everyone has good and evil in them. Maybe you brought out his goodness."

"How would I do that?"

"He fell in love with you, Ricos. That's what I think. He fell in love with a woman outside his world, and now he's between a huge rock and the proverbial hard place. It must be a terrible place to be."

"No, he's not in a hard place. He's dropped out of my life."

"I bet he hasn't."

That was when the sheriff called to tell us about Ms. Whitson's visit and to ask about Morton and William. Barney blabbed our whole plan. I couldn't believe it.

"I'm coming down there right now," barked Sheriff Duncan. "You two sit tight and I'll be there in an hour or less."

Barney didn't have much choice but to agree. Then the sheriff cut the call.

"Barney! Why did you tell him?"

"Well, he asked what we were doing, and he wanted to know if we had any more info about the truck that was stolen. I can't lie to the sheriff."

"Of course you can. Besides, you don't have to lie, just omit certain things. He's the boss, and employees are expected to lie to their bosses. It's the American way."

"Now he's coming to kick our asses."

"I'm sure he has other reasons for coming."

"Such as?"

"Maybe he wants to ride in the Porsche."

He didn't; he wanted to kick our butts. He never mentioned the Porsche. We had to listen to him tell us we were doing a dangerous thing, and he should have been told about it, and he went on and on the way bosses do.

"It's a good idea," he said and surprised us. "I should

have thought of it. It's good, with one big exception."

"What's that?" asked Barney.

"We should use a set-up vehicle and involve the Texas Rangers in our plan."

"We don't need them," I said.

He frowned. "I believe we do. They're trying to get this Sotol character. It's their case, if you'll recall. I suppose you're going to waltz across the river, grab him, and bring him back over here yourself?"

"Maybe," I said, "but I wouldn't waltz. I was trying to think of a way to lure him to this side so we could nab him. Barney and I aren't afraid of him."

"Well you should be afraid of him," snapped the sheriff.

Barney gave me a look that said *shut up right now.*

"What do you mean by a set-up vehicle?" I asked.

"I mean we bring a vehicle that's attractive and leave it with the keys in it or at least leave it open so it can be hot-wired. You know what I mean. We can't stand by and let Morton and William steal a tourist's vehicle right under our noises. What if they got it to Mexico and it was never seen again? We can't have our office involved in that. If you see someone stealing a vehicle, you'd damn well better stop them."

"I see your point," said Barney, the ass kisser.

"We have the perfect truck at the county impound. It's a new Chevrolet, fully loaded, 4X4. It even has those fancy rims that twirl around."

"Spinners," said Barney.

"It was used to haul two hundred pounds of marijuana across the border five months ago, and I don't believe the drug dealer who owns it will ever see it again. I can get that down here tomorrow, and we'll set it up near the river with the keys left in it. Maybe the Trading Post would be a good place to leave it."

After the sheriff let the truck talk rest, I gave him the information I'd gotten earlier. "Luis Garza sent me a message today. He's hiding in fear for his life. Bill Hayfield was murdered because he no longer wanted to buy from Sotol since he's broken away from the Martez cartel. Luis was forced to participate in the murder. Also, he was insistent that Sotol is an American citizen, for whatever that's worth."

"Who brought you this information? Is it from Emilio Martez?"

"No, it's not from him, but I'm not at liberty to say who.

I have my sources."

"Margarita, I'm the Sheriff of this county and—"

"Yes sir, and because you are, I'm sure you know sources are crucial to the work we do, and if I give them up then I no longer have those sources."

He looked at me a long time. "Is this a source you trust?"

"Yes, or I wouldn't repeat anything to you."

"You believe in it enough to call the Rangers?"

"Yes."

"Ask for Sergeant Martinez. He's the one heading up the investigation, and I imagine he wants Sotol as much as you do."

That was unlikely.

Sheriff Duncan went on to explain that he'd send the decoy truck later, with an undercover Ranger. He expected Sergeant Martinez to be involved. Someone else would come with him, either another Ranger or a state trooper. They would ride around, show off the truck, and try to catch the attention of Morton and William. The hope was to catch the local boys and Sotol at the same time.

I had questions about his plan but kept them to myself. I guess what bothered me most was that it was being taken away from us—again. I wanted Sotol for personal reasons—not a good thing in law enforcement—but that didn't stop me from wanting him.

The Sheriff went to play golf after making it clear we were going to do things his way.

"We should've known golf would be involved in his trip," I said.

"You're gonna get us in trouble with that mouth of yours," grumbled Barney.

"*Me?* You're the one who blabbed everything."

"Let's not fight. We get the evening off."

"With our luck, this'll be the night those idiots make their move."

"If they do, it won't be our fault," Barney pointed out. "The sheriff told us to back off and that's what we're doing."

* * *

That night I was helping my father paint his store when I received a call.

"Deputy Ricos?"

Because the caller spoke Spanish, my heart skipped a

beat. "Yes, speaking."

"José here," he whispered.

My heart sank. "Yes José."

"Señora, van a pasar otra troca."

"They're going to pass another truck?"

He told me in an excited jumble that Sotol and his sidekick were back with another man nobody knew. They were drinking beer in their truck, an older one with Mexican plates, and going to the river every twenty minutes to look.

José said when he passed them Sotol stopped him to brag that he was getting a new truck tonight, better than the first one. I thanked José for calling me and stood looking at the phone. The Sheriff had told us to wait for his sting operation, but they were doing it now, or that's what it sounded like.

I called Barney, who took so long to answer I thought he wasn't going to.

"This better be good, Ricos."

I told him what I knew.

"Call the Sheriff because we're going," he said. "Can you pick me up? I'll be dressed by the time you get here."

"I'm on my way."

I was still speaking with the sheriff as I pulled up to Barney's. He remained calm when I told him Barney and I were headed to the river to stop a truck theft in progress. He wanted to argue, but I reminded him that we couldn't ignore a crime; he had said so himself. There was nothing he could do but agree and wish us luck.

CHAPTER 27

Barney flew out his front door tucking a wrinkled uniform shirt into his jeans. A pair of night vision binoculars on a strap bounced against his chest. He was wearing a faded red Terlingua Ghost Town cap and sneakers without socks. He looked thrown together, but he still had me beat. Paint splotched my old cut-offs as well as the long-sleeved white blouse I reserve for house cleaning and yard working. A battered and abused pair of river sandals completed my handywoman look.

"What did the sheriff say?" Barney asked as he climbed in.

"He said to be careful. Where'd you get the binocs?"

"I borrowed them from a friend a few days ago. You're kidding about the sheriff, right? All he said was to be careful?"

"He doesn't like it, but I pointed out that we couldn't ignore a report of a crime going down. He had to agree after that little rant he pulled yesterday."

"Huh. Is he coming?"

"No."

"Is he sending back-up?"

"Not unless we call for it. It would take back-up more than an hour to get to the river from Alpine, so we're on our own."

"I'm having trouble believing this after all the fuss he made yesterday."

"What can he do, Barn? He hired us, and he did a lot of our training. It'd look bad if he had no faith in us. And if that was the case, he'd get rid of us."

"It's the 'getting rid of' I want to avoid."

"He knows we can handle this. He didn't like it that we were tailing Morton and William without his knowledge. It's okay if it's his idea. You know how old men are."

He made a fake pouty face. "Poor old sheriff can't get no respect from you."

"I respect him plenty, but he does have his ways."

"Do you think you'd be a better sheriff?"

"Oh, hell no."

He chuckled. "When the sheriff hired you, did he say

small town work is rewarding and that things are usually tranquil in Terlingua?"

"Yep."

"So he lied to you, too."

I laughed. "It wasn't a lie; how would he know it would get like this?" A few miles whizzed past. "Would you want to be the sheriff?"

"Nope."

"Well then, I guess the old guy would heave a sigh of relief to know that."

Barney smacked me with his cap.

We were traveling fast—my favorite way—with the lights on but no siren. There was little traffic, and the few cars there were pulled over when they spotted the lights.

Barney kept looking over at me.

"What?" I looked down to see if I was missing a piece of clothing.

"You're unarmed?"

"What do you think?" I patted the console. "You think I'd leave my piece at home when I'm dying to shoot that murderer?"

"Ricos, if you in-real-life killed somebody, I don't think it would be as great as you think. I bet it would wear on you."

"I didn't say I was going to kill him, only disable him enough to drag him back to the U.S. Maybe Agent Fillmore would accept Sotol as a peace offering."

"Fillmore wants the big-dog criminals, not the little ones. No offense to Lover Boy."

It was hard to imagine spicy hot/sweet Lover Boy as a "big-dog criminal." I tried, but my brain spit it out in my face.

"What were you doing, anyway? Painting your house?"

"I was helping my dad paint his store."

He sighed as if life as we knew it was over. "I was making love to my wife."

"I'm sorry, but that's a small price to pay for the glamorous job you get to do."

He shot me an angry look I ignored.

"Take heart. You'll have another chance to make love to your wife."

"That's what you think because you don't have a three-year-old and a one-year-old living at your house."

"You say when and I'll watch them for you. It's not like I have a life."

My pity party was interrupted by the ringing of my cell phone. The sudden noise made both of us jump. Barney grabbed it off the seat and answered.

"It's José," he informed me, "calling to say that a truck is being passed right now." Then he spoke to José again. "We're almost there. You go home and stay there, and keep your family in. Thanks for calling."

Barney flipped the phone shut. "It looks new, José says, but he has no proof that it's stolen. He was trying to tell me something else, but the reception was breaking up and then we got cut off."

We arrived in Lajitas, and I clicked off the lights and slowed. We swung into the Ocotillo's parking lot to take advantage of its bird's eye view of the river. Headlights were already halfway to the other side. A vehicle appeared to be stuck there but it was hard to tell.

Barney scanned the river through the binoculars. "Let's go. It's our bad boys, and they're hung up on something."

We took our vehicle as far as a dirt path that goes to the river and left it at the bottom of the hill by a stand of tamarisk. We were still a little way from where they were crossing, so we hurried, stumbling in the ruts.

Long pants would have been nice, and I wished I'd taken the time to change before charging off on my white horse. The breeze off the river was cool, and we had to shove and smack our way through thickets of mesquite and other thorny plants that stabbed at my legs.

After about twenty yards, we came to a narrow clearing along the bank. We stood still and quiet while Barney again studied the scene through the binoculars. My cell phone vibrated, but I ignored it. Whatever it was would have to wait.

"They do appear to be stuck," he whispered. "It's the same truck they were looking at Thursday night. What idiots."

"Do you see Sotol or anyone else you recognize?"

"People are waiting on the bank." He kept watching. "Yeah, that's him. I can tell by that gaudy bling. He's with what's-his-name with the missing fingers."

"Ruben."

"Uh-oh, the truck is moving again."

My cell vibrated but I ignored it again. "We can't stand here and watch these guys steal this truck. But if we jump out there and make them stop, we'll lose Sotol."

"Not to mention we might get shot," Barney pointed out.

He was still watching through the binoculars. "Yeah, light that cigarette, jerk. That gives me a real good look at your ugly face. Okay. What're we gonna do, Ricos? Bad guys are up to no damn good and the good guys are watching; now what?"

The stolen truck's front wheels were now on the Mexican bank, headlights blazing into the bushes. People moved back and forth in and out of the light.

"I think," I started to say when there was a gunshot and an agonized scream. I was halfway across the river, which was up to my waist; it made the going slow. Barney was right behind me.

"Stop! Police!" I yelled. My pistol was out in front of me, but there was too much confusion to take a shot at anyone.

Then there was another shot, and at first I thought they were shooting at us. Then I saw the body on the bank, motionless.

"Stop! Police!" Barney yelled in his booming voice.

Another shot blasted into the night, and a bullet whined past us. Barney fired a warning into the air. *"Manos arriba!"* he roared, but no hands went up.

Men darted around yelling at each other in Spanish. A truck started and then headlights blinded us. It backed up in a cloud of dust and was gone in a second. The new Ford truck sat at the edge of the river with the motor still running and the lights on, but we saw no more movement near it.

When we got to the bank, William was sprawled there with a hole in his forehead; it was a sickening sight. Barney spit, "Hell," with feeling, and began to move around the truck, gun held high, wary of someone sneaking up on us. Everyone had gone.

"Over here," he called.

Morton was crumpled in the mud looking at us with frightened eyes. He'd been shot in the chest and looked bad. His face was white and pinched-looking, and his breathing was strained and shallow. I dropped to my knees beside him and took his hand while Barney called 911 for the ambulance.

Morton struggled to speak. "So—So—"

"Rest," I said. "The medics are on the way."

"So—So—"

"Are you trying to tell us that Sotol shot you?"

He managed a slight nod.

"Yeah, we figured as much," Barney grumbled.

"Why did he shoot you?"

Morton tried to answer my question then closed his eyes instead.

Barney patted his hand. "It'll be okay, just rest and don't worry."

I stood. "Let's get this truck back to the U.S. We can put Morton in the back seat. Look—there's tarps back here." I began getting them out of the bed.

Barney helped me spread a couple of them out, and then we lifted Morton to the seat. He appeared to be unconscious.

We took another tarp, spread it on the bank, and lifted William's body onto it. We carried him to the bed and laid him there. Since we were dripping wet and muddy, we draped a tarp across the front seat as well.

Barney asked me to drive because I'm more familiar with the crossing, thanks to my papi. We had no problems and were back on the American side within two minutes. Barney went to get the Explorer while I stayed with Morton.

I nearly jumped out of my skin when he spoke. "Wha—bout—Will?" Every syllable sounded strained.

"I'm sorry to tell you, but William is dead. He was shot in the head."

"Bastard!" he groaned with more passion than I had ever heard from him.

"Yes," I agreed.

Headlights approached the river on the Mexican side, followed by more. I scrambled out of the truck, moved to the passenger side, and waited with my weapon poised. Both trucks stopped and several men got out. I could tell by the talk that they were local guys, not the thugs. They were looking around to see what happened and were horrified by all the blood.

My phone vibrated again and I answered. José was anxious to tell me that someone overheard Sotol say he was going to kill the two gringos. That's what he was trying to tell Barney earlier.

I explained what happened. He said Sotol and his entourage left town in a cloud of dust and skidding tires. We had witnessed that escape.

Barney pulled up in the Explorer. "Well, at least he didn't get the truck," he said as he joined me.

"That's a small consolation."

"Yep; instead of gettin' the bad dude, we have a dead

guy and an injured one."

"I—die—too." Morton's breathing was rattley, wheezy.

"No. You're not going to die," Barney assured him.

"So—tol—did—not—want—to—pay—us," Morton said. "He—kill—me—too."

"The medics are coming, and you'll be fine," I said.

"No." He gasped and the rattley wheezing stopped.

"Morton?" When he didn't answer, Barney checked. "He's gone too."

We stared at each other.

"This makes five murders by the same sick sonofabitch," Barney fumed. "These guys didn't deserve to die over the stupid stuff they did."

"They didn't know who they were dealing with. They were nothing but petty criminals trying to make a quick buck. Morton and William were scumbags, granted, but they didn't deserve this."

"Don't speak ill of the dead, Ricos."

"Sorry." The wail of the ambulance siren announced their approach, which made me think of our boss. "I guess I should call the sheriff."

"Yeah, before he thinks the medics are coming for us."

Sheriff Ben assured me he wasn't sleeping and had been waiting to hear from us. He was relieved to hear Barney and I were unharmed.

He asked if Morton and William had been armed, and I told him I doubted it. They could've been and were relieved of their weapons, but it was unlikely. They were lazy opportunists who took what they wanted, but they weren't killers. Because of the sneaky, non-violent way they operated, they probably never felt the need to arm themselves.

Mitch and another medic arrived on the scene. Mitch hugged me and rubbed my back. "Thank God you weren't hurt," he whispered.

I rested my head against his chest a second. "I'm okay," I insisted, even though I was a long way from it. I wondered if he knew I had chosen the wrong man.

Mitch left to take the bodies to Terlingua, where they would await transport to Midland by hearse. Barney and I took the truck back to the hotel in search of its owner. He was one of the mid-level managers of the resort, Roger Lawrence, and he was grateful that we had saved his new truck. We explained about his tarps and offered to bring them back but he declined.

"You should inspect your truck for damages, and let us know if you find anything to report," Barney said.

Roger ignored my partner and seemed more interested in my wet clothes.

Barney moved between us. Sometimes he knows exactly what to do. "Roger, I'm trying to talk to you about your truck."

"Yeah, yeah, I heard what you said." He paused for a beat and added, "Thanks," which I assumed was because of the look on my partner's face.

"I'll just wait for you in the vehicle," I said to Barn.

"Sure. Go ahead. I'll be right there."

Roger started to come after me. "Hold up. I'd like your phone number."

Not happening.

On the way home, we talked about the latest incident from beginning to end, venting our frustrations at the outcome. We had saved a truck, but other than that the evening was a depressing failure.

I'd had about all the stress I could take. "Could I get time off, Barney? I know I have to talk to the sheriff, but I want to be sure you don't have anything planned."

"When do you want it?"

"Tomorrow." I laughed at the look on his face. "I guess I could wait a few days."

"You aren't flying off to meet Lover Boy somewhere, are you?"

"No. I think Lover Boy has turned back into Cartel Boy. I was thinking of going on the river by myself a few days to think and lick my wounds."

"I have no plans. If the sheriff says you can go, then go."

For a long time we were quiet, each with our own thoughts.

"Could you speed it up?" Barney blurted. "I want to finish what I started before the babies wake up."

CHAPTER 28

My plan was to spend two days on the river in an inflatable kayak, taking nothing but camping essentials and a notebook. The Rio Grande is a healer, and Santa Elena Canyon intensifies its power; I needed a mega-dose. According to several river guides, the water was high enough for a kayak, but still too low for a raft.

Craig agreed to protect my house, although what I hoped was that it would protect him. He didn't think I should go on the river alone. Under other circumstances, I would have invited him along, but I didn't want to have to be good company, even for someone as undemanding as Craig. I felt almost desperate to be alone for a while.

Barney took me to the Lajitas Crossing put-in point in his pick-up before he went to work. He eyed the Mexican side suspiciously, but even the boatman wasn't there yet.

"I don't like this, Ricos," he said at least a dozen times.

I was getting ahead of any commercial trips that would follow, so I could take my time and still have backup for going through the Rockslide rapid. It's what its name implies, and can be tricky at almost any level but often treacherous at low water. If a raft or kayak gets stuck in the maze of boulders, you have to get out and stand on slippery rocks to free your boat. It's safer to have others around in case of injury or other mishap.

"Aren't you afraid to go alone?"

"I'm never afraid on the river. What's to fear?"

"Bandidos, wild animals, or drunk college kids for starters. And what about river guides?"

"College kids are in college. Rafters don't carry much money, so the river doesn't attract bandidos, and wild animals have never bothered me before, so I assume they won't start. I can handle river guides."

"I still think it's a bad idea. Do you have your phone?"

"Yes, but it won't work once I leave Lajitas, so don't expect me to call."

"What if I told the sheriff it's an emergency, and I need to go with you?"

"Well, for one thing you'd need your own kayak. Mine is

made for two, but with a big man like you and gear, I don't think it'll float."

"Is that an insult?"

"No. I'm stating a fact. We'd need a lot more food and water."

"And beer."

"Yeah, well see? I don't have any beer."

"Okay, but it seems wrong to go on the river without beer."

"Yes. It does to me too, but I need to be able to think."

Barney's protests grew weaker, and soon I had pushed off and was waving to him from the middle of the river. There, I was half in the U.S., half in Mexico, and I liked it that way. I was raised in both countries and love them equally.

On the river, peace reigned. Turtles were sunning themselves on rocks or logs along the bank. Some held their ground as I glided past; others freaked out and nose-dived into the water. For a while a family of ducks followed me, quacking and demanding a handout.

I released a long breath of heartbreaking, he-done-me-wrong, no-hope-for-the-future blues, and breathed in the damp, cool, morning smell of the Rio Grande. It raised the serotonin level in my brain, and then a miniscule fire of hope for the rest of my life began to burn. Ten minutes into a river trip and things were looking up.

The muted colors of sunrise had left the cliffs, and the sun was doing its best to warm the day. Soon I passed a herd of goats drinking from the river and a shy goatherd waiting in the shade of mesquite and tamarisk brush. He squatted and drank water from an old-fashioned canteen. His cap was pulled low over his eyes, so it was hard to tell if he saw me, but when I waved he waved back. I slowed to watch baby goats drag their long, silky ears in the water as they drank.

In another few hundred yards I would round a bend and leave all signs of civilization. Ahead I could see a pair of great blue herons poking in the shallows near the shore. I didn't see the men watching me with binoculars from a hill on the Mexican side. Therefore, it surprised me when two guys stepped out of the brush just before I got to the bend in the river that would've taken me away from them.

Surprise is the wrong word. I was terrified. They had automatic rifles aimed at me and told me in Spanish to stop. I considered not stopping. Dying in the river wasn't the worse thing I could think of and didn't seem so bad for half a second. In the next half-second, I thought about being twenty-six, and how sad it would be to give up my life without a fight.

One of the men took aim. I steered to shore, willing to take a chance that I might get out alive. Craig wouldn't be saving me this time. I was on my own.

"We're not going to hurt you," claimed one of the men, but as soon as I was on the shore they covered my head with a black hood and handcuffed me. I figured him for a liar. All sense of safety, even the hope of it, left me. They lifted me, one on either side, and carried me through brush. It whipped at my face and legs, stinging and making me itch. The rough men made me want to cry.

"Can you ride a horse?"

"Yes."

"We're going to set you on one. We're seating you behind Felipe so don't panic. He isn't going to hurt you."

I had no faith in their promises, but what was I going to do? I tried a question. "Where are you taking me?"

"To a helicopter."

"And then?"

"To a man who wants to see you."

"Is this a man I know?"

"I don't think you do. No more questions. You'll know everything soon enough."

I thought if I knew it in the next second it wouldn't be soon enough, but I stayed quiet. Felipe smelled like spicy aftershave, cigarettes, and leather. Someone removed the handcuffs, but before I could appreciate freedom, each hand was cuffed around Felipe and then to his belt, forcing me to hug him. I had to lay my cheek against his back or have my nose mashed and possibly broken by the movement of the horse.

"Hang on," he said when we started to move, and then he laughed. "Don't be shy." I wanted to bite him.

We rode to what I supposed was a path and then we began going uphill. I thought I knew where we were headed—to a bluff overlooking Paso Lajitas, where there was the perfect landing spot for a helicopter. I was right too, not that it made me any freer or less frightened. They removed the handcuffs, lifted me in, and fastened me to a seat. A man sat on either side of me in a tight fit.

Once we were in the air, and I was confused about

which direction we were headed, they removed the hood. There were two men in front, two guarding me in back. My first impression was that they were all goons who worked for a drug cartel. Talk about jumping to conclusions. Still, I jumped. I was sure they were taking me to a Martez stronghold, but had no idea if that would be Monterrey, Chihuahua, Cancun, or south of Mazatlán. One of the men offered water or soda. I chose water.

If Diego had sent for me in this way, I would kick his ass all over Mexico. I began to seethe, but at the same time, I wanted it to be him. *Please let it be him.*

"Are you taking me to Emilio Martez?" I asked.

"You wish."

Yes. I did.

They had a laugh at my expense, so I stayed quiet, but I thought I was right and relaxed a little. No matter what else Emilio/Diego might be, I didn't think he would hurt me. That someone else in his organization might didn't occur to me then.

We were headed south, judging by the sun. I didn't know if the men thought I couldn't figure it out, or if it didn't matter, or if they had only meant to terrify me with that hood. I stayed quiet on the subject because I didn't want to wear it again.

In spite of my silence, the hood was replaced after an indeterminable amount of time passed. The men talked about fútbol, horse racing, nightclubs, and women. They gave no hints about their employer.

When the chopper landed, I was cuffed again but to the front, which is more comfortable.

"It won't be long now," one of the men said when I was lifted out. I didn't know if that was good or bad. Not long until what?

The breeze was brisk but smelled like a city, not the sea and definitely not the mountains. The air was cooler than where I had been. I was wearing shorts, a bikini top, and a long-sleeved shirt. I was underdressed for whatever awaited me and that alone was terrifying. But not one of the men had touched me or hinted about it, or said anything about my clothing or lack of it. To me, that said Emilio had sent for me and they didn't dare.

We were on a helicopter pad on top of a building, maybe a house. That part was hard to tell and didn't matter anyway.

Soon we were descending in an elevator, but it was a short ride. Then we walked, a door opened, and I was told to sit. I had to trust there would be something there. It felt like a sofa.

We waited—or I waited; I thought I was alone but couldn't be sure. When I lifted my hands to the hood to peek, a voice across the room said, "Don't do that, please."

After a while a big commotion entered. "Take those handcuffs off her right now, Armando," a man barked.

As soon as my hands were free I buttoned my shirt. Nobody stopped me.

"And a hood?" He continued admonishing his flunky."What were you thinking? Do you think?"

The angry man's Spanish was distinct and elegant, but something about him was malevolent. For one thing, he was barking orders and for another, there were five goons in the room who looked ready to jump out the window if he so ordered.

The man was short, good-looking, in his fifties, and dressed in expensive clothes. He had the air of royalty. He sat across from me and dismissed all but one of the men guarding us. I guess I didn't look intimidating enough for five.

"So this is the famous, fabulous Margarita Ricos," he said. I wasn't sure if he was making fun of me but assumed it.

"I'm not famous."

"Let's say I've heard a lot about you. Do you know who I am?"

"No, but I assume you're Emanuel Martez, Emilio's father."

"What makes you think so?"

"You have a helicopter and a lot of bulked-up men guarding you."

He chuckled and then studied me a while. "You are correct. I understand my son wants to marry you and you've agreed."

"Does he know I'm here?"

"No. He does not."

"I don't believe he intends to marry me."

"You're wrong, Señorita Ricos. He very much wants to, but there are only two ways that can happen. One is if you fully understand what being married to him will entail and agree to that. The other is if he runs away with you and you're able to successfully hide from me for the rest of your lives. I believe that is what my son intends, so I've brought you here to talk you out of that option."

"Shouldn't your son be here?"

"He's indisposed."

"In what way is he indisposed?"

"He's unable to join us."

"Where is he? Is he hurt?"

"It's touching that you ask. He's unharmed, but he's being held against his will, I'm sad to say."

"By you?"

"Yes, by me."

"But why?"

"With all due respect, señorita, this is between my son and me."

"Is he far from here?" I suddenly wanted to see him like I never had. He hadn't abandoned me. He was being kept from me. The man seated in front of me now seemed more sinister than handsome, and his son looked nothing like him.

"Señorita Ricos, this is between us and does not involve you."

"I don't mean disrespect, but if you're keeping him from me, it does involve me. I thought he had abandoned me, but that's not true, is it?" *You cold sonofabitch.*

"No. If he had his way, he would have gone to you by now, but the FBI would have grabbed him. If that happens, he won't see the light of day again—if they don't kill him in a feigned accident before he goes to trial."

"He's not stupid. He knows the FBI wants him. He wouldn't have come to me in the United States no matter what."

"Señorita, do you understand that we are the Martez cartel?"

"Sí señor."

"And you understand what that entails?"

"Sí."

"Are you willing to give up the life you have for a different kind of life? It will be a lavish life, and you'll never want for anything, nor will your children. However, you come from a law enforcement background, and I wonder how it will set with you."

"I'm unwilling to talk about this without Emilio."

I must have had a face full of stubborn because after studying me a long time, he decided to cooperate. "Very well, I'll send for him."

I wasn't about to tell him his son and I planned a different life from the one he envisioned for us. I also didn't correct his use of *señorita*. A woman who has been married is *señora* even if she's young and even if her husband is dead. To mention it would be like letting him further into my life. Not happening.

"Bring Emilio," he ordered the man guarding us. "Would you like something to drink?" he asked me.

"I'd like a soda."

"Do you mean a cola or soda water?"

"A cola would be fine."

He picked up a phone and called a servant with instructions that included glasses of ice and cola for three and cookies. He added that there would be three for lunch. After that, he spent a long time talking to a secretary over an intercom. It gave the impression of him as a busy businessman, but I couldn't think of him like that.

Two men came with Diego—I still thought of him as Diego. He was walking with a limp and his face was marred by bruises. He had been hard to subdue.

I jumped off the sofa and went to him. Two men tried to stop me.

"Let them be," Martez, Sr. said.

"Oh, Margarita," Diego sighed. He looked unbearably sad.

My hug caused him pain. He didn't complain, but I felt him wince.

I was near crying. "Diego," was all I could manage to say.

"How'd you get here?" he asked, then took in the shorts and river shoes and turned to his father. "You had her brought here, didn't you?"

"I wouldn't have come dressed like this." I indicated my clothes. "And I don't know where this is."

He hugged me to him. "At first I thought you'd come to rescue me," he whispered, "and my father captured you." He spoke in English, and it angered the elder Martez, but I soon learned that he spoke the language in a limited way himself.

He told us, in English, to be seated on the sofa, and then he dismissed the men in Spanish but asked them to wait in the hall.

"Padre, you're giving my soon-to-be wife a bad impression of our family." He returned to Spanish. He took my hand as he spoke.

"Whose fault is it, Emilio? What choice did I have but to send for her?"

"You couldn't have invited her like a normal guest? So she could come dressed for the occasion? How do you think she feels? She must have been terrified." He took off his shirt and gave it to me, exposing more bruising on his arms. I wrapped the shirt around my waist to make a sort of skirt.

"I apologize," said Emanuel Martez. "It never occurred to me you would come of your own free will."

"Of course I would. I wanted to meet my future in-laws." But now I wished I never had.

"Did they grab you while running, or were you on the river?" Diego asked.

"What difference does it make, Emilio? I had her brought to me, but she refuses to speak without your presence."

"How did you know where I would be?" I asked.

"You can thank your Federal Bureau of Investigation for that. They've been tracking you, and we've been watching them. They could learn a few things from us."

"I don't think Margarita is impressed by your espionage skills, Padre. You answered her question. There's no need to preen and strut."

There was a knock on the door, and when instructed, a woman in a maid's uniform came in with a tray of refreshments. She wasn't acknowledged and began setting up on a sideboard. She wordlessly served me a plate of cookies and a tall glass of soda on ice. Then she served the father, and last, the son.

"Will that be all, señor?"

"Yes Dorothea, thank you."

The smell of the cookies made my mouth water. I'd had nothing to eat, thinking I would enjoy a breakfast of fruit and energy bars on the river.

"What do you hope to accomplish?" Diego asked his father.

"I want to explain to Señorita Ricos how things will be if she marries you. I don't think you've been truthful with her, Emilio. I want to hear you tell her what we do for a living in the Martez family."

"She knows what we do."

"All of it, Emilio. I know you haven't told her all of it."

"Please don't do this, Padre."

He studied his son the way a rattlesnake watches its prey. "Tell her, son. Tell her what you do."

I didn't want to know, but the old drug lord was going to force me to hear it. Diego looked so pained it hurt me.

"It's okay," I encouraged him, "You can tell me anything."

"This is cruel, Padre, even for you."

"Tell her and you'll feel better."

"Margarita, I love you." He spoke to my hand. "I never expected that. Loving you changed everything for me. Suddenly I knew I couldn't keep doing the things I was doing. You make me want to be a better man." He looked at his father, then at me. "My father scoffs, but he's always scoffed at me."

"Tell her Emilio, or I'm going to."

"I lied to you, Margarita. I have killed people—more people than I've counted. It had to be done for one reason or another. Someone stealing, someone suspected of stealing, someone being insubordinate or getting in the way, someone who didn't pay on time. I've done terrible things. The FBI has me on their most wanted list with good reason. I deserve to die, but I want to live. For the first time since I realized what I am, I want to live. I don't want to kill anymore. I'm willing to walk away from Martez money and power, but I'm not being allowed to walk."

He glanced at me, but his attention returned to my hand. "If you agree to marry me we'll be married, but we have to live here in the Martez compound. And I have to continue to help the family. I have to do whatever my father tells me. I will no longer be allowed to go to the United States for fear of capture."

He looked at me then with tears rolling down his face. "I want you to leave. That's what he wants, too. You're from outside and he scorns your clean way of living and your work. In different circumstances, he would have you shot. Please hear what I'm saying, Margarita. We can't be together. It's impossible. I regret with all my heart having dragged you into this. I never meant to."

"Well done, son."

I wanted to kill that old man. He had himself surrounded by thugs so he could piss people off and keep on living.

Diego spoke again. "Tell him you'll go home and never see me again, and he'll return you today. You won't be harmed."

"What about you?"

"I stay here. Someday I'll be released from house arrest and continue my work. I'll never bother you again."

"That's not what I want."

"What do you want?" the father from Hell inquired.

"I want to be able to speak with your son about this in private. I want to marry him, but I don't think I can live the Martez cartel way. I have parents and friends in the United States, and I'm not going to give them up and stay here sequestered the rest of my life."

"You don't have to give them up. You misunderstand. You may visit them as you wish. If you interfere in the Martez business in any way, you'll be eliminated and so will your husband."

"You would kill your own son?"

"I do what I have to do, señorita. I doubt you want any part of this."

No kidding.

"Since we're being so fucking honest," growled Diego, who had never used a curse word around me, "why don't you tell her the truth about our relationship?"

The older man glared at him but said nothing.

"I'm not his son," Diego continued, "and he's never forgiven me for being another man's bastard. He's made my life hell, and that of my mother. My mother killed herself when I was ten because of him."

"Your mother was unworthy of the Martez name."

"Yes, because she had a heart."

"That's enough, Emilio."

"My mother had to turn to another man for love and comfort."

"I said that's enough."

"I'm not through," Diego said, but for a moment he and the elder Martez only glared at each other.

"You could let me go," Diego pleaded.

His father said nothing.

"You're doing this for spite. You never loved anyone so you don't think I could love someone the way I love Margarita."

"Spare me the emotional *chorradas*. You were married to the perfect wife, but you willfully ruined what you had."

"I didn't love her. And we've driven this subject into the ground."

"There's more to a successful marriage than love."

"I feel sorry for you."

"You needn't."

"I have four brothers to carry on your work, and they have your blood in their veins. Why can't you be satisfied with that?"

"Emilio, we've had this conversation before. You know the details of our business, and you're smarter than your brothers, better suited to it."

"But I'm not suited to it at all!"

"You could ruin us with what you know."

"But I won't. I don't care what you do as long as you let me go."

"You could tell what you know to the FBI. I'm certain you could go back to the United States if you made a deal to help them catch me."

"I'm sure you're wrong."

"You're on their Most Wanted list, but they would want me more than you."

"Maybe so, but you're not a U.S. citizen; you never go there. That's why I'm on the list and you're not on it too."

"Regardless, you know too much, Emilio. You could destroy us."

"I would never hurt my whole family like that and you know it."

"You would do anything to hurt me."

"How can you say that? I have no desire to hurt you. All I've asked is freedom to marry the woman I love and to live where we choose and in the manner we choose."

"Yes, Emilio, and all of us here know it isn't that simple. And you don't know for sure if this young lady wants to marry a murderer and a narcotraficante."

They looked at me.

"I'd like to speak with Emilio in private."

"I will not allow that. Anything you have to say can be said to both of us."

"In that case I have nothing to say."

"Very well, then. Jorge, will you show Señorita Ricos to her room?"

"Wait—"

It was too late. I was grabbed off the sofa by Jorge, a

stern-looking stunt double for Rambo. A tattoo darkened one side of his face, adding a sinister attribute to a face that didn't need help to be frightening. I thought it was a fire-breathing dragon, but I was afraid to look at him long. I didn't want his company later, in the dark.

In the hall I resorted to begging. "Please, Jorge, don't put me in a room alone. I need to be with Emilio."

He was not without compassion. "I'm sorry, señorita," he whispered. "I'm following orders. If I know Emilio, he'll figure out a way to come to you."

CHAPTER 29

The room was far from being a bleak dungeon. It raised comfort to the level of a five-star hotel, plus a star or two. It overlooked manicured gardens and a beautiful terrace where no one sat or walked. Past that there were tall buildings. Monterrey, I thought. I wasn't blindfolded, chained, or even locked in, but when I opened the door there were two stone-faced muscle men in the hall. One shook his head at me. It was a slight movement, but I got the message.

I had been exploring the opulence for ten minutes when an intercom brought Emanuel Martez's voice into the room. "There are clothes and shoes in the closet that will fit you. You may bathe if you wish. Lunch will be served in about an hour. Please make yourself at home."

Like hell.

I bathed on the off chance I would get to spend time with Martez, Jr. I couldn't think coherently, nor could I explain how I could still be in love. Look up "stubborn" in the dictionary. It reads: willful, pigheaded, obstinate, strong willed, hardheaded, mulish, example: Margarita Ricos.

The clothes were too fancy for my tastes, but I dressed in purple palazzo pants and a blousy shirt in a lighter shade of the same color. I felt tempted to wear the sexy high heels but instead chose practical sandals. What I needed were running shoes but there weren't any. Escape was on my mind.

* * *

Rambo came to escort me to lunch. I made a mental note of every door we passed and every window. I would've counted steps, but he kept talking to me. I wasn't interested until he stopped, cleared his throat, and spoke in a low voice. "Emilio is my friend. He asked me to give you this. After you read it, destroy it. If someone else reads it, we will be killed."

I took a sliver of paper from him. "Thank you, Jorge."

I turned away, although I supposed he already knew how it read. *Mi amor, go home. Tell him you want no part of this. I will figure out how to get to you, but you must go home today no matter what he offers. I love you with all my heart, Emilio*

I put the paper into my mouth and chewed until it was

wet enough to swallow. Jorge gave me an appreciative smile. Then he opened the door to the dining room. I took a deep breath and stepped in.

Seated across from each other at the largest table I had ever seen were Mafioso Martez and his heartbreaker son. A frosty silence hung in the air and I was sure they had been arguing. Diego appeared somehow worse and wouldn't look at me. I wanted to attack the old man who was all smiles and courtesy once I came into the room.

"How lovely you are! *Sientese, señorita.*" He indicated a chair next to him. No way would I sit there and play nice.

"I'm not going to sit, Señor Martez. I can't eat here."

He smirked at his son. "Do you understand now, Emilio?"

Emilio did not speak or acknowledge any of us.

"I would like to return home. I won't bother you or your son again."

"How quickly you give up, Margarita. I would have thought a fiery, outspoken American woman like you would have a lot more fight in her."

"I would if we were fighting fair, but what will fighting with you accomplish? You have everything stacked in your favor."

That angered him. "Jorge, please return the señorita to her room. I'll have lunch sent there."

"I don't want lunch. I want to go home."

"Padre, you said you would let her go."

"I need to think about it. I may have spoken too soon."

"You promised me. You can't keep her here against her will!" Diego jumped to his feet but still didn't look my way.

"How arrogant you are, Emilio. Of course I can do whatever I want with her. You're here against your will, aren't you?"

"Are you going to keep us here under guard the rest of our lives?"

"You would be together. Isn't that what you want?"

"I want to go home," I repeated, starting to feel panic.

"What if I let you spend tonight with my son?"

"Are you serious?" I asked. "Or are you torturing us?"

Emilio turned to me. It was the saddest look I ever saw. He didn't speak, and I wondered if he wanted me to stay. Then I remembered his note, *you must go home today no matter what he offers.*

"If I torture you, you'll know it, señorita."

The younger Martez slammed his hands on the table with so much anger the heavy wood shuddered. "Padre!"

The older one didn't apologize. "I'm sincere in my offer to let you stay with my son," he said. "I'm not an unreasonable man."

"I need to go home."

"All right; home it will be." He glared at his son and didn't look at Jorge as he addressed him. "Jorge, escort the señorita to the helicopter and wait for me there. Emilio and I will come to say farewell, but there is something I have to do first."

Jorge grabbed me by the arm and hurried me out, practically dragging me.

"I should get my clothes and leave these."

He gave a negative shake of his head.

"But these aren't mine and—"

"No." He pulled me towards the elevator. When the doors shut, he reached up and removed two bullet-proof vests from behind a panel. "Put this on," he whispered. "Can you run?"

"Yes."

"When we get to the roof, follow me. We have to move fast."

"But—"

"Please trust me. It's our only chance."

I nodded, even though I didn't have a clue what was going on. This man had said he was Emilio's friend, and my instincts said that much was true.

When the elevator opened, I followed him across the roof at a dead run. We ran past the empty helicopter and climbed down a service ladder that took us into a maze of air-conditioning units and other machinery that didn't register. My attention was focused on Jorge's back. We came out to what looked like the rear of the house. He grabbed my hand, and we dashed across the street as someone opened fire from the Martez roof.

Jorge cried out but didn't stop. A dark red stain spread across the back of his pants at the thigh. We threw ourselves into thick shrubbery across the street and stopped to catch our breath.

I started to ask if he was all right, but Jorge silenced me. *"No todavía,"* he mouthed. Not yet. With his hand, he motioned for me to stay while he forced his way through the shrubs to the front of them and tied a red bandana there.

"For Emilio," he whispered when he returned, "so he knows we're out." He took a deep, shuddering breath. "Let's go!"

"But you've been hit."

"We'll be getting it in the head if we don't go."

"Lean on me," I suggested, but he didn't.

We began to run again, following the line of shrubbery through several yards and on and on until we were in a commercial area full of storage units and construction equipment. Jorge opened a door and threw himself into an old Ford Bronco that had been stripped of its roof. He cried out as his leg hit the seat. I dove into the backseat and lay still, trying to get my breath.

Jorge took a key from his pocket, started the engine, and we roared away. As we did, I looked out the back. Two men burst into the lot carrying automatic weapons. They fired and the noise was terrifying, but we were out of range by then. It felt like I was having a nightmare after a night of heavy drinking, but I couldn't make myself wake up. I squeezed my eyes shut and opened them, but I was still there.

After a while, I crawled into the front seat. Jorge looked pale and was sweating. Blood was everywhere.

"Let me drive," I said.

He was hauling ass through whatever town we were in. He ran several red lights and then stopped at one. "Can you drive fast?"

"That's the way I drive."

"I can't stop yet and anyway, you don't know the city."

"You can direct me."

"The helicopter was going to explode," he said hoarsely as we lurched forward.

"What? How do you know?"

"We have to get far from here and then I will explain. Up here, we're going to change vehicles. Then you drive."

He parked the Bronco on a downtown side street and we ran several blocks to a parking lot. Jorge dragged himself in a limping gait and his breathing was labored. It was scaring me. He collapsed against a pick-up, struggling to get his breath. Then he opened it with the automatic button on a key ring he fished from his pocket. The truck was newer than the Bronco, but it was still an older model.

"Please get in," he gasped.

I got behind the wheel and watched as he pulled an automatic weapon from behind the passenger seat. Then he got in and handed me the key. "Pull out and go left to the light, then left again."

He was now sweating profusely and his eyes were glassy. I thought he was going to pass out. Instead, he shut his eyes and let out a long, impassioned string of curse words. *Hijo de la chingada* (loosely translated as "son of a bitch") was the least of them. When he ran out of filthy words and curses in Spanish, he threw in a few choice ones in English.

"You need a doctor, Jorge."

"Not yet. We have to get out of here."

I had hundreds of questions but held them because he began yelling instructions. "Don't stop at that light, but you have to stop at the next one. Slow down! But not too much! If a traffic cop gets after us keep going. Don't stop for anything. Most of the cops here are Martez cops, if you know what I mean. Everyone is terrified of him." He sighed and leaned against the headrest a second. "Damn, this hurts like a fucking, bitchin' whore of a motherfucking bastard. Son of a bitch!"

I started to ask a question but again he started directing. "Run this next light; just hit the horn and keep going. The one after that, turn right and floor it until you come to the next intersection, which will be about a mile." He tried to turn around in the seat but groaned and remained facing forward. "Check the mirrors. Do you think we've been followed?"

"No. I've been watching."

"I know they're coming," he said in a voice that made my blood freeze.

I had turned right and floored it. People were trying to cross the street from shop to shop, but I hit the horn and kept going. I could drive like this all day, but I would have preferred not to feel so terrified. My hands were trembling.

"So you had this escape planned," I correctly guessed.

"Yeah, ever since I got in the cartel. This is the first time I've had to use it."

Jorge reached under his seat and brought out a bag. He put a cap on his head and pulled it down tight. "We're going to have to change clothes. Pull into that big parking garage ahead on the right."

We had to stop for a claim ticket. "Pull in up there in that dark corner, get out, and get re-dressed, and don't forget the vest. I won't watch, but anyone else who comes is going to." He handed me a bundle of clothes. It was a uniform that was too big but workable. Except wearing sandals with it looked weird, and I didn't think it would fool anybody.

As he spoke he was putting on a uniform shirt, but his had a badge that read: AFI, Jorge Alvaréz. The number of questions I had doubled.

"Up on the next level," he instructed, "is a black Dodge Challenger. Here are the keys. Get it and bring it, please. I would go but my leg is killing me. And please stop for me. If you don't, it will be the same as murdering me, you understand?"

"Of course I'll stop for you."

"I'm sorry. I—I just don't trust anybody anymore."

"I know how you feel."

I ran to the next level and didn't have to look around long for a Challenger, the best ride in the place. It started with a powerful hum. *Oh, baby.* I drove it down to the next level and stopped for Jorge, who was sagging against the truck, his head down.

He got in and collapsed against the headrest. "I need water," he groaned pitifully, and in the next breath, "What are you waiting for? Let's get out of here. Just go straight through that barrier, turn left, and haul it."

I was behind the wheel of a Dodge Challenger. Nobody had to tell me to haul it. The parking lot barrier cracked like dry twigs as we sailed through it.

"Martez wasn't going to let you go," Jorge said suddenly. "I should tell you I'm with Agencia Federal de Investigación, AFI. It's a federal agency that was set up in 2001 to fight corruption and organized crime, similar in some ways to your FBI. On this case we're working with them. It took me three years to get where I am in the cartel, and I just lost my position and have a bullet in my leg."

"What was your position?"

"I was in the inner circle. It was a difficult place to get and avoid doing killing for hire. Go right up here then left. Among other things, I now protect Emilio Martez. The thing I never expected was to become friends with him. He's not your average cartel—but back to Martez, Sr. Now go left three times and you'll be on Avenida Hidalgo. There won't be any stop signs or lights for at least a mile after that."

He took a deep breath and kept talking. "Martez, Sr. can't let you marry his son because he can't control you. He was dismayed when Emilio told him he was in love with an American woman, not to mention one in law enforcement. Imagine how that hit the old gangster. He's not stupid. Emilio is no longer cooperating and he blames you, so what's left but to eliminate you and hope that Emilio will get back on board? I hate to tell him, but that ship sailed. Emilio has had one foot out of the cartel ever since I've known him."

"How do you know the helicopter was going to explode?"

"I'm in the inner circle. I told you that. Except nobody was supposed to tell me about the bomb because the old man thought I'd tell Emilio, which I did. It was going to kill me, too. Emilio knew nothing about it, and of course he asked me to save you—and me. Martez, Sr. had one of his guys rig a bomb with a remote trigger. His plan was to bring his son to the roof and when our transport was a safe distance away, let him watch the love of his life explode in midair."

"Sentimental old man, isn't he?"

"Oh, you have no idea. He loves to overstate a point, the flashier the better. Okay, up ahead the road forks. Bear right and you'll be in the countryside after about two miles. Have you noticed anyone following?"

"No."

"We're going to an AFI helicopter. It's not far now. You'll have to help me get into it, but I can fly it. There might be an agent waiting, but I don't know if he's had time to get there."

"What's going to happen to Emilio?"

"I can't say. It depends. If his father knows he was involved in our escape, I can't say what he'll do. If he blames his men, then he'll kill them. If he suspects Emilio, then he may be killed too."

"He would kill his own son?"

"Emilio is technically not his son. But let's hope for the best. Emilio has dealt with this man all his life, so he can handle him."

"We should go back for him."

"We can't go back. They're hunting us and I'm injured."

"I could go."

"No offense to you, señorita, but you have no idea what you'd be dealing with. And you're unarmed. I can't let you go back. You would be killed on sight."

"You could arm me. I could sneak in."

"How? There's no sneaking into that place. And I cannot legally arm you."

"I don't care about legal. Martez can't legally be armed or sell cocaine or kill people he doesn't like. That doesn't stop him, does it?"

"No, but I still can't arm you."

"You said he would kill all his men. Without them, it would be easy to get in."

"He'll kill them, but not until he has replacements. Again, he's not stupid. And he won't have to replace all of them. The guilty ones may have already jumped ship."

We arrived at our destination and two men with weapons met us. They didn't look much different from the Martez thugs, but I assumed they were good guys based on Jorge's reaction to them.

I continued arguing.

"Don't make me tie you up," he threatened.

"I'd like to see you try it. You're in no shape to do anything."

He rolled down his window. "Gregorio step over here, please."

"Sí, Jorge, *que necessita?*" Gregorio was as large as Barney and ten times more intimidating.

"Margarita, do you see this man? He'll do it if I tell him I need help."

"Okay," I relented, "You've made your point."

"What do you need, Jorge?" Gregorio asked again.

"Will you help me get into the chopper? And keep your eye on this woman. Meet Margarita Ricos, Greg. Margarita, this is Gregorio Taranga. She wants to go back for Emilio Martez."

Greg raised one eyebrow and made a 'huh' sound. We shook hands, and then he reached in, took the keys to my ride, and tossed them to the other guy.

"Daniel will take the car to headquarters after we take off," he said.

Daniel nodded at me in greeting but said nothing.

I was hustled into a waiting helicopter before I could ask questions about anything. Greg insisted that Jorge remove his pants and lean against the open door so he could examine the wound.

"I bet that hurts a lot," he said when he saw it.

Jorge spit a long list of things not complimentary to Greg's mother.

"We'll leave you at the hospital once we get to Chihuahua."

"I'll go to Dr. Salazar after we get Margarita back," Jorge said.

They had a typical man argument involving a lot of inventive swearing as if I wasn't there or wouldn't understand. As he insulted the injured man and most of his family, Gregorio gave us water and got Jorge situated. He was laid stomach-down, covered by a blanket, on a seat behind the two front seats.

"Seatbelt," Gregorio reminded me.

"I don't want to whine, but I don't want to go to Chihuahua. I need to go home."

"You won't be in Chihuahua long. I have to get Jorge back, and then I'll turn you over to the FBI at the bridge in El Paso. They'll take you home."

Panic hit me like an 18-wheeler at full speed. "Please don't do that. I can take a bus from Chihuahua to Ojinaga and someone will pick me up. The FBI thinks I'm aiding and abetting Emilio, and they can put me in prison for being in Mexico, and people won't even know where I am. It could be months before I'm brought to trial if I ever am, and for all you know I'll be tortured, and I don't even know anything useful."

Greg looked around at Jorge. "I told you nobody trusts those guys."

"Listen, Margarita," Jorge said. "They know you were picked up by Martez against your will, and they're going to protect you until—"

"No, Jorge!" Greg cut him off. "You can't tell her anything about that!"

"That's all I can say for now."

"They're going to protect me until when, the end of time or what?"

"Please don't push it."

"I want to know what's going on."

"It's classified information. I'm sorry."

The men stopped talking and were so quiet I felt frightened by what they weren't saying. I decided then that I would get away from the AFI and get home on my own. No way would I let myself be put into the hands of the FBI even if I had to hide in Mexico for a while.

I had no way to know that the FBI had ceased caring what I did. Their Operation Martez was about to close.

CHAPTER 30

When we landed, several other agents were waiting. They were more concerned with Jorge and his injury than with the woman accompanying him. I stood around being quiet and looking innocent while they asked questions one on top of another.

When Jorge began relating the events at the Martez stronghold, I slipped away and walked through the building as if I belonged there. I wandered out the other side and ran as hard as I could towards a highway. When I reached it I kept running.

Before long I saw an ancient pickup pulled to the side of the road, stacked high with hay. An old rancher-type was checking the tires.

He looked alarmed when I ran up to him. *"¿Que pasa, señorita?"*

"Ayúdame, por favor," I panted. "Bad men are chasing me."

"Get in."

In Mexico, women can get anything they want. A man's first reaction is to help a woman, and an older man, like the one I had the good fortune to find, was a certainty. Within seconds, we were headed away from the 'bad men.' I felt guilty calling them that when they had saved my life, but I couldn't trust them to have my best interests at heart just because they were with a government agency.

"You're wearing a uniform," he observed, "but it isn't yours. It's too big."

"Yes. Would you exchange clothes with me?"

"My clothes are dirty, señorita, and too big for you."

"I don't care. I have to change my appearance."

"I can take you to my house and my wife will give you clothes."

"I don't have any money, not even a peso." Yeah, that would make hiding out in Mexico or going home impossible. I tried to stay calm but panic was gaining on me.

"Come with me, and we'll take care of you. Then I'll take you wherever you need to go. Do you have family around here?"

"My family is in the United States. I was captured by criminals and brought here against my will."

"You don't want me to call the police?"

"No. Please don't."

He looked relieved. Mexicans don't necessarily trust government agencies, either.

* * *

The rancher was Alberto Gomez, and he lived in a humble adobe home on the outskirts of Chihuahua. He had a few acres of land, not a ranch. There were goats in a pen, chickens scratching around in the dirt, and a fenced vegetable garden.

Señora Gomez welcomed me with open arms. She looked so much like my grandma that when she hugged me to her, I began to cry. That caused her to hover and call me *mija,* as is Mexican custom. More affectionate people than Mexicans you will not meet.

It never occurred to them that I could be a wanted criminal running from the law. Or if it did, they didn't care. I was a young woman wearing a too-big uniform, and I was a wreck, so they treated me like their own family.

I was fed corn tortillas hot off the comal with fresh asadero cheese. Señora Gomez set salsa and a plate of avocado slices on the table beside me. During that long day I hadn't eaten anything except a sugar cookie and a love note.

My ravenous hunger further endeared me to my new friends. They watched me with real caring in their eyes. It made me want to cry again. These are the kind of people hurt the most by the so-called war on drugs. The vicious cartels don't care who gets in their way, they kill their way past anyone, and often for no reason except that they can. A mental image of Emilio Martez ended that train of thought.

When I had eaten as much as I was able, I asked to use the phone. When I explained that it would be long distance, Señor Gomez waved his hand as if it didn't matter. And it wouldn't. No decent Mexican man would ever stand in the way of a daughter and her parents.

"Papi," I sobbed into the phone when he answered.

"Mija, we've been so worried. Where are you?"

"I'm in Chihuahua Papi, and I want to come home."

"What do you need?"

"I don't have any money for a bus or plane and bad men are looking for me."

"Explain to me where you are and I'll come for you."

"But Papi, you could wire money."

"I would have to go to Alpine for that, and it could take hours for the money to arrive in Mexico. And how will you get it without identification? I know you don't have it because they found your kayak, and your wallet was in the dry box, along with your cell phone."

It felt like I was in one of those nightmares where you have to be somewhere and everything you do is a failure. "Okay, Papi. Come for me, and please bring extra money · because I owe these people who've been helping me. Will you let Barney and Craig know I'm okay? And Mom, too."

"Of course; I'm leaving right now. It'll take me about four hours. Are you safe?"

"Yes, Papi, I'm going to put Señor Gomez on the phone so he can explain where I am. I love you."

"I love you, Mija. I'll be there soon."

* * *

"I thought we had lost you," my papi said tearfully when I met him at the door.

The Gomez couple insisted on feeding us dinner before we left, even though it was past midnight. It was as if they had always been our friends. I was wearing Señora Gomez's clothes, a simple homemade skirt fastened with a safety pin, a plain blouse, and a threadbare sweater. I didn't want to take them because I knew she didn't have any to spare, but all I had to wear was an AFI uniform. They thought their grandsons would enjoy playing with it so I left it.

When we said adiós, I promised to return the clothes. With typical generosity she said I could keep them, but I wrote down their address. I planned to bring them back, along with others, when I was no longer wanted by the AFI or the FBI or the Martez Cartel. Papi left them fifty dollars which they insisted was too much.

"You helped my daughter when she needed it," he said. "No amount of money can ever repay you for that."

"You owe me nothing, señor. I'm glad I was there to help."

* * *

On the way home I tried to explain to Papi what had happened and why. He had already heard the truth of Diego's identity from Barney. He was horrified, as any parent would be, but didn't argue when I said I was still in love with him and feared for his life.

After I told the whole story he said, "We won't be able to cross at the bridge. Won't the FBI have alerted them?"

I hadn't thought of that. "I don't even know if they want me. It's that they were so sure I was aiding and abetting Diego. I'm afraid they'll hold me if they catch me coming back from Mexico. They can say I'm a threat to homeland security, and it could be a long time before I'm released."

Papi scowled at that. "I can take you to the river by way of Paso Lajitas. If there's no Border Patrol there, I'll drive across. If there is, you can sneak across and I'll come back through Ojinaga."

"I can't go to Paso Lajitas, Papi."

"Why is that?"

"There's a fifty-thousand peso bounty on my head."

That made him furious. "How long has this been going on? Why hasn't anyone told me? Why is your father the last to know anything?"

"I'm sorry, Papi. The point is I shouldn't go there."

"So you've made everybody mad, huh?"

"Yep, good guys and bad guys are after me, and I'm afraid of all of them. And speaking of that, what if the FBI is at the river?"

"Why would they be there?"

"They were there before, when the Martez goons took me."

"Then why didn't they stop them?" My father had a look on his face that said he would take on the FBI and they'd be sorry.

"I don't know. Maybe the goons outnumbered them. They don't care if I'm harmed. They see me as one of the enemy."

"How stupid can people be?"

"Pretty stupid, from what I've seen so far. Anyway, I can't blame them for being suspicious. I refused to cooperate with them."

"That's the girl I raised! The Ricos family doesn't bow to government assholes."

"Right, Papi."

"Damn right."

"I'm in a big mess, Papi. I shouldn't have called you."

"Are you crazy? This is the reason God gave you a father."

"True; that's one of the reasons. What I meant is, now I have involved you. They could take away your resident status for aiding and abetting someone they think is aiding and abetting a wanted criminal."

"Let them try. I haven't done anything any other father wouldn't do."

Men like Agent Fillmore would feel differently, but I stayed quiet and tried to think what to do.

We decided to stay in Ojinaga for the night. It was late and we were exhausted. We called my mom so she wouldn't worry.

Early the next morning, I called Barney at his house.

"I guess you don't know this, Ricos, but the FBI is no longer interested in you. It's all over the news that the AFI, FBI, DEA, and a bunch of other agencies with initials I don't remember have taken down the Martez cartel. They killed Emanuel Martez, and arrested the son in charge of his Juarez operation, and another in New York City, and a third in Miami. The fourth son was killed in Mexico City trying to escape."

"Barney, you know I only care about one son. What have they said about him?"

"Nothing; it's assumed he escaped when they stormed the compound in Monterrey but that's unconfirmed. He wasn't among the dead."

"You're sure the old man is dead?"

"As a stump. A bunch of his men are dead, too. I guess when the old man took you the FBI swung into action. The word is they were just a few weeks away from closing in anyway. They've been working on this case a long time."

"Yes, about four years, according to the AFI. One of their guys got me out."

"Your Texas Ranger father told me that. He also said you escaped from them in Chihuahua. That pissed them off. They thought it made them look inept to the FBI." He laughed and made me laugh too.

"They were going to turn me over to the FBI at the bridge in Juarez. I begged them not to, but they wouldn't listen."

"So I want to hear that whole story when you get back."

"It'll make you laugh."

"I figured that. Your extra father has called here about a hundred times, but don't try to call him now. He's gone to the border to help bring back guilty parties. Are you safe, Ricos? You'd better be."

"I am."

"Your papi tore out of here like an avenger."

"I'm with him now. Will you let Craig know that all's well?"

"Sure, I'll tell him. I'll feel better when you're home."

"How will I find out about Diego?"

"I'm sure he'll contact you as soon as he can."

"His whole family has been annihilated. They were all criminals, but they were still his family. I know he loved his brothers."

"I know; that's tough, but at least he's free of his father."

"The only person I know that's as evil as Martez, Sr. is his understudy, Sotol. Have you heard anything about him?"

"Not a peep. I think he's history in this part of the world, and for all you know, Diego killed him and that other guy."

"I doubt it. He's been held hostage by his father ever since he told him about me. I still can hardly believe that he was going to blow me up right in front of his son."

"Yeah, and I call you cold because you shoot off a couple of fingers."

"You haven't seen cold, Barney."

* * *

Later that morning, I bought jeans and a shirt in Ojinaga. Well, my papi bought them. Señora Gomez's clothes were in a bag behind my seat when Papi and I crossed the International Bridge at Presidio, Texas. They searched us, used their drug dogs, but could find no reason to detain us. After wasting our time, they had to wave us through. It was good to no longer be a threat to my country's security.

When we got to Terlingua, I asked Papi to leave me at the office. We hugged good-bye, and I promised to be careful.

He handed me the bag. "Don't forget to send these back to the señora. I doubt if she has a lot of clothes."

"Yes. I know, Papi."

He sighed. "None of this would've happened if you were working in my store."

Papi always has to have the last word.

* * *

Parts of my story did make Barney laugh, but in telling

it I realized how lucky I was to be alive. And I owed a debt of gratitude to AFI agent Jorge Alvarez and to Diego, who saved both of us.

Barney said the sheriff had ordered that I take a few days off to recuperate from the trauma. I thought I needed to work, but I lost patience with everyday tasks and couldn't keep my head on anything. Even my hill didn't interest me.

I gave up after twenty minutes, went home, and took a long bath. After that I took a drive through the national park in my Mustang, trying not to think of what it must have been like in the Martez compound when half a dozen agencies from two governments stormed in. I was also trying not to think about how smooth and warm and comforting a bottle of tequila would be.

Had Diego gotten out or was he among the dead? If I drank an entire bottle, how long would I be unconscious? How would Diego have gotten out? Had he gotten a tip from someone? Wouldn't it be better to start with beer and work up to tequila?

No matter what the subject, I always had more questions than answers. If the mountains had answers, they were stoic in their silence.

* * *

It was dark when I pulled into my driveway. For a moment, the headlights swept over Craig sitting in a chair on the porch with what looked like an automatic weapon across his lap. What? How would he get one?

When I turned out the lights, the porch and everything on it plunged back into darkness, and I thought I had imagined the scene.

As I approached, Craig whispered hoarsely, "I'm keeping watch." He lifted the weapon as if that explained it. I thought maybe he had lost it.

"You should be sleeping." I had a hundred questions but didn't ask them.

Marine popped his head out of his jacket, blinked, then disappeared again.

"Don't be alarmed when you go in," Craig whispered.

"Okay; why would I be alarmed?"

He handed me a note in his own shaky scrawl: *Diego is here. You never know who might be watching. I'm on duty. Don't worry about anything.*

I stared at him in disbelief. He nodded and indicated

with a slight sideways movement of his head that I should go on in.

Diego was lying on my bed. I sat on the edge of it like it might explode under my weight. My heart was pounding so hard it was a wonder I heard his greeting. He pulled me to him and as always, everything else disappeared.

"Mi amor, mi amor," he whispered and held me close.

"Oh, Diego, I love you so much. How am I going to stop?"

"Please don't stop. Please don't."

He cried about the deaths of his brothers, and the fact that he was a wanted man in the only two countries he knew. Then he described the horror of the final moments in the Martez compound. He said the raid was so perfectly executed that at first they thought it was a rival cartel, not government agencies.

He described the deafening sounds of the automatic weapons, how blood had run on the floors, the screams of dying men, and the awful panic he felt when he thought he'd never see me again.

"Jorge saved my life," he said when I asked how he got away, "because I had saved his. He's my true friend, even though he was working the whole time to bring my family down."

We talked and made love and ignored whatever the morning would bring. I chose to ignore the fact that he was a killer. And that he had come from a family that stood for everything I stood against. I chose to ignore that the AFI, DEA, FBI, and the Texas Rangers were hunting for the man holding me. Everyone wanted him, but I had him.

And the part about having my heart shredded by the tragedy that was as sure to come as the winter winds? It was a matter of when.

But it wasn't that night.

CHAPTER 31

Diego left before dawn, accompanied by Craig. I didn't ask him how he'd gotten to me or if this was his big plan—to sneak in and out in darkness for the rest of our lives. Besides, I knew it wasn't and dreaded what his plan would be. I didn't ask him where he was going when he left. I was afraid to know.

As he went out the door, he handed me an envelope. In it was five thousand dollars in cash, a driver's license, birth certificate, and a U.S. passport in the name of Angela Garcia, and a letter.

Mi amor, this is not drug money. I have a legitimate business in Chihuahua. I'll explain later. This is to tie up loose ends so you can meet me in Ojinaga this afternoon. We're going to Cuba if you'll agree to go. We'll come back when things calm down. I can't be extradited from Cuba. I have all the documents we need. Please come with me. I don't think I can live without you.

Don't worry about packing. I'll buy whatever you need. I already have a Cuban bank account. I've been thinking of this since I met you.

There is a room reserved in Ojinaga at the Valentino Hotel in the name of Angela Garcia. Enclosed is a driver's license in that name with your photo and a birth certificate should you need it.

Please be there at 4PM. Leave your car at the bridge and come in a taxi. Bring Craig and he can take your car back. At 5, I'll come to your room dressed as a delivery man. I've been over this plan with Craig, and he thinks it's sound. The question is whether you'll go with me. Please, mi amor, run away with me. I love you so much.

With all my heart,

Diego

As I read, my brain screamed *no, no, you can't* because my heart wanted to go.

I sat on my porch to wait for Craig. I watched light begin in the east behind the Chisos Mountains and grow brighter as the sun rose. Wisps of clouds turned purple then pink and then golden. Sunlight burst onto the land I love, moving mountains, spotlighting spires and crags, then plunging them into shadow. I took little notice. I was going to have to let Diego go, and it was more than I could bear.

* * *

Craig didn't ask to know my decision, nor did he explain how he got Diego to my house or how he got him away or where they went. I didn't ask.

I think he felt the sadness in my heart and already knew my decision. "Let's go to our office," he suggested when he couldn't take my mopey silence any longer.

Our "office" was a crumbling native stone dwelling on Highway 118 on the way to everywhere and in the middle of nowhere. It was three road miles from my house, shorter going cross country. Others whizzed past and never seemed to see the old ruin that was our secret meeting place. This was the building I had tried to claim when I was eleven, where I had declared myself boss of the whole Big Bend. As a child it had been a place of daydreams, games born of my wild imagination, and secret thoughts and wonderings. In a lot of ways, it was still all that.

We stepped over a low window sill into what had once been a bedroom, looked around, and backed out because a wide-eyed barn owl was nesting there.

The wooden frames were still in the windows and doorways of the house, but they looked splintery and buckled now. There were two open doorways in front. We went through one into a space that was once a living room. It held a rusted-out umbrella table without an umbrella and two ancient folding chairs, all of it discarded by my parents and dragged there by me when I was ten.

I positioned the chairs in front of a glassless window so that the wide crack in the distant mesa, Santa Elena Canyon, was framed in it. If you can't be there, the next best thing is to look at it. I sat with my feet up on the old sill, and breathed in fresh desert air and old memories.

I patted the chair next to me. "Will you tell me a story, Craig?" Those were the first words spoken since we left my house.

We had often sat there through the years I was growing up, admiring the view, telling stories, or just being together.

Craig sat. "Shall I tell you the Native American tale about how the canyon was formed?"

"I want to hear the one about the blue of the sky."

The roof of our office had deserted its position long ago and if anything was left of it, it was in pieces out in the desert somewhere. This was the only kind of building Craig tolerated because the view of the sky was unhampered. We leaned our heads back to watch it while he told me the tale I knew by heart.

* * *

I spoke the last line along with Craig. "That's why the desert sky is so blue and it goes on and on forever."

A few seconds passed. "My heart is broken, Craig."

"I know, Little Boss. I know it is. My heart is broken, too."

* * *

"I'm going with you," Craig insisted. "You might need me."

"No, Craig. I'm going to say good-bye to Diego. I won't need you to bring the Mustang back. I'll drive it home tomorrow."

"But what if you change your mind?"

"I'm not going to, but if I do, I'll call my father and you and he can come for it."

"I'm going with you. I'll get a room near yours and I won't bother you. You'll know I'm there in case you need me."

"But you won't be able to take Marine back and forth across the bridge." I thought that would stop him.

"Marine is already with your mother."

"Oh, I thought he was in your jacket."

"You've had a lot of things on your mind."

"You're not going to budge, are you?"

"No. I'm a stubborn old marine."

"Let's go then, you stubborn old marine."

We drove wordlessly to Ojinaga, parked the Mustang on the U.S. side, and took a taxi across the bridge. Craig went ahead of me into the Hotel Valentino, rented a room, and waited on a bench in a courtyard between two rows of rooms.

After a few minutes, I walked in and claimed the room reserved for Angela Garcia. I wasn't asked for identification so didn't show it.

When I rejoined Craig he looked up at me. "Room fifteen."

"I've got room eighteen."

It was four o'clock.

"Everything is going to be okay, Little Boss."

I knew it wasn't. "See you later, Craig. We'll come get you for dinner, depending on what Diego says."

I went into the room, set my overnight bag on a stand, and sat on the bed. Would I really be able to let him go?

CHAPTER 32

At five o'clock Diego was not there, nor did he come at six. At seven-thirty I went to Craig's room.

"Give him a little more time," he said. "Maybe he's run into a problem or there's a danger here he didn't anticipate."

"Was he bringing the Skycatcher?"

"No. It was confiscated during the raids."

That made me so sad. I didn't think I would ever forget how Diego had looked in the moonlight, making love to me in the deluxe skybox seating for two. I had to remind myself over and over that I was letting him go. I couldn't breathe when I thought of it.

"He has other plans to get to Florida and then to Cuba, but I don't think you want to know them, do you?"

"No."

"I know it's hard, Margarita, but I think you should keep waiting."

"Will you come to my room?"

"Yes, of course, just let me get a few things."

At ten there was still no word from Diego.

"We should eat something," Craig said. "We can leave him a note."

I agreed because I was about to start screaming if I stayed in that room. I had memorized the ceiling pattern, studied the paintings, counted the fake flowers in the cheap vases, read a Spanish language version of *People* from cover to cover twice, and checked the TV ten times for anything besides novellas. I wasn't in the mood to watch someone else's life fall apart.

I left a note explaining where we were going to eat and said we would be at the plaza after that, and then we would come back to the hotel.

We walked about ten blocks to a taco stand that has great food, made while you drool. We ordered beef taco plates and sat on stools watching people and drinking Mexican cokes. They're made the old way so they still have flavor and are sweet enough to rot your teeth on contact.

I found myself compulsively studying every man, looking for one. He'd said he wouldn't look like himself, but he wouldn't be able to change his size or mannerisms.

"I hope you know you're like a daughter to me," Craig declared, apropos of nothing, "and the best friend I have."

"You know I love you, Stubborn Old Marine."

"Yeah, I know. I wish life would be kinder to you, but sometimes it's not kind. You wonder why you keep going."

Amen to that.

He shifted on the stool so he could see me better. "I didn't want to go to that war, Margarita, but I was drafted. My country needed me, so I went."

"You have medals, don't you, Craig? I think they're in that little wooden box you don't want anyone to open."

"Do you know what kept me going?"

"No, but I'd like to hear about it."

"It was a woman. I stayed alive for her. Every day I pretended I could speak with her. When I was a POW, and even when I was being tortured, I put my head on her instead of what was happening."

"What was her name?"

"Evelyn, but I called her Evie. We were engaged." He hesitated so long I didn't think he was going to continue but he did. "When I came home, she had moved on, married. She had given up on me, Margarita. You can't imagine how that felt. I should have died over there, and the reason I didn't was the conversations I had with Evie in my head every day. I imagined holding her, smelling her, touching her. I don't mean to make you cry."

He handed me a napkin. Somehow, I already knew this story even though he had never told it.

"I'm telling you this because I think your love is what's keeping Diego going. I'm not saying you should go with him, but I think you should wait for him. If Evie had waited for me I could have told her how much I loved her. That would have meant so much to me, just to be able to say it.

"Because she didn't hear from me, and nobody knew what had happened to me, she lost faith. She lost it before it was time, so our story never had a chance to play out. I think you should give yours a chance. Maybe Diego has thought of some other way, but whether he has or not, he needs to know how much you love him."

"He knows I love him, Craig. He's a wanted criminal, and I can't live a life on the run. And I still have a problem with him murdering people over drugs, and he even admitted

that sometimes it was over nothing. At the same time, I know how good he is. I've seen that side of him, and it's killing me."
* **

After we ate, we walked to the plaza where mariachis were performing. We sat on a bench and watched people dancing and having fun.

"I wonder if I remember how to dance," Craig said.

"Do you want to find out?"

He offered his hand. "Would you dance with a stubborn old man?"

"I would love to."

"I've still got it, don't you think?" he asked after the third dance.

"I'll say." I kissed him on the cheek. Then I froze. In the crowd of dancers, we had been gradually pushed towards the street. When I looked up, I saw Sotol and Ruben sitting on the tailgate of Tom Thomason's truck talking to some other hoodlum types.

"Keep dancing, Craig," I said into his ear, "but move me away from here, and don't look towards the street."

He began doing what I asked without question. We were moving away from him, but Sotol had already spotted us.

"Hey! You! Nosy American bitch! Hey! I should've shot you at the river. Hey!

"When I say go, we're going to run like hell into the crowd and then zigzag towards the bank building. Take my hand and don't let go. Now, Craig—Go!"

I took off, dragging him along, into a crowd of people. They began screaming and scattering, so I assumed Sotol had pulled a weapon, or one or all of the goons had. We were in a side street running left and right and then back. I expected to be shot dead at any time, but we dove into a narrow alley between the bank and a drugstore seconds before the blasting began. Bullets pinged into parked cars and smashed out windows. Several hit the corner of the bank building and filled the air with dust.

I was unfamiliar with the back alleys of Ojinaga, but I followed one into another without seeing, terrified Craig would have a heart attack if I kept pushing. We needed a place to rest, even if it was for a minute. When we came to the backdoor of a restaurant I ducked in, pulled Craig along, slammed the door shut, and locked it.

The startled cooks began yelling. It was two old women.

One was stirring a skillet of sizzling meat and the other was making flour tortillas.

"Please. We need to hide. Bad men are following us."

"We don't want bad men in here," the tortilla-maker said. "Get out!"

The other woman watched us with sad eyes, so I appealed to her. "Please help. My father can't keep running. We have to rest. Please help us."

Without speaking, she opened a door and indicated with her hand that we should go in. "Buena Suerte." She wished us luck as she locked the door behind us.

At first I thought she had locked us in a pantry, but as my eyes adjusted to the dim light, I saw a set of stairs. Above those were stars.

"Wait here."

Craig looked ready to pass out, but he nodded and slumped against the wall, gulping in air. I ran up the stairs to a roof. It was perfect. I went back down so fast I stumbled.

"If you can go up the stairs, we can rest on a roof. Come on, I'll help you."

Once I had Craig settled, I crawled to the edge and looked over. There was a maze of alleys and back doors. I saw a man with an automatic rifle go by, but he made a wrong turn and was moving away from us. Another man followed, but he passed the door we had entered and continued on down the alley.

I crawled back over to Craig.

"Those are the sons-a-bitches that killed that boy, aren't they?" he asked.

"Yes, and they've killed a lot of other people, too."

"That one with all the jewelry, he's the ringleader, and he's evil."

"Yep, he is."

It was cold up there and the later it got, the colder it was. Craig began to shiver.

"Let's get out of here," I said.

We picked our way across the roof to an adjoining one, then another, and found a fire escape going down the side of one of the buildings into a dark alley that stank of rotting food. From there we crept to the street. We waited because a vehicle was coming. It was a dark Blazer, like the one that brought the cocaine to the empty house in Terlingua, and Sotol was driving it. He looked from side to side, searching for us but couldn't see us waiting in the shadows of the alley.

"Maybe he's looking for his men," Craig whispered from behind, startling me.

"Maybe so," I said but doubted it. He was looking for us.

When the taillights of the Blazer disappeared, we tore out of there, down that street to another and kept running in the direction of our hotel, taking side streets and alleys where possible. Without making a sound, a man stepped out of an alley we had just passed and fired a shot at our backs. It went wide and we kept running. The shooter began yelling to someone else. There was nothing to do but run.

After a couple of blocks, I dragged Craig into an alley where we crouched behind a dumpster. He was severely out of breath and couldn't speak. I could speak but couldn't think of a thing to say. What in the hell were we going to do? I squeezed his hand with affection, and he managed to squeeze back.

Running footsteps went by the alley.

"Do you have your knife?" I whispered.

He nodded.

"We might need it."

"Jacket pocket," he gasped. "Take it."

I managed to get it out of his pocket but it was worthless in my hand. He was the commando with a knife. I'd be more likely to stab myself. What I needed was a gun—any gun—and we'd have a chance.

"If someone comes in here," I whispered to my friend, "we'll attack." Oh yeah, there's a plan. One old man who can't breathe and an unarmed woman who can't think hold off mean Mexican mobsters.

Crazy as it sounds, that's what happened, and it happened fast—that has to be the reason it worked. People were running by on the sidewalk again, but one set of footsteps came into our alley. Craig gripped his knife. His gasping had subsided to heavy breathing. I crouched, ready as I would ever be.

When the footsteps passed the dumpster, I nodded at Craig. I bolted out first and jumped on the man's back. He gave a little cry of surprise, and the pistol flew out of his hand. Craig came from behind, picked it up, and held it out in front of him.

"*Manos arriba!*" Craig yelled, as if he spoke Spanish

fluently.

I dropped down from the hoodlum's back, but he turned and lunged at me.

"*Hijo de la chingada,*" he growled. He called me a son of a bitch and put his rough hands around my throat. It was the cigar-smoking goon with the pocked face who had been in Paso Lajitas shoving people around, looking for me, and tacking up reward posters of fifty thousand pesos. He was the *hijo de la chingada.*

When he came at me, Craig shot him in the leg. He screamed in pain but didn't let go of my neck. I thought I was going to pass out. Craig shot him again and he dropped me, but pulled a small pistol on Craig. When the goon turned towards him, Craig shot him dead.

At the commotion, another man aiming a pistol ran into the alley and Craig shot him, too. I picked up the first man's extra pistol, which was a Walther P 99 semi-automatic. Then I took the 9MM Jericho from the second man.

"It's been a long time since I held a gun." Craig was looking at it in amazement.

"Well, you didn't forget how to use one, did you, you stubborn old marine?"

He grinned, but it was short-lived.

So many things happened at once that it's still a jumble in my head. From the direction of the plaza came the sound of automatic gunfire. The noise was deafening. Craig and I looked at each other and began to run. I had one thought: I'd told Diego we would be on the plaza.

Before I had another thought, a Blazer pulled up and Ruben began firing at us. Craig moved in front of me, holding his arms out to the side in an attempt to shield me. One second he was standing there, the next he was a heap on the ground.

I fired at Ruben and hit him in the head. It was so gruesome it would've made me throw up, but Sotol had gotten out of the Blazer. He was taking aim at me, so I had to kill him, too. I did it without even thinking about it.

Other men came running up, yelling to drop the weapons. They wore uniforms and seemed like law, but it was hard to tell.

Someone yelled, "Margarita!" I thought it was Zeke and wanted to say something but more shots were being fired and pain came over me like fire. I fell on top of Craig. Sounds from the plaza had stopped, but now gunfire seemed to surround me.

From somewhere, I thought I heard Diego's soft, sweet voice. "Pancho met his match you know, on the deserts down in Mexico. Nobody heard his dyin words; ah but that's the way it goes."

"Love you," I murmured and my world went black.

CHAPTER 33

Before I opened my eyes, I heard my parents whispering with a third person. Voice number three left before I figured out who it was, and then it was only my parents. I didn't care, felt no pain, and was floating, floating. My brain was too fuzzy to focus.

Why were my parents there and not Craig? My parents were in Terlingua. I had been with Craig. All day. Sure of it.

I floated a while longer, but bit by bit I remembered and hesitated to open my eyes, afraid of what reality would bring.

My mother was looking at me the way she alone does.

"Where?" I croaked.

She took my hand and her eyes were so sad I didn't want to look at her. "You're in the hospital in Ojinaga. Do you remember being shot?"

I nodded or tried to.

"You took a bullet to the shoulder. I know it hurts, and you lost a lot of blood, but you'll be fine. They put your arm in a sling to keep it still so your wound will heal."

"Craig?"

"Sweetheart, he's hurt," she said softly. "They don't know if he will live."

"Save him, Mom. You're a doctor."

"I've spoken with his doctor and he's doing everything he can."

"But you can save him."

"Craig is injured in a serious way. I can't work magic, Margarita."

Oh yes you can! She did it all the time. She was always doing it.

"He's a marine," I said. "He survived Vietnam." For Craig not to survive a trip to Ojinaga was just—wrong. And the thought was unbearable.

My father took my hand after my mother let it go, and the sadness on his face said this was serious. Craig had jumped in front of me to protect me. I remembered him going down. And those other men were there to—do what?

Papi was saying I could see Craig when I felt stronger.

"Now," I said, "he's all alone."

"Don't worry, we've been checking on him."

"Not the same," I insisted, but had no energy to argue. I sank back into pillows and floated away.

* * *

When I woke again, Zeke was there talking with my parents. His was the third voice I'd heard earlier. It was too weird, and at first I thought it had to be a drug-induced dream.

"She's coming around now," my papi said. *Papi.*

"How are you feeling, Mija?"

Can I get in your lap? "Better," I said.

"Your mom and I are going to get something to eat. Zeke wants to talk to you."

I looked at Zeke standing there all official-looking with his shiny star badge and his cowboy hat and his face like mine, and I knew I didn't want to hear what he had to say. I shut my eyes tightly, but he didn't go away.

"Margarita," he said, coming nearer the bed, "may I speak with you?"

"I guess so."

"Thank God you're all right. I got there just in time to see you go down."

"I thought you were there. I didn't know if I was imagining it."

"I heard all the commotion and could hardly believe my eyes when I saw you. I sent your weapons back to the U.S. with a man who will leave them at your office, so no questions will be asked. As far as the police know, various cartel goons shot and killed each other. It happens all the time and they took it in stride, so the Mexican authorities won't be looking for you."

"Wait. Those weren't mine. I know better than to bring weapons to Mexico."

"How did you get them?"

"Craig and I took them off criminals. It's a long story I'll tell you another time."

"You had come to Ojinaga to meet Emilio?"

"Yes, to say good-bye."

He took my hand and studied it, which was a dead giveaway of bad news coming. "I'm so sorry to have to tell you that—"

"Don't say it. That can't be, Zeke. I don't want to hear you say it."

"I'm so sorry, but the AFI and FBI took Emilio Martez down on the plaza in a joint operation that has been in place for over four years."

"You're a liar!" I screamed, and in practically the same breath, "Does *take him down on the plaza* mean he's dead?"

"Yes; that's what I came to tell you."

"Who shot him?"

"Many men shot him at once."

"Were you one of them?"

"No. The Texas Rangers don't participate in assassinations, which is what it was. Emilio Martez was unarmed and was coming out of the church. He was ordered to halt and he did, but they began firing. Someone said he reached into his pocket for a weapon, but the only thing on him was a cell phone."

"This is my fault," I sobbed.

"How can it be your fault?"

"I left him a note to meet us on the plaza."

"He never saw your note, Margarita. The FBI was watching the hotel so he never went there. He couldn't."

"Where is he now?"

"I don't know," Zeke said.

"Who will know where they took his body?"

"I think the FBI took it." He cleared his throat. "I can find out for you, but it might take some time. I'm so sorry, Margarita."

"Everyone thought he was bad, but he wasn't."

Zeke pulled a chair close to me and held my hand. "I think you knew the real man. Everyone else knew the criminal."

A long time passed before Zeke spoke again. "I wasn't there, so what I've told you was related to me by someone else." He cleared his throat. "If you can keep your perspective on this from a law enforcement point of view, you'll consider that the man shot was a Martez, a drug trafficker, and a wanted criminal in two countries."

"I'm a woman, Zeke, and that comes before anything I'll ever do for a living. From a woman's perspective, he was a man I loved."

* * *

Craig had taken two bullets to the chest; one missed his heart by a hair. The doctors hadn't thought he'd survive the surgery but he did. He had survived worse than that, the stubborn old marine, but I never mentioned it to them.

On my third day at the hospital, which was also my last, I stood by his bed, holding his warm hand. "I love you, you stubborn old marine. You have to stop saving my life if it means risking yours." Tears threatened so I stopped talking. If he could hear me, I didn't want him to know how upset I was.

I didn't speak until I regained control. "I have to go out for a while, but I'll be back. Please wake up so we can go home."

That afternoon he did wake up, but I wasn't there.

* * *

I promised to call my papi when I was released from the hospital but I didn't. I had already told him my Mustang was at the bridge, so I didn't know what the point would be if he came. I had things to do that didn't need to involve him.

The plaza was a couple of blocks from the hospital so I walked there, bought a cup of sliced fresh peaches from a street vendor, and sat on a cement bench pocked by bullets from a century of shootouts between rival drug lords.

The peaceful quiet of the old cathedral and the comical bobbing pigeons belied the bloody slaughter that had taken place a few nights ago.

The AFI and FBI took Emilio Martez down on the plaza. I wanted to know where.

First I tried the police. Their office was at the plaza and they had to know. Maybe some of them were involved. How many shooters does it take to kill one man?

I approached an officer at a desk in front. He was interested in me but not my problem and claimed not to know anything.

"Surely you're aware of the shoot-out at the plaza a few nights ago? It was more of a shoot-at than a shoot-out. Emilio Martez was gunned down."

"I heard it was AFI and FBI that got him. We weren't involved."

Are you really that callous? "Do you know where he died?" I persisted.

He flipped through papers on his desk. "No."

"Do you know what happened to his body?"

He shrugged. "The federales took it, I guess."

"Was it taken to a city morgue or a funeral home or where?"

"It was taken away. That's all I know."

"What I need to know is where to take a dead body in Ojinaga."

"Why? Do you have one you want to turn in?"

Yours, if you keep this up, I was tempted to say. He had no clue how close to the edge I was.

I should have told him I was an investigator or somebody official, but instead I tried the truth. "Can't you see I've been shot?"

I began to cry. My shoulder burned and throbbed. And my stomach too, from the unbelievable, heartless way Diego had been murdered and the frustration of talking to Mexican police and the aching in my heart.

"I loved the man who was shot on your plaza," I said in a voice that was tightly controlled but breaking anyway. "Is it too much to ask to bury him? I'm begging you for help. What is wrong with you? Why are you trying to make it worse?"

"Please don't cry señorita. I'll find out where they took him." He pulled a chair over and handed me a box of tissues. "Sit here. I'll be right back."

He was gone a long time or maybe it wasn't that long. I cried and couldn't quit.

Another officer came, and he spoke with respect. "The body of Emilio Martez was taken away by the U.S. Federal Bureau of Investigation, back to Texas. Are you a relative?"

"We were going to be married."

"I'm so sorry. Do you need help calling them?"

"Yes, please."

"Come to my office, señorita."

"Gracias," I said to both men.

The one at the desk smiled sadly and nodded. The other one led me to his office. He was the police captain, but even with his rank he couldn't get a straight answer from the FBI; nor could the mayor of Ojinaga when he tried. All anyone knew was that the FBI had flown him back to the U.S., claiming the body using a foot-high pile of warrants they carried around like the tablets of Moses.

"He was wanted by the Mexican government too," said the captain, "but the man was dead, for God's sake. The AFI saw no reason to argue over his remains."

* * *

I went into the ancient cathedral for reasons I can't say. I was just sitting there in a daze, not seeing anything, when a priest came up to me.

"I apologize for interrupting you, señorita," he said softly.

No problem, I was just sitting here cursing God and everybody else.

"That's okay," was what I really said.

He slid into the pew next to me. "Aren't you the young woman looking for information about the man they shot on the plaza a few nights ago?"

"Yes."

"I wanted you to know I took his confession moments before he was killed. He left, walked down the steps, and the gunfire started. When it was over, I came out and prayed over him. I wouldn't let them take his body until I finished."

"What did you say—to God I mean?"

"I would have administered Last Rites, but he was already gone, so I sprinkled holy water on him, and I said, 'May God Almighty have mercy upon your soul, forgive your sins and bring you to everlasting life.' I have continued praying for him."

"Thank you, Padre."

"You loved him."

"Yes."

"In that case, I think this was meant to be yours." He fished a velvet box out of the pocket of his robe and put it into my hand. "He mentioned that he was going to be married and that his betrothed was meeting him in Ojinaga."

I turned the box over and over in my hand but didn't open it.

"When I knelt to pray over him," the priest said, "I saw the little box on the ground next to him. I took it, believing you would come."

"Thank you."

"Would you like to pray with me?"

"I want to know where he was when he—when he fell."

"Come with me."

We walked together onto the plaza and he showed me the spot. There was nothing there, nothing left of him; every trace of his blood had been washed away.

"He died instantly," the padre said. "I hope that gives you comfort."

At my request he left me alone, and there I sat for a long time.

* * *

Somehow Barney found me. Men and women scattered when he strode up to the bar, leaned against it, and stared.

I stared back.

"You picked a fine time to leave me, Lucille," he sang with a straight face and in English.

"Go away, Barney."

"What are you doin', Ricos?"

"Drinkin' tequila."

"Do you think that's wise?"

"Go home to your family and leave me alone."

"I promised your papi I would find you."

"Well, you can tell him you did."

"Have you eaten anything?"

"What is it with you and eating? Did you bring me a Dr. Pepper?"

"Don't you dare make fun of me, Ricos. This is serious."

"If you're hungry, go eat something."

"I want you to come with me."

"At least have a drink first."

He chewed on his bottom lip as he watched me. "Okay, Ricos, we can do this the hard way or the easy way; you choose."

"I'm stayin'."

"Does she owe you any money?" he asked the bartender in Spanish.

When the man said my account was paid, Barney hoisted me onto his shoulder.

"You can't do this, Barney. Put me down!" I struggled against him even though I knew it was useless. "I'm a grown woman."

Regardless of that, he carried me away from there.

* * *

Two weeks later my stubborn old marine was allowed to come home with me. He was weakened by the ordeal, but the sparkle had returned to his eyes. I slept on the couch and let Craig have my bed, something he fought but without enough strength to win. He still had to spend a lot of time resting, but his little gray kitty cuddled next to him and did his part to make him whole again.

CHAPTER 34

When the man walked into my office, I thought for a second it was Diego, but an older version of him. My heart began to pound in the same old way. More than anything else it was the eyes. This gringo was responsible for Diego's beautiful eyes and also why he was tall.

"I don't mean to startle you, Ms. Ricos."

By now I don't need to say I was staring out the window at my hill.

I stood and took the hand he offered. "He looked just like you."

"Yes. I'm proud that he did. I'm Chris Walden, Emilio's father."

"I'm Margarita Ricos."

"You're just as beautiful as he said."

"Thank you."

"Could we go somewhere private?"

No, but I took him to the rock wall above the Rio Grande because no one could hear us, yet it wasn't remote. I couldn't trust Chris Walden because he was tall and had his son's eyes.

On the way, he talked about the unspoiled beauty of the area, and said he lived in Chihuahua as an expatriated American. I answered the usual well-meaning questions about being in law enforcement on the frontier.

When we got to the wall, Emilio's father said he managed the restaurant where his son and I had eaten on our dinner date. The restaurant was named Emilio's and belonged to him. I had never given a thought to the name of the place and wouldn't have recognized the name anyway.

"I knew when I saw him with you his life was going to change," he said, "I wish he could have met you earlier."

"Why didn't he introduce us?"

"He had told you his name was Diego Romero."

"Oh, that's true."

"The man you fell in love with was my son. The criminal was Emanuel Martez's son. He spent his whole life torn between two worlds. The Martez story ended the only way it could have, and I think he always knew it would."

"Did you get his body away from the FBI?"

"Yes, I did. I wanted to invite you to the funeral, but there wasn't time. After their autopsy, he had to be buried right away."

"Why did they do an autopsy when they're the ones who shot him?"

"They wanted to be sure the body belonged to Emilio Martez."

It was unbelievable. Tears welled in my eyes.

"Where is he buried?"

"In Chihuahua. If you ever come there, come by the restaurant and I'll take you to his grave."

"I will do that."

"I had a hard time getting permission to take his body back to Mexico."

"Why is that?"

He shrugged and looked inconsolably sad. "I guess the Mexican authorities are still afraid of him."

"That's ridiculous."

"His body had more than seventy-five bullet holes." Chris Walden's voice was so faint he was hard to hear. "There wasn't much left of him."

I was so outraged I couldn't speak.

"Ms. Ricos, I came to tell you that Emilio left a bank account that was to become yours in the event of his death."

That news freaked me out. It's a wonder I didn't start screaming and jump into the Rio Grande.

"I want to assure you it's money he earned with the restaurant, not with drug trafficking. He knew how you felt about drugs."

"I don't want his money no matter where it came from."

"But surely—"

"I don't want it. Please don't tell me about it. I loved him, not his money. What good does his money do me? What good did it do him?"

"He wanted you to have it. If you won't take it, I don't know what to do."

"Give it to a charity or keep it for yourself."

"But it was his desire that you have it. He was a hell of a businessman and his restaurant was the one work he could feel pride about. It would hurt him for you to shun it." He thrust a file at me. "You'll have to complete the paperwork, but your name is already on the account."

I took the file out of frustration. "Are you sure you don't want it?"

"He left me the restaurant, which is worth a fortune and provides a good income. I don't want to accept the money because I know Emilio wanted you to have it. I think he'd approve if you donated it to charity, as long as it's in your hands first."

That month the orphanage in Ojinaga received a gift of one hundred thousand dollars in the name of Emilio Martez. My mother's non-profit clinic, Doctores Fronterizos, received the same amount in the same name.

After a lot of thought, I bought a certificate of deposit for one hundred thousand dollars in my name. Diego wanted me to have it, and I thought I should keep some of it "just to see." Maybe I could put it to good use in memory of him.

The last two hundred thousand plus was put into an interest-bearing account in Craig's name to insure that if something happened to me he wouldn't be penniless. I didn't want him to ever be at the mercy of our community or to have to be put into an institution. He would have to sign the paperwork, and getting him to accept the money would be tricky, but I would cross that bridge when he felt better.

* * *

Three weeks later, I took Craig to my thousand-acre mesa for the first time. We went on my ATV, moving slowly. The road that climbs to the top is rutted and nearly impassable. The jolting caused pain in my shoulder, but I was more mindful of the still-recovering hero sitting in back of me.

"Oh my God," Craig exclaimed more than once.

When I stopped so we could admire the view, he took Marine out of his jacket. "Look at this, little man!"

It was a warmish day in early December, one of those perfect days when the sun is bright but not hot and everything sparkles without becoming hazy. The sky was bluer than blue and cloudless. A cool breeze ruffled our hair. Yellow wildflowers still bloomed in profusion along the bottom of the hill. Even halfway up seemed high, and the view became long-distance. The world seemed to change up there.

At the top, Craig was more awestruck. "How did you say you got this land?"

"It was given to me by a man who appreciated some detective work I did."

"Well I guess he must have. Lordy, lordy, lordy."

I had never brought anyone to my mesa who wasn't impressed, though I brought few people. I came often, usually running, and it still struck me too. Huge stands of prickly pear and strawberry cactus, giant ocotillo, and yuccas looked perfectly placed across the top. There was also just the right number of giant creosote bushes. Up there in December, the wildflowers were white, low to the ground, and less profuse than they'd be in spring and summer, when they'd be joined by purple and red ones. Doing a three hundred-and-sixty-degree turn, there were buttes, bumps, surrealistic rock formations, arroyos, and well, more mountains than you could count.

Craig and I sat on a quilt near the edge, overlooking the Terlingua side. Cimarron Mountain seemed closer, but somewhat smaller, from the top of my mesa.

"I have something to tell you, Craig."

"Well, here I am," he said in his dry way.

"Diego left you some money. It turns out he had a restaurant in Chihuahua, so it's not drug money."

His eyes filled with tears. "Why would he do that?"

"He revered you and he knew what you meant to me. I don't know all the reasons why, but he wanted you to have it."

"I don't need his money."

"You might, Craig. Diego's money will keep you free. If you have money, people can't shove you around. I put it into an interest-bearing account at my bank, but we should try to find one that pays more."

"I'm afraid to ask how much."

"It's two hundred and forty-eight thousand dollars and a few hundred more."

"What is an old man like me going to do with that kind of money?"

"Just keep it. Know you have it, and know that Diego thought you were a brave, honest, good man—a real hero. He aspired to be like you."

Craig took my hand. "He was all those things, too," he said softly.

We were silent a long time.

"Up here," Craig said softly, "Terlingua seems inconsequential, doesn't it? The cars and buildings are so small—everything is small. And I don't see any people. What a blessing that is."

"Yes. I keep all that crap they're saying away from me

up here. I'm above it all when I'm on my mesa."

"What do they say?"

"There are good people who've expressed their sadness at my loss. But there's a faction saying I was part of a drug cartel all along. They want to know why I'm still working in law enforcement. Sheriff Ben has been getting a lot of heat about it, but he supports me."

"People are stupid."

"Some of them think I'm an idiot for dating a drug dealer in the first place, as if I knew that from the beginning. Some even say I'm on the FBI's Most Wanted list. I guess they think I'm hiding in plain sight since I'm still here doing my job and using my own name and with the same face."

"They don't think before they speak. And they make stuff up."

"Craig, I thought of one way you could use some of your money, if you want to."

"How is that?"

"We could build you a place up here. I'm going to build a house one day, but you can pick out a spot anywhere you like."

"Oh, I couldn't."

"You can see there's plenty of room. I was thinking a small, snug place for when it's cold and the wind howls. You could have a lot of patio space, or an open porch, or both. We could make a roofless sleeping room for when the weather is fabulous. You could be inside or out, and nobody will even see you up here. And you're still within walking distance of the grocery store, although thankfully you can't see it because of that hill. We'll get you an ATV. You'll be King of the Mountain."

He chuckled. "You've given this a lot of thought, haven't you?"

"Yes. I want to keep you near me, Craig, but I know you don't want to be in a regular house."

"I don't want to be underfoot, either."

"You'll have your own place decorated how you want. We can build it exactly the way you design it. My papi will help us. I know he will. He knows how to build and he can teach us. I could stay with you sometimes while I build my house. Please say yes Craig, because if you say no, another chunk of my heart will break off."

"I wouldn't break your heart for anything."

"Is that a yes?"

He laughed. "Yes. It's the best idea I ever heard. I can be your own personal security system up here."

"I was thinking that too."

After a while, we moved over to the national park side of the mesa, effectively turning our backs on Terlingua and the petty crap going on down there. On the park side there is no sign of civilization except for a narrow two-lane road that winds into the park and disappears among the rugged mountains.

"Are you going to be all right, Margarita?"

"Yes. I have faith that I will. It will help keep me focused on something positive to build a little empire up here."

He laughed softly.

"I know you need a little more recovery time," I said, "but when you feel up to it we'll start building. There's no electricity or water, so we'll have to figure out what to do about that. We can put in solar and wind energy. There's always wind, and for now we can haul water."

Craig sighed and we were quiet for a while. Marine ran around jumping on anything that moved.

"I can hardly believe I'm so blessed." Craig turned to me. "It feels like a place for God alone. Are you sure, Margarita?"

I leaned my head against his shoulder. "Yes, Craig. Every fabulous mesa should have a marine to guard it."

ABOUT THE AUTHOR

Elizabeth A. (Beth) Garcia has lived for more than thirty years in the Big Bend country of far west Texas. She has hiked, rafted, explored, and earned a living in this wild desert-mountain land near the Rio Grande, on the border of the United States and Mexico. It was experiencing the deep canyons, creosote-covered bajadas, and stark, jagged mountains; the wide-open spaces and dark, starry nights that eventually brought her to writing.

Darker than Black is her fourth published novel and the third in the Deputy Ricos Tales series. One Bloody Shirt at a Time was the first, and The Beautiful Bones was her second. These are the first three of many Deputy Ricos tales.

Beth is also working on several other novels, unrelated to Deputy Ricos. One of them, The Reluctant Cowboy, was published earlier this year.

deputyricos@yahoo.com

https://www.facebook.com/ElizabethAGarciaAuthor

WWW.DEPUTYRICOS.COM

Made in the USA
San Bernardino, CA
01 August 2018